MURDER BY SACRILEGE

D. R. Meredith

BALLANTINE BOOKS • NEW YORK

 Published in the United States of America by Ballantine Books, a division of Random House, Inc., New York, and simultaneously in Canada by Random House of Canada Limited, Toronto.

Library of Congress Catalog Card Number: 93-90517

ISBN 0-345-37693-5

Manufactured in the United States of America

First Edition: December 1993

Praise for D. R. Meredith's John Lloyd Branson mysteries:

MURDER BY IMPULSE

"The crime is imaginative, the characters memorable, the West Texas locale evocative, and the story hair-raising."

—*New York Newsday*

MURDER BY DECEPTION

"The first mystery I've seen in which the truth is more frightening than fiction, the only mystery I have ever read in which I felt that *I* might be one of the ultimate victims."

—SHARYN MCCRUMB

MURDER BY MASQUERADE

"A delight for the gourmet of mayhem: sparkling characters, a diabolically dovetailing plot, and some of the most brittle writing this side of McBain."

—LOREN D. ESTLEMAN

MURDER BY REFERENCE

"John Lloyd Branson is the West Texas equivalent of Lord Peter Wimsey—a sleuth to be treasured.... One of the best and most distinctive mystery series in America. Superior in every respect."

—CAROLYN G. HART

Also by D. R. Meredith:

MURDER BY IMPULSE*
MURDER BY DECEPTION*
MURDER BY MASQUERADE*
MURDER BY REFERENCE*
THE SHERIFF AND THE PANHANDLE MURDERS*
THE SHERIFF AND THE BRANDING IRON MURDERS*
THE SHERIFF AND THE FOLSOM MAN MURDERS*
THE SHERIFF AND THE PHEASANT HUNT MURDERS*
A TIME TOO LATE

**Published by Ballantine Books*

Any resemblance between my characters and any persons actually living in Canadian, Texas, or Amarillo, Texas, is coincidental and utterly unintentional. The events portrayed here are a figment of my imagination and not meant to mirror actual events, past or present.

Canadian, Texas, is a very real town of brick streets, giant cottonwoods, and old Victorian houses. Neither the Church of the Holy Light and its congregation nor the Reverend David Hailey actually exist. John Lloyd Branson does not exist either, although you may believe in him if you choose.

My thanks to
Marlys Millhiser, who is not an anthropologist, for sharing her name; and to Tom Ellzey, who is, for sharing his knowledge

FOREWORD

ECCENTRIC CHARACTERS AND CONVOLUTED PLOTS DO NOT excuse the mystery writer's responsibility for creating a realistic courtroom drama. I may stray from the probable but never from the possible, no matter how outrageous my characters' courtroom behavior may seem to those not familiar with legal procedure. Truth is stranger than fiction, and never more so than in a criminal trial. Nothing John Lloyd or Maximum Miller could do or say in court can equal the stories I hear from real prosecutors and defense attorneys who often admonish me "to put that in one of your books." I seldom do. No one would believe it.

PROLOGUE

ON THE FIRST DAY OF DECEMBER, THE MEMBERS OF THE Church of the Holy Light in Canadian, Texas, erected a life-size nativity scene.

Mildred Fisher and her brother, Virgil, donated mannequins from their ladies' ready-to-wear store, and Agnes Ledgerwood, church secretary, ran up costumes on her twenty-year-old Singer. Hank Gregory, church deacon, and Roy O'Brien hammered together a mock stable and raided a local taxidermist's establishment for a variety of stuffed animals.

"I don't believe there were chickens in the stable in Bethlehem," said Agnes Ledgerwood, tugging on Mary's voluminous garment to cover the mannequin's feet, which, she had observed with disapproval, possessed painted toenails.

"Don't know why not," replied Mildred Fisher, shrugging off the comment with the ease of a lifetime spent bickering with Agnes. "I'm sure they ate eggs the same as us. Besides, don't look a gift horse in the mouth. We needed stuffed animals and the taxidermist was kind enough to loan us what he had. We couldn't turn up our noses at what he offered."

"That's no reason why we couldn't have courteously refused the chicken,'' retorted Agnes. ''And another thing. We need a real sheep, not that mountain sheep with curly horns. I *know* they didn't have mountain sheep in ancient Israel.''

''You don't know any such of a thing, Agnes Ledgerwood. You're just complaining because *you* didn't think of asking the taxidermist and I did. And if you don't stop pulling on that garment, you'll split the shoulder seams.''

''I will not. I sewed this costume myself, and if there's one thing I know how to do better than you, it's sewing. I double-stitched every seam. And if you wouldn't paint the toenails on your mannequin, I wouldn't have to worry about covering her feet.''

''*I* didn't paint them! Virgil did—for the swimsuit-and-sandal window display at the store. Virgil likes the mannequins to look as lifelike as possible, and most women paint their toenails.''

''I don't,'' said Agnes firmly. ''And I'll bet you don't, either.''

In Agnes's opinion it was a safe bet. Mildred had a bunion on her right foot and would sooner expose her chest in a see-through blouse than her feet in some flimsy sandals. Besides, Mildred Fisher held thrift in too high a regard to waste a nickel's worth of nail polish on what wouldn't be seen.

Agnes forgave herself for her momentary, very un-Christian flash of triumph at the other woman's miffed look and hummed as she adjusted the folds of the Virgin Mary's robe. After nearly fifty years of friendly—and not so friendly—rivalry that usually ended in a tie, Mildred owed her an unqualified win.

''What we do is beside the point, Agnes,'' said Mildred finally. ''Our generation is too mature to appear in public in swimsuits and sandals.''

It was Agnes's turn to feel miffed. It was bad enough to notice gray hairs and wrinkles, to feel as though one's skin was a casualty of gravity without Mildred Fisher making light of it.

''Mature, my hind leg! You mean *old*, Mildred Fisher, so

you might as well admit it. Well, maybe you're ready to be put out to pasture, but I'm not."

"Ladies."

At the sound of the Reverend David Hailey's deep voice, Agnes immediately felt guilty for her irritation with Mildred. With a single word—and not even an overtly religious word at that—the rector could inspire more remorse in the bosoms of his parishioners over minor transgressions than the average preacher could with an hour's sermon. Agnes didn't understand how he accomplished such a feat and had often wrestled with explanations while typing up the church bulletin. It was nothing so cheap as charisma, a trait she had no use for, associating it as she did with slick politicians and sleazy television ministers. But neither was it saintliness. She no more believed in saints—living or dead—than she believed in the tooth fairy. No, the Reverend David Hailey was not a saint—else he wouldn't have taken Amanda Hailey to wife—but he wasn't an ordinary, run-of-the-mill minister either.

She gave the Virgin Mary's gown a last tug and turned to face David Hailey. Mildred, she noticed, was looking at the rector with an expression somewhere between defensive and sappy. Mildred seldom bothered feeling guilty since she thought she was never in the wrong. Agnes envied her self-assurance.

"Agnes and I were discussing the mannequin's painted toenails, Mr. Hailey," said Mildred. "Agnes feels they're sacrilegious."

Agnes lost her guilt in favor of outrage. "I never said any such of a thing, Mildred Fisher! I just think they're inappropriate on such a symbol of innocence and goodness." Actually, she did believe there might be at least a semblance of sacrilege involved, but she didn't feel it was her place to point it out. That's what ministers were for, after all.

"If Mary were living today, she might very well wear cosmetics—as most of our teenagers do," David Hailey finally said in that deep, patient voice that never failed to hold the attention of his congregation. "Because that's what she was, a teenager, a young, unwed mother living in a small village who heard the voice of God. Today we would say she was suffering from schizophrenia and commit her to an institution. In her day I'm certain she suffered unkind gossip. I'm also certain there were times when she was frightened and confused, perhaps even angry that her neighbors judged her on appearances."

Agnes didn't like losing an argument, even to a minister. "You make her sound so ordinary."

"But she was!" interrupted the young woman hanging on to the minister's arm. "I never thought of her that way until now, but David's right. She was an ordinary woman—like any of us. That makes this whole Mother of God thing easier to relate to."

Agnes wasn't sure what her own face revealed, but Mildred's was a study in shocked outrage, as well it should be. Referring to the Virgin Mary in terms better suited to describing a rock star was outrageous. Next Mrs. David Hailey would be calling the birth of Christ a "gig in Bethlehem."

Amanda Hailey brushed a lock of curly red hair out of her eyes and glanced first at Mildred, then at Agnes. "Did I say something wrong?" She looked up at her husband. "Did I hear you wrong? Didn't you mean Mary was ordinary? I mean, she wasn't a saint or anything. That came afterwards, didn't it? No one starts out as a saint. That would be a bummer for the rest of us because no one would stand a chance to be blessed like Mary was unless they were born to it." She wrinkled up her lovely—and very young—forehead. "That would be like predestination. Isn't that what it's called, David?"

The minister smiled and patted his wife's hand. "That's right, Amanda."

She turned back to Mildred and Agnes. "I don't think much of predestination," she announced firmly.

Agnes wasn't certain about it either. Sometimes she stood foursquare in favor, sometimes she didn't, but one thing she knew for certain: Amanda Hailey had *not* been born to be a preacher's wife. If there was anything to the doctrine of predestination, then Amanda Hailey was predestined to bring disaster to her husband's ministry.

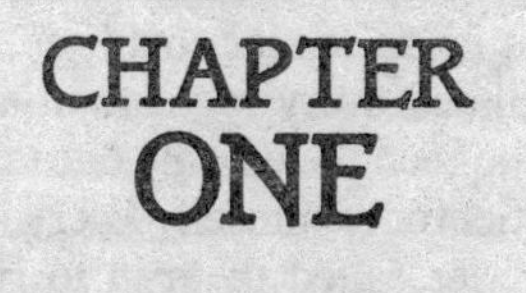

CHAPTER ONE

Amarillo, Texas—December 3

SERGEANT LARRY JENNER HAD JUST MADE THE DRUG BUST of his career. He had stopped a black rental car with Florida tags for a minor traffic violation and the driver had tried to cut and run. He might have escaped, too, if he hadn't tried to cross six lanes of I-40—or if he'd looked where he was going while he was at it. As it was, the driver broadsided a cattle truck and knocked himself unconscious. Jenner figured he had probable cause to search the rental car and found ten kilos of cocaine in the trunk. He was posing beside the open trunk for a photographer from the *Amarillo Globe News* when the phone woke him up.

He burrowed his head under his pillow and tried to hang on to his dream. Damn it all, that dream was the best thing that had happened to him since last September. That was the month the chief had temporarily transferred him to the Special Crimes Unit and into the hands of Sergeant Ed Schroder. For disciplinary reasons, the chief said. Because he'd broken regulations by going undercover when he was technically suspended. Sergeant Schroder was going to teach him proper procedure, teach him how police work was a team effort.

Jenner hadn't had a good day since.

If Chief Mostrovich had really wanted a ten-year veteran of the Amarillo Police Department taught respect for regulations and team effort, he shouldn't have chosen Schroder as the teacher. As far as Jenner could see, Schroder folded, stapled, and mutilated every regulation in sight if it suited his purpose, and he recognized only one team and it boosted only one player: Schroder himself. Everyone else sat on the bench until Schroder called them in to run a play he had already set up.

The way Jenner saw it, Schroder had conned Chief Mostrovich for reasons of his own. He just wished he knew what those reasons were.

He might have successfully ignored the phone if his wife hadn't elbowed him in the gut. There was probably some law of physics that explained how a woman weighing a hundred and fifteen pounds dripping wet could knock the breath out of a man seventy pounds heavier and seven inches taller without using a weapon, but Jenner had no idea what it might be. Physics hadn't been his best subject at Amarillo High.

"Yeah," he gasped into the receiver.

"I'll pick you up in fifteen minutes."

There was a click as the caller hung up without identifying himself, but he didn't need to; Jenner recognized the voice. It often provided the narration for his nightmares. Had his respiratory system not been paralyzed, he could have probably even smelled the caller's ashtray-scented breath over the telephone wires.

A chimney didn't smoke as much as Sergeant Ed Schroder.

Nor was a homeless wino in the last stages of alcoholism as untidy, Jenner thought as he climbed into Schroder's battered ten-year-old green Ford (with one red door) exactly fifteen minutes later. If Schroder didn't actually sleep in his clothes so he didn't have to waste time pulling on his pants when he got called out to a crime scene, he always *looked* as though he did. His frayed shirts always crawled out of his pants of their own volition; his sports coats (and Jenner never saw him wear anything else no matter what the weather) always lacked at least one button; his trousers had creases where the manufacturer never intended them; and his shoes were always cracked, scuffed, runover at the heels, and needed new soles and a polish. As for Schroder's ties, the less said the better.

Rumpled was the kindest observation Jenner could make about the barrel-chested sergeant of Special Crimes—and slovenly was the worst. Both words were misleading. *Rumpled* made Schroder sound like a shambling, kindly uncle when Jenner knew he was about as kindly as a grizzly bear with hemorrhoids, and *slovenly* made him sound careless. The last man who thought Schroder was careless wasn't due his first parole hearing for thirty years.

On the other hand, in Schroder's business, his clients didn't care that he dressed like a walking rummage sale or that he smelled like day-old ashes or that he would never win a Mr. Congeniality contest. His clients were all murder victims and Sergeant Ed Schroder was the best friend they had.

"There's coffee and doughnuts in that sack," said Schroder, nodding toward a greasy paper bag that looked as if it had been recycled one time too many.

Of course, everything connected with Schroder—from his clothes to his car—looked to have been recycled, but that wasn't what alarmed Jenner. "Why did you buy coffee and doughnuts, Schroder? The way you drive like a bat out of hell, there's no place in Potter or Randall counties you can't get to before my coffee cools down enough to drink. And you know I can't eat just before I look at a dead body. It unsettles my stomach."

Schroder lit an unfiltered Camel with his dented Zippo lighter that looked of WWII vintage—except Jenner knew Schroder was too young to have fought in that war. "You ought to work on overcoming your weak stomach, son. It's a character flaw in a homicide detective."

"I'm not your son! And I'm not a homicide detective! I'm a traffic cop. It's what I'm good at, Schroder. I can unsnarl a traffic jam or investigate an accident like nobody you ever saw."

A cloud of cigarette smoke erupted from one corner of Schroder's mouth, and Jenner broke off the argument to cough and roll down his window. "Never saw the difference myself between pulling a mangled body out of a wrecked car and looking at a murder victim," said Schroder. "One's just as dead as the other. Besides, your stomach will settle by the time we get to where we're going."

"There's a big difference between an accident and a murder, Schroder," began Jenner, fanning the cigarette smoke away from his side of the car, then freezing as his internal alarm bells clanged louder. "What do you mean, *by the time we get to where we're going*? Where are we going?"

"Canadian."

"Wait a minute! Special Crimes operates in Potter, Randall, or Armstrong counties. Canadian is in Hemphill County."

Smoke curled out of Schroder's nostrils and rose slowly to the top of the car. Jenner wasn't sure what color the interior of Schroder's car had been originally, but ten years' worth of nicotine smoke had coated it a uniform mucky brown.

"Sheriff Taylor requested our help with a little problem he's got."

"A murder?" Jenner asked, then cringed at the expression in Schroder's eyes.

"Son, asking a question like that ain't gonna convince me you're stupid, so you might as well save your breath. If it wasn't murder we wouldn't be going. Special Crimes doesn't investigate anything but suspicious deaths."

Jenner took a deep breath of the cold—but smoke-free—air blowing in from his open window and tried a different tack. "If Sheriff Taylor's got a big enough problem to call in Special Crimes, then he's not going to want an amateur like me. I'll just be in everyone's way, and with a murderer on the loose he won't like my slowing down the experts like you." Flattery had never worked with Schroder before, but what the hell, there was always a first time.

"Murderer's already in custody."

Jenner felt sweat beginning to bead his forehead despite, the cold air and flailed around for another reason to avoid the investigation. Other than the real one, which was that looking at murder victims nauseated him. That wouldn't work. Schroder would just tell him not to throw up close to the crime scene.

"Then it's just a straightforward crime-scene investigation—labeling evidence and so forth—and I'm not an evidence technician, Schroder. I'd just be standing around with nothing to do, and that's a waste of the taxpayer's money. No point in paying me overtime for taking up space. The county can't afford it." He nodded his head as he warmed to his subject. "There's a budget crunch, you know. It's everyone's responsibility to hold costs down—and you can start by letting me out. You don't even have to waste gas by taking me back home. I'll walk. I need the exercise."

He heard a deep rumble from the other man, like the sound an avalanche made just before a man found himself ass-deep in snow. He had heard that sound before. Not often, but enough to recognize it. Schroder was laughing.

"I haven't heard so much hot air since the presidential election, Jenner, but you're still wasting your breath. Save it for questioning witnesses."

"Why are we going to be questioning witnesses? Isn't that Sheriff Taylor's job? I mean, all Special Crimes will do is work the crime scene and turn over the physical evidence to the sheriff. If he's already arrested the murderer, he doesn't need us in charge of the investigation. He can handle it himself. That's what Hemphill County elected him for."

Schroder stubbed out his cigarette in the car's overflowing ashtray and immediately lit another. Jenner wondered if he ought to mention that smoking was a form of drug addiction, but decided against it. He wondered if he ought to point out the dangers of secondhand smoke, but decided against that, too. Schroder was in a good mood—for him—and Jenner didn't want to spend ninety miles closed up in a car with the detective when he was pissed off from being lectured about the vices of nicotine. A barracuda made a friendlier traveling companion. Instead Jenner decided he'd just hang his head out the window like a dog.

"You just hit the nail on the head," said Schroder.

"I didn't know I had a hammer," Jenner muttered under his breath.

Other than giving him a sharp look, Schroder ignored him. "You see, the sheriff is elected. That makes him a politician whether he likes it or not. Mostly Taylor doesn't, but if he wants to keep his job, he's gotta pay attention to how he steps on the citizens' toes. Canadian is a small town, and most of the voters in Hemphill County live there. Now if there's one thing certain about small towns, it's that everybody knows if the sheriff is stepping on toes equally. At the same time there are toes the voters agree shouldn't be stepped on at all and others they believe ought to be amputated at the ankles."

Schroder shook his head, and an inch of cigarette ash broke free and sprinkled gray cinders on his shirt. "You have to feel sorry for county sheriffs like Taylor. They don't hardly know where to step without ending up knee-deep in horse shit. The smaller the county, the more likely the voters will see the sheriff scraping his shoes."

"So what are you saying? That the sheriff called us in to scrape his shoes?"

"Everything is politics these days, Jenner. A man can't hardly do his job anymore for all the self-styled advocates waiting to ambush him."

Jenner figured Schroder was speaking rhetorically rather than from experience. Anybody stupid enough to try to ambush the burly detective was likely to end up eating whatever cause he was advocating. Schroder didn't have much use for any causes but his own.

"So who did the sheriff get crosswise with, Schroder? The environmentalists? The vegetarians? Animal rights? The Women's Christian Temperance Union? They still have an active branch in Canadian, you know." Jenner snapped his fingers as another candidate occurred to him. "I know who the sheriff's afraid of. I should have thought of him sooner since Canadian is his home ground. The sheriff arrested one of John Lloyd Branson's clients, didn't he? No wonder he yelled for help. Branson's worse than all the other advocates put together."

Schroder's right eyelid started twitching. "Branson has

nothing to do with this case. Branson's name was not even mentioned by the sheriff." The detective whipped his head around to glare at Jenner. "That's because the sheriff is smarter than certain traffic cops I know. He knows better than to say Branson's name out loud. The son of a bitch might be listening. Worse, he might answer, and Sheriff Taylor's in enough trouble without having the Panhandle's would-be Perry Mason sticking his long, skinny nose in this business."

"Did anybody ever tell you that you're getting paranoid, Schroder? You're talking about Branson like he was omniscient."

"That's because he damn near is! Nothing happens in this whole north end of Texas that Branson doesn't hear about sooner or later—generally sooner. Let a man stab his wife and Branson hears about it before the blood dries on the knife."

Jenner thought the detective was exaggerating, but not by much. John Lloyd Branson did have a knack for showing up at a crime scene, but there was nothing supernatural about it. Since he was the Panhandle's best-known criminal defense lawyer, it was only natural that anybody afraid of being charged with murder would call Branson before the victim was cold. To use Schroder's example, a smart man would call Branson *before* he stabbed his wife.

Jenner noticed that Schroder's eyelid was still twitching, glanced at the Ford's speedometer, and swallowed hard. He was sorry he had ever brought up the attorney's name. Since Schroder always drove as close to the speed of sound as his old Ford could manage, anything that obscured the detective's vision—such as a nervous eyelid—was to be avoided.

"Take it easy, Schroder. Not every murderer hires Branson as his attorney. It just seems that way because he's so hard to miss." Which was no exaggeration. John Lloyd Branson stood six feet four inches in his stockinged feet, had graying blond hair and the blackest eyes Jenner had ever seen, dressed in three-piece suits, and wore either a string tie or a bolo. If it weren't for the Phi Beta Kappa key on his watch chain, he could pass for a lawyer of the last century. Or maybe an undertaker—since he almost always wore black.

Schroder's eyelid twitched once more before he expelled a smoke-laden breath and relaxed. "You're right, son. I'm jumping and I ain't even been bit—yet. And maybe I won't be on this one because I'll give Branson some credit for defending murderers he thinks have some redeeming quality about them. That doesn't mean they do. It just means he persuades a jury they do. Anyhow, that ain't the case here as far as I could tell from Sheriff Taylor's phone call. He wasn't exactly operating on all cylinders when he talked to me, but then a thing like this is liable to leave most men a little shaky."

Jenner felt himself break out in a sweat while at the same time his stomach felt like a block of ice. "A thing like what, Schroder? What kind of murder is so heinous that you think even Branson will back off? God Almighty, he defended his secretary when she was tried for dismembering her husband with an ax. What could be worse than that?"

Schroder lit still another cigarette and snapped his lighter shut. "Mrs. Dinwittie did a little more than just dismember her husband. If he had been a log, you might say she chopped him into kindling."

Jenner gagged and stuck his head out the window again. The wind whipping around the car was full of sleet, and he figured a few minutes' exposure would freeze his ears right off his head and he wouldn't have to listen to Schroder describe a gory murder scene.

Schroder's voice rose above the wind's shriek. "But this is worse than any do-it-yourself Lizzie Borden."

The old bastard's voice was almost hypnotic, Jenner thought, and wholly against his will, he wondered what could be worse than John Lloyd Branson's harmless-looking secretary wielding an ax against her dearly beloved.

"No, sir, Jenner, this ain't your garden variety of murder case," Schroder continued. "This killer is going to make the headlines. Might even make one of those afternoon talk shows."

Jenner listened impatiently for Schroder's next line, but all he heard was the older detective whistling tunelessly. He pulled his head in out of the wind and rubbed his numb ears. Not that he was curious, but he might as well humor Schroder by listening. Besides, his health insurance probably didn't cover plastic surgery for self-inflicted mutilation.

"Well?" he asked.

Schroder looked at him and drew on his cigarette. "Well what?" he asked, expelling a cloud of smoke.

"What kind of case is it?"

Schroder's lips stretched into what Jenner recognized as a smile. On anyone else it would qualify as a grimace. Jenner recognized something else.

He had just been conned.

Sheriff William G. "Buster" Taylor, sheriff of Hemphill County, Texas, huddled inside his fleece-lined sheepherder's coat in front of a white clapboard church. He looked almost as stiff and lifeless as any of the mannequins in the nativity scene.

Except one.

Jenner stood next to Schroder and looked at the pale figure seated on a bale of hay and leaning against the wooden backdrop with its freshly painted scene of a manger. Each gust of wind lifted the long, curly red hair off the figure's shoulders and whipped it across her face like a veil. At those moments she looked almost alive—until the wind died and her hair drifted back to her shoulders to reveal the lax mouth and still green eyes.

No one could ever mistake the eyes of the dead for the eyes of the living.

At the sight of a stuffed lamb curled up at the figure's bare feet, its fleece no whiter than the flesh it touched, Jenner felt his eyes sting and didn't try to kid himself that the wind-driven sleet was responsible. For the first time in his ten-year career as a hard-nosed, thick-skinned cop, after seeing bodies mangled, burned, and crushed in car wrecks, after observing murder victims who had been strangled, stabbed, shot, tortured, bludgeoned, battered, and drowned, Sergeant Larry Jenner cried. He stood in front of a nativity scene built by the congregation of a small nondenominational church in a town whose population was smaller than the enrollment of Amarillo High and cried. Not because the victim had met a hard death—if any death is easy when you're only nineteen—and not because her husband had killed her—one is more likely to be murdered by one's nearest and dearest than by a stranger—but because Amanda Hailey had been forever denied the privacy of the grave and what little respect it owed the dead. By substituting her body for the mannequin of the Virgin Mary, David Hailey had ensured his wife immortal infamy.

Jenner wiped his wet eyes on the sleeve of his coat and looked again at the corpse's narrow, childish feet with their red-polished toenails. If disposing of his wife's body in the midst of a religious symbol wasn't bad enough, David Hailey had dressed her in the thin cotton clothing of the Virgin Mary. In a cold, blustery December David Hailey hadn't even thought enough of his wife to dress her corpse warmly. Not that Amanda Hailey would ever feel warm again, but it was the callousness of the act that bothered Jenner.

The sleet-covered ground was so cold, and her feet were so bare.

For the first time Jenner was glad he was a member of Special Crimes. He would show David Hailey as much mercy as the good rector had shown his wife.

Sheriff Taylor cleared his throat. "We haven't touched anything, Schroder. Soon as I got the call from the chief of police, who was running over with thanksgiving that the church was just outside the city limits and out of his jurisdiction, and I saw what I was up against, I set up barricades to keep folks away and put in a request for Special Crimes. I sure appreciate your board of directors responding as fast as they did seeing as how it was the middle of the night." He broke off and studied the nativity scene with its lonely corpse. "If you hadn't gotten here so fast, I probably would have moved the body and to hell with preserving the crime scene. It's about more than I can stand—her sitting there in the cold to be stared at while her killer's warm and cozy and out of the public view in the county jail. It kind of chaps me to have to keep him safe, if you want to know the truth. I'd like to wring his neck myself and that's no way for a sheriff to be thinking. That's why I called Special Crimes to take over the investigation. I don't trust myself to be objective, and the folks here in Canadian don't *want* me to be objective, and I can't fight them and myself, too. It's better if somebody outside the community takes charge, and you're used to working with Maximum Miller."

Jenner felt a chill that owed nothing to the weather run down his back. "Maximum Miller? What's he got to do with this? He's an assistant district attorney in Amarillo. He doesn't have jurisdiction in Hemphill County."

The sheriff tugged his coat collar up to cover his ears. "He does now. Glen Williams, our own district attorney, disqualified himself and asked for a special prosecutor. Miller was given the job."

"Phone lines sure were humming between here and Amarillo tonight," said Schroder. "You explained why you didn't want to handle this investigation, but what's your D.A.'s reason? Once the evidence is collected and Hailey is charged, a prosecutor isn't supposed to be objective. He's supposed to go for the throat."

"Maximum Miller sure will," said Jenner, buttoning his coat up under his chin. "He'll go for any exposed throat like a vampire. He'll suck everybody dry—defendant, witnesses, the other attorney, cops." He reconsidered his analogy. Comparing Maximum Miller to a vampire might not be entirely accurate. Vampires only inflicted tiny fang marks; Miller tore out throats like a giant pit bull.

The other two men ignored him. "Glen Williams can't prosecute," said Taylor. "He's a witness."

"You mean he saw the reverend murder his wife?" asked Jenner.

Taylor lifted his Stetson and ran his fingers through his graying hair. "Not exactly. What he saw was Hailey disposing of his wife's body. The whole church budget committee saw it."

"What?" yelled Jenner. "He dumped his wife in the nativity scene in between discussing entries on a balance sheet?

What the devil was he thinking? That he'd save money on the water bill if only one person showered in the church parsonage?"

Taylor replaced his Stetson, pulling it low over his forehead as though to shade his eyes from the still figure staring sightlessly past them at the cream-colored Special Crimes van parking at the curb behind Schroder's old Ford. "According to the church secretary's notes, the budget committee was voting on taking bids to replace the roof on the Sunday school wing. We had a hailstorm earlier this fall that put paid to a lot of roofs in town."

"So nothing happened in the budget meeting that might account for the preacher suddenly excusing himself to go kill his wife?" asked Schroder, rolling an unlit cigarette from one side of his mouth to the other.

"Not that I know of," replied Taylor. "Of course, I haven't talked much to the witnesses except for Glen Williams, and that was a real short conversation. Glen said he was excusing himself and for me to call Special Crimes. We both agreed it was best not to handle this ourselves. We didn't want a defense attorney saying we were railroading the preacher because of what he had done. Got to watch out for a defendant's civil rights."

"For God's sake, the man killed his wife!" yelled Jenner. "Unless you people in Canadian usually overlook a crime like that, then you're not railroading him. You're prosecuting him. You're exacting justice. You're protecting society. You're avenging the innocent."

He felt Schroder grab his shoulder. "That's enough, son. You're sounding like one of them vigilante movies. Next thing I know, you'll be leading a lynch mob."

Jenner twisted out of the detective's grip. "Everybody's so damn calm about this. What about her civil rights?" he demanded, pointing to Amanda Hailey's pale body. "Didn't she have a right to be safe in her own home? Didn't she have a right to die of an accident or a disease or old age? Didn't she have a right not to be—" He stopped suddenly. "How did she die, anyway? I don't see any bullet hole or stab wound or marks of strangulation."

Taylor cleared his throat. "The right side of her head in back of her ear is crushed. I did check that much after I found what I figured was the murder weapon in the Hailey's bedroom. At least it had blood and long red hair stuck to it, so I reckon it's the weapon. The minute I saw it, I knew what the preacher's motive was, and if he had left her body where it fell instead of defiling a religious symbol the way he did, then I figure folks around here might be a little more sympathetic toward him. Or maybe not. We expect our ministers to live by higher standards than the rest of us. A preacher is supposed to walk the straight and narrow, and God help the poor bastard if he steps off the path to smell the flowers. He's not supposed to even know there are flowers. If David Hailey hadn't been a minister, the town might have thought his marrying a girl half his age and twice his worldliness was funny. We might have snickered behind his back and waited for Amanda to make a fool out of him, but instead we were all uncomfortable. It's one thing for a minister to lead a sinner to God. It's a horse of a different color to personally escort her."

"So David Hailey married the town bad girl and killed her when he learned he couldn't reform her?" asked Schroder.

Taylor scratched his chin. "Judging by the weapon, it appears that way."

"What is the weapon?" demanded Jenner.

The sheriff turned and pointed toward the front of the church. "See that flower bed full of dead stalks to the left of the church door? See the vacant spot in its rock border? Well, I found that missing rock in the preacher's bedroom. I reckon you might say David Hailey stoned his wife to death."

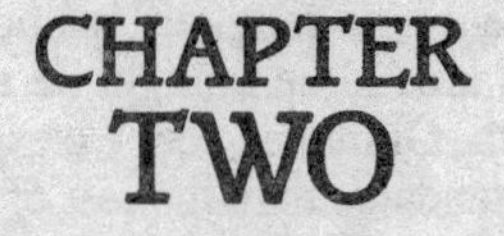

CHAPTER TWO

Canadian, Texas—December 3

LYDIA ANN FAIRCHILD YAWNED. FIVE-THIRTY ON A COLD December morning was an obscene time to be sitting in John Lloyd Branson's living room. In Lydia's opinion any hour before at least eight o'clock was obscene, which was why she never signed up for any class at Southern Methodist School of Law that met before nine in the morning. Nine o'clock was a civilized hour to listen to lectures on such weighty subjects as the Uniform Commercial Code (the single most boring example of bureaucratic regulations out of control), Oil and Gas (almost as bad), and Contracts. Five-thirty was not a time at which Lydia was interested in even her first love, Criminal Law, nor was it a time when she wanted to be confronted by her legal mentor and erstwhile boss dressed in his usual three-piece suit and Phi Beta Kappa key. No one human should look so wide awake, so in control and ready to face the day as John Lloyd Branson. He could at least have misbuttoned his vest or cut himself shaving, Lydia thought resentfully, instead of looking as though he wrapped himself in cellophane and slept in the refrigerator all night to preserve his perfect appearance.

"It appears that your Christmas break will not be wasted after all, Miss Fairchild, if the call from our local district attorney is any indication," John Lloyd said in his usual slow drawl.

Lydia yawned again. "I hadn't planned on wasting it. I was planning on sleeping late." She wondered why John Lloyd's eyes weren't as red and swollen as hers. After sitting up talking until two A.M. any normal person would have bloodshot eyes. Of course, John Lloyd Branson wasn't normal. He probably had absolute control over his blood vessels. He probably hadn't even lain awake with tingling thighs after that sizzling good-night kiss they had shared. John Lloyd Branson didn't allow any part of his body to tingle without express written consent.

"Miss Fairchild, you are far too young to develop the bad habit of wasting half the day in such a frivolous pastime as sleeping late."

Lydia glared at him. "For your information, God doesn't turn on the lights until eight in the morning."

John Lloyd arched one eyebrow—another example of his control that irked any normal person. At the best of times, which this was not, Lydia's eyebrows rose in tandem or not at all. "My dear Miss Fairchild, your theology is shocking."

With an effort Lydia raised her eyebrows. "You don't look shocked."

Without slumping in his chair, John Lloyd stretched out his long legs and crossed one impeccably polished, custom-made black cowboy boot over the other while linking his hands together over his lean belly. For him it was an informal pose. "I did not say *I* was shocked. However, your flippant remarks concerning the Almighty may distress the local residents, particularly in this instance."

"What instance?" demanded Lydia, pouring herself another cup of coffee from the silver pot. Leave it to John Lloyd to serve coffee in silver and china. She, on the other hand, would be lucky to find two mugs in her own kitchen that weren't chipped. Her command of domestic chores was as lacking as her theology.

"Mr. Glen Williams, our aforementioned district attorney, was rather brief in his explanation over the phone, but I gather one of our local ministers is experiencing certain legal difficulties."

"Legal difficulties?"

"I gather he is suspected of murdering his wife."

"What! Why?"

"Why is he suspected, or why did he murder her? You really must learn to phrase your questions so that your listener has some hope of understanding you, Miss Fairchild." He held up his hand when she opened her mouth to protest. "However, I have learned to decipher your verbal shorthand. Your *what* I shall assume is an expression of disbelief that a minister could break one of God's commandments. Unrealistically, we expect better of them. As for why he is suspected, according to Glen, it is because the Reverend Hailey substituted his wife's dead body for the mannequin of the Virgin Mary in his church's nativity scene."

"Nativity scene! My God!" exclaimed Lydia.

"I doubt that He had any hand in tonight's events, Miss Fairchild. In spite of our calling His name to justify our petty actions, I believe man commits evil deeds of his own free will whether it be bearing false witness, coveting his neighbor's property, or murder. I have little sympathy with those who commit crimes, such as planting bombs in school buses, in the name of some higher purpose, be it religion or politics."

John Lloyd rose awkwardly when his doorbell chimed. "As for why he murdered his wife, perhaps our esteemed district attorney will enlighten us."

"Why? You're asking me why, John Lloyd? Why?" asked Glen Williams a few minutes later as he sipped his coffee after being introduced to Lydia. She liked him immediately. For one thing he needed a shave, and for another his eyes were red-rimmed from lack of sleep. He was human.

John Lloyd frowned. "Glen, I am a patient man"—he ignored Lydia's snort—"but I have already suffered through several of Miss Fairchild's incoherent echoes. I am beginning to feel as though I am the only man on the planet whose hearing is not impaired.''

Glen Williams carefully set his cup on John Lloyd's coffee table and rubbed his hand over a haggard and rugged countenance whose attractiveness Lydia would rate in the average to above-average range. A woman wouldn't lose her breath at the first glimpse of his wavy brown hair, square jaw, and hazel eyes, but her pulse rate might accelerate just a bit.

She wondered why hers didn't.

''Speak up, man,'' demanded John Lloyd.

Williams cleared his throat. ''I don't know why, John Lloyd. He won't say why he killed her. He won't even confess that he *did* kill her. As a matter of fact, he won't talk at all. According to the sheriff, since the moment Hailey dumped his wife's body, he hasn't said a damn word. Of course, I haven't dared question him. I'm a witness.'' He broke off and drew a deep breath, looking over at John Lloyd with an expression of surprise mixed with horror. ''It's the first time I've ever witnessed a crime and I don't like it. Makes me feel dirty somehow—like I fell in a puddle of filth that won't wash off. I never expected to feel this way. I've prosecuted all kinds of felons, some of them guilty of crimes I don't want to talk about in mixed company, but I've never felt this way before. What I saw last night made my skin crawl and I can't figure out why.''

''Interesting,'' murmured John Lloyd.

Lydia shivered and rubbed her arms. ''Interesting? Is that all you have to say? It's unspeakable! It is''—she fumbled for another word—''cold. It is . . .''

''Sacrilege,'' finished John Lloyd. He touched his palms together in a prayerful attitude and nodded. ''By desecrating the nativity scene, David Hailey deliberately committed an act of sacrilege, and it is that act rather than the murder itself that you and Glen find most disturbing, Miss Fairchild. Your reactions are what I find interesting. Such sincere outrage is unexpected in our secular age.''

Glen Williams hesitated, his face pensive as if he found his thoughts uncomfortable, then slowly nodded. ''I don't want to agree with you, John Lloyd, but I have to. As a prosecutor I ought to be able to focus on the murder, but I can't. Murder is such a sordid, commonplace crime, but what Hailey did afterwards isn't and it shocked the hell out of me. Even if I wasn't a witness, I'd still disqualify myself. I'm a member of that man's congregation. I thought I knew him. To discover he's capable of desecrating a symbol of his own religion shatters a lifetime of trust. Damn it all, we expect the men who stand behind the pulpits to be stronger than we are. We expect them to resist temptation more often than we do, and when they do sin, we expect the sins to be minor ones. We *don't* expect them to marry sexy, young waitresses, and if they do, we *don't* expect them to knock their wives in the head with a rock when they catch them straying. Most of all, we don't expect them to *spit* at God like David Hailey did!"

John Lloyd gripped the arms of his chair and leaned forward, staring at the man seated on the couch in front of him. "Stoning was the frequent punishment in biblical times for a woman guilty of committing adultery. Was she guilty?"

"My God, John Lloyd!" yelped Lydia, feeling an outrage of her own.

His thin, ascetic face betrayed no emotion as he turned toward her. "The fact that our society frequently treats adultery as somewhat less serious than jaywalking does not mean that every age was so lenient, Miss Fairchild. Adultery used to be considered a felony, and in many parts of the world still is."

"That's not what I meant!"

"Then I suggest you use complete sentences, Miss Fairchild. The purpose of speech is, after all, communication."

Lydia drew a deep breath, unclenched her jaws, and silently counted to ten. It was unprofessional to point out in front of a visitor that John Lloyd's convoluted speech would tax the understanding of anyone who wasn't a student of Victorian novels. Not only was it unprofessional, it was useless. No one in the late twentieth century spoke like John Lloyd Branson, and it was one of his less endearing personality traits that he didn't care.

"I mean," said Lydia through gritted teeth, "that it doesn't matter if Mrs. Hailey committed adultery or not. David Hailey had no right to murder her."

"I am not suggesting that he did, Miss Fairchild. I am only trying to ascertain if the murder weapon also had religious significance to David Hailey."

"What difference does it make?" demanded Lydia. "He killed her, and all this talk of religious symbols and sacrilege doesn't change that."

"I disagree, Miss Fairchild. The weapon may suggest a motive, and motive is important in understanding David Hailey." He turned back to Glen Williams. "To your knowledge, was Mrs. Hailey guilty of adultery?"

Williams shrugged. "Amanda Hailey had quite a reputation in town before he married her, but I don't know whether she was carrying on with somebody behind Hailey's back or not. If she was, I can almost understand his losing his temper. My God, they'd only been married twelve days."

Lydia catapulted from her chair. "Twelve days? He killed her after only twelve days? That doesn't say much for his Christian forbearance, does it? What a pompous, arrogant, murderous, sexist pig! He carries religious hypocrisy to new heights."

"Sit down, Miss Fairchild. You're in danger of frothing at the mouth like a mad dog."

She whirled on the attorney. "I wish I were a mad dog. David Hailey would be the first man I'd bite."

"If David Hailey was not a minister, the twelve-day span between his marrying Amanda Hailey and his murdering her might seem—if you took the most charitable view—an adequate length of time for a man to understand how badly he has been fooled and for his resentment to build to murderous levels."

"Well, I don't take a charitable view!"

"Your expression leaves me no room to doubt your feelings, Miss Fairchild. But to continue: unlike the science of physics, in human behavior there are no formulas specifying the length of time before emotions reach critical mass."

"Are you trying to make excuses for him?" asked Lydia, swallowing back a sob. She wasn't entirely certain why she felt like crying except that it suddenly seemed very important that someone feel sorry for Amanda Hailey.

John Lloyd uttered what sounded like an expletive—except that John Lloyd Branson was more likely to utter a contraction than a profanity, so Lydia assumed her own hearing must be impaired. Flooded eustachian tubes, perhaps. All her tears had to go somewhere if she didn't shed them.

The lawyer rose from his chair with such a swift motion that only those who knew him well noticed that his right leg took most of his weight during the maneuver. He clasped Lydia's shoulders, turned her around, and gently pushed her down into the chair he had vacated. "You are distraught, my dear."

"I am not distraught!" She sniffed. "What did you call me?"

John Lloyd raised an eyebrow. "I called you my dear. Unprofessional under the circumstances, perhaps, but it did serve to remind you that I am not insensitive to your distress."

She reached up to catch his hands. "I just don't want to hear you defending him, John Lloyd."

"I was merely pointing out that disillusionment and hurt pride have buried many an erring wife, Miss Fairchild, and neither time nor the husband's calling will dam up primitive urges."

Williams cleared his throat. "Uh, Miss Fairchild, I don't want to cause trouble between you and John Lloyd, but there is the matter of David Hailey's defense."

Lydia jerked her head around to stare at him. "You want John Lloyd to defend that coldhearted hypocrite? You do, don't you? I should have guessed. Why else drive over here in the middle of the night?"

"It's not exactly the middle of the night," said Williams. "And I didn't drive. I walked. I didn't want any of the neighbors to recognize my car and guess what I was up to. My God, if the voters knew I was trying to arrange for David Hailey's defense, they'd organize a recall election. If they didn't do something worse. There was already a crowd of onlookers at the church when I sneaked away. I overheard one grandmotherly woman who I would have sworn before tonight didn't have a nasty bone in her body say that she thought we ought to burn David Hailey at the stake—since Canadian is the only town in the Panhandle with enough wood to build a decent bonfire. By this time tonight half the men in town might be out chopping wood."

Williams took a deep breath. "But David Hailey must have an attorney. He must be defended. We can't just take him out and wring his neck like a chicken."

"Then let someone else do it," said Lydia. "Why should John Lloyd risk ending up tied to the same stake as David Hailey?"

"Because he's the best, Miss Fairchild, and because John Lloyd won't be ostracized like any other attorney. His reputation for integrity is so inviolate that he could defend Judas for betraying Christ and no one would hold it against him—provided he didn't get Judas probation."

Lydia clutched John Lloyd's hands tighter. "Don't do it. Mr. Williams is pandering to your ego."

John Lloyd freed his hands. "Miss Fairchild, my ego is hardly so fragile that it requires pandering." He snapped off his words as he would an icicle.

Lydia swallowed. When John Lloyd dropped his slow drawl, it was generally safest to change the subject or leave the room. She could do neither. "John Lloyd, please don't take this case. Let him hire an attorney from Amarillo."

"He can't," said Williams. "The church won't pay his salary and he has no outside income. Hailey will have to take potluck with an attorney appointed by the court, and I don't want him claiming inadequate counsel when the jury finds him guilty. I don't want any bleeding hearts saying that local prejudice interfered with justice. And I damn sure don't want some lawyer out to make a name for himself holding my town up to ridicule by claiming Canadian is full of gun-toting rednecks who slap their women around and David Hailey just went too far following local custom. Hailey committed a terrible crime and I don't want my town tried for it. I remember what folks said about Dallas after Kennedy was shot."

"Now you're appealing to John Lloyd's patriotism, Mr. Williams," said Lydia.

"Miss Fairchild, I'd bribe him if I thought it would work. You're a stranger here. You don't know this town, but I do. And John Lloyd does. We grew up here. This is a decent community and I don't want any outsiders criticizing us for what one man did."

Williams wiped his forehead on his sleeve and directed his gaze on the silent figure who had walked over to the fireplace and stood with his back to the room's other occupants. "I'm begging you, John Lloyd. Will you defend David Hailey?"

Lydia stared at John Lloyd's back and waited. The mesquite logs in the fireplace occasionally snapped as pockets of sap burst open from the heat. The quiet, regular ticking of an antique grandfather clock against the wall by the front door and the muted sound of the wind blowing sleet against the double-paned windows underscored the heavy tension gathering in the room. And such a lovely room, she thought, with golden oak floors contrasting with the subtle jeweled tones of red and blue and cream Persian rugs dotting its surface; solid bookcases flanking the marble fireplace while a massive piano sat opposite it across the room; comfortable furniture upholstered in a nubby cream-colored fabric; and polished mahogany end tables holding glowing Tiffany lamps. In one corner a massive red-cedar Christmas tree ascended to the ten-foot ceiling, while boughs of the same fragrant wood wound around the banisters of the broad staircase that led toward the second floor.

It was such a gracious room—such a civilized room—a room filled with peace and the symbols of the Christmas season.

It was not a room in which murder should be discussed.

Lydia couldn't wait silently another moment. "John Lloyd?"

The lawyer turned toward her, a tiny, ceramic figure held delicately in one hand. He met her eyes, his own holding a regret, and she knew before he spoke what his decision was. He glanced toward the district attorney. "I will defend David Hailey if he agrees."

Lydia could hear the district attorney releasing a pent-up breath. "Thank God, John Lloyd."

John Lloyd stiffened. "Glen, you may be giving thanks prematurely. I said that I will defend David Hailey. He is my client, not you and the sheriff, not the congregation of his church, and not the citizens of Canadian. I will investigate the charges against him and I will defend him to the best of my ability, which as you know is considerable."

"Damn it all, John Lloyd!"

"By the legal canon of ethics I can do no less."

Glen Williams sighed as he rose and put on his coat. "I guess I knew that all along, John Lloyd. That's why I asked you in the first place. I guess nobody can complain if you act the way you always have—with integrity. But I wouldn't count on any help from your client. He hasn't said a damn word about what he did, and my gut tells me that won't change."

He walked to the door before he turned back to look at Lydia. "I'm sorry, Miss Fairchild. If I'd known how it was between you and John Lloyd, I might not have come over here this morning." He rubbed his chin thoughtfully. "On the other hand, I probably would have. I make a lot of decisions that lose me sleep at night. This might be one more." He nodded abruptly. "Good morning, John Lloyd."

The door had barely closed behind him when Lydia rose and stalked toward John Lloyd. "I know I'm just a law student and might be missing something, but in spite of what your friend said, any lawyer could handle Hailey's defense because there is nothing to be done. It's open-and-shut, a done deal, hopeless. He's guilty, John Lloyd, and you can't save him. You *shouldn't* save him."

She laid her hand on his chest and wasn't surprised to feel herself trembling. "I know that even after I graduate and join you full time, there will be instances when we disagree. But I had hoped that if I felt strongly against taking a case, you would at least listen to me. But you won't, will you?"

He clasped her hand and kissed it, then pressed her palm against his chest. "Not this time, Lydia, and I would ask you to accept my decision on faith."

She shook her head. "No. We aren't talking about religion here, John Lloyd. We're talking about your accepting me as an equal. Tell me why you took the case."

He studied her, a faint—very faint—smile on his face. "You have grown up, Miss Fairchild. Only a few months ago you might have physically assaulted me for refusing you an explanation for my actions."

Lydia smiled back—insincerely. "Don't push your luck, John Lloyd. Primitive urges and all that."

His smile faded away. "Did I disillusion you, or merely hurt your pride?"

She lost her own smile. "You hurt me—period. I thought I had won my spurs, so to speak, when I helped you solve the murder at the Panhandle Plains Museum. I thought I'd made it. I thought I'd earned my place beside you, but now you're acting like you expect me to walk two paces to the rear again. I may be a little flawed in some respects, but I don't deserve that kind of treatment."

"If you ever walked behind a man, Miss Fairchild, it would only be to kick him in his posterior. Otherwise your objections are valid. You do not deserve to be left in ignorance"—he looked at her—"but you may wish that you had remained so."

"Why?" she asked, her throat suddenly tight.

"Because in spite of the possibility that you might throw my own silver coffeepot at my head and quit my employment in a fit of hurt feelings and moral indignation if I failed to consider your wishes, I accepted the case anyway, and would do so again. In this instance David Hailey's need takes precedence over your wishes."

"I see." She turned and walked away.

"I doubt that you do, Miss Fairchild. There is more at stake here than whether a man murdered his wife in anger."

She whirled around. "Like what? What is more important than a woman's murder?"

"David Hailey's soul."

She stared at him in disbelief. "You're losing it, John Lloyd. Next you'll be hearing voices and running off to live in the desert and eat cockroaches and honey."

"I believe you mean locusts and honey, Miss Fairchild."

"Don't tell me what I mean!" she yelled.

"I am endeavoring to tell you what *I* mean if you would refrain from interrupting me."

Lydia curtsied, stalked back to her chair, and sat down, folding her hands in her lap and fluttering her eyelashes. "You have the pulpit, John Lloyd."

He glanced down at the ceramic figurine he held, then

looked back at Lydia. "I will disregard your last flippant remark, Miss Fairchild, in the interests of mending the tears in the fabric of our relationship. . . ."

"Personal or professional?" asked Lydia.

John Lloyd sighed. "Miss Fairchild, even Glen Williams, who is not overly intuitive in such matters, recognized that our relationship has evolved beyond the strictly professional in spite of my best efforts to avoid such a disruption to my emotional tranquillity. Had my own nativity scene on the mantel not caught my eye, I would almost certainly have refused Glen's request out of deference to your feelings."

He sat down beside her. "Hold out your hand, Miss Fairchild."

Had his voice not held such a note of urgency, Lydia might have demanded an explanation first. Instead she extended her hand palm-up. John Lloyd Branson had a way of commanding obedience that required more strength of character to resist than Lydia possessed before sunrise. It was another inequity in their relationship.

John Lloyd placed the ceramic figurine in her palm. It was warm from his body heat and faintly slick, as though his hand had been sweating. Lydia decided that her sense of touch must be faulty. John Lloyd Branson didn't possess sweat glands, or if he did, he had disconnected their power source.

Lydia studied the figurine. "What is it?"

"Not what but who, Miss Fairchild. It is the Virgin Mary, the ultimate symbol of sexual innocence, of chastity, of purity, of unsullied maidenhood. Just as I was preparing to refuse Glen's request in the interests of our relationship, I glanced at the figurine and realized that the most important question in this case was not why David Hailey murdered his wife. The most important question is: why did David Hailey replace Mary with the body of a woman who was anything but sexually innocent, if we are to believe Glen Williams?"

"Mary is the only woman in the traditional nativity scene, John Lloyd. Hailey didn't have any other choice."

The attorney shook his head. "Incorrect, Miss Fairchild. David Hailey had several choices. He need not have moved the body at all. Or he could have added it to the nativity scene without the necessity of substitution. He certainly could have chosen to dispose of his wife's body in secret. Instead he deliberately called attention to his act of desecration by committing it in front of witnesses. I ask you again: why did he choose the Virgin Mary?''

''He's a religious nut?'' guessed Lydia.

''If by that remark you mean he is a religious fanatic, I doubt it, Miss Fairchild. Traditionally, fanatics—religious or otherwise—hardly wait to complete whatever reprehensible actions they are engaged in before commanding the microphone or the television camera to pontificate endlessly on their motives. In fact, murderers in general tend to babble once they are apprehended, particularly in the case of a domestic murder such as this one. Indeed, I have often wished in the past that certain of my clients had been stricken with a paralysis of the vocal cords. To summarize, one seldom finds a silent murderer or a mute fanatic. Yet David Hailey is apparently both.''

''Not exactly,'' said Lydia. ''Actions *do* speak louder than words, and in this case David Hailey is practically shouting.''

''But what is he shouting, Miss Fairchild?''

''I *don't* know! And it doesn't matter anyway, John Lloyd.''

''It matters to me. Though a minister, David Hailey is, after all, subject to the same human frailties as the average man and might murder his wife, but I find his subsequent actions inexplicable. I do not like the inexplicable. It violates my sense of order. Furthermore, I do not like what appears to be uniform condemnation of David Hailey. It violates my sense of fairness. David Hailey is indeed shouting, Miss Fairchild, but I seem to be the only one listening.''

''And your arguments violate the rights of the victim, John Lloyd. Symbols and shrines and icons and sacrilege and desecration and your sense of order and of fairness are all intangibles. But Amanda Hailey's husband hit her with a very tangible rock.''

CHAPTER THREE

IF ONE IGNORED THE SEVERAL STRANDS OF CURLY RED HAIR and the brown smears, it was an ordinary grayish rock of approximately the size and shape of a softball with one side bulging out in a blunt tip, smooth as though rushing water had ground away its rough edges. Which was probably the case, thought Jenner, since the town of Canadian hugged the banks of the river of the same name. That rock and the others like it marking the borders of the flower bed in front of the church probably came from the riverbank, picked up by members of the congregation on some warm Sunday afternoon. No way any of them could know that on a cold December night their preacher would turn a decorative rock into a blunt instrument. In the minds of most congregations, murder and minister have nothing in common except that both words start with the same letter.

"Pretty modest parsonage," said Schroder.

"I hadn't noticed," muttered Jenner.

"I ain't surprised. You've been staring at that rock for the past ten minutes. If you think you got it memorized by now, you might try looking around the room, figure out how the murder happened."

"He hit her in the damn head, Schroder. It doesn't take a rocket scientist to figure that out."

"Damn good thing it doesn't, too, considering what you got to work with. I've heard brighter comments coming from addicts who fried their brains on drugs."

"That's some kind of remark coming from somebody who single-handedly keeps the tobacco industry afloat."

The older detective sucked on an unlit Camel. Jenner had never seen Schroder actually smoke at a crime scene, but he had never seen him without a cigarette either. The old bastard had probably forgotten how to talk without a cigarette hanging out of one corner of his mouth.

"Quit trying to change the subject, and reconstruct the crime for me, Jenner. We got no time to waste while you act cute. Soon as I get a handle on what happened here, I want to interview the witnesses, then head down to the jail and talk to the preacher before some shyster persuades him that confession isn't good for the soul."

Jenner glanced around. Schroder had been right on the money. If the master bedroom was any gauge, then the parsonage was modest. Less than modest, in fact. Genteel poor was a better description. The room was not much larger than twelve by twelve with a tiny closet and a half-bath barely large enough to cuss a cat in, if the cat was a kitten. The double bed with a bookcase headboard, a vanity dresser, and a bureau were of blond wood, and Jenner figured they dated from about the time he was born. The carpet was green and worn in spots, but clean. As a matter of fact, everything in the room was dusted, polished, pressed, fluffed, and almost painfully neat. However lax Amanda Hailey's moral habits might have been, she was Donna Reed when it came to keeping house.

The only objects out of place were a crumpled piece of paper covered with numbers in the middle of the bed, the overturned vanity stool in front of the dresser, and a jar of cheap cold cream lying on the floor to one side of an open sliding glass door that led onto a tiny patio. And the rock, of course. Dropped by the murderer halfway between the dresser and the glass door.

"It's pretty clear what happened, Schroder. Amanda Hailey was sitting on the stool creaming her face when the reverend comes storming in, all ready to explode judging by the way he crumpled up what I guess is the budget report. He accuses her of misbehaving. Or maybe he doesn't accuse her. Maybe he just walks up behind her and smashes in the right side of her skull, but I doubt it. I think the average husband would say something, even if it's just calling her a name. I sure as hell would."

He glanced at Schroder for his reaction, but the detective just looked back at him out of faded blue eyes, so Jenner shrugged his shoulders and continued. "At any rate, he smashes her skull, she falls off the stool, knocking it over in the process, and the jar of cold cream drops out of her hand and rolls across the floor. He drops the rock, picks her up, totes her outside, and sticks her in the manger scene. End of reconstruction."

Schroder rolled his unlit cigarette from one side of his mouth to the other. "Where's her clothes?"

Jenner blinked. "Well, uh, let me think a minute." He chewed on a thumbnail while he glanced around the room again. "I think she'd be in her nightie, Schroder. My wife always takes a bath, puts on her nightie, then rubs goo on her face. Supposed to keep wrinkles from forming or erase wrinkles that she already has or maybe keep her skin soft. I don't know. I'm not an expert in women's skin care."

"Where's her nightie?" asked Schroder.

"You mean she wasn't wearing it under that robe?"

"She was naked as a jaybird."

"You mean Hailey stripped her and put her clothes away before he dumped her body? Now that's coldblooded, Schroder. The bastard probably has to wear insulated underwear to keep his own blood from freezing him to death."

Schroder nodded. "Could be. Or Mrs. Hailey might have been creaming her face in her altogether."

"That doesn't sound like any preacher's wife I know."

One corner of Schroder's mouth—the corner not sprouting a cigarette—curled up in his version of a smile of approval.

"That's the point, son. I don't think Amanda Hailey was your average preacher's wife."

"She most certainly was not! You can't imagine anybody less suited to be a minister's wife, Sergeant."

Agnes Ledgerwood was on the far side of fifty and fighting it. Her dark brown hair was a little too dark and a little too brown not to owe its color to chemicals; her complexion owed its matte finish to an expensive makeup base and Agnes's refusal to move any muscle in her face lest a line, crease, or wrinkle be revealed; and her bosom owed its youthful firmness to the victory of an uplift bra over gravity and her good sense in never exposing her wrinkled cleavage in public.

Jenner admired her efforts and thought it a shame that her wattled neck, the age spots on her hands, and the varicose veins beneath her support hose gave her away.

Schroder lit a cigarette and took a small, glass ashtray out of one of the sagging pockets of his jacket. While the burgeoning campaign against smoking had not decreased Schroder's consumption of tobacco by a single cigarette, he had taken to carrying his own ashtray. He set it on Agnes Ledgerwood's desk in the small church office within easy reach of his right hand, expelled a cloud of smoke, and smiled at the secretary. Jenner wished Schroder wouldn't smile, or if he did, that he not do it before breakfast.

"Now, Mrs. Ledgerwood, not being in the religious line of work, Sergeant Jenner and I don't know a lot about how a preacher's wife ought to act, so why don't you give us a job description? What should a preacher look for when he's in the market for a wife?" Schroder asked as he turned on a cassette recorder to tape the conversation. Jenner didn't think it had as much to do with producing a legal record of the witness's statement as it did with Schroder picking apart the words looking for ways to trip up a witness later.

Agnes cocked her head to one side and gazed at the ceiling as though considering how to answer the question. Jenner figured the pose was less for thoughtful reflection on her answer than it was to tighten up her double chin. "I had never thought of a job description for a minister's wife, but I believe it would be a good idea. Perhaps a church seeking to hire a new minister should scrutinize his wife at least as closely as they do him. You have no idea the kind of discord an unsuitable wife can cause in a congregation.''

''Did Mrs. Hailey create discord?'' asked Schroder.

''She played secular music in the parsonage. It was very embarrassing when church members arrived for marriage counseling to be greeted by some country singer wailing of broken hearts and wild women. It didn't set the proper tone.''

Jenner didn't like her opinion of country-and-western music. ''It beats hell out of some rap songs that call for killing cops and raping women.''

''Young man, profanity is out of place in a church,'' said Agnes.

So was judging one's fellow man—or woman, in this case—but Jenner didn't notice it stopping Agnes Ledgerwood.

''Shut up, Jenner,'' said Schroder. ''Mrs. Ledgerwood isn't interested in a lecture on music appreciation and neither am I.'' He smiled at the woman sitting behind her desk. ''Go on, ma'am.''

The church secretary appeared dazed by Schroder's smile and sat staring at him for a moment before recovering her voice and her visual focus. Jenner wasn't surprised. Schroder could stun a rattlesnake at ten paces with one of his grimaces.

Agnes cleared her throat. ''She—Amanda Hailey—was late to her first meeting of the Women's Missionary Society, then rushed in wearing jeans and a sweater. Slacks would have been appropriate, but jeans?'' Her voice rose in a question as if inviting Schroder to share her disgust.

''Oh, I don't know,'' said Jenner, a little disgusted himself. ''Jeans are the clothes of choice if you're young, and Mrs. Hailey looks—looked—like she was pretty young.''

Schroder nudged him in the ribs. ''Shut up, Jenner. Mrs. Ledgerwood isn't interested in your opinion of fashion either.''

Agnes sniffed. ''She was barely nineteen, young man, but

that's no excuse. I'm sure there are many girls as young as she with a better sense of what's appropriate."

Jenner moved out of range of Schroder's elbow. "How old is Hailey?"

"Thirty-five."

"Sort of stole from the cradle, didn't he?"

"It is a vulnerable age for a man when faced with temptation, I believe," said Agnes, pursing her lips in disapproval.

"In my opinion age has nothing to do with it. A man either is tempted or he isn't, and Hailey apparently was."

Schroder glared at him. "Quit arguing with the witness, Jenner, or we'll be here the whole damn day."

"That was another trait of Amanda Hailey's," said Agnes, apparently ignoring Jenner. "She argued with the minister in public. She thought he spent too much time ministering to his flock. She had the audacity to tell him he should render more to Caesar. Render more to the flesh was what she really had in mind."

"Well, they probably hadn't been married very long," began Jenner.

"Twelve days," said Agnes.

Jenner noticed that even Schroder reacted to that bit of information. He put out his cigarette before he'd smoked it more than halfway, then immediately stuck another in his mouth. "Twelve days?" asked Schroder in a low growl. "He killed her after only twelve days? Must have had a low tolerance for secular music and blue jeans."

Agnes looked unsure of herself for the first time. "I don't think so, Sergeant. Reverend Hailey was rather . . . liberal in many ways. He never criticized his wife, just said that Mrs. Hailey possessed the tastes of her generation in music and clothes and that there was nothing sinful about either. He said we shouldn't judge on appearances."

She reached in her desk drawer for a tissue and dabbed at the tears that suddenly rolled down her cheeks. "Reverend Hailey could make one feel so guilty for falling short of his own standards. He expected so much of us. That's what makes this so awful, Sergeant. He committed a horrible sin, but I'm the one feeling guilty. Can you explain that, Sergeant? Can you explain it, young man?"

Jenner shook his head. Teary-eyed women made him feel inadequate. He'd let Schroder answer. Nothing made him feel inadequate.

Schroder leaned over and patted Agnes's shoulder. "It's common for a murderer's family to blame themselves, to sit around wondering what they did wrong to make their son or husband or brother kill somebody. Well, I figure his congregation is Hailey's family, so it's natural for all of you to feel guilty. Just don't feel sorry for David Hailey, Mrs. Ledgerwood. He made his choice when he killed his wife and he has to take responsibility for it."

Agnes twisted the tissue in her hands as she looked at Schroder. "But I don't feel sorry for him, Sergeant. It's the other way around. David Hailey feels sorry for us."

Jenner noticed that Agnes Ledgerwood's revelations were having a positive effect on Schroder's tobacco consumption as he watched the detective stub out an unlit cigarette. "I don't think I understand what you're saying, Mrs. Ledgerwood," Schroder finally said. "Or else you're confused."

Agnes laughed without humor. "No, I'm not, Sergeant. I know what I saw. While the budget committee was standing on the sidewalk in front of the church admiring the nativity scene, David Hailey came walking out of the parsonage carrying his naked wife in his arms. Well, you can just imagine how shocked we were. We were speechless—except for Roy O'Brien. He cursed, but then Roy's a truck driver and I imagine all that long-distance driving tries a man's patience until profanity becomes a habit. Goodness knows, when I get caught behind a slowpoke on the highway or some teenager cuts in front of me in traffic, I'm tempted to cut loose myself. At any rate, Roy was the only one who said anything then. The rest of us were just frozen, unable to believe what we were seeing. Even when Reverend Hailey laid his wife on the ground, then stripped the robe off the mannequin, we didn't move. Not until he propped his wife on the bale of hay and pulled the robe over her head did we finally move. And we still didn't run. We walked slowly, very slowly—as if we were wading through mud—toward that manger scene. Roy was cursing with every step by then. I guess he was the only one of us who realized she was dead. *I* certainly never imagined it, and I don't believe Mildred Fisher did either."

Agnes closed her eyes for a second, then opened them, but Jenner didn't think she was seeing him or Schroder. Agnes Ledgerwood was seeing her minister dress a dead woman in a virgin's robe. Jenner figured she'd be seeing that image over and over again for a long time.

"When we got close, Roy spoke. 'What the hell do you think you're doing, Reverend?' is what he asked," continued Agnes. "But David Hailey didn't answer, Sergeant. He carefully arranged Amanda's hair over her shoulders before he turned around. And he *still* didn't answer. He just looked at us, his eyes so full of pity and sorrow that even Roy couldn't say anything. We stood there looking at him, and he stood looking at us until finally Glen Williams asked if he should call an ambulance. I mean, by then we all knew something was wrong with Amanda Hailey. It's the eyes, you know," she added.

Jenner knew.

"When did you know Amanda Hailey was murdered, Mrs. Ledgerwood?" asked Schroder.

She blinked, as if realizing she was sitting behind her desk in her own office and not standing in the cold staring at a man Jenner figured had to be mad as a hatter or mean as hell. "When David Hailey told us. 'Amanda is murdered' were his words, and those were the very last words he said. Then he just stood there looking like he felt sorry for us until the sheriff came."

She wiped her eyes and threw the tissue in a wastebasket, then leaned across the desk toward Schroder. "I hope you lock up that man for a long, long time. He committed murder, he *vandalized* a holy symbol, and he tried to manipulate us into feeling guilty. And he succeeded! With me at least. And, Sergeant, he knew what he was doing every minute. He wasn't dazed or shocked or reacting like a puppet controlled by some irresistible impulse. We were the puppets and he certainly pulled our strings and watched us dance."

"What do you think, Jenner?" asked Schroder after Agnes Ledgerwood had stumbled out of the church office.

"It makes me want to turn back the calendar to September when I was running up and down Amarillo Boulevard hunting the Boulevard Butcher. Now there was an honest, straightforward killer, Schroder. He was a damn sociopath who killed because he liked it, but at least he didn't try to shove the blame off on anybody else. But David Hailey's a different piece of work. He's slimy. You can't get hold of him because your fingers slip. He can't just off his wife. He's got to make some kind of statement about it nobody understands so everybody will forget he killed her in the first place!"

Jenner heard himself shouting and realized he was standing over Schroder, but he didn't remember getting out of his chair. He abruptly closed his mouth and sat down again. He didn't have anything else to add anyway, and his legs were shaking. So were his hands, he noticed when he wiped the sweat off his forehead. He hadn't even met David Hailey, but the damn man already had him tied up in knots.

"Get hold of yourself, Jenner. We can't convict Hailey by letting him sidetrack us with religion."

Jenner looked up. "We can't convict him with all this gossip about his wife either. We're doing the defense attorney's job for him. We're proving his wife was a tart and that Hailey had a good reason for killing her in a fit of rage."

The detective shifted his bulk in his chair. "We haven't proved it yet, but we're getting there."

"Damn it! Why?"

"Because Maximum Miller doesn't like surprises. He has to disclose every damn thing to the defense, but the defense doesn't have to tell him jackshit. He can't even tell the witnesses for the state not to talk to the defense. He can tell them they don't have to, but he can't order them to keep their mouths shut. What he can do is prove up a good defense so he can practice shooting holes in it before he gets to the courtroom. What he *doesn't* want is some shyster sneaking up behind him and kicking his ass while he's leaning over tying his shoe. If that happens, and if Maximum Miller decides it's our fault, guess whose ass he's gonna plant his size fourteens on?''

Jenner flinched. ''Ours?''

Schroder showed his nicotine-stained teeth in what passed for a grin. ''Nope. Mine. I'll kick yours myself. Now let's get another witness in here and find out more about Mrs. Hailey besides the fact she liked loud music.''

''I don't have to like it,'' muttered Jenner, wiping his brow again.

''Never said you had to,'' said Schroder, lumbering to the office door and summoning the next member of the budget committee from his seat on a church pew along one wall of a small foyer. ''Just keep your opinions to yourself unless you're talking to me. Until you've worked a few more murders you don't have any credibility with Maximum Miller anyway. He likes his homicide detectives the way he likes his bourbon—aged.''

Aged was a good word to describe Hank Gregory, a deacon in the Church of the Holy Light and a member of the budget committee. What hair remained on his head was a soft white, and his skin was tanned the color of leather from a lifetime spent farming under the hot Panhandle sun. He looked experienced, seasoned, mellowed, venerable, and undoubtedly bursting with wisdom.

Maximum Miller ought to love him—if Hank Gregory lived long enough to testify.

Because the old man also looked infirm. Judging from the way he clutched his chest, he was more likely to pass through the pearly gates than a courtroom doorway. Witnessing a murder apparently had been hazardous to Hank Gregory's health.

''Are you all right, Mr. Gregory? Do you need a doctor?'' asked Jenner, rising to grasp the old man's arm and help him to a chair.

Gregory's eyes were so light a blue, they appeared almost clear—clear enough to reveal a flash of humor. ''You mean because I'm holding my chest? Well, don't worry about it. I'm just checking to see if my heart's still beating. When you pass the ninety-year mark, it's a good idea to do that once in a while, just to remind yourself something still works same as it did when you were twenty. Sure as hell nothing else does. Your joints creak, your eyesight and hearing and kidneys weaken, your prostate swells, and your pecker don't. The truth is, longevity ain't all it's cracked up to be."

He lowered himself gingerly into Agnes Ledgerwood's secretarial chair and peered across her desk at Schroder. "So what do you make of this business, young man?"

Jenner would bet nobody had called Sergeant Ed Schroder a young man since the Eisenhower administration, if then, but other than a slow blink, the detective didn't react. "We hoped you could tell us, Mr. Gregory," he said.

Gregory folded his hands and shook his head. "I purely don't know and that's the truth. When I first seen him carrying his wife's naked body, I thought they were gonna fool around and I'll confess to feeling envious. Any man who could keep his mind on that kind of business when a forty-mile-an-hour wind is blowing sleet on his bare behind is a better man than me. But it didn't take long for me to forget that notion. Mrs. Hailey was just too limp, like maybe she was unconscious. Then, when he laid her on the ground while he stripped the clothes off that dummy, I knew something was bad wrong. That ground was covered with sleet and cold enough to rouse anyone short of the dead, which by then I figured she must be. Except I didn't really believe it. Nobody would, Sergeant. A man can't shift gears that fast. You keep looking for an explanation that makes sense. Well, I'm still looking and I ain't found it yet."

"You have no idea why David Hailey murdered his wife?" asked Schroder.

The old man rubbed a palsied hand over his face. "That ain't the explanation I'm talking about. It's not common for a man to kill his wife, but it ain't unheard of either—not like a preacher who mocks God."

"Mocking God isn't against the law unless you vandalize a church or create a disturbance during the Sunday-morning sermon, Mr. Gregory, so there's not much I can do about it except charge Hailey with mistreating a corpse," said Schroder, lighting another cigarette.

Gregory studied his folded hands, then looked up again. "That might be it, Sergeant. Hailey killed his wife because she was a disturbance and he liked things peaceable. It used to be a preacher's wife looked like she wore homemade underwear. A man never thought of her as a woman at all. A man couldn't hardly think of Amanda Hailey as anything else. It was mighty hard to keep your mind on the sermon with her sitting in the same church, and I don't think David Hailey could handle it. I think he decided the leopard couldn't change her spots, so he killed the leopard."

Suddenly the old man hammered his fist on the desk. "That's it, Sergeant! That's why he did what he did. He couldn't change her into what he wanted her to be. He couldn't guide her the way he did the rest of us. He couldn't *control* her if she was alive, but dead he could make her into whatever he wanted. He could stick her body in that manger scene and pretend she was pure. That's using religion for your own ends without any regard for what other folks might feel and that's a worse crime than murder."

"Just a damn minute!" exclaimed Jenner. "That manger scene is just lumber and paint and stuffed animals and a bunch of mannequins. Amanda Hailey was a woman."

"She's just another mannequin now, ain't she, sonny?"

"Not to me she isn't!"

Gregory sighed and suddenly looked as old as Jenner knew he was. "Well, that's good. She ought to mean something to somebody, and I don't mean to be saying that Hailey's killing her wasn't wrong. It was. But that manger scene means something, too. It's a symbol of God's love, and David Hailey turned it into a symbol of man's hate. There wasn't no call for that. No call for it at all."

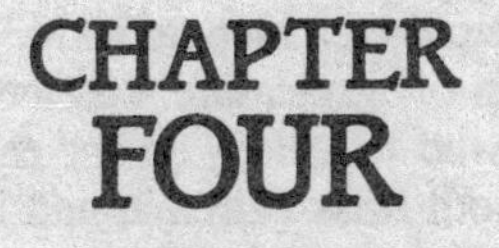

CHAPTER FOUR

TO LYDIA'S EYES THE MINISTER'S FIRST NAME WAS APROPOS. He looked like Michelangelo's David: tall, slim, curly hair, large, wide-set eyes, full pouty lips (she'd never liked pouty lips on a man), and cold and still as marble. A closer look disclosed differences: his hair was a pale brown—almost champagne; his eyes were blue, with fine lines fanning out from the corners; his skin very lightly tanned. And he was alive, of course. She could see his chest rise and fall with each breath. Still, she couldn't get over her initial impression: David Hailey was a cold, hard man, and John Lloyd would be better off appealing to the statue his client resembled.

Not that John Lloyd would listen to her. At least he hadn't so far. Lydia pressed her lips together so tightly they ached. It was better than letting her mouth tremble, which it had a tendency to do ever since her argument with John Lloyd. Damn it, but she hated women who cried when men disappointed them. She hated the old adage that crying made a woman feel better. Tears never made her feel better; they just made her throat hurt, her nose drip, and her makeup run.

Tears were not her idea of an adequate substitute for throwing a silver coffeepot—or a right hook.

Sometimes acting like a mature professional had little to commend it.

The only lift to her sagging self-esteem was that occasionally even John Lloyd couldn't have it his way. Occasionally even John Lloyd's ego received a blow to its id. And he didn't like it if his expression of displeasure was any indication as he glared at the man who sat quietly on one end of a bunk bed.

"Mr. Hailey, both Miss Fairchild and I are familiar with the lack of amenities offered by the average jail. We are familiar with both the odor of disinfectant and that generated by guests whose personal hygiene is nonexistent. We are familiar with the lack of privacy and with the poor tailoring of the common jail uniform. In short, there is little about the conditions of your incarceration that we do not already know. Therefore, refusing to leave your cell to speak to us serves no useful purpose except to call attention to your self-styled martyrdom, and I have no patience with martyrdom, self-styled or otherwise. As I told you, I have been requested by a member of the community to act as your attorney—"

"Who?"

David Hailey's voice was deep and resonant and so persuasive that Lydia had actually relaxed her lips enough to answer when John Lloyd intervened by tapping his cane on the concrete floor. "By no one who believed you innocent, sir," he said. "To the contrary, the individual is quite convinced of your guilt, so you need not expect any emotional support from that quarter. Nor from any other. Judging from the extraordinary number of people gathering on every street corner in Canadian in spite of the miserable weather, I suspect that Idi Amin would be more likely to find forgiveness for allegedly feeding his political foes to the crocodiles than you will for committing sacrilege."

"Sacrilege?"

David Hailey closed his eyes for a brief second, and Lydia debated pressing herself against the cell bars. If the minister's closed eyes and upturned face meant he was praying, then in her opinion he was seriously courting being struck by light-ning for his hypocrisy and she didn't want to be anywhere in the vicinity.

On the other hand, steel bars were good conductors of electricity if God's aim was careless.

She stepped behind John Lloyd. At five feet ten inches in her stockinged feet and over six feet in her high-heeled boots, she could peer over his shoulder at Hailey and still be shielded from any untoward divine retribution. She didn't worry about John Lloyd. God made a point of staying on John Lloyd Branson's good side.

"Sacrilege," repeated Hailey as he opened his eyes to look at John Lloyd. "I'm sorry to distress so many people. It wasn't my intention."

Lydia thought she might like to exact a little divine retribution herself. "You didn't think murdering your wife and playing Barbie doll with her body would *distress* people? You didn't *intend* to cause strain or anxiety or discomfort? In other words, you're not sorry you killed your wife, but you're oh so sorry to upset the neighbors!"

"That is enough, Miss Fairchild," said John Lloyd, flinching and stepping to one side. "Not only will our client be sufficiently pilloried by others without your adding to the outcry, but your skulking behind my back and hissing over my shoulder is distracting."

"He's not our client yet. He hasn't agreed to let us represent him," Lydia pointed out. "And I wasn't hissing. I was shouting."

"And your remarks are hardly a recommendation for our employ, Miss Fairchild, but perhaps Mr. Hailey will overlook them. Your passionate nature often generates comments you later regret."

Lydia considered denying that she would ever regret a word she had said, but decided against it. John Lloyd's expression was enough to make a saint examine his conscience.

Satisfied that he had quelled rebellion, John Lloyd turned back to the minister. "However, Miss Fairchild's outburst has reminded me that we do not yet have a professional relationship. Do you wish us to represent you?"

David Hailey studied the attorney. "Why do you want to?"

John Lloyd arched one eyebrow. "Defending the accused is what I do, Mr. Hailey."

"You didn't say you defended the innocent."

"My clients are usually guilty. The innocent seldom need defending. In spite of television's and novelists' fondness for stories of the innocent victim who is sent to prison for crimes he did not commit, the reverse is usually true. Criminals are usually guilty of the offense or offenses for which they are convicted as well as numerous others with which they were not charged. Unfortunately, man is flawed and reality more sordid and much less romantic than fiction."

Hailey leaned forward on his bunk, an expression in his eyes so intense that Lydia found herself holding her breath. "Then why do you defend the guilty, Mr. Branson? Surely they deserve to be sent to prison?"

John Lloyd straightened. "Because, Mr. Hailey, out of a hundred thousand guilty, there is one who is not. Someone must believe in him."

Lydia wondered if John Lloyd would ever feel as much passion for her as he did for the law.

Hailey nodded his head. "Then our professions are similar, Mr. Branson. We are both shepherds searching for the lost sheep."

Lydia seriously considered gagging. She settled for rolling her eyes toward the ceiling.

"An adequate metaphor if not carried too far," replied John Lloyd. "Are Miss Fairchild and I suitable shepherds?"

Hailey didn't answer but turned his head to look at Lydia. "Would you defend me, Miss Fairchild?"

Lydia felt as if she were caught in a spotlight. It was his eyes, she decided. They were like blue lasers burning through one's skull to secret thoughts beneath. Much as she would like to hide, she could not. "No! I'm on your wife's side," she blurted.

"Amanda," Hailey whispered, and he looked away, but not before Lydia saw the grief in his eyes. Grief, not regret and not remorse. The minister might mourn his wife, but he didn't regret killing her.

The silence stretched out until Hailey's sigh finally broke it. He looked up at John Lloyd. "I'll accept your offer to defend me."

"A wise decision, and one not too swiftly made. I expect the police will want to talk to you shortly, and I want to hear your explanation of last evening before they interrupt with their questions, which I do not intend for you to answer in any case. Miss Fairchild, your notebook, please."

Hailey clasped his hands loosely and leaned forward again. "I don't think you understood me, Mr. Branson. You may defend me, but I will not defend myself."

Lydia huddled deeper into her coat and shivered. She was nearly as cold sitting in John Lloyd's Lincoln Continental as she had been standing outside. Leather seats might be luxurious, but sitting on them in winter weather was too close to sitting on a block of ice. Her hips and thighs were going numb.

"Aren't you going to turn on the heater, John Lloyd?"

John Lloyd started the car. "My apologies, Miss Fairchild. I was preoccupied and failed to remember that you are unused to a Panhandle winter."

"You don't have to apologize, John Lloyd. A person in shock does have problems dealing with ordinary tasks."

His head whipped around and he glared at her. "Miss Fairchild, preoccupation is not synonymous with shock. My mental faculties are not the least disturbed."

"Maybe not, but your physiological reaction to David Hailey's comment was something to behold. I hope you have a backup cane at home, because you certainly splintered that one when you slammed it against the floor. It's comforting to learn that even your professional demeanor cracks occasionally. Makes you seem more human, more like an average guy."

"I am *not* an average man, Miss Fairchild, and my professional demeanor did not crack."

"Looked like it to me—unless mistreating inanimate objects and calling your client a fool constitute acceptable professional behavior." She folded her arms and smiled at him. "I think the evidence proves that more cracked than just your cane."

She watched muscles tighten on either side of his jaw and wondered if he was grinding his teeth. "Miss Fairchild," he finally said, sounding as if he were forcing his words out between clenched teeth. "I merely responded to a verbal stimulus in a somewhat physical manner."

"That's what I said. You cracked." She leaned over and patted his shoulder. "It's all right, John Lloyd. You don't have to make excuses for yourself on my account. I probably would have broken the cane over his head."

He brushed her hand away. "Miss Fairchild, that does not reassure me. The thought that your propensity for resorting to physical violence to relieve frustration might be contagious is nearly as disturbing to me as learning that I have a self-made martyr for a client."

"Client! You can't still be considering defending him, John Lloyd. Not now. Not after what he said. Putting aside the fact that he's guilty, you can't represent a man who won't talk to you."

John Lloyd tapped his fingers on the steering wheel, something Lydia had noticed him doing whenever he was feeling provoked—usually with her. "If he does not speak, then he cannot lie. Never forget, Miss Fairchild, that the criminal defendant is frequently a consummate liar and will all too often lead the gullible astray with self-serving statements. I am at least spared that possibility, remote as it may be, since I do not make a practice of believing my clients without supporting evidence."

Lydia rubbed her temples. As usual, John Lloyd's logic was giving her a headache. "Then why did you get so angry at Hailey?"

"I despise self-made martyrs, Miss Fairchild. By going like a lamb to the slaughter, David Hailey is making a great show of suffering in order to win sympathy. He will find instead a multitude eager to pick up the sacrificial knife and slit his throat. His behavior will avail him nothing and it seriously undermines both his defense and his relationship with God. The Almighty will not accept his posturing and neither will I."

Lydia wished she didn't feel compelled to defend David Hailey. She wished she hadn't seen the grief in his eyes and thought of a psychological explanation for his behavior. Most of all she wished John Lloyd was right and she was wrong because she hated giving David Hailey's character the benefit of a single doubt. But the fact remained that John Lloyd's thinking was tied up in religious symbolism and hers was not. That made her the more objective observer.

"I don't know what God believes, but I think that you're misinterpreting his behavior, John Lloyd. I think David Hailey is refusing to talk because he knows he's guilty of murder, wants to be punished, and doesn't intend to help you prevent it."

John Lloyd tilted his head as he looked at her. "An interesting observation, Miss Fairchild, and although based upon an unproven assumption, it still has merit."

"What unproven assumption?" demanded Lydia.

"We have not yet proved that David Hailey is guilty of murder in addition to sacrilege."

Lydia took a deep breath, let it out, and took another. Deep breathing to control one's temper had an advantage over counting to ten. There was always the possibility that she would hyperventilate and pass out, thus avoiding any further discussion of John Lloyd's growing obsession with religion over reality. "He's not in jail for sacrilege or desecration or even creative undertaking, John Lloyd. David Hailey was arrested for murder. Period. Finis. End of story."

John Lloyd frowned. "Miss Fairchild, you are confusing an arrest with a conviction. While most of our clients are not innocent, it does not necessarily follow that they are guilty. The prosecution must prove beyond a reasonable doubt that David Hailey committed murder, which means I must prove it first."

Lydia rubbed her temples again. If anything, her headache was getting worse. "John Lloyd, I am a reasonably intelligent woman. I am also a reasonably logical woman. I don't believe in crystals, the power of pyramids, the Bermuda Triangle, a conspiracy to kill Kennedy, reading palms or Tarot cards, splattering rooster blood over an altar, or the existence of supernatural beings such as vampires and werewolves, but I'll be damned if all the aforementioned aren't more logical than you!"

"I fail to see how I may be compared to a palm reader," replied John Lloyd.

"All this talk of religion has short-circuited your brain. Your synapses aren't snapping. You are a *defense* attorney. You do *not* prove your client guilty. You prove your client is *not* guilty—although in this case maybe you better just aim for a hung jury."

"The most beloved principle of both generals and football coaches also applies to defense attorneys. The best defense is a good offense. I cannot prove my client innocent without first proving him guilty, using the evidence and witnesses provided by the prosecution. Once I win a conviction in my own mind, I can reverse my strategy to win an acquittal from an actual jury. It is elementary, my dear Miss Fairchild."

Sherlock Holmes used to say the same thing to Watson, and if Lydia remembered those stories correctly, Watson didn't always understand either. However, she had more sense than Watson. She wasn't about to ask for further explanations.

"Your observation of David Hailey's behavior has merit in other respects, Miss Fairchild," John Lloyd continued, pulling away from the curb in front of the Hemphill County jail.

"It does?"

"It suggests that he is not by nature a liar. It would in part explain the inexplicable. Faced with the necessity of either lying or confessing—and unable to force himself to do either—he remained silent then and allowed his actions to speak for him. He remains silent now for precisely the same reason. He cannot tell a lie."

"Damn it, John Lloyd, he's not George Washington!"

"He's not the Devil either, Miss Fairchild, although you persist in casting him in that role."

"Me? Not me. I'm not the one speaking in metaphysical tongues. I want to get back to basic English—as in guilt, innocence, murder, son of a bitch."

"That is the third possibility inherent in your observation, Miss Fairchild."

"What? That he's a son of a bitch?"

"That he is an innocent son of a bitch."

"W-what?" gasped Lydia. "W-what?"

"I believe you may be right, Miss Fairchild," said John Lloyd after a quick glance at her.

"W-what?" If she was right, then John Lloyd was wrong, but it wasn't like him to admit it.

"I believe you might indeed be suffering from sleep deprivation. I understand it often manifests itself in slurred or indistinct speech. I shall take you home before I drive to the Church of the Holy Light. Perhaps a few more hours of rest will enable you to speak without stuttering."

"I'm not stuttering!" yelled Lydia. "I mean, I was stuttering, but not because there is anything wrong with my synapses. I was temporarily shocked. You used a profanity."

John Lloyd frowned. "I suppose it is possible your use of vulgarities is also contagious as well as your propensity for violent reactions."

Lydia debated releasing her seat belt and giving him a firsthand—or first-fist—demonstration of her propensity for violence. A jab to his ribs or a right hook to his pompous jaw perhaps. But then he might lose control of the car on Canadian's ice-covered brick streets and crash into one of the town's ancient cottonwood trees or smash through someone's Victorian home.

He would blame her, of course.

No admission of extenuating circumstances.

No confession that his own remarks had driven her to violence.

A martyr.

Like David Hailey.

Guilty of the act but innocent of the intent.

Suddenly she knew how to prepare David Hailey's defense and it didn't have a damn thing to do with religion. Psychology, not theology, was the smoking gun. Or perhaps, in this case, smoking rock.

AD INTERIM

SACRILEGE!

He never meant to commit sacrilege, and not meaning to he did not consider that others would see his act in that light. He distressed—no, not that word—he wounded and confused his flock just as the tall young woman said. What was her name? Lydia? Yes, it was Lydia, but he doubted she was much like the Lydia of Philippi, the first Christian convert of Europe who opened her home to Paul. He could not see her sitting quietly at Paul's feet being instructed in Christianity. She had too much fire, too much passion, as John Lloyd had said. She would have gone toe to toe with the apostle over some of his opinions on women. She was not a meek woman.

Neither had Amanda been.

Amanda was not humble, nor did she allow herself to be easily imposed on. Despite all of his counseling, Amanda had not grown in patience. She had been too young, too impulsive, too defensive when reproached. And at the last, when he should have been tolerant and forgiving of her, when he should have wiped her tears, he had been silent. He had let his anger overcome him and he chastised her.

He covered his face. "Forgive me, Amanda."

CHAPTER FIVE

JENNER FIGURED THE CHAIR HE WAS SITTING IN MUST HAVE come from a seventh-grade Sunday-school classroom. It was a wooden seat and back bolted on a tubular-steel frame and was exactly two inches too small in every direction for his six-foot body. He felt like Ichabod Crane: all knees, elbows, neck, and feet perched on a slab of wood that left one inch of buttock hanging over either side. Every few minutes he shifted his weight from one cheek to the other to keep the circulation going. It was going to be a near thing whether his butt went numb and fell off or Schroder ran out of witnesses to interview.

He would bet his money on waddling out of the church office unable to feel anything between the back of his knees and his shoulders, because Schroder showed no inclination to hurry. His considerable bulk rested comfortably on an adult-size wooden chair with sturdy legs, his cigarettes and ashtray within easy reach, and his faded blue eyes half closed like a sleepy turtle sunning itself on a rock. Schroder was enjoying himself doing what he did best: adding this witness's story to that witness's story until the sum equaled five years to ninety-nine for the murderer.

"What time did the budget meeting start, Ms. Fisher?" asked Schroder, and Jenner wondered when the other cop's consciousness had risen above addressing a woman as Miss or Mrs. depending on her marital status. He would have bet that Schroder's acknowledgment of changing social customs stopped at 1956.

On the other hand, Mildred Fisher didn't fit anybody's stereotype of a small-town maiden lady. Dressed in a woman's version of a man's suit, including vest and what looked to Jenner like a real necktie, with her hair cut short and brushed behind her ears, Mildred Fisher looked to be in charge of her life and anyone else's who might have the misfortune to come under her influence. There was nothing soft about this woman. She was all hard edges and uncompromising angles, and Jenner suspected her unmarried state was by choice. Either no prospective husband had ever measured up to her standards or she had never felt the need for one. He would bet on the latter.

She folded her hands with their medium-long polished nails. Jenner was surprised. Mildred Fisher and hot-pink nail polish didn't fit together. "The meeting began promptly at ten o'clock, Sergeant Jenner. I am the chairperson of the committee and I believe in starting on time."

"Ten o'clock," interrupted Jenner. "Why so late?"

"It is the Christmas season, and many of our merchants stay open until nine in the evening. Our store certainly does. Ordinarily we don't have a budget meeting in December at all, but Mr. Hailey was insistent. The hail-damaged roof had to be replaced before the heavy snows began. He was right, of course. An accumulation of snow on the roof could very easily cause leaks. We should have replaced it back in November, but the minister's personal life interfered and the budget committee voted to paint the parsonage instead. Not me, of course. I voted against it and so did Agnes, but there are four men on the committee and they let Amanda Hailey's woebegone face sway them. I was appalled. She wasn't even officially married to Mr. Hailey yet—only engaged—and I didn't think we ought to waste paint on an engagement."

She clenched her hands until Jenner noticed that her knuckles were turning white. "I was still hoping that the minister would come to his senses and realize that Amanda wasn't a suitable wife. At my age I should have known better. A man's brain goes south when he gets next to a cheap woman."

Jenner didn't need to ask how far south a man's brain went. He'd done a little thinking with his gonads when he was younger. Every man did—except maybe Schroder—but that didn't mean sexual attraction was wrong. Just sometimes futile.

Schroder leaned forward. "Any particular reason why you didn't think Amanda Hailey was suitable?"

"Sergeant Schroder, I never give an opinion without a reason."

Jenner would bet his next paycheck on that.

"She was too young, stood too close, and touched too much," continued Mildred. "She had no idea of what was proper."

"Couldn't keep her hands off the preacher?" asked Schroder, his sleepy turtle eyes looking a little less sleepy and a little more like those of a different reptile—one with rattles on the end of its tail.

Mildred's lips thinned. "She couldn't keep her hands off any man. The way she played up to Hank Gregory made my skin crawl. She was always patting his hand or his cheek, and the old fool would wiggle like a puppy. And it didn't stop with him either. She'd touch Glen William's arm and hug Roy O'Brien when he teased her. She'd even hang on to my brother Virgil's arm whenever she came into our dress shop. Well, I soon put a stop to that, I can tell you." She nodded her head abruptly and leaned forward. "I told her that if she didn't keep her hands to herself, I would be forced to speak to Mr. Hailey."

"And did you?" asked Schroder, his eyes wide open now and his head jutting forward like a snake ready to strike.

Mildred Fisher slumped back in her chair. "No, I didn't. I was a moral coward, Sergeant. I just couldn't talk about her behavior with Mr. Hailey. I'm the wrong generation to feel comfortable talking about"—she hesitated and her face flushed an ugly pink—"physical things."

"You mean sex?" asked Jenner, thinking that she had done a damn good job of talking about it so far, at least by innuendo.

Her flush deepened in splotches until she looked as though she had a rash. "I don't like your tone of voice, young man! It's your generation who has turned sex into a spectator sport, and you're judging me because I don't want to watch it. I couldn't talk to David Hailey about his wife without feeling like I was peeking in their bedroom window, so in the end I said nothing."

She swallowed and looked away, the flush gradually fading. "She brought on her own judgment, but even dead, he wasn't free of her. Even dead, she continued to corrupt. When David Hailey put her body in that nativity scene, he was saying that all women were tarred with the same brush. We were all impure in thought and deed."

Abruptly Mildred Fisher stood up. "If that is all, Sergeant, I must open the shop. The whole town will be watching, and I have no intention of hiding. What is done is done, and it solved nothing, least of all for David Hailey."

"Well, it sure solved the reverend's marital problems," said Jenner.

Mildred paused as she opened the office door and looked over her shoulder. "But it was too late, Sergeant. David Hailey had already lost his innocence."

"Lost his innocence, my Aunt Fanny!" Jenner exclaimed as the door closed behind Mildred Fisher. "She's talking about that bastard like he never had a naughty thought until he married Amanda Hailey and learned about the birds and the bees. Maybe she believes that, but I don't buy it. The meanness was already there. And another thing, Schroder, how many more reasons do you think we'll hear for Hailey's dumping his wife's body?"

Schroder lit another cigarette. "We got three more witnesses, so I figure we'll hear three more reasons. Put them all together and we've got a multiple-choice test with seven possible answers."

Jenner counted on his fingers. After three hours' sleep and a look at a dead body, he didn't trust himself to be able to add in his head. "We got six witnesses, Schroder. That's six answers."

Schroder opened the door and motioned to the next witness. "You forgot about the last choice, Jenner."

Jenner shifted his weight from one buttock to the other and wondered if the numbness in his behind was creeping to his brain because he was damned if he could figure out exactly what Schroder meant. "What are you talking about, Schroder? What choice?"

"None of the above."

Jenner thought about how he had always hated multiple-choice tests for that very reason: there was always a trick question with four or five parts to it and all the parts were correct but one—and that one contradicted all the rest, and what looked right was wrong—and he always missed the answer every damn time.

He listened to Virgil Fisher identify himself for Schroder's tape. It was easier than thinking about David Hailey, who was one big trick question.

"I'm Mildred Fisher's brother, Virgil Fisher," said the slender, middle-aged man, and Jenner felt a stab of pity. He suspected that Virgil Fisher had introduced himself in just that way all of his life, like he didn't have an identity apart from his sister's.

Certainly he looked like a man who always stood in somebody's shadow. His face was dead white with soft hazel eyes that looked slightly unfocused behind his wire-rimmed bifocals, a tiny button nose that he wiggled periodically, and a chin that receded just enough to be described as weak. Jenner decided that Virgil Fisher looked a lot like a timid rabbit.

"You're on the budget committee with your sister, Mr. Fisher?" asked Schroder. "Isn't it unusual to have two members of the same family on a committee?"

Virgil's nose twitched. "We're a nondenominational church with a small congregation and sometimes it's hard to get enough volunteers to serve on committees. And it's not like we're a voting block, Sergeant. Sometimes Mildred and I don't agree at all. The difference between the masculine and the feminine viewpoints, you know."

Jenner wondered which viewpoint Virgil represented.

"Did you agree on Amanda Hailey?" asked Schroder, lighting a cigarette from the stub of another.

Virgil shook his head. "Sometimes I did and sometimes I didn't. Amanda wasn't suited to be a minister's wife—anyone could see that except David Hailey—but Mildred was too hard on the girl. Amanda might have changed her ways eventually, but the more Mildred criticized her, the more stubborn she got. Cutting off her nose to spite her face. If everyone hadn't been so critical, or if David Hailey hadn't been so naïve, maybe Amanda would still be alive. Reverend Hailey always expected us to be more divine than we are. I think he was surprised when the congregation didn't take to Amanda being his wife. I think he just got frustrated and felt like he was caught in the middle between his ministry and his wife. And Amanda didn't help by always flirting with men."

Virgil glanced over Schroder's shoulder like a furtive rabbit searching for the fox. "Could I have a cigarette, Sergeant?" he asked in a whisper. "I don't smoke in front of Mildred—or behind her either. I usually go outside and always use breath freshener afterwards so there's no tattletale smell, but with all the smoke in this small room, she'll think it's all secondhand. I don't usually talk behind my sister's back, but she does have her faults. She has an obsessive personality, and smoking is one of her obsessions."

It was one of Schroder's, too, and the homicide cop had the closest thing to a recognizable smile that Jenner had ever seen. "Help yourself, Virgil."

Jenner blinked. Schroder had called a witness by his given name. Schroder never did that. Schroder had never even called *him*, Sergeant Larry Jenner, by his given name. Of course, *he* didn't smoke, and Jenner decided it was a circle-the-wagons mentality of smokers against the attacks of nonsmokers. On the other hand, this was a homicide investigation, and Schroder had no business buddying up to a witness.

Jenner coughed and cleared his throat. "So was Amanda Hailey at the budget meeting?" He ignored Schroder's frown. Somebody had to get this interview back on track if for no other reason than so he could rush outside for a breath of unpolluted air.

Virgil smiled. "Amanda—she always asked everyone to call her that rather than Mrs. Hailey—wasn't a member of the committee, but she did come in to serve coffee about eleven-thirty. She told the committee that the minister needed his sleep and we should make up our minds and take a vote—that is wasn't like we could refuse to fix the roof. She was wearing a caftan, a soft gold-colored one that complemented her hair," he added with a smile and an even more unfocused look. Jenner had seen the same expression on adolescent boys trying to rent adult videos with a false ID.

Virgil exhaled a lungfull of smoke along with a burst of words. "It was a very modest garment and inexpensive, but Amanda was one of those few women who could literally wear sackcloth and ashes and look absolutely"—he hesitated a moment before settling on a word—"gorgeous."

Jenner had the feeling that what Virgil really meant was that Amanda Hailey looked sexy, but was afraid to say so for fear his use of the *s* word would get back to his sister.

"Mildred and Agnes were horrified," continued Virgil. "In fact, Mildred told Amanda that she wasn't dressed for a church meeting and that she ought to leave because she was embarrassing her husband. Amanda hugged herself, glanced toward David Hailey, then dropped her arms and straightened up and stared right at my sister. She told Mildred that no one appointed her an arbitrator of fashion."

He stopped, a malicious smile on his face. Virgil Fisher had clearly enjoyed seeing his sister put in her place by Amanda Hailey. "I have to be honest, gentlemen. Mildred deserved a comeuppance." Then the smile disappeared and he continued. "But poor Amanda was outmanned from the start, I'm afraid. She mispronounced *arbitrator*, but before Mildred could correct her—which, believe me, Mildred would have—Reverend Hailey hustled Amanda out of the room."

"How long was he gone?" demanded Schroder, leaning forward until he was almost in Virgil's face.

Virgil flinched backwards. Most people flinched when Schroder got that close, but Jenner figured that this time it didn't have anything to do with the sergeant's nicotine-scented breath. Rattlesnakes always intimidated rabbits.

"I don't know. I wasn't watching the clock, but even five minutes seems like a long time when people are shouting."

"Who was shouting?"

"Roy O'Brien and Mildred. Roy has always liked Amanda and he doesn't always like Mildred. In fact, I don't think he has *ever* liked Mildred. They're too much alike. Both opinionated and not afraid to let you know it. Then David Hailey came back. He had been outside—I saw the sleet in his hair and on his jacket—but the cold air hadn't cooled his temper at all. His face was red under his tan and he was breathing hard. But he didn't say a word. Not a single word. But Mildred did. Sometimes Mildred can't leave well enough alone. 'Did you speak to her?' she asked, and David Hailey looked her straight in the eye and said, 'Yes, but you won't speak to her again.' His voice sent a chill down my spine, Sergeant. Sometimes David Hailey can be a very stern man."

"Son of a bitch!" said Jenner, and received a stern look of his own from Schroder for interrupting. He didn't care. He was tired of everyone dumping on Amanda Hailey. He was tired of all the civilized euphemisms like 'stern,' 'loss of innocence or control,' 'naïve expectations' for what was a deliberate homicide after all.

David Hailey didn't go outside in a sleet storm to cool his temper. He went outside to pick up a rock.

"Did anybody see Amanda Hailey after that?" asked Schroder.

Virgil stubbed out his cigarette and rubbed his soft white hands together. "The others did, of course, when David Hailey carried her out."

"You didn't look, Virgil?" asked Schroder.

"I wasn't there. As soon as the budget meeting broke up, I rushed out to warm up the car. Mildred is very sensitive to the cold. I didn't even know what had happened until Mildred came to the car to tell me, and even then I didn't understand at first. Not that Mildred was incoherent—Mildred seldom is—but I simply didn't believe what I was hearing. Finally I accepted it—Mildred was quite insistent—but I didn't run to gawk at Amanda. I couldn't force myself out of that car until the police came."

He looked at Schroder, his eyes glistening behind his bifocals. "I'll never forgive David Hailey, Sergeant. No matter what Amanda did, it didn't excuse being disrespectful to the dead."

"You got a problem, son?" Schroder asked after dismissing Virgil Fisher with his usual warning that he might want to talk to him again. "Your face is turning red and your eyes are bulging out of your head."

"Disrespectful to the dead!" exclaimed Jenner. "Jesus, Schroder. Doesn't anybody care that Amanda Hailey was murdered?"

"I do."

Jenner whipped his head around to stare at the husky, balding man who stood in the doorway. Just under six feet, with broad shoulders and a torso beginning its middle-aged slump into a paunch, the speaker had a fringe of black hair around his square head and piercing gray eyes. Dressed in Levi's, boots, and a red-and-black-checked flannel shirt, he was blue-collar and comfortable with it.

The man stepped inside the office and closed the door. "I'm Roy O'Brien, and I figure you must be Sergeant Jenner. Hank Gregory said you were pissed off as hell about Amanda. It's time somebody was."

"Sit down, Mr. O'Brien," said Schroder.

O'Brien walked past Agnes's desk. "If you don't mind, I'll just lean against the windowsill instead. I drive trucks for a living and spend most hours of every damn day sitting on my butt. I stand every chance I get."

"Suit yourself, Mr. O'Brien," said Schroder.

"I usually do—every chance I get," replied O'Brien.

Jenner watched Schroder's bushy eyebrows drawing together in a frown and wanted to snicker. Schroder didn't like witnesses who were too independent. They tended to compete with the detective for control of the interview. They usually lost, but the competition always put Schroder in a bad mood.

"I understand you and Mildred Fisher had a little disagreement during the budget meeting," Schroder began.

O'Brien chuckled. "You must have heard that from Virgil. Nobody else would bother since Mildred and me have a knock-down-drag-out over something anytime we're in the same room at the same time. If the same thing happens over and over, it becomes a habit and folks ignore it until ignoring it becomes a habit, too. But Virgil never misses a chance to tattle on his sister if he thinks it'll make her look like a fool. Can't blame him much for biting the thumb that squashes him."

"What was the fight about this time?" asked Schroder, his brows now a straight fuzzy line across his forehead. Jenner figured the detective was just being contrary since a) they already knew what the fight was about, and b) it didn't matter anyway since it didn't trigger Hailey's violence. He was already busy killing his wife and didn't witness it.

O'Brien folded his arms and leaned back against the windowsill, his gray eyes intent. "You mean Virgil didn't tell you?"

Schroder rolled his cigarette from one corner of his mouth to the other, a feat other smokers told Jenner was next to impossible. "Even cops have habits, O'Brien, and one of mine is that I don't tell one witness what another witness said. Just answer the question."

O'Brien inclined his head. "I ain't sure what you're after since I figure you already know, but I ain't got anything to hide. Mildred was being a bitch about Amanda and I didn't like it. It's none of her business if Amanda walks around buck naked in the parsonage. She didn't have any call to come down on her like that and I told her so. Called her a jealous woman and she blew up like a firecracker. She accused me of being soft on Amanda and I exploded like a goddamn bomb. I was feeling so damn guilty anyway and I didn't need to hear her crap—"

"What did you have to feel guilty about, O'Brien?" interrupted Schroder. "Did you and the preacher's wife have something going?"

O'Brien straightened like someone had jerked him up by his hair and clenched his fists. "No, damn it! And you watch your mouth. I don't give a hoot in hell if you are some kind of fancy cop. I'll kick the shit out of you anyway and take my chances on jail."

"Hey!" said Jenner, stumbling up and grabbing the edge of the desk to keep from falling until circulation returned to the whole lower half of his body. "Take it easy, O'Brien. Schroder's just trying to get a handle on the, uh, interpersonal relationships involved here." Actually, he thought Schroder was being a crude jerk and he couldn't figure out why.

O'Brien stood breathing hard, then finally unclenched his fists. "He ought to be more polite."

Jenner thought his legs might hold him up and let go of the desk to spread his hands in a gesture of helplessness. "What can I say? Schroder's not very subtle sometimes."

"Sit down before you fall, Jenner. I've seen drunks who didn't weave around as bad as you." Schroder switched his attention back to the truck driver. "If you've finished with your white-knight act, O'Brien, you can tell me how come you're so quick to jump to Amanda Hailey's defense when sure as hell nobody else is. Who appointed you her guardian angel and why the hell do you feel guilty about it?"

"What difference does it make?" demanded O'Brien. "I didn't kill her!"

"Every murder begins with a victim, and in a domestic murder like this the victim is the most important person. So talk to me, O'Brien, but don't waste your breath and my time talking about any plaster saint. Amanda Hailey stirred up trouble worse than a whore on a Sunday-school picnic and I want to know why."

O'Brien wiped his face on his sleeve and took a deep breath. "She didn't mean to rile people. That's the first thing you have to understand about Amanda. She didn't always stop to think how folks might look at things. Hell, Amanda didn't *know* how they looked at things. She didn't *know* how she was expected to act. She wasn't even much of a churchgoer until she got engaged to the preacher. She was just young and friendly and undisciplined as a pup, and like a pup, she was playful. That's why I introduced her to the preacher in the first place. He needed to learn to play and she needed somebody to pull up on the leash before she got too rambunctious and hurt herself. He needed to be more human like he was always trying to make folks from the Bible seem human, like Joseph was a working-class stiff and Mary was a housewife."

"So you just gave her to David Hailey like she was some mongrel puppy he could housebreak and maybe train to fetch the newspaper?" Jenner asked, glad he hadn't eaten any of Schroder's doughnuts because O'Brien was making him sick enough to puke. "I know a pimp in Amarillo named Jo-Jo Jefferson who I like a lot more than you. He's at least honest about being in the business of selling women, but he does it for money. What did you get out of this deal?"

O'Brien's face turned red from his chin to the top of his balding head. "Damn it, it wasn't like that! I didn't count on their getting married. I thought the preacher would maybe counsel her like a big brother, get her interested in doing something with her life besides slinging hash in a two-bit truck stop, and she'd teach him to laugh. She was such a funny little girl. I didn't know the preacher would fall for her like she'd poleaxed him. I never would have introduced them if I'd known that because there's something else you have to understand about Amanda. Come down hard on her and she wouldn't cower like a whipped pup. She'd turn around and nip you just like she did to Mildred. The harder you swatted her, the deeper she'd dig her teeth in. Maybe if everybody had left her alone or if the preacher had tried to smooth her rough edges, things would have worked out. But everyone kept at her, and she ends up dead."

O'Brien took a deep breath and wiped his eyes on his shirtsleeve. "Everybody else is more upset about David Hailey's sacrilege than about Amanda's murder, but not me. I'm more pissed that he killed her."

"Why do you think he did it, O'Brien?" asked Schroder.

The truck driver rubbed the back of his neck as if the long night had stiffened his muscles. "I don't know, unless he figured it was the only way to stop her."

"Stop her from what?" demanded Jenner. "Damn it, what exactly had she done?"

O'Brien looked at Jenner. "For all his talk about how Joseph and Mary and the disciples were ordinary folks like us and even Christ had a human side, he didn't see himself that way at all. He stood off to one side like he was better than average, and Amanda proved him a liar. David Hailey found out he could be as possessive and jealous and foolish over a woman as the next man and I don't think he liked finding that out. Amanda made him human, and killing her was the only way to deny it. I'm not surprised he's not talking. If he doesn't confess, then he doesn't have to admit to himself that he's so damn human that he killed his wife."

"What about his putting her body in the manger scene in front of witnesses?" asked Schroder.

O'Brien raised his eyebrows. "What about it?"

"I'd call that a confession."

"If he'd buried her, *that* would be a confession. At least burying a body shows more than just trying to hide what you've done. It shows you care some. But trading a body for a plastic figure? Sitting Amanda out in the cold to rot and for the animals to chew on? Hell, Sergeant, he was just putting out the trash."

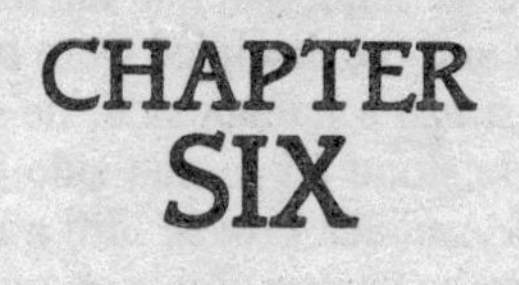

CHAPTER SIX

The Church of the Holy Light was built in the form of a cross, with two wings at the rear and on either side of a narrow, jutting sanctuary that reminded Lydia of a Currier and Ives print: all white clapboard and black trim with a belltower and a portico with wooden pillars that stretched across the front of the building. In the exact center of the portico were two doors at least eight feet high and four feet wide. A wide concrete sidewalk ran from the street to the front of the church. On one side of the walk was the nativity scene and on the other stood a gigantic Christmas tree whose outdoor lights were still blinking off and on in the gray winter morning.

The tree was a secular note in a religious theme, but its incongruence didn't disturb Lydia as much as the yellow crime-scene tape around the manger scene.

"Interesting," murmured John Lloyd.

"Obscene is more like it," said Lydia. "What a rotten thing to do. I'll never be able to look at another nativity scene without wondering which of the figures ought to be at the local funeral parlor."

"That was not my point, Miss Fairchild. I was referring

to the fact that the manger more closely resembles a common Panhandle stable than one in the Middle East."

Lydia tilted her head and examined the manger. "Well, it is made of wood and there is a saddle hanging on the back wall and there are bales of hay stacked around and that cow looks like a Texas longhorn, but maybe the congregation was just using the materials at hand. The figures are dressed in robes like you would expect."

John Lloyd stepped over the crime-scene tape and walked closer. "The robes are Pendleton blankets, Miss Fairchild, and if I am not mistaken, Joseph is wearing long underwear underneath."

Lydia followed him reluctantly. Amanda Hailey's body had been taken away before they arrived, but all of the remaining mannequins' heads were turned to look at the empty hay bale by the cradle as though waiting for her to return. The sensation of Amanda Hailey's absence as being only temporary was so strong that Lydia caught herself glancing toward the parsonage—almost in expectation of seeing the young woman walking across the lawn. Perhaps she had gone to fetch a bottle or another blanket for her newborn son, but wherever she was, she would be back.

"Miss Fairchild?"

Lydia blinked her eyes and shuddered. John Lloyd's harping on the supernatural—and religion certainly went beyond the laws of nature—had her seeing things. Or rather, sensing things that weren't real, and she didn't like it. "I'm sorry, John Lloyd. What did you say?"

John Lloyd's eyes were nearly as piercing as David Hailey's. "The costumes, Miss Fairchild. Joseph's long underwear, and I believe the three wise men are wearing boots and Levi's under their robes."

With a muttered apology to the nearest wise man, Lydia twitched aside his robes and saw that he was dressed more like a cowboy than a king, and a hard-riding cowboy at that. His boots were scuffed, his Levi's worn and faded. Like the Magi, he had ridden far to see the Christ child. That he rode a horse instead of a camel, that the manger was a rough stable in a desolate plain in Texas instead of a sun-hardened mud shelter in Bethlehem made no difference. She stared at the mannequin with its glassy eyes and faint smile on the plastic lips. In the dull gray light and blowing sleet, his rigid features softened and took on life.

Lydia felt herself begin to shake and fought against the panic that threatened her. She didn't need surreal visions. She needed practical, unimaginative, feet-on-the-ground reality. "Why?" she whispered. "What was he doing? What was David Hailey's point?"

"David Hailey believed that if the holy family and the wise men looked like people you met every day, then they would seem real and, by extension, so would Christ's birth."

Lydia screamed and whirled around, her fists clenched.

Glen Williams threw out his hands and backed away. "Hey, it's me, Miss Fairchild."

She felt John Lloyd clasp her shoulders from behind and felt like a big, crimson-faced idiot, and from the expression on Glen Williams's face, he thought so, too. "I'm sorry. I was thinking of something else and didn't hear you walk up. You . . . you startled me. But I wouldn't have hit you."

Williams looked as though he doubted that, and Lydia actually wasn't too sure herself. "I wouldn't have hit you," she repeated firmly. "I just don't like people sneaking up on me."

Williams nodded. "It's okay, Miss Fairchild. I understand."

He might, but Lydia doubted it, not unless she explained about being trapped in a room by a serial murderer and how defenseless she had felt; not unless she explained how the Boulevard Butcher had haunted her for months after she'd killed him in self-defense; and not unless she explained that the experience had left her a legacy of fear. But worse than the fear was the sensitivity to things unseen and feelings unspoken. Before the Butcher she would never had stood in front of this nativity scene and imagined that Amanda Hailey was not dead so much as she was waiting out of sight.

But waiting for what?

She felt John Lloyd squeeze her shoulders. "Miss Fairchild, are you all right?"

Lydia took a deep breath. Perhaps more oxygen would clear her head. "I'm fine, John Lloyd. It's just that all this—the manger, the mannequins—it's eerie, and I don't like eerie. Not anymore."

"Ghosts again, Miss Fairchild?" asked John Lloyd, turning her around so he could study her face.

She shook her head. "Not the kind you mean. I've buried the Butcher. I just lost my objectivity for a minute and felt too much empathy for Amanda Hailey. And I can't do that. I have to take David Hailey's side against his wife's. The legal canon of ethics is very clear. I have to defend my client to the best of my ability."

"If it will make you feel any better, David Hailey will go down for life no matter what you and John Lloyd do, so there's no point in getting yourself in an uproar," said Glen Williams.

Lydia twisted around to face him and opened her mouth to argue, but then swallowed back her words. Williams was not only a prosecution witness, he was a prosecutor himself, and a defense attorney never revealed strategy to a prosecutor. She couldn't tell him that whatever else David Hailey was guilty of, technically he wasn't guilty of murder, and she intended to prove it.

Lydia would rather see the minister in hell, but that was her problem and she would have to handle it.

She had no choice.

She smiled at Williams. "Do you think I could see the parsonage? That's where the deadly deed was done, wasn't it?"

Williams frowned. "I don't know about that, Miss Fairchild. It's a crime scene and I don't think Sergeant Schroder and Special Crimes would appreciate your getting in the way. And I know damn well Maximum Miller would throw one of his ring-tailed fits."

"Sergeant Schroder," murmured John Lloyd. "And Maximum Miller. A formidable team, but one that Miss Fairchild and I have bested in the past."

"You won't beat them this time, John Lloyd," said Williams. "When the budget meeting broke up, David Hailey followed us out. I saw him nudging the rocks around the flower bed with his foot.'' He pointed toward the front of the church. ''Then he leaned over and picked one up. I'll testify to that in court and not even one of your bloodletting cross-examinations will make me drop the ball on this one.''

Lydia walked over to the flower bed and studied the round depression in the frozen ground, then glanced toward the parsonage, which was a good fifty feet away. ''Then what did David Hailey do?'' she asked, turning around to face Williams and John Lloyd, who had followed her.

Williams frowned. ''You know, Miss Fairchild, I haven't been officially interviewed yet, so I think I'd better stop talking out of turn. You can read my statement after Sergeant Schroder takes it.''

''What difference does it make?'' asked Lydia, frowning back at him. ''Are you planning to tell Sergeant Schroder one thing and me another?''

Williams pulled a handkerchief out of his pocket and wiped his face. ''I see John Lloyd's trained you, Miss Fairchild. You like to play hardball, too.''

''I don't understand why men always have to reduce everything to sports terms,'' snapped Lydia. ''Must you resort to locker-room mentality when you don't want to answer a woman's question?''

Williams flushed. ''Damn it all, John Lloyd. She keeps this up and she's going to be meaner at cross-examination than you are.''

John Lloyd shrugged, a casual motion that barely lifted his shoulders, but Lydia noticed that his eyes were anything but casual. Beady—or predatory—might best describe them. ''Miss Fairchild has never subscribed to the theory that honey catches more flies than vinegar.''

Lydia wasn't sure whether he was complimenting or criticizing her and didn't particularly care. At least he wasn't lecturing her on professional courtesy. ''That's because a splash of vinegar is more likely to get an honest reaction.''

The D.A. looked startled, then shook his head and smiled. ''I don't mean to give you a hard time, Miss Fairchild, but for just a minute there you sounded a little like Amanda

Hailey—a little on the tart side. I heard her giving David a hard time once about always talking in Bible terms." His smile disappeared. "To most men sports is a common language. To David Hailey it was the Bible. He and Amanda just flat didn't have a common language," he added. "I used to wonder how they talked together at all."

"Well, it was a short conversation in any case—twelve days' worth," said Lydia, thinking that as an apology, his comments weren't bad. As an answer to her question, they stank. If vinegar didn't work, there was always nagging. In her opinion, it was a much, underutilized legal tactic.

Wrapping her arms around herself and shivering as she walked toward the parsonage, she asked, "So what did David Hailey do after he picked up the rock?"

"Persistent, aren't you, Miss Fairchild?" asked Williams, shaking his head. "So was Amanda Hailey sometimes."

Lydia didn't intend to allow herself to be diverted by listening to any more parallels between herself and the victim. Defending David Hailey was hard enough as it was. Besides, the effectiveness of nagging depended on endless repetition, like water dripping on the stone-hard heads of men.

"What did David Hailey do next?" she repeated.

Glen Williams threw up his hands. "All right, I'll answer. He went back to the parsonage and closed the door behind him."

"He *walked* back?" asked Lydia. "He *ran* back? He *skipped* back?"

Williams frowned again, his eyes straying back toward the flower bed. "He straightened up and stared at the rock in his hand, then walked rapidly toward the parsonage. I guess some might say he was in a hurry."

"Thank you, Mr. Williams. Now what happened immediately prior to his picking up the rock?"

"Nothing happened! We said good night and walked away. Then Mildred Fisher insisted we all walk over to look at the nativity scene. I wasn't much interested to tell the truth. It was colder than a gold digger's butt in the Klondike, and I helped build the damn manger, so I didn't need to look at it again, but Mildred was on her high horse, and I guess we all wanted to calm her down."

"Why did you need to calm her down?" asked Lydia. "And who is Mildred Fisher?"

"She and her brother, Virgil, own the dress shop across the street from John Lloyd's office. You've probably seen it."

Lydia had. She had even gone in once but had left without trying on a single dress. In fact, she had been afraid to touch anything in the store. The prices were so far above her Kmart budget that she broke out in a sweat and was afraid she'd leave a perspiration stain on anything she touched and have to spend next semester's tuition buying the ruined garment.

"Mildred's rigid about a lot of things, and she took offense at what Amanda Hailey was wearing last night. Some kind of a gold robe or something. Anyway, the two of them sniped at one another until David Hailey took Amanda out of there, then Roy and Mildred got in a fight over the way Mildred had talked. They were going after each other and Agnes Ledgerwood, the church secretary, was trying to make peace the way she always does. I got disgusted and went outside for a smoke with Hank Gregory. It was cold as hell but a lot more comfortable than sitting around the preacher's dining-room table. Pretty soon Mildred whips out of the door and stomps off in the dark toward the parking lot on the other side of the church, and I knew the fight was over. Mildred always stomps off for the car when she loses a fight."

"So that was the end of the budget meeting?" asked Lydia.

Williams laughed. "Lord, no! Mildred can't drive a lick and as long as she's got Virgil to do it, she doesn't need to learn. A person would think she would be at Virgil's mercy, but it's the other way around. She's been ordering Virgil around since before he wore long pants. Sure enough, here comes Virgil through the door to coax Mildred back to the meeting with Agnes trailing behind him. Standard operating procedure for a budget meeting. Anyhow, we're all sitting around the table with Roy and Mildred glowering at each other when the preacher comes back in like a breath of cold air and tells Mildred that she won't speak to Amanda again."

"Interesting," murmured John Lloyd as he took Lydia's

arm. "I think we should get Miss Fairchild out of the cold, Glen."

"Just a minute, John Lloyd," protested Lydia.

"Don't thank me, Miss Fairchild. You're shivering and I've been remiss in my care of you. We'll continue this discussion later." He pulled her along toward the parsonage, and Lydia stumbled after him in a state of shock. John Lloyd Branson had used four contractions in a row, an unheard-of lapse of his customary syntax.

"John Lloyd! Wait!" said Glen Williams. He was uttering several expletives Lydia considered inappropriate for a church deacon when he stepped on a patch of ice and made a three-point landing on the frozen ground.

Lydia pulled back. "Wait, John Lloyd. Your friend might be hurt."

John Lloyd pushed her through the front door of the parsonage. "No one capable of such an outburst of scatological vernacular is seriously hurt, Miss Fairchild. Besides, for the duration of this case Glen is a prosecution witness and therefore not a friend." Impatiently he urged her through the parsonage living room. "Hurry, before our friendly prosecutor recovers his feet and his injured dignity and pursues us. I want to see the murder scene without any further delay."

Lydia's fleeting impression of the parsonage was that it was caught in a time warp: furniture from the late Fifties, freshly painted plaster walls, worn avocado-green carpet, and not a single object out of place. Magazines, mostly religious, were fanned out on the coffee table like a deck of cards, and sheet music was neatly displayed on a black upright piano whose chipped and yellowing ivory keys reminded her of an aged woman in need of dental care.

John Lloyd pushed Lydia down a short hall but caught her arm before she could enter the master bedroom, which was too crowded with Special Crimes personnel garbed in disposable clothes in any case to allow one more person elbow room. "Do not step inside, Miss Fairchild. I do not want to risk Maximum Miller's ire by contaminating the scene," he whispered.

"Then what do you want me to do?" Lydia asked aloud. Several of the Special Crimes evidence technicians looked up, and one, an attractive woman in her forties who reminded Lydia of her librarian mother, started toward the door.

"Be silent and, for the moment, just observe," John Lloyd answered so softly she could hardly hear him. "I will, of course, demand to see the videotape of the scene, but I want your impressions. Your woman's impressions, for it is a woman at the heart of this crime." He raised his voice as the evidence technician blocked the doorway. "Ah, Mrs. Watson, it is delightful to see you again."

Mrs. Watson lowered a molded-paper surgical mask and smiled at John Lloyd, ignoring Lydia completely, a reaction that no longer surprised Lydia. John Lloyd had a potent effect on most women—herself included—that defied any logical explanation based on the attorney's physical appearance, unless tall, lean men with faces similar to those found in paintings of fourteenth-century monks happened to make your thighs tingle.

Lydia admitted that her thighs were susceptible—and so were Mrs. Watson's if her adoring expression was any guide—but decided the catalyst was not so much John Lloyd's physique or face or even his deep, slow drawl and reputed wealth. It was his absolute self-assurance, a will more powerful than that of other men, and a sexual self-control that challenged any woman between puberty and death to tempt him. John Lloyd Branson was a mountain a woman wanted to climb because it was there. So far as Lydia knew, every woman who had tried to do more than scale the lowest heights had stubbed her toe and fallen flat on her face.

She suspected that Mrs. Watson's mountain-climbing expedition wasn't going to be any more successful, but at least her attempts kept her too occupied to notice Lydia's slipping just inside the bedroom door and studying Amanda Hailey's private quarters.

The room was small, cramped, and despite the fingerprint powder dusted on every surface, the disarray of drawers pulled out, the bedspread flipped up, and the tiny closet door standing open, the room was painfully neat. Even Amanda Hailey's vanity was bare except for a small hand mirror and a comb and a brush. No cosmetics at all.

The room was also chilly, although the sliding-glass door was closed and there were no windows to let in cold air. It was as if Amanda Hailey had taken the room's warmth with her when she died.

Lydia hoped so.

The grave was reputed to be a cold, cold place.

"Where's the murder weapon?" she asked abruptly.

Mrs. Watson whirled around, a shocked expression on her face. "My God, how did you slip past me? Out of here! This is a crime scene and you've got no business tramping around."

"Where's the murder weapon?" Lydia repeated. "You know, the rock?"

Mrs. Watson pointed at the door. "Out! You and Mr. Branson can visit this room after Special Crimes finishes, and you can look at the evidence after it's been processed."

Lydia shrugged and walked out of the room. She might have known that nagging wouldn't work on a woman.

"My apologies, Mrs. Watson. I am shocked by Miss Fairchild's behavior," said John Lloyd with a purr in his voice like a tomcat who had just licked up a gallon of cream. All he needed was a long black tail to swish.

"You damn hypocrite!" Lydia hissed at him when he caught her arm just as she was opening the front door. "You chauvinistic manipulator. You tin-plated bastard." She jerked her arm free. "And quit grabbing at me. If you want to handle somebody, go handle Mrs. Watson. I'm going to the car—to which I have the keys if you remember—and I'm driving home, pouring myself a glass of your bourbon, which happens to be illegal since this county is dry, and examine my options."

John Lloyd grasped her wrist. "Later, Miss Fairchild. I want to examine the dining room."

It was the absence of his usual slow drawl as much as the urgency in his voice that made Lydia allow herself to be tugged away from the door. John Lloyd didn't drop his exaggerated drawl unless he was moving in for the kill, but there was absolutely no prey that she knew of in the minister's dining room.

There was, in fact, nothing in the dining room except an old mahogany table, a matching breakfront holding sparkling-clean but modest china, seven chairs—one of them a vinyl chair from a kitchenette set—a few dirty coffee cups, some pencils, and six copies of the church budget. Glancing over the figures, Lydia noticed that the Church of the Holy Light had an astonishingly healthy bank balance.

Again, like the rest of Amanda's home, the room was neat, painfully clean, and one step above poverty. She felt her temper begin to rise. Given the church's bank balance, there was no excuse for the state of the parsonage. Modest was one thing. People expected ministers to live modestly. But this bordered on Third World poverty, and Lydia was incensed that Amanda Hailey was offered no better.

"This is rotten!" she burst out.

John Lloyd turned abruptly from his study of the dining-room table. "What is, Miss Fairchild?"

Again there was the urgent note in his voice, but Lydia paid no attention to it. She spread out her hands. "This. This house. The church could afford better. It's not fair, John Lloyd. I don't care if Amanda Hailey stood on the street corner every night and gave away"—she remembered she was standing in a parsonage regardless of its condition and substituted general terms for specific acts—"sexual favors, she deserved a more comfortable home. And she tried so hard." Lydia blinked back tears brought on by the sad emptiness she felt in the mean little room. "She tried so hard to make a home. I've never been in a house so clean and polished."

John Lloyd nodded as he glanced around the room before looking at her. "An astute observation, Miss Fairchild, or rather your interpretation of available facts is astute. I had, of course, noticed the excessive cleanliness, but had not considered that it might be because Amanda Hailey was trying to please. The question now becomes why did she cease to care."

"But she didn't, John Lloyd. At least she still cared enough yesterday to dust and vacuum and polish the glass and the brass drawer-pulls on the breakfront.'' She shook her head. ''The important question is: why did David Hailey murder the bride who was trying to please him? That, and when did he do it?''

''Excellent, Miss Fairchild! You also caught the significance of Glen's statement. Did David Hailey murder his wife when he removed her from the budget meeting, as his remarks to Miss Fisher seem to indicate when he told her that she would not be speaking to Amanda again? Or did he murder her after he allegedly picked up the rock? Two opportunities for murder and the prosecution will have to choose one or the other. In my experience juries do not like either/or scenarios in a murder case.''

Lydia started to tell him that she didn't believe this was a murder case—technically—but a deep voice that sounded like the speaker had gravel in his throat interrupted her.

''Branson, what the hell are you doing here?''

Lydia turned toward the speaker, hesitated a moment, then smiled at the untidy, square-bodied figure who stood in the open doorway flanked by a disgruntled Glen Williams and an Amarillo cop who seemed to have difficulty standing. ''Sergeant Schroder, do you have something in your eye? Your right eyelid is twitching.''

CHAPTER SEVEN

Canadian, Texas—December 5

JENNER FIGURED HE HADN'T SAT IN A COMFORTABLE CHAIR in two days, and the wooden theatre seats in the Hemphill County Courthouse were no exception. But at least he had a seat. The courtroom was so full of spectators, including newspaper, radio, and television reporters—some from as far away as New York—that the standing-room overflow lined the walls. No doubt about it. Canadian's murdering preacher made good copy.

Of course, so did the prosecutor. Built like a fullback gone to seed, Cleetus "Maximum" Miller was big, black, balding, and racially color-blind. Not that Miller didn't see people in terms of black and white—he did—but neither term had any relation to race. Black was guilty and white was innocent, period, and anybody foolish enough to suggest that his terminology might be politically incorrect earned himself a lecture on First Amendment rights and a permanent place in Maximum Miller's Hall of Fame for Ignorant Assholes. Anyone who wondered whether or not he was already elected to that dubious honor only had to glance at the list of names on the wall behind Miller's desk.

Maximum Miller gave a whole new definition to the term *blacklisted*.

Certain defense attorneys had been known to lose their breakfasts in the men's room just before facing him in a courtroom. One attorney had gone so far as to say that opposing Maximum Miller was worse than taking the bar exam three times. Miller had retorted that "the stupid son of a bitch ought to know since that's how many times he had to take it before he passed."

Maximum Miller passed the bar exam the first time with the second highest score for that year.

John Lloyd Branson beat him by a single point—or so Jenner had heard. He wasn't about to ask for confirmation. Mentioning John Lloyd Branson to Maximum Miller was the only thing in the known universe that gave the assistant D.A. indigestion. A loud belch punctuated any reference to the defense attorney, followed by the crunching sounds of antacid pills being consumed.

Miller hadn't belched yet, but Jenner figured it was only a matter of time, especially given the fact that Canadian's district courtroom had only one counsel table instead of two, and the prosecution and the defense sometimes literally rubbed elbows. Jenner thought setting an open can of kerosene next to a campfire might be safer than seating Miller and Branson side by side. Less chance of an explosion.

He guessed Maximum Miller's boss, Potter County District Attorney Robert Benson, thought so, too, because he was sitting between his assistant and the defense team. Actually, he was sitting between Miller and Lydia Fairchild with John Lloyd Branson seated on the other side of his blonde assistant. Jenner wasn't sure either Benson or Lydia could actually prevent an explosion, but maybe they could stamp out the flames before anybody got burned.

Schroder's wooden seat creaked under his weight as he leaned over to whisper to Jenner. "Sure can tell Bobby Benson will be running for reelection come January."

Jenner flinched away from Schroder's tobacco-scented breath. "How can you tell that?"

"This is what you call a high-profile case. That means we got more reporters than we got jackrabbits—and this country's sure as hell got plenty of jackrabbits. Benson couldn't buy this much publicity if he had a million dollars, and he's gonna need every mention he can get. He's got an opponent in his own party sniffing at his heels this time around. A man can't be responsible for sending people to prison without making enemies of every mama, papa, brother, sister, aunt, uncle, and cousin of the defendant. After eight years in office I figure Bobby's got a list a mile long of prisoners' relatives who wouldn't vote for him if he wore a halo and could raise the dead. His only hope for reelection is a big turnout at the primaries so maybe the voters who ain't mad at him will outnumber the ones who are. That means he needs a lot of publicity between now and April to get the vote out."

"I figured he came along to keep Maximum Miller and Branson from fighting," said Jenner, thinking that Benson would be lucky if the reporters paid enough attention to him to even spell his name right. No reporter who valued his job would write about an elected official who kept his nose clean and his pants zipped when he could interview instead John Lloyd Branson, the Perry Mason of the Panhandle, or Cleetus "Maximum" Miller, who always asked for the maximum sentence and got it.

"He'd sooner have a chance of stopping a tornado," said Schroder. "Besides, this is just an arraignment, not a trial. There's no jury to impress, just the judge, and all he's hoping to do is read the charge and ask the preacher how he's going to plead. Branson might ask to have the charge dismissed, just as a matter of form, but that's about all that he'll do." Schroder rolled his unlit cigarette to the other corner of his mouth. "Nope, I don't see that there'll be any fireworks between Branson and Cleetus today."

Jenner looked first at the back of Branson's graying blond head and the tense set of his shoulders, then shifted his gaze to Maximum Miller, who sat with thick shoulders hunched over the counsel table like a tackle ready to sack the quarterback. Maybe Schroder thought this would be a peaceful scrimmage, but Jenner had his doubts. There was something about the way both men were all tensed up that reminded him of the Cowboys and the Redskins awaiting the opening kickoff of an NFC championship game.

The only calm individual at the counsel table appeared to be the preacher, who was quietly reading the Bible as though the proceedings had nothing to do with him.

Damn cold-blooded hypocrite!

"All rise," the bailiff said in a monotone, and Jenner watched David Hailey carefully mark his place with a narrow purple ribbon before closing his Bible and rising as the judge entered the court.

Lydia Fairchild was watching Hailey, too, Jenner noticed, and judging by what he could see of her expression, she didn't like the preacher either. Her lips were pressed together so tightly that white lines bracketed her mouth. Jenner could almost feel her effort to keep her mouth closed against whatever outraged comments he felt she wanted to make. Her hands were clenched in fists, and she shifted from one foot to the other while Judge Myers seated himself at the bench.

"Be seated," said Judge Myers in his Panhandle drawl as he tucked an unlit pipe in the corner of his mouth, sucked on it, and frowned unhappily.

Distracted by the inroads the nonsmoking ordinances were making in the criminal justice system, Jenner only saw the end of Lydia Fairchild's altercation with David Hailey, which resulted in her possession of his Bible. However, since his and Schroder's seats were directly behind the counsel table, he did hear her whispered order to the minister.

The judge, however, did not. He cocked his head and spoke around his pipe. He was nearly as good at talking out of one side of his mouth as Schroder. "Did you address the court, Miss Fairchild?"

Jenner watched a red flush creep up the back of her neck as John Lloyd rose to his feet and clamped his hand on her shoulder to prevent her from rising. "Miss Fairchild was merely reminding our client to listen carefully to the charge, Your Honor."

Euphemistically, that was one way to put it, Jenner supposed, but he much preferred Lydia's actual words: "Pay attention, you hypocritical jerk, and give me that Bible before I break your neck and feed you to the wolves!"

The judge looked as though he believed John Lloyd may have misinterpreted his clerk's comment, but not even a judge went against the defense attorney if he had any other alternative. Myers cleared his throat instead, placed his unlit pipe in an ashtray out of habit, extracted the complaint from the court file, and peered over the bench at the defendant.

"Reverend"—the judge's mouth twisted as though he had trouble spitting out the word—"Mr. Hailey, are you represented by an attorney?"

Hailey sat silently until John Lloyd sighed and rose to his feet again. "I am representing the Reverend David Hailey, Your Honor."

Judge Myers cocked one eyebrow at the silent minister before continuing. "Mr. Hailey, you are before this court charged by the state of Texas with the offense of murder. The complaint alleges that on or about the second day of December of this year you did intentionally and knowingly use and exhibit a deadly weapon, to wit, a rock, that in the manner and means of its use and intended use was capable of causing death and serious bodily injury, and did then and there cause the death of an individual, namely Amanda Ruth Hailey, by striking Amanda Hailey with said rock, against the peace and dignity of the state of Texas."

The judge laid the complaint aside and folded his hands. "How do you plead to the charge, Mr. Hailey?"

Again the minister sat silently and John Lloyd finally answered for him. "My client pleads innocent, Your Honor."

Maximum Miller pushed back his chair and stood up. "Your Honor, the state requests that Mr. Branson plead his client in the usual and acceptable manner. That is, the state requests that Mr. Branson plead his client guilty or not guilty since his alleged innocence is for the jury to decide."

John Lloyd inclined his head toward Maximum Miller, and Jenner saw several reporters who were leaning against the walls surreptitiously straighten and edge toward the counsel table. "Your Honor," said John Lloyd in a deep, slow drawl. "Innocence is what is at stake here. I do not believe that the Texas Code of Criminal Procedures forbids a defendant from so stating that innocence at his arraignment. However, it is possible that I have overlooked such a statute, so if the illustrious assistant district attorney from Potter County could indicate his authority for objecting to my client's plea, I will of course amend said plea to conform to the law." He cocked an eyebrow at Miller. "If it is the law, and not Mr. Miller's private preference."

"Your Honor," began Maximum Miller.

Judge Myers held up his hand. "Just a moment if you please, Mr. Miller." He picked up his pipe and chewed on its stem while staring at both attorneys, then returned it to the ashtray and cleared his throat. "John Lloyd, I've never known you to overlook *anything* in the Texas Code of Criminal Procedure, and God knows I and every other judge wish to hell that you would—just once—so we wouldn't feel so damn inferior. An attorney isn't supposed to know more than the judge *every time*! It gets embarrassing!"

John Lloyd bowed his head briefly. "My apologies, Your Honor. It is never my intention to embarrass the court, only to defend my client."

The judge waved his hand. "Never mind the apologies, John Lloyd. Humility doesn't become you. But to get back to the point, if you say that your client can plead innocent instead of not guilty, then I'm not about to argue with you unless Mr. Miller can cite chapter and verse. Can you, Mr. Miller?"

Jenner heard Maximum Miller belch. "Your Honor, it's a matter of precedence. Our criminal justice system uses the terms guilty or not guilty."

"I will agree with Mr. Miller, Your Honor," said John Lloyd. "Those are the terms used, but neither adequately define my client's plea. Guilty means culpable of wrongdoing. Not guilty means legally blameless. My client is neither. He is innocent—which means he is uncorrupted by evil, malice, or wrongdoing. He is sinless!"

"Give me a break," Jenner heard Lydia mutter under her breath.

Bobby Benson grabbed his assistant's arm. "Drop it, Cleetus," he said in a low voice that carried to Jenner's ears but no further. "The reporters already have their evening headlines, and I guarantee you're going to look like a fool. Now ordinarily that wouldn't matter since both you and I know that you aren't. But this isn't ordinarily. This is twenty-six days before I have to file for reelection, and I can't afford to have my assistant look like a fool. So give in gracefully. It's just a matter of semantics anyway. It's nothing important."

Jenner thought the district attorney had a good point, but Maximum Miller shook his head. "You give that son of a bitch an inch and he'll take a goddamn mile, Bobby. Now I ain't for sure what the devious bastard's got on his mind, but I'll guarantee it's more than semantics! Getting the judge to let his client plead innocent rather than not guilty is important or else John Lloyd Branson wouldn't bother arguing about it."

"Mr. Miller," interjected the judge. "Can you cite a particular passage in the Texas Code of Criminal Procedure that specifically denies the defendant the right to plead himself innocent?"

Maximum Miller sighed. "No, sir, Your Honor, I can't, but I still argue that the court is setting a dangerous precedent."

Judge Myers chewed on his pipe thoughtfully before replying. "I've no doubt you're right, Mr. Miller. However, I can't think of a reason to rule against Mr. Branson—at least, not a reason that will hold up to scrutiny—so you win, John Lloyd. Your client may enter a plea of innocent."

John Lloyd inclined his head, and Jenner thought the lawyer's shoulders looked less stiff. "Thank you, Your Honor. And if I might step outside legal precedence again . . ."

"I told you so," muttered Maximum Miller to his boss. "Branson's got something up his sleeve besides his arm."

". . . and submit a motion for a change of venue at this time."

The judge looked thoughtful. "Well, it's irregular, but I believe I'll allow it. I'll set the date for a hearing on the motion for the first Monday after New Year's, if that would be acceptable to the prosecution. Mr. Miller, do you have any objections to that date?"

Maximum Miller hesitated, swinging his head to stare at John Lloyd. "No objection, Your Honor," he finally answered.

"Well, then—" began the judge.

"I object, Your Honor," interrupted John Lloyd.

"What happened to his drawl?" whispered a bewildered reporter Jenner knew wasn't from the Panhandle. In the first place he wore his hair in a ponytail, and in the second place he didn't recognize John Lloyd Branson's nut-cutting voice.

Maximum Miller did, though. His head came up and his nostrils flared as though he was sniffing the air for the scent of danger. "Your Honor, Mr. Branson can't object to his own motion."

"It is not to my motion that I am objecting," answered John Lloyd, his enunciation as clean and sharp as a scalpel. "It is to the date of the hearing."

"Give Mr. Branson some more time if he wants it, Your Honor," said Maximum Miller. "The prosecution has no objections."

"It is not more time that interests me, Mr. Miller," said John Lloyd. "It is less. I would ask for a ruling this afternoon."

"This afternoon! What are you trying to pull, Branson?" demanded Miller, leaning around the slighter figure of his boss to glare at the defense attorney.

John Lloyd spread his hands in a gesture of innocence. "Given the small population of Canadian and the extensive media coverage of my client's alleged offense, it is unreasonable to expect to be able to seat a jury who has not already heard of the case and formed an opinion. In the interest of justice, I hardly think you and Mr. Benson would object to a change of venue."

"We'd have to hold the trial in Timbuktu. They might not have heard of Hailey there," said Miller. "But we've damn sure heard of him in Amarillo and every other city in Texas. A person can be illiterate and know about the preacher. He's all over CNN worse than fleas on a dog. His case is even pushing Elvis sightings and alien kidnappings off the *National Enquirer*'s front page."

"I do not believe that Texas has jurisdiction in Timbuktu," replied John Lloyd.

"I didn't say it did!" shouted Maximum Miller.

"My client will, however, agree to your suggestion of Amarillo," continued John Lloyd.

"I didn't suggest Amarillo!"

Judge Myers's head had swung back and forth between the two attorneys as though he was watching a tennis match, his mouth opening and closing like a fish out of water before he finally pounded his gavel. "I've heard enough!" he shouted. "If either of you make another remark that isn't addressed to the court, you'll both be spending Christmas in the Hemphill County jail for contempt."

He leaned over the bench to stare at the two, neither of whom appeared to Jenner to be the least bit contrite. "Now that the point of behavior is settled—for the present at least—I'll address the point of law. Mr. Miller!"

"Yes, Your Honor?"

"Are you planning to argue against a change of venue?"

"No, Your Honor," said Bobby Benson before his assistant could do more than draw a deep breath.

"Who's the doofus in the three-piece suit?" asked the ponytailed reporter in a low voice.

Not low enough, though, thought Jenner as he watched the district attorney's ears and the back of his neck turn bright red.

Benson turned halfway around so that he was facing the reporter. "Your Honor, as Potter County's district attorney, whose office has accepted the responsibility of trying this case, I wish to assure the court that the prosecution is as interested in justice as Mr. Branson and has no desire to argue against a change of venue."

"He must be running for reelection," remarked the reporter. "That sure as shit sounded like a campaign speech."

A few spectators chuckled, and Benson's ears turned an even brighter red. Jenner decided that being a politician was a lot like being a cop: neither professional got any credit for good intentions.

Judge Myers hammered his gavel again. "Change of venue is granted. Are you sure about Amarillo, John Lloyd? That's just a hop, skip, and a jump from Canadian. I don't want you filing an appeal later claiming that your client couldn't get a fair trial in Amarillo."

"My client will waive his right to appeal on that point, Your Honor."

The judge leaned forward and rested his arms on the bench, a worried frown wrinkling his forehead. "Are you certain your client understands what he's giving up, John Lloyd?"

The defense attorney sighed. "Your Honor, Mr. Hailey does not wish the taxpayers of Hemphill County to bear the cost of a lengthy trial in some far corner of the state. He feels that his neighbors have better uses for their money than paying for food and lodging and travel for the witnesses, the attorneys and their staffs, and for the court. He does not wish to be a burden."

The judge cleared his throat. "We don't measure justice in dollars and cents, Mr. Hailey, and you mustn't either. Don't let the possible cost of a trial influence your decision."

"He is adamant on this point, Your Honor," said John Lloyd softly.

"I'd like to hear him say so himself, John Lloyd," replied the judge in a testy voice.

"Mr. Hailey refuses to speak on his own behalf. He trusts me to speak for him."

The judge capitulated. "All right, since everyone is in agreement, the trial will be moved to Amarillo on a change of venue."

John Lloyd leaned forward slightly. "Mr. Hailey also demands a speedy trial."

The judge nodded. "I believe I have room on my docket in March. Trial will begin on the fifteenth of March. Is that agreeable, Mr. Benson and Mr. Miller?"

The district attorney blotted his forehead with a handkerchief and shifted from foot to foot. He cleared his throat, looked at Maximum Miller, then nodded. "We agree, Your Honor."

Schroder leaned over and muttered in Jenner's ear, "Poor bastard's between a rock and a hard place. If something goes sour with this case, then the voters won't have time before election day to forget that he screwed up."

"But I thought Maximum Miller was trying the preacher," whispered Jenner.

"He is, but it doesn't make any difference. If Cleetus loses, Benson's the one the voters will hang. His opponent will see to it. If the judge had moved the trial to El Paso or Dallas—someplace far enough away so that the voters wouldn't pay much attention—then Bobby wouldn't have his ass hanging out like he does. But Branson did everything but turn somersaults to make sure that the trial will be held in Bobby's backyard." Schroder's brows drew together until they looked like a fuzzy caterpillar stretched lengthwise over his eyes. "Why the hell did he do that, Jenner? What's that shyster up to?"

The shyster in question stretched his six-foot-four-inch (and then some) frame to its full height. "Your Honor, my client does not agree to the date."

The judge looked puzzled but nodded anyway. As long as a defendant wasn't acting like a complete jackass, Myers was willing to be agreeable. Jenner figured it cut down on appeals in the long run.

"I can set the date for the first week in May, John Lloyd, if that will suit your client better."

John Lloyd shook his head slowly. "Justice is measured in minutes and hours, Your Honor. When a man is accused of such a heinous crime, each passing minute deepens the wound to his reputation and the goodwill he has accrued over time bleeds away until soon even justice cannot restore his good name to health. When that man is a minister, he is wounded more deeply and bleeds more quickly. My client demands swift justice. He wishes to go to trial in two weeks."

"What!" yelled Maximum Miller, bouncing to his feet

and glaring at John Lloyd. "That's damn impossible and you know it, Branson. No one but God himself can get ready to go to trial on a murder case in only two weeks. *No one*—including you!"

John Lloyd Branson turned slowly to face the assistant D.A. "The defense will be ready." He looked steadily at Robert Benson, Potter County District Attorney—and a desperate man. "Will the prosecution be ready to see justice done?"

The D.A. nodded his head vigorously. "Oh, absolutely, Mr. Branson. Cleetus will be raring to go, won't you, Cleetus?"

AD INTERIM

THE ANIMOSITY OF THE CROWD FOLLOWED HIM BACK TO HIS cell, and he sank to his knees beside his bunk. Had he been wrong to do what he did? Had he offended God with an act of sacrilege? Had his act blinded those he ministered to? Should he have chosen a more worldly course?

He shivered, chilled by the anger he had felt from the town, repulsed by the curiosity of the unbelievers. And afraid. He was afraid he had taken the wrong path. Afraid he would turn back. But if he did, if he rendered unto Caesar before God, then he would condemn a soul to damnation. Until God was asked for forgiveness, he had no response except to go on.

He wished he could confide in John Lloyd. But he could not. Nor could he confide in Lydia Fairchild. He must trust the wisdom of one and pray for the understanding of the other even though understanding did not always lead to forgiveness. He did not believe Lydia Fairchild would ever forgive him for what he did.

But he believed that Amanda had.

CHAPTER EIGHT

LYDIA STOMPED OUT OF THE COURTROOM AND DARTED across Canadian's redbrick main street and around the corner to John Lloyd's office. A reporter for *The New York Times* had filed a story about the eccentric and modest defense attorney whose nondescript office was located above a drugstore, which only showed how little that journalist knew. John Lloyd might be eccentric, but he certainly wasn't modest. And once past the small reception area, which was as far as the reporter got, his office was anything but nondescript. On the contrary, it was furnished with museum-quality antiques, including a rolltop desk that, according to rumor, had originally belonged to Temple Houston, a son of Sam Houston and a legend in the Panhandle for his legal brilliance and his eccentricity.

All of Canadian believed that John Lloyd Branson was the modern reincarnation of that pioneer lawyer. The fact that John Lloyd never used contractions and his syntax was straight out of the nineteenth century lent further credence to that belief. Lydia had little patience with that theory. John Lloyd was too damn arrogant to settle for being anyone's reincarnation.

Lydia bypassed the elevator in favor of running up the single flight of stairs. She had read somewhere that physical activity reduced stress. Obviously the author had not known John Lloyd Branson any better than the reporter for *The New York Times*. A twelve-hour day spent picking cotton wouldn't be enough physical activity to reduce the stress levels engendered by that skinny, devious, sneaky, morally dishonest, unethical, and *enraging* jerk. Between the Reverend David Hailey and John Lloyd Branson, Lydia wasn't certain but what she liked Hailey better.

She slammed open the door to John Lloyd's reception room, heard the rattling thud as it bounced against the wall, followed by the ominous crack of breaking glass. She whirled around to see a sunburst of cracks in the door's frosted-glass inset.

"Damn it!"

"Miss Fairchild! You broke Mr. Branson's door. Oh dear, he will be so upset."

Mrs. Dinwittie, John Lloyd's legal secretary, was the only person Lydia knew who could say "oh dear" without sounding affected. She was also the only person Lydia knew who could wear glasses with heart-shaped pink lenses without looking silly. In spite of her lurid past as an acquitted ax murderer, Mrs. Dinwittie possessed an innate sweetness that overcame such drawbacks as cliché-ridden speech, ridiculous glasses, dyed black hair set in crimped waves such as no woman had worn since the Thirties, and blush applied in a perfect circle on each round cheek. She looked like a Kewpie doll—and no one could really dislike a Kewpie doll.

At the moment, though, Mrs. Dinwittie's large black eyes were snapping with fire, and Lydia felt a flicker of uneasiness. She wondered if Mr. Dinwittie had seen that same angry expression in his wife's eyes just before she chopped him into Little Friskies.

"I didn't mean to, Mrs. Dinwittie. The door just slipped out of my hand." Lydia felt unbidden tears stop up her nose. She sniffed. "I was just so angry I didn't notice what I was doing."

Mrs. Dinwittie plucked a tissue out of the box sitting on the windowsill and tottered around her desk toward Lydia.

"Gracious, Miss Fairchild, I didn't mean to upset you. Now dry your eyes and blow your nose and tell me all about it. Did the arraignment go badly? Did the judge refuse bail?"

Lydia blew her nose. "We didn't ask for bail. John Lloyd thought Hailey would be safer in jail."

The secretary nodded her head and teetered back and forth on her three-inch heels. "Mr. Branson is as wise as an owl sometimes. He knows that feelings against the reverend are at fever-pitch right now. Why, I believe certain people would hang him from the highest tree if they had half a chance." She reached up to pat Lydia's shoulder. "Now don't you worry your pretty head. Mr. Branson knows best. And don't worry about the door. I'll just tell the insurance company that the wind blew it open."

"Mrs. Dinwittie, there isn't any wind in the hall," said Lydia, aghast at the secretary's plan. "That would be defrauding the insurance company."

Mrs. Dinwittie twittered. Lydia had never heard anyone else who actually twittered. "Miss Fairchild, you're just as honest as the day is long, but sometimes you're too honest for your own good. After all, if there was wind in the hall, it might blow open the door, and we can't say for certain that it didn't happen just that way because sometimes there is a draft created when the door to the street is opened. . . ."

"Mrs. Dinwittie! I'll pay to have the door fixed!" shouted Lydia.

The secretary tilted her head to one side and smiled. "You will?"

"Yes! Just don't file a false insurance claim."

"Well, I'm just as pleased as punch that you'll face up to your responsibility. I thought you might, but sometimes even honest people need a tiny bit of persuasion to do what's right."

"Just send me the bill, Mrs. Dinwittie," said Lydia, and fled into John Lloyd's private office, slamming the door (a solid-core wooden one) behind her. She sank into one of the comfortable-for-an-antique armchairs in the sitting area at one end of the office and burst into hysterical laughter. She had been conned by a Kewpie doll! She wondered if Mrs.

Dinwittie came by her manipulative skills honestly or if she had picked them up from that past master of manipulation: John Lloyd Branson.

She heard his deep, slow drawl on the other side of the door and leaped out of the chair and shrugged off her coat. This confrontation might end in unarmed combat, professional behavior be damned, and she didn't want to be hampered by a fleece-lined car coat. She faced the door, waiting.

John Lloyd entered and carefully closed the door behind him. He studied her with expressionless black eyes—always so startling when his blond hair and fair skin led one to expect blue eyes—as he removed his overcoat and laid it neatly over the back of the Victorian sofa.

"Do I have choice of weapons, Miss Fairchild?" he asked.

"I'm in no mood for your archaic humor, John Lloyd."

"I had no intention of being humorous, Miss Fairchild. Even if your precipitous departure from the courtroom had not forewarned me, the sight of your clenched fists and heaving bosom most definitely indicate that your propensity for violence is about to overcome your hard-won self-control. I only wished to ascertain whether or not you would allow me to choose the means by which you hope to defeat me."

As he spoke he walked past her with only the faintest hint of a limp and sat down at his gigantic rolltop desk and tossed his Stetson over his shoulder in the direction of his hat rack. The fact that the Stetson settled nicely on one of the hooks did nothing to calm Lydia's temper. Even John Lloyd's damn hat did exactly what he wanted.

She stalked through the archway that separated the sitting area from the office proper and faced him with fists clenched. "You conned them!"

He cocked one eyebrow and made a temple of his hands as he leaned back in his chair. "Them?"

"Them! The prosecution! You conned them, John Lloyd. All that . . . that *crap* about pleading your client innocent instead of not guilty and then manipulating the judge into changing the venue to Amarillo—which is not nearly far enough away—was all a smokescreen so that you could sneak up behind them and stick a knife between their ribs."

"I believe it is next to impossible to ambush Maximum Miller."

"It wasn't Maximum Miller you ambushed. It was the district attorney. What you were really doing was backing that poor man into a corner so he would agree to an early trial date. Maximum Miller had no choice but to go along. What else could he do? Tell his boss to take a hike?"

Lydia paced back and forth in front of the silent but watchful attorney, her footsteps loud on the polished hardwood floor. "Oh, but you were good, John Lloyd. You were so smooth that I doubt Bobby Benson realizes yet that he was conned."

"I prefer to think of this morning's work as creative defense strategy," said John Lloyd, stretching out his legs and crossing them at the ankles.

"Bull"—she caught herself before finishing the profane expression for bovine manure—"hocky!"

John Lloyd's lips twitched in what might have been the beginning of a smile, and Lydia stopped and leaned over him, shaking her finger in his face. "Don't you dare laugh!" she shouted.

"I would not dream of it, Miss Fairchild," he replied, gently pushing her hand out of his face.

She felt tears burn her eyes and blinked furiously. She absolutely, positively would *not* cry. "Why did you do it, John Lloyd? How could you endanger your client by tricking the prosecution into such an early trial date? Maximum Miller is right. We won't be ready. We *can't* be ready. The paperwork will hardly be finished. The ink won't be dry on the pathologist's signature on the autopsy protocol. Test results on blood and hair and fiber won't be back from the FBI lab. You will be defending your client blindfolded and with both hands tied behind you."

"And so will Maximum Miller. We will be evenly matched, the better to see whose side the angels take."

"For God's sake, John Lloyd, angels aren't members of the Texas Bar Association! They can't practice law in this state!" she exclaimed, then gritted her teeth. She was arguing about angels as if they actually existed, something she wasn't sure she believed in spite of a lifetime spent in Sunday school.

"Have faith, Miss Fairchild."

She clutched her head in frustration. "Faith is for church, John Lloyd. This is a secular matter."

"It is both, Miss Fairchild. A man's faith is at stake in a secular court."

Lydia imagined that the eyes of the knights of Arthurian legend had held the same expression of earnest fervor and unshakable faith when they set out in search of the Holy Grail as John Lloyd's did now. She wondered if the attorney was completely sane. Perhaps his psyche was cracking under the weight of a lifetime spent suppressing all outward signs of human weakness. Perhaps all the frailties he had denied for years were bursting free in the form of religious fanaticism.

"John Lloyd," she said in as quiet and rational voice as she could manage. "David Hailey is a hypocritical little shit!"

John Lloyd's lips twitched again. "Perhaps I should be thankful that you refrained from using that particular scatological term for our client at the arraignment this morning, although calling him a jerk was also unprofessional. Your behavior was inexcusable, Miss Fairchild."

Lydia felt a quiver of guilt—but only a quiver. "Don't you judge me after what you did. I won't put up with it." She wasn't sure what she would do. Break his hat rack over his head perhaps.

"Ah, yes, my conning—that was the vernacular you used, I believe—Mr. Benson and Maximum Miller."

"Well?" demanded Lydia.

He tilted his head back to study the ceiling, and Lydia resisted the urge to do the same thing. There were no answers to be found on its plaster surface. The answers were in John Lloyd's devious mind.

"Don't you have anything to say for yourself? Don't you have any explanation or defense?"

He finally looked at her, his face as stern and resolute as she had ever seen it. "I had no choice. I had to gamble and trust that Mr. Benson would not call. I *will* have that early trial date, Miss Fairchild, if I have to stipulate that Amanda Hailey died as a result of blunt-force trauma, if I have to stipulate that the blood on the rock was indeed hers—which I have no reason to doubt in any case—and if I have to stipulate that she was murdered in the bedroom. I will stipulate every apparent fact except that David Hailey is guilty as charged. I will go to trial if I have not read a single statement by a single witness or examined a single piece of evidence. But I *will* go to trial!"

He slammed his fist on his desktop and Lydia flinched. She had never thought of John Lloyd as a man who might punch holes through walls or break furniture or indulge in the kind of petty violence lesser men might commit when they were angry. Now she wondered if she had misread his character or merely misjudged the strength of his determination. One fact was very clear: she didn't know John Lloyd Branson as well as she thought she did, and she didn't know the John Lloyd Branson facing her at all.

She retreated to the library table—her temporary desk—that stood at right angles to his enormous rolltop and sat down in her chair, turning to face the brooding figure whose body was within her reach and whose mind was beyond her grasp.

It wasn't a situation she planned on allowing to continue.

She drew a deep breath and laid her hand on his arm. "Why, John Lloyd? Tell me why."

He turned to look at her, examining each feature as though she were the stranger and not him. Finally he smiled and it was both sad and resigned. "You misjudged me, Miss Fairchild."

"Tell me how, John Lloyd."

"Although you do not believe it, I was sincere in part this morning. Every hour that David Hailey sits in jail is another hour for public opinion to harden against him. Despite their careful use of the word *alleged,* the media presents him to the public as a vicious criminal. Eventually, an allegation endlessly repeated buries the truth beyond recall. It wears away reasonable doubt in one's mind as surely as constantly dripping water will wear away stone. The sooner we reveal the truth at his trial, the better for David Hailey, his congregation, and Canadian."

"What is the *truth* you're referring to, John Lloyd!"

He blinked slowly like the owl Mrs. Dinwittie had called

him, and his eyes were as expressionless. "I am not certain, but in this case, as in all human acts, the truth must be interpreted from the proper perspective."

"Unfortunately, the budget committee had a pretty clear perspective, John Lloyd. Not even a tree to obstruct the vision."

He shook his head impatiently. "That was only the finale and meaningless except for its shock value because we do not yet know what the opening acts were. I cannot discern the theme of our pageant or hope to understand the motive of our main character until I hear the lines delivered by our supporting cast. Given the brief time between arraignment and trial, I doubt that the witnesses' statements will be ready for my perusal much before the opening gavel, and I shall be forced to ad-lib until such a time as the plot becomes clear to me."

"Why don't you just demand to hear the recordings under the rules of discovery?" asked Lydia.

John Lloyd's head snapped up and his black eyes were as sharp as a laser. "Sergeant Schroder recorded the witnesses' statements?"

Lydia smiled. "According to Sergeant Jenner, he did."

John Lloyd rose and grabbed Lydia's hands to pull her up. "Miss Fairchild, you are more precious than pearls. You are invaluable."

"I am?" asked Lydia, staring into his smiling face. She wasn't certain she recognized this John Lloyd either, although she preferred him to the brooding stranger.

He pulled her into his arms and waltzed her around the office. "You are, Miss Fairchild, and as a gesture of my esteem for you, I will pay for the glass to be replaced in my door. And might I caution you to be more circumspect in your behavior in the future?"

She pulled away. "My behavior? What about Mrs. Dinwittie? She conned me into offering to pay in the first place."

"Surely you're mistaken. Mrs. Dinwittie is a pillar of rectitude—so long as she doesn't have a sharp-edged weapon in her possession."

AD INTERIM

GRADUALLY HE STOPPED SHIVERING. HE HAD NEVER thought of himself as a physical coward before, but the revilement he had felt in the courtroom had frightened him. He was a man like any other and he did not want to be hated and spat upon. Neither did he want to go to prison. The prospect of it dried his mouth and cramped his belly. He would pray for courage and ask forgiveness for his fear. With God's help he could face the revilement and forgive those who felt it and not allow them to sway him from his chosen course.

He would also pray for those he had injured and ask God that their faith not be weakened by what they saw as an act of sacrilege. He knew now that their understanding was less perfect than he believed. They still saw symbols as important in and of themselves and did not seek the meaning behind them. They still did not understand that those who were in the manger that long-ago night were like themselves. They still did not believe that Mary gave birth with the same blood and pain as every woman before and since. They still did not believe that Joseph, a common carpenter from an isolated and undoubtedly conservative village, had to overcome a sense of betrayal to believe that Mary did not bear the fruit of adultery. They still credited those biblical men and women with virtues and understandings beyond their own. They would not see that they were only common people with uncommon faith.

He prayed that they might experience an epiphany, and rose from the floor with his heart soothed and his conscience clear.

CHAPTER NINE

JENNER SQUIRMED IN THE CONTOURED GRAY CHAIR THAT the Potter County district attorney's office furnished for a short-legged, vertically challenged individual with middle-age spread who happened to be unfortunate enough to visit Maximum Miller. Between Sunday-school chairs, the lumpy, rump-sprung front seat of Schroder's Ford, and Potter County's idea of comfortable furnishings, Jenner figured his hindquarters and lower back were permanently impaired. He wondered if he would be eligible for work-related disability pay. Probably not. Given the county's budget, nothing short of permanent paralysis would qualify. Besides, most of the employees in Potter County who had ever had dealings with Maximum Miller might consider a numb behind an advantage. At least you couldn't feel it when the assistant D.A. kicked your ass.

And Maximum Miller looked to be ready to kick somebody's ass, and since he couldn't kick John Lloyd Branson's and he couldn't kick Bobby Benson's, Jenner figured the black prosecutor would settle for the next best person's, which could belong to anybody who might be unlucky enough to get on his wrong side. Unfortunately, since the arraignment Maximum Miller didn't have a right side.

The burly assistant D.A. leaned forward in his sturdy, high-backed chair and placed a massive hand in the middle of a thick manila folder. His forehead had more furrows than a freshly plowed field and his black eyes were nearly lost under his bushy gray eyebrows. "I spent the weekend studying this case file, and just so you won't misunderstand how important I take my responsibilities, I even missed watching the Cowboys whip up on the Giants to do it. And, Sergeant Schroder, I don't like to miss the Cowboys. I don't like reading about the game on the sports page the next day, but at least the goddamn sportswriter laid out the action so I could imagine the game. He told me what happened. He didn't describe forty-seven options for every play called. That's more than you've done as the investigating officer of record—feebly assisted by the youngest Hardy boy here—of the case the newspaper is calling the Virgin Mary case."

"That's rank!" Jenner exclaimed before he thought.

Miller's massive head swung slowly toward him. "You got something pertinent to say?"

"I go to church every Sunday when I wake up in time, and I find the paper's name for this case offensive. It lacks sensitivity to religious feelings." Jenner had more to say, but the expression on Miller's face told him he had already said more than enough.

Miller swung his head back to Schroder. "Tell the Hardy boy here that I've got no time for literary criticism. John Lloyd Branson"—he belched and reached for a package of Tums—"was in here this morning bright and early before I had a chance to digest my breakfast with an order from the judge allowing him to Xerox every damn piece of paper in the case file, including the autopsy protocol. Speaking of which, I never knew the pathologist to get his protocol written up so damn fast. He would have to turn efficient on this case when I'd just as soon he had turned in his report five minutes before trial. It's not good tactics to give Branson any more time to cogitate on the evidence than you absolutely have to."

"I didn't see anything at the autopsy that's going to help Branson," said Schroder. "And I didn't take my eyes off that body from the time the doc cut her open until he sewed her back together."

Jenner swallowed hard. He wished the fat slob of a detective would be a little more euphemistic.

Maximum Miller glared at Schroder. "You and the fumblebutt here had better not have missed anything. I still remember the body in the farmer's cornfield. That case looked so open and shut, too, until I read the autopsy report and learned the victim had been stabbed twice, but eight hours apart, something you didn't tell me because you stepped outside the morgue to hold Junior's head while he threw up."

Miller switched his gaze to Jenner, and Jenner swallowed hard again. He wondered who told the assistant D.A. that he'd bolted out of the autopsy room to hang his head over a convenient bedpan. Somebody had to have told him. Maximum Miller wasn't omniscient; he only seemed that way.

"I didn't leave the room once," said Jenner. He didn't mention how many times he had closed his eyes. As long as Schroder was watching the autopsy, too, he didn't see any reason why two pairs of eyes were better than one. Schroder didn't miss much.

Maximum Miller made a sound suspiciously like a snort but at least didn't pursue the topic, turning back to Schroder and the previous subject. "Branson sat in that very chair where you're sitting, Schroder, looking as comfortable as a well-fed tomcat on a satin pillow—although how anybody could look comfortable in one of those chairs is beyond my comprehension—and asked to view the video of the crime scene. *And* to listen to the tapes of the interviews. I tried to foist off the written statements on him instead, but no, he wanted both and gave me some legal bullshit about his right to compare the transcript with the original tape under the rules of discovery. Frankly, I don't know if I have to provide him with those tapes or not. You might say that as a legal area it's quicksand. I don't know if I'd be sucked under or he would if we went before the judge, and it's not worth the fight. There's nothing on those tapes that's going to help him save the preacher's butt just like there's nothing that's going to help me nail it to the barn door for more than twenty years maximum. Because''—he slammed his fist down on the manila folder—''I don't have a goddamn murder case here!''

Jenner reared up out of the chair. ''What are you talking about? Damn it, the preacher went outside to pick up that rock, then walked back in the house to off his wife.''

''Son, you better stick to literary criticism. You're a hell of a lot better at that than you are at criminal prosecution. You just write a few letters to the editor and let me take care of the preacher.''

''If it isn't murder, then what is it?'' demanded Jenner.

''It's voluntary manslaughter! I got a corpse, I got a murder weapon, I got *six* motives, I got *two* opportunities—which is one more than I need and for damn sure one more than I want—but I don't have a single witness who actually *saw* David Hailey kill his wife. If he walks like a duck, talks like a duck, and looks like a duck, then he's a goddamn duck! You know it, and I know it, and Branson knows it, but I can't prove it—not beyond a reasonable doubt. My gut tells me the jury won't buy premeditation. They're gonna believe that the reverend obliviously beaned his wife in a sudden fit of passion. That's voluntary manslaughter, and it's the best I think we can get, but at least it gets the son of a bitch out of the pulpit and off the streets for two to twenty years.''

''But he went outside!'' insisted Jenner. ''Doesn't that prove premeditation? I mean, if he killed her in a sudden passion, wouldn't he have used the jar of cold cream?''

Miller smiled—or at least showed his teeth. ''I'll be damned, Schroder. The little Hardy boy is not as dumb as he acts sometimes. He might even grow up to be a decent homicide detective.'' The smile disappeared. ''But he won't grow up to be a lawyer because he's looking at things the way he *knows* they are instead of the way I can *prove* they are and the way the jury will *believe* they are. Those are three horses of three different colors. I can *prove* David Hailey picked up that rock, but the jury won't *believe* he was in control of himself because he didn't try to hide what he was doing from the witnesses. He picked up that rock in full view of everybody who happened to be looking. Now that's not a real good picture of somebody planning to commit a murder. The assumption is that when you premeditate murder, you try to conceal your intentions. And you damn sure try to dispose of the victim so no one suspects you had anything to do with the crime. You goddamn sure don't parade around in front of witnesses carrying a dead body. I can talk myself blue in the face that David Hailey planned the murder from start to finish, but nobody is going to buy it because when the bastard dumped his wife's body in the manger, he set himself up a defense that I can't get around. The jury is bound to think that he was crazy as hell when he did that—like he was operating on automatic. In other words, an irresistible impulse that kept pushing him from one act to another. He had an irresistible impulse to stone his wife and then to cleanse her. If the jury doesn't see that for themselves, you can bet your last nickel that John Lloyd Branson will point it out to them. If I was arguing to a Canadian jury, I might—*might*—be able to pull it off since I figure the folks in Canadian are predisposed to amputate that pecker's head at the neck, but I'm not arguing to a Canadian jury. Thanks to that sneaky son of a bitch, we got an Amarillo jury. Now an Amarillo jury ain't gonna like what the preacher did any more than a Canadian jury, but they're a damn sight more likely to believe Hailey was crazy."

Miller scratched the top of his balding head, then the graying fringe of hair that looped around his head from one ear to the other. "But Hailey isn't crazy. If he was, Branson would already be demanding a sanity hearing—and he isn't. Because Branson knows Hailey is as sane as I am." Jenner watched Miller chew a handful of Tums and thought that one grown man letting another grown man give him indigestion wasn't the best sign of strong mental health. However, for the sake of his own physical health, he thought it best not to mention it.

The prosecutor belched and continued. "That means the skinny son of a bitch has to be going for voluntary manslaughter, too, so I'll just plan my courtroom strategy around that fact and beat him to the punch on Amanda Hailey. I won't try to whitewash her reputation. Besides, from what the witnesses said, there's not enough whitewash in Amarillo anyway. Everybody paints that girl in primary colors—mostly red."

Schroder blew a cloud of smoke out of one side of his mouth. "Cleetus, it sounds to me like you've got a game plan already. You picked a motive and you picked an opportunity. You can damn sure prove the opportunity and you don't have to prove motive, so I don't see what's got your bowels in an uproar."

Miller slapped his hand down on the desk. "Schroder, you're not a fool, so don't talk like one. Juries watch *Perry Mason* reruns. They watch the crime-of-the-week shows. They watch that Jessica What's-her-name, the one who's always tripping over bodies. If that woman were real, she'd be under investigation as a serial killer. Anyhow, juries expect prosecutors to prove motive. This case has too many motives, and you sure as hell don't want to give somebody like Branson any options! He's liable to turn this trial into a write-your-own-murder mystery and I'll end up with a hung jury in search of a publisher. Damn it, Schroder, I'm guessing what that skinny, slick, cold-blooded son of a bitch is planning and I don't like to guess!"

"You just got pretrial jitters, Cleetus," said Schroder.

Miller's nostrils flared as he drew several audible breaths, and Jenner braced himself. "Schroder, I *do not have* pretrial jitters. I *give* opposing attorneys pretrial jitters." He belched again. "I'd like to know how the hell Branson knew you made tapes, Schroder. You got a mole in Special Crimes?"

Jenner got up and edged toward the door. He could feel the sweat run down the sides of his body and guessed no anti-perspirant on the market was equal to the sweat generated by the possibility that Maximum Miller was about to kick his butt.

"I guess I might have mentioned something about it—just sort of a vague word or two—to Lydia Fairchild. She just kept asking and asking why Sergeant Schroder didn't tape his interviews and I finally said something to the effect that he did." Jenner wiped his sweaty forehead on his sleeve and tried to smile. "I never noticed that woman being such a nag before. I figure Branson is a bad influence on her."

Maximum Miller rose up from his chair like the wrath of God. "Skip Miss Fairchild's personality profile and tell me just exactly what you said to her!"

Jenner slid one foot outside of Miller's cubicle and tensed himself to turn and run for the big double doors at one end of the district attorney's suite. "I said 'Yes, Miss Fairchild. Sergeant Schroder always tapes his interviews' as best I can remember." He stealthily eased his body a little farther out the cubicle. "And I just remembered something else. I got another appointment."

He would have made it through the double doors, but he had forgotten that the district attorney had recently installed a security gate by the receptionist's desk. The gate was only waist high and he figured he could have vaulted it and been out the door if his butt hadn't been so numb.

As it was, he caught his heel on the top of the security gate and fell backward. Maximum Miller plucked a fistful of shirt and jerked him off the floor. "Jenner, when a man tries something stupid, he's got two ways to save himself. One is quick thinking and the other is quick reflexes—you lose on both counts."

CHAPTER TEN

Amarillo—December 20

THE POTTER COUNTY COURTS BUILDING LOOKED JUST AS Lydia remembered it from her last visit: a block-long building sheathed in gray marble that curved around unexpected corners; a large section of triangular-shaped smoked panes of glass out of which jutted the front entrance; and a hard, stone floor in the foyer. There were only two differences: the parking lot had been paved and the inside of the building was as cold as a deep freeze. Lydia had heard rumors that every office was cluttered with space heaters because the heating system, while brilliant in design, was woefully inadequate in reality. The courtroom, being an interior room without windows and whose walls were fabric-covered curves, was marginally warmer. Lydia thought her legs would be frozen to the knees before court had been in session an hour. Tomorrow she would wear furlined boots, woolen tights, and an insulated vest over the warmest sweater she owned. She might look a little unprofessional for an anal-retentive lawyer, but she wasn't anal-retentive and she wasn't a lawyer yet, just a law student on Christmas vacation, and she'd rather be warm than shivering. Besides, frostbite and chattering teeth weren't very professional either unless one was an ice skater giving an outdoor exhibition performance in the middle of the Arctic.

John Lloyd, of course, showed no signs of noticing the chill in the courtroom. It was the best indication she'd had in the last ten days that he actually was warm-blooded. The way he hibernated in his office during the day and in his study during the evening was more like a reptile than a mammal. He had stared without blinking at those photo reproductions of the crime scene, or listened with headphones to the taped interviews with the slack-jawed attention of a teenager with enlarged adenoids listening to sexual fantasies on a 900 number. Except the teenager at least would have shown some signs of physical response, even if it was only an erection. For all the attention John Lloyd had paid her in the last ten days, Lydia thought she could climb into his lap stark naked and he'd merely ask her not to block his reading light.

Not that he had physically or verbally responded to anything he had read in the file or heard on the tapes either, and for all her self-professed sensitivity she'd hadn't an inkling as to his thoughts. He was a black hole: devouring light and matter, but giving back nothing.

A pet rock was better company.

She'd taken to reading the newspaper from front to back, including the classified ads, and discussing interesting articles with Mrs. Dinwittie to break the silent monotony of the office. She could tolerate the secretary's clichés better than John Lloyd's silences, although Mrs. Dinwittie's constant defense of him irritated her almost as much. The woman acted as though she believed John Lloyd Branson could walk on water.

Yesterday morning was a typical example of Mrs. Dinwittie's uncritical esteem for John Lloyd's character, wit, charm, physical appearance, and mental acuity. Lydia had been reading aloud an article from the *Amarillo Globe-News* and offering a running commentary on its contents . . .

"Listen to this headline, Mrs. Dinwittie," said Lydia, clearing her throat and straightening her shoulders. " 'Battle of the Titans Begins Tomorrow,' referring of course to Maximum

Miller and John Lloyd as opposing attorneys. It should read 'The Devil and Daniel Webster with the Devil Defending.' "

The secretary wagged her finger. "Now, Miss Fairchild, you shouldn't call Mr. Miller names. It's not polite and might violate his civil rights."

Lydia gritted her teeth. "Mrs. Dinwittie, I was calling John Lloyd the devil."

The secretary rolled her eyes toward the ceiling and gave a theatrical sigh. "Oh, Mr. Branson is such a devil sometimes. So mischievous and as handsome as the devil—or as the devil is supposed to be."

Lydia sank down on a chair in the reception area. Hearing John Lloyd described as mischievous disoriented her. If she was easily shocked she might even faint. Or swoon. One never did anything so modern as faint in John Lloyd's office. Other than the word processor on Mrs. Dinwittie's desk and a few magazines on a marble-topped table, there was nothing made later than 1900 in the reception area. Even the telephone was a mock antique.

"Mrs. Dinwittie," said Lydia, speaking slowly. "I don't think you get my joke. You know the Stephen Vincent Benét short story, 'The Devil and Daniel Webster'? A farmer sells his soul to the Devil, then hires Daniel Webster to defend him."

"Why ever would he do that?"

"Well, you see, the Devil came to claim the farmer's soul and Daniel Webster . . ." Lydia began.

Mrs. Dinwittie waved her hands. "Oh, no, Miss Fairchild, that's not what I asked. I guess I'm just as clear as mud today." She twittered, and Lydia swore she heard an apologetic note. It was amazing the range of expression the secretary could instill in a simple twitter. "I meant, why did the farmer sell his soul?"

Lydia drew on her reserve of patience. "For material gain, Mrs. Dinwittie. Anyway, as I was saying, he hired Daniel Webster to defend him against the Devil—"

"Just like Reverend Hailey hired Mr. Branson," interrupted the secretary. Her bright smile faded and she tilted her head. "Oh, Miss Fairchild, that story is nothing like our little soap. Reverend Hailey didn't sell his soul. He forfeited it instead. And it wasn't for material gain. He wanted to be quit of his wife and he couldn't divorce her. Oh, my, no. He's a preacher and divorce would be such a scandal."

Lydia pressed her hand against her forehead where a dull ache was beginning, undoubtedly caused by confusion. She had a feeling that she was speaking one language and Mrs. Dinwittie another. Or perhaps Mrs. Dinwittie's brain was scrambling the message.

"What are you saying? That murder is more desirable than scandal?"

Mrs. Dinwittie clasped her bosom. "Oh, no! Not at all. Murder is much worse than a scandal." Her eyes grew misty. "There are exceptions, of course. You were right as rain to kill that terrible Butcher. And there is Mr. Dinwittie"—she shook her head—"but enough of that."

Lydia hoped so. She wasn't up to hearing a recap of the Lizzie Borden story as lived by Mrs. Dinwittie. "Then exactly what do you mean?"

"Appearances are so important if you are a minister, Miss Fairchild. You live in a glass house and everyone is so ready to throw stones. Just the silliest thing and your congregation is up in arms and ready to fire you. Perhaps Reverend Hailey was so concerned with appearances and avoiding gossip that he temporarily lost his head and killed his wife. Sometimes the ordinary person becomes so flustrated that he or she does something foolish. I don't imagine that ministers are any less human, do you?"

Lydia didn't answer. She was too caught up in wondering if *flustrated* was a real word or one that Mrs. Dinwittie made up. A few minutes of conversation with the woman and Lydia felt as though she had fallen down the rabbit hole—or was it a well?—or stepped through the mirror into Wonderland. Given Mrs. Dinwittie's familiarity with axes, she supposed her analogy was a good one. She could almost imagine the secretary dressed as the Queen of Hearts screaming "Off with his head!"

"Miss Fairchild?"

Lydia blinked. "Yes?"

"Are you quite all right? Your eyes glazed over. You don't

have petit mal seizures, do you? I had a cousin on my mother's side who did, and her eyes would glaze over and she'd stare straight ahead just like you. That was before treatment, of course. Now she's just right as rain."

"I'm all right, Mrs. Dinwittie!" said Lydia. "I was just distracted by an errant thought. Did you ask me something a moment ago?"

"I asked if ministers were any less human than other people?"

"I'm no expert on ministers, but I imagine they feel the same temptations and lusts and dislikes as any other person. We just don't expect them to succumb. I mean, don't they develop an immunity in divinity school?"

"Of course," said Mrs. Dinwittie thoughtfully. "Reverend Hailey was different. If he sinned at all, it was an oversight rather than something he did deliberately. He was as close to being a saint as a man can get—and still be alive, that is."

"Saints don't kill their wives, Mrs. Dinwittie!"

"They don't abandon their God either, Miss Fairchild, and Reverend Hailey did both in one night. I wonder which came first."

"I don't know. I try to avoid metaphysical discussions."

Mrs. Dinwittie waved her hand. "Oh, you mean religious. But isn't that a religious story you were telling me about the farmer and the Devil?"

"Not exactly."

"How does it end, Miss Fairchild? Does Daniel Webster save the farmer from the Devil?"

"Uh, yes. He won the farmer an acquittal from a jury of lost souls who already belonged to the Devil."

Mrs. Dinwittie clasped her hands together. "Just like Mr. Branson. I do believe he could win a soul from the devil, too, Miss Fairchild."

Lydia reached into her reserve of patience again and found it empty. She rested her head on the back of the chair and closed her eyes. "If you say so, Mrs. Dinwittie."

"Miss Fairchild! If you could forgo a morning nap, I need you."

Lydia's eyes snapped open at the deep sound of John Lloyd Branson's voice and she scrambled to her feet. "It speaks, Mrs. Dinwittie."

John Lloyd's eyebrow arched. "Miss Fairchild, I have been fluent in the English language since I was eight months old. Although I must confess my vocabulary was somewhat limited until the age of three." He looked toward his secretary. "Mrs. Dinwittie, if you would be so kind as to serve coffee when I call."

"You just sing out, Mr. Branson, and I'll come quick as a bunny rabbit."

"A leisurely stroll will be satisfactory, Mrs. Dinwittie." He looked toward Lydia and inclined his head like a royal potentate. "Miss Fairchild, if you would join me, please—now!"

Lydia imitated the bunny spoken of by Mrs. Dinwittie and scurried into his private office, although she thought a nearly six-foot-tall blonde made a less than convincing bunny unless it answered to the name of Harvey and hung around bars with Jimmy Stewart.

As soon as he closed the door, she flung her arms around his neck. "Thank God, John Lloyd!"

She heard him grunt when she slammed against his chest, but he didn't try to escape her grip. In fact, his arms came around her and he stroked his hands up and down her back from shoulders to hips. She felt her thighs begin to tingle. Perhaps she should have been assertive much sooner. Perhaps she really should have crawled naked into his lap. Perhaps . . .

On the other hand, his behavior had been inexcusable, abominable, and enraging.

"Miss Fairchild, much as I find this a highly enjoyable interlude, I must confess that it is unexpected. Ordinarily you would have bristled at my admittedly sharp tone and refused to come at all, or you would have sashayed into my office with the fluttering eyelashes and exaggerated hip roll of a morally loose Southern Belle. If you could perhaps tell me what I did that pleased you, I shall endeavor to repeat the behavior at frequent intervals in more private surroundings."

"You've been a jerk," muttered Lydia, her face buried in

the side of his neck. "And if I weren't so glad you're finally speaking, I'd probably hit you."

"What?" he asked. "Miss Fairchild, not only are you endangering my self-control over certain physical reactions, but you are wilting my collar and making no sense at all."

She inhaled his bay rum cologne and lifted her head to meet his eyes. "After ten days of indecipherable grunts when sounds passed your lips at all, you finally spoke to me. I was so desperate for conversation that I . . ." She took a deep breath and began again. "John Lloyd, I was trying to explain a joke to Mrs. Dinwittie."

He smiled and Lydia caught her breath. He really was handsome as the proverbial devil when he smiled. "While Mrs. Dinwittie is an estimable legal secretary and a woman of high moral character—if one overlooks her one lapse—she is wanting in conversational skills. My apologies for leaving you with idle hands or, I should say, an idle mind. However, I am about to rectify that. Sit down at your desk, Miss Fairchild, and peruse the case file for the State of Texas versus David Hailey, listen to the tapes of the witnesses, then . . ."

"Then what?" asked Lydia.

"Then let us talk, Miss Fairchild." He sank down in his chair and waved his hand. "To work, please."

Eagerly she opened the file. Even with all of the religious symbolism involved, the David Hailey case had to be more straightforward than a conversation with Mrs. Dinwittie.

Two hours later she wasn't so sure.

"Eenie, meenie, minie, mo, catch a preacher by his toe," Lydia recited in a singsong voice as she turned off the cassette recorder and pushed it out of her way. "I think we ought to ask for a sanity hearing so that if our first line of defense is breached, we'll have insanity to fall back on."

John Lloyd raised one eyebrow. "And what in your estimation is our first line of defense, Miss Fairchild?"

"Voluntary manslaughter, of course. Hailey was subjected to increasing criticism by his congregation until he finally snapped the night of the budget meeting. It fits with the expression I caught in his eyes when we first tried to interview him. He was sorry Amanda was dead, but he didn't accept the blame for causing her death because he believed her own actions were responsible. She pushed him too far." Lydia leaned toward the attorney, who for once seemed to be listening to her with full attention. "The way I see it, John Lloyd, he dumped her body in the manger in an attempt to cleanse her soul of her wrongdoing—or what he saw as her wrongdoing. He was a preacher to the last, just a crazy one. He was trying to save his wife's soul after he killed her."

He laced his hands behind his head and leaned back in his chair, stretching his legs out and crossing them at the ankles, a relaxed pose totally unlike him. "An interesting hypothesis, Miss Fairchild, but unfortunately you are starting with the finale." He turned his head to look at her. "Not that I entirely disagree with you at present, but by beginning at the ending, you are leaving out certain facts essential to your defense. Let us backtrack to the second act. When did David Hailey kill his wife?"

Lydia nibbled at her thumbnail to give herself time to think. She had been so involved in listening to the tapes from the perspective of how the witnesses supported her theory that David Hailey had succumbed to an irresistible impulse, that she hadn't given all that much thought to the timing of the crime.

"I think after the budget meeting, when Glen saw him pick up the rock."

"Then why did he tell Mildred Fisher that she would not speak to Amanda again?"

"Uh, because he thought he could forbid the two women from speaking again and everything would be all right."

"If he believed that, why was it necessary to kill Amanda?"

Lydia felt rattled. "Maybe he brooded on his whole situation during the rest of the budget meeting and decided forbidding conversation wouldn't work. Mildred Fisher doesn't sound like a woman who would take orders from anyone. By the end of the meeting Hailey decided to stone his wife and cleanse her soul in the manger scene."

"If that scenario is true, Miss Fairchild, then David Hailey is guilty of premeditation. He had sufficient time during the second half of the budget meeting to plan his crime, and if he planned the crime, he is guilty of murder rather than voluntary manslaughter.''

Lydia shook her head. ''No, he's not guilty of murder—at least not in the legal sense. I saw grief in his eyes, John Lloyd, but not guilt.''

John Lloyd lowered his hands and turned his chair to face her. ''Perhaps you were mistaken in your evaluation of his expression. You have frequently called him a hypocrite, Miss Fairchild.''

''Well, he is a hypocrite. He doesn't regret killing his wife, and he sits there in that cell with a nasty-nice expression on his face like he's justified in what he did.''

''But surely a hypocrite is capable of misleading you.''

Lydia twisted her hands together as she thought, then slowly shook her head again. ''No, I'm not wrong. He's a cold, cold man and I don't like him, but maybe *hypocrite* is the wrong word. Hypocrisy means that a person is insincere, and I know he's sincere in his belief that he is blameless in her death and he's sincere in his grief. I'd know it if he wasn't. I'd sense an emptiness—and I didn't.''

She glanced at him and quickly looked away when she saw the curiosity in his eyes. ''I can't explain it any better, John Lloyd. Call it a sixth sense or call it ESP—except I don't believe in ESP—or call it empathy, call it whatever you want, but I can sense emotions where I couldn't before. . . .'' She stopped abruptly and clasped her hands together in her lap to hide their tremor.

''Before the Butcher?'' John Lloyd asked after a pause.

''Yes! He's dead, but he left me a legacy of this whatever it is.'' She laughed and heard tears in her laughter. ''It isn't even a dependable sixth sense. Sometimes I can't sense anything about a person even when I want to so badly I ache. About you, for instance. Sometimes I can't even make a guess about what you're thinking or feeling, or I guess wrong. Like when I lost my temper at the arraignment and accused you of being a con artist.''

She felt him grasp her hands and squeezed her eyes shut. She didn't want to see sympathy or, worse, pity in his eyes. ''Don't you dare feel sorry for me. I'm not deaf or blind or infirm or mad. Well, maybe I'm a little mad—still functional—but a little mad. Maybe I should go see a counselor like you told me to after my encounter with the Boulevard Butcher. No one escapes being a victim of a serial killer without wounds of some kind, but I couldn't tell some stranger who probably didn't believe in evil any more than I did before I met the Butcher that I was haunted. I'm illogical, I know. I don't believe in ESP, but I believe I was haunted. Was—past tense. I'm not haunted anymore, but I'm still cursed with this sensitivity or whatever it is. I don't think a psychologist would understand it any better than he would understand being haunted." She rubbed her hand over her forehead. "My Lord, I sound as ditzy as Mrs. Dinwittie."

She felt John Lloyd gently trace the hairline scars that crisscrossed her palms, mementos of the Butcher's knife. "You are not mad, Lydia, and you are not psychic, but perceptive and highly imaginative. Neither is your sensitivity a legacy of the Butcher although he was responsible for its present form. You were always sensitive to others, but it was the sensitivity of a child, inexperienced and often even unaware of the infinite complexity of human nature in all its forms. When you killed the Butcher, you killed your own girlish innocence at the same time. You no longer view the world through the rose-colored glasses of girlhood, but through the eyes of a woman who saw evil. Now you see beneath the masks we all wear, and being intelligent with more self-control than previously, you see more deeply than the average woman."

She jerked her head up to stare at him. "Self-control! I still want to punch you in your supercilious nose sometimes."

He squeezed her hands, then released them. "Ah, but, Miss Fairchild, I never said you were perfect. Somewhere inside you dwells the impulsive girl just as there dwells within me an adolescent boy."

"John Lloyd, you were never an adolescent! You were born a hundred years old!"

He tilted his head, a thoughtful expression on his face. "Upon reflection, I believe my analogy in respect to myself was inaccurate, but my point is that you are not a saint, Miss Fairchild, for which I am grateful. I believe a saint would try the patience of even so tolerant a man as I to a much greater degree than do your slight imperfections. Since I also possess a certain number of faults—"

"In the double digits," Lydia muttered under her breath.

"—we complement each other whereas David and Amanda Hailey did not. Realistically, when saint and sinner dwell together, one would expect the sinner to murder the saint if for no other reason than resentment. To be constantly forgiven by one's mate for ordinary human weaknesses must be wearing. To constantly strive to match the saint's perfection and to just as constantly fail must certainly lead to frustration, and frustration, Miss Fairchild, is fertile ground for the seeds of murder."

He leaned toward her. "So why was Amanda Hailey, whom we know from Mr. O'Brien's testimony had a temper and did not hesitate to defend herself, the victim? Why did she not instead murder David Hailey whose expectations she could not meet?"

"But that's not right, John Lloyd. It wasn't David Hailey's expectations she couldn't meet. It was the congregation's—or rather the members of the budget committee's. According to Agnes Ledgerwood, who as church secretary certainly was in the best position to know what was going on behind the parsonage door, David Hailey was tolerant of Amanda's behavior. The real question is: why didn't Amanda Hailey murder everybody on the budget committee except Roy O'Brien?"

"Exactly, Miss Fairchild!" exclaimed John Lloyd, slapping his desk again. "Now we are at the opening act—when the curtains go up—and the question we must answer is elementary to our plot. Why did David Hailey murder his wife?"

Lydia licked her lips. "Uh, she committed adultery. Otherwise, why would he stone her?"

"Perhaps because the stone was there, Miss Fairchild. We do not know that every prop in our drama is a religious symbol."

"You're the one who said it was!"

John Lloyd shook his head. "Your memory is at fault. I said that I needed to ascertain if the murder weapon had religious significance to David Hailey. However, in view of his refusal to speak, we have no way of knowing one way or the other except by hearsay, and might I remind you that hearsay is inadmissible in court. We cannot prove that Amanda Hailey committed adultery merely because the murder weapon was a stone. Nor do I believe Maximum Miller can prove it, so I ask you again, Miss Fairchild, why did David Hailey murder his wife?"

"For God's sake, John Lloyd, we don't have to *prove* adultery. We only have to plant a reasonable doubt in the jury's mind, and you can do that with the prosecution's own witnesses. We have the witness list. Other than members of Special Crimes and the pathologist, Maximum Miller isn't calling anybody to testify except the budget committee and we already know what they're going to say. Just ask them their opinions of Amanda's behavior and their knowledge of her reputation in the community, and David Hailey is home free. It all became too much for the preacher, and when Amanda came to the budget meeting in a slinky caftan and fought with What's-her-name, Mildred Fisher, it was the straw that broke the camel's back. He took her back to the bedroom and killed her!"

"So now you theorize that he killed her during the budget meeting?"

Lydia nodded. "We have to go with that scenario, I think. Otherwise, as you pointed out, he had time to premeditate." She nodded again. "Yes, with a little juggling, I think that scenario will work."

"Perhaps you would care to explain how he murdered her with a stone that he did not have in his possession until after the budget meeting, Miss Fairchild."

Lydia rose and began to pace around the office. The stone! How could she have forgotten the stone? But she had to be right. The more she thought of David Hailey pulling his wife back to the bedroom, undoubtedly furious with her, the more the emotions rang true. She closed her eyes and tried to imagine herself in Amanda Hailey's place. How would Amanda Hailey feel? She felt goose bumps spring up on her arms as she saw the scene playing itself out against her closed eyelids. Amanda would be furious also—furious with Mildred Fisher and furious with her husband for not defending her. And he didn't! No witness mentioned David Hailey coming to his wife's defense, only his pushing her out of the room. In Amanda's place she would be furious enough to kill her husband.

But that's not what happened.

She squeezed her eyes more tightly shut and mentally shuffled through the crime-scene photos. The judge's order hadn't specified that John Lloyd could make copies of the photos, but it hadn't forbidden it either, so there were copies in the file on her table. And there was something in those photos that teased at the edge of her mind, something that could be used to refute Glen's testimony.

Her eyes snapped open and she rushed back to her table. Hurriedly she pawed through the copies of the photos and lined them up in a row. Her eyes darted from one copy to the next, then she began nodding her head. Centered on a page, each photo was in black and white and rather indistinct—as indistinct as any object would be seen from a distance through a raging sleet storm. She felt a growing sense of elation. She was right! Her theory would work! Maybe it wouldn't explain everything, and it depended on John Lloyd's skill at cross-examination and his unequaled ability at delivering a persuasive closing argument, but it should be enough to plant a reasonable doubt in the jury's collective mind that Hailey had committed premeditated murder. She was reasonably certain the jury would return a guilty verdict to a lesser offense—mainly, voluntary manslaughter. That was the best she and John Lloyd could do, but with a little luck they could do it. . . .

"Miss Fairchild."

Lydia felt herself being shaken and blinked her eyes. John Lloyd was leaning over the counsel table, his hands holding her arms. Behind him she saw Judge Myers craning his neck to see her. On her left she heard the whispers of the just-seated jury.

Maximum Miller crossed the aisle from the prosecution's table and hovered at John Lloyd's shoulder. "You want me to ask the judge for a recess, Branson? She looks peaked to me."

Lydia straightened up. "I'm sorry, John Lloyd. I was thinking about yesterday, about the strategy. I didn't realize we were ready to start." She squeezed the assistant D.A.'s arm. "Thank you, Mr. Miller, but I don't need a recess. I looked peaked because it's colder than a well digger's butt in here."

She realized what she had said a second after she saw John Lloyd flinch and heard Maximum Miller's belly laugh. At least she didn't have to worry about looking peaked anymore. Her face had to be cherry-red with embarrassment.

She felt someone lay an overcoat on her lap and tuck it around her nylon-clad legs. She turned her head quickly to meet David Hailey's eyes. "What are you doing?"

"You are cold, so I gave you my coat," he answered as though he wondered why she needed to ask. "Please, don't refuse it."

His face was drawn and pale and he had lost weight during the past two weeks in jail, but his eyes had not changed. They still saw too much. He knew she wanted to throw the coat back in his face.

She hesitated, then nodded. "Thank you."

"It will keep you warm," he said, then sat back in his chair and folded his hands, his head only slightly bowed. Not bowed enough for prayer, but as if he was too weary to hold it up.

Lydia felt warmth seeping back into her cold legs and told herself she kept the coat because it would prejudice the jury if she refused it. Besides, she *was* cold and it would be stupid to turn down a perfectly good coat. Two very good, very logical reasons, and both were lies. She kept the coat because she felt the need in David Hailey. He was a shepherd alone without a flock and he needed a lamb to care for. For the duration she supposed she was that lamb.

She looked at him out of the corners of her eyes. Why *had* David Hailey killed his wife?

AD INTERIM

HE KNEW LYDIA FAIRCHILD HAD WANTED TO REFUSE HIS coat, but she hadn't, and he had sensed a bewilderment and a seeking in her. She was not a prophet—would never be a prophet as she would always be more of this world than of the next—but she felt the need in him. She had a kind heart, a goodness about her, that would always respond to another's need. But she would not understand a need—a duty—that asked you to sacrifice the one you loved for the spiritual good of another. He doubted she would ever sacrifice John Lloyd Branson for the good—spiritual or temporal—of any number of people.

Amanda was like that. She would never have sacrificed him, but he believed she had loved him enough to allow herself to be sacrificed. He could almost feel her beside him, curled against his body, her soft voice whispering in his ear, "You do what you have to do, sweetie, and I'll back you all the way."

He lowered his head so that no one would see his tears.

CHAPTER ELEVEN

JENNER BLEW ON HIS HANDS AND RUBBED THEM TOGETHER to restore the circulation. First a numb butt, then numb hands. If this case lasted much longer, no part of his body would have any feeling left. He wished he was back in the witness room drinking hot coffee with Schroder. At least his stomach would be warm. But he wasn't on the witness list. Everything he could testify to, Schroder could also, and he guessed Maximum Miller trusted Schroder more in the witness box. Not that Jenner blamed the assistant D.A. As a member of Special Crimes, Schroder had a lot more practice testifying in murder trials. Besides, as a spectator Jenner expected to enjoy himself. Maximum Miller and John Lloyd Branson were better entertainment than going to the movies. Or watching a prizefight, which their clashes sometimes resembled.

Jenner guessed the press thought so, too, because the courtroom was full of reporters, including the ponytailed one from out of state. Certainly Judge Myers had his gavel handy and was leaning forward as though he was ready to dive over the bench into the fray if necessary. In his place Jenner figured he'd dive *under* the bench instead. The last judge who became physically involved in one of Miller's and Branson's trials fell over the jury-box railing and broke his arm.

Maximum Miller and John Lloyd Branson were hard on judges.

Jenner slouched down in his seat to listen to Branson's opening statement. Maximum Miller had already given his, describing Amanda Hailey as "prone to improper actions and whose impropriety disrupted her husband's ministry." Miller's statement would have been more effective, Jenner thought, if the prosecutor hadn't kept looking over his shoulder to see if Branson was going to object. Finally the judge, the jury, and all of the spectators started watching Branson, too, like cats watching a mouse hole. But that particular mouse didn't twitch a whisker although he did flinch several times when Lydia Fairchild elbowed him in the ribs and hissed "Object, damn it" in his ear.

By the time the tall, lean attorney stood up to address the jury, Jenner figured there wasn't a person in the courtroom, including Maximum Miller, who wasn't afraid to breathe for fear of missing a word. If nothing else, Branson knew how to build suspense.

Branson tugged his vest down and flexed his shoulders, then stood casually in front of the defense table—just out of reach of Lydia Fairchild's elbow, Jenner noticed—and looked directly at each juror.

"Ladies and gentlemen, Amanda Hailey was a whore!"

There was the sound of a courtroom full of breaths sucked in at the same time, and Maximum Miller surged to his feet. "Objection!"

"According to the prosecution," finished John Lloyd smoothly.

Judge Myers held up his hand. "Just a minute, John Lloyd. I believe Mr. Miller has an objection. Mr. Miller, would you care to elucidate?"

Maximum Miller opened and closed his mouth twice and Jenner figured he had objected by reflex action rather than on a specific legal point and his brain had to catch up to his mouth.

"I never called the victim a whore, Your Honor, and I

object to the defense putting words in my mouth,'' Miller finally said.

Myers cocked an eyebrow at the attorney. ''John Lloyd, you got a rebuttal?''

The attorney held out his hands in a gesture of innocence. ''Your Honor, I only stated bluntly what the prosection stated by inference. I believe in speaking plainly.''

''I'd sooner believe that Santa Claus has joined Weight Watchers, John Lloyd, but I'll let your exaggeration pass this time. Overruled, Mr. Miller. Your statement left the door open to Mr. Branson. You should have expected him to waltz through it with his own interpretation.''

John Lloyd nodded to the judge and turned back to the jury. ''I cannot disagree with the prosecution's claims. Witnesses will testify as to Amanda Hailey's reputation with men, to her inappropriate behavior, to her disruptive influence, and to her final appearance in a seductive robe more suited to the boudoir than to the budget committee meeting. We will not refute this testimony. Amanda Hailey was everything the witnesses claim—and more.''

The courtroom was silent—spellbound or thunderstruck, Jenner couldn't decide which—by a defense attorney who provided his client with enough motives for multiple murders, much less one.

David Hailey broke the silence with a strangled cry as he bolted upright, and John Lloyd whirled around. The bailiff leaped out of her chair and started for the defendant while Lydia Fairchild lunged across John Lloyd's empty chair to grab Hailey's wrist.

''Stop!'' commanded John Lloyd, his voice a close approximation of how Jenner always imagined God's might sound. It drowned out the sounds of women's gasps, men's brief expletives, and the judge's gavel and his repeated demands of ''Order in the court!''

Jenner froze halfway out of his seat, the bailiff stopped dead halfway across the courtroom, and Lydia clung to Hailey's arm like a paralyzed limpet. Even the judge hesitated, his mouth hanging open and his gavel poised for a downward swing.

"Mr. Hailey, does the sheep doubt the shepherd who watches over it, who leads it to pasture, who finds it the sweetest pasture, who fends off thieves and the wild beasts of the field? Does the sheep flee from the shepherd who seeks to save it?"

John Lloyd took slow, measured steps toward the minister as he spoke, his voice soft but not low. It carried to every corner of the courtroom, mesmerizing all who listened, caught up in the spell woven by the tall, lean man who halted in front of the minister. Suddenly John Lloyd raised his arm and pointed his finger.

"Or does the sheep trust the shepherd to lead it even though the path is stony?"

Jenner just barely kept from shouting amen and decided that the lawyer from Canadian would have made one whale of a preacher. He craned his neck for a better view of David Hailey and wished he could see more of the minister's face than just his profile. Profiles were fine on coins but not if anyone is interested in reading a man's expression. As it was, he had to guess by watching the jury's faces, and that was like looking at someone else's reflection in a funhouse mirror. You got the general idea, but the image was distorted. And this image was more distorted than most because there were fourteen mirrors, if you counted the alternate jurors, and every one of them reflected something different: curiosity, confusion, sympathy, grief—although for whom, Jenner couldn't be sure—excitement, anger, indecision, anticipation, pity, disbelief.

Whatever John Lloyd saw in Hailey's face, it satisfied him and he nodded his head. "Thank you, Mr. Hailey, and sit down, please."

Jenner heard the sound of breaths expelled as though John Lloyd had released everyone in the courtroom from his spell at the same time he released his client. Seats creaked as spectators wiggled and shifted and looked around to see if everyone else had been as afraid to move or breathe as they themselves. Jenner sat down, too, but he wasn't interested in what everyone else thought or felt. He was too busy trying to figure out why, just for an instant, just before he turned back to the jury, John Lloyd Branson's eyes had held the expression of a man who had just found the piece of a puzzle he thought was missing.

Jenner heard a nasal whisper behind him. "What the hell was that all about? Was Branson quoting from the Bible or what?"

Jenner didn't need to turn around to know that it was the ponytailed reporter from out of state. His question as much as his accent gave him away. Everybody local knew John Lloyd Branson could make a grocery list sound like it came from the Bible.

"Ladies and gentlemen," John Lloyd continued as though there had been no interruption at all. "We will prove Reverend David Hailey innocent of the charge of murder. Thank you."

There was another buzz from the spectators, and Judge Myers stared at the attorney with disbelief. "Is that all, John Lloyd?"

"It's damn sure enough," Jenner heard Maximum Miller mutter to Bobby Benson. "Give Branson any more time and he'll just preach another sermon. I wouldn't know if I was in the courtroom or in church except at least that skinny shyster didn't bring his own pulpit."

John Lloyd turned toward the bench. "Not quite, Your Honor. The defense requests a recess until tomorrow morning—"

Maximum Miller was on his feet. "Objection, Your Honor! The state has already given way to enough of Mr. Branson's unreasonable requests, including asking the citizens of this county to sit on a jury only a week before Christmas when they should be free to be thinking of their families. The state is ready. Mr. Branson said he was ready. Let's get on with it."

"—in order that Reverend Hailey may attend his wife's funeral," John Lloyd finished as though there had been no interruption.

Maximum Miller whirled toward the lawyer. No one could say the assistant D.A. didn't have an expressive profile. His eyes looked as though they were bugging out of his head.

"What? You want to let your client pay his last respects to the woman he murdered? Damn it all, Branson, that woman has been mistreated enough by him. Can't she at least go to her final rest without his hanging over her coffin?"

"Does everybody in this part of the country talk like a backwoods preacher?" the ponytailed reporter asked in a whisper.

John Lloyd walked behind the defense table and placed his hands on the defendant's shoulders. "My client has not been convicted, Mr. Miller. Only accused. To forbid him to attend his wife's funeral when he still stands before you as innocent as the next man might be construed as a violation of his civil rights."

"Don't threaten me with a civil rights suit, you—"

Whatever else Maximum Miller might have said was smothered by Bobby Benson's palm, which was tightly pressed over his assistant's mouth. "Your Honor, the state finds Mr. Branson's request insensitive to the victim, whose civil rights were most heinously violated, but we can think of no legal reason to object to his motion. None that would be upheld on appeal, that is."

"Unfortunately, I can't think of one either, Mr. Benson, so I'll declare this court in recess until tomorrow morning. Mr. Miller, you will arrange for Mr. Hailey's attendance at his wife's funeral, *but* you'll do it in such a way as to cause the least disturbance. Sit him in the back of the church, or rope off the upstairs and stick him up there. If it weren't winter, I'd leave him outside to listen through a window. But whatever you do, I don't want a riot!" He pointed his gavel at John Lloyd. "Did you hear me, John Lloyd? I'll let your client go, but I'll be damned if I'll have an ugly confrontation between Hailey and the townspeople at that poor girl's funeral. You go with the officers who escort Hailey, and you keep him from making a spectacle of himself. You're the only person with enough moral authority that the folks in Canadian might—*might*—respect you enough to keep their indignation within reasonable bounds, but I'll tell you right now for your own good, I think you're spending that moral authority at a faster clip than you're earning it. Be careful you don't end up bankrupt."

Jenner opened the back door of Schroder's old Ford and reached in to help David Hailey out. He wasn't sure how John Lloyd had talked the judge into letting Hailey ride to Canadian in Schroder's car. It didn't have bars between the front and back seats; didn't have a screen; wasn't missing its inside door handles on the back doors. In other words, it wasn't suitable for transporting a prisoner. Hailey could have reached over the seat and knocked Schroder in the head. He could have opened a back door and jumped out. He could have done damn near anything.

Or he could have if he hadn't been sharing the backseat with the man who slid out after him. "Damn it, Schroder, that's the filthiest car seat I ever rode in," said Maximum Miller. "I found a newspaper that was two years old, a blanket the Indians must have woven before Columbus sailed, enough paper cups to stock a Dairy Queen—if they hadn't already been used—and enough soft-drink cans to bankrupt the recycling center if you ever tried to redeem them. And when was the last time you took this junk heap to the car wash?"

"Look at all the damn press," said Schroder, ignoring the prosecutor's question, but then Jenner had noticed that the detective always ignored criticism. Either he didn't hear it or he didn't care. Jenner bet on the latter.

Maximum Miller drew himself up and squared his shoulders at the sight of the crowd in front of the church sprouting cameras and microphones of every size, description, and national origin. He grabbed Hailey's arm and whirled the slighter man around to face him. "Preacher, you got any idea of making some kind of teary-eyed statement to those newshounds, you can forget it. Schroder, get Sheriff Taylor to station a couple of his deputies at the church door. Nobody with a camera of any kind gets through, and freedom of the press be damned. I'm not having that girl's funeral showing up on the six o'clock news. She didn't die in peace, and her body's been poked and prodded ever since, but by God, she's gonna be buried in peace."

"Thank you," said Hailey, and Jenner looked at him in shock. It was the first time he'd heard the man say anything, and he couldn't quite reconcile the gratitude in that deep, slow voice with the man who thought so little of his wife that he propped her up in the manger for everybody to stare at.

Miller must have been a little shocked, too, since it took him a few seconds to answer. Maximum Miller was usually quicker with a comeback. "I ain't doing it for you, Hailey. I'm doing it for her."

The preacher nodded. "I know, and I'm thanking you for her. Amanda frequently suffered from the lack of understanding of others. And I was guilty of it, too." He swallowed and closed his eyes briefly. "She would appreciate your kindness today."

The assistant D.A. gave Hailey a look that Jenner couldn't quite read. "Here comes your legal escort, preacher, and I hope you remember that it's his butt on the line today. You cause any trouble, you provoke anybody else into causing trouble, and it's John Lloyd Branson the judge will ream. And it's him this town will blame. I don't know why he took your case, and I sure as hell don't know why he's using the legal strategy he is, but I do know this. He's got to live in this town after we send you to Huntsville, and you can pay me back for keeping the press out of your wife's funeral by not making Branson live to regret he ever decided to defend you. Frankly, I don't think you're worth the misery you're gonna cause him."

Hailey gave the assistant D.A. a long look, and Jenner was shocked all over again by the approval he saw in the minister's eyes. "You're a good man, Mr. Miller. You are worrying about another and not about the possible embarrassment I might cause you."

Maximum Miller stuffed his hands in his pockets and not quite but almost avoided the minister's eyes. "My hide's so thick I don't worry about being embarrassed, and even if I did, I don't live in this town. Let's just say you owe me and this is the way I'm demanding payment and leave my motives out of it."

Hailey smiled. "I understand."

Jenner wasn't sure he did. Unless Maximum Miller thought getting caught doing John Lloyd Branson a favor might ruin his reputation as a hardnosed prosecutor who could fight the defense attorney to his last breath. Jenner didn't figure it would do Miller much good if the word got around that he was a little soft around the edges.

"Mr. Miller, it was unnecessary for you to accompany my client, but I must admit I appreciate your presence to block," said John Lloyd Branson, escorting a solemn Lydia Fairchild and swinging a plain wooden cane. Jenner wondered what had happened to his silver-headed one.

"What do you mean, block?" asked Maximum Miller.

"You did play collegiate football, I believe. For the University of Texas?"

"*A&M*!" the prosecutor yelled, looked around, then lowered his voice and shoved his face close to John Lloyd's. "I played for Texas A&M, you ignorant, Ivy League shyster!"

"Yes, I know, Cleetus," said John Lloyd. "But you were looking so uncharacteristically unsure of yourself a moment ago that I feared an imminent mental breakdown. I thought a stimulus in the form of righteous anger might restore your usual belligerent but basically sound personality, and nothing provokes righteous anger in the breast of a Texas Aggie quicker than being mistaken for a graduate of the University of Texas."

Miller jabbed a finger in John Lloyd's chest. "One of these days, Branson, I'm going to forget my professional standing in the community and belt you one right in the mouth."

Lydia stepped between the two men. "Stop it, both of you! Save your macho posturing for some other time."

Maximum Miller looked a little abashed, Jenner thought, but John Lloyd seemed to shrug off his clerk's criticism. "You misunderstand, Miss Fairchild. Mr. Miller was feeling out of sorts for doing me a favor, and I merely restored the balance of our relationship."

"What favor?" asked Lydia.

"You got good ears, Branson," Miller said with a steady look at the attorney.

"I have always had acute hearing, Cleetus. Now, as Texas A&M's greatest blocker, perhaps you could lead the way into the church by opening a hole in that line of journalists while Sergeant Jenner and I take Mr. Hailey's flanks. Miss Fairchild, please bring up the rear and do not be reluctant to use that oversize bag of yours as a weapon if an overly eager reporter threatens to step on your heels."

Maximum Miller cracked his knuckles and lowered his head in the attack position. "Grab his arms and let's go!"

Jenner wondered if anyone else heard John Lloyd's whispered comment over the shouted questions of journalists. "Thank you, Cleetus."

AD INTERIM

He had not asked to attend Amanda's funeral and did not know why John Lloyd was so vehement that he do so. He had already said goodbye to Amanda the night she died. The gray metal coffin did not hold her spirit, only the clay from which her physical being had been molded. Still, he shrank from looking at the coffin.

He did not want to think of her as dead.

He did not want to admit that her time had been brief and his time with her even briefer. God forgive him, but thoughts of seeing her in heaven did not bring him comfort. They would not be husband and wife there, and being Amanda's husband had been his happiest time. Love between man and woman was truly God's greatest gift.

He lowered his head, fighting his anger that he had been able to enjoy that gift for such a short time. He must not give way to spiritual weakness again. He had done so this morning when John Lloyd had judged Amanda so harshly. Had John Lloyd not reminded him of the path ahead, he would have failed in his ministry. An immortal soul would have been lost.

Like Maximum Miller, he did not understand his lawyer's

strategy, but he would not mistrust his shepherd again. He would not forget again that love had not disappeared from the world with Amanda. He saw it in a tough, cynical prosecutor of one race and in the satiric tones of a defense attorney of another race. Unlike Lydia Fairchild, he understood the actions of both men. A man's nature is such that he finds it difficult to give or receive favors without denying that such favors spring from love. It is easier to speak of debts owed or debts paid. Unlike woman, a man hides his love deep within his own heart for fear knowledge of it will put him at a disadvantage with other men. That is why men need women. So that they might bask in unselfish love.

It is also why they need God.

CHAPTER TWELVE

LYDIA SAT NEXT TO DAVID HAILEY AND WISHED SHE HADN'T. Maybe if he was sobbing, or rending his clothing, or pouring ashes on his head, or engaged in any of the other biblical rituals of grief—if there were any others—she might feel different. But he was doing none of those things. Maybe she had been wrong when she thought she saw grief in his eyes that day at the jail. She certainly hadn't seen it since. He didn't even have the decency to look at Amanda's coffin. Of course, she wasn't either, but she hadn't been married to its occupant. Besides, she didn't like open-casket funerals, and that casket was most certainly open. After her first startled look at all that bright red hair against a white silk pillow, she had concentrated on looking anywhere but at Amanda Hailey's white dead face. Psychologists could say what they wanted about the denial of death prevalent in the twentieth century, when families no longer sat up at night with the deceased in his coffin in the living room, or made mourning brooches out of the dead loved one's hair, but she was in favor of it. She didn't believe in making a cult of the dead or in throwing an elaborate funeral to prove how much you loved the deceased. It was too late then and, as Lydia remembered her great-grandmother saying: "The fancier the funeral, the guiltier the mourners."

Granny Abby hadn't given the human race much credit for sincerity.

She wondered what Granny Abby would have said about the Reverend David Hailey. Not much, probably, since the old lady hadn't held preachers in as high an esteem as one expected of a member of her generation. But Granny Abby had an explanation for that, too. "Lydia Ann," she had said, gripping the arms of her rocking chair with arthritis-twisted fingers and leaning forward to peer at the five-year-old version of her own face. "I've lived too long to have much faith in what people call themselves. A pig can call himself a Thoroughbred, but he still swills from a trough. A man can call himself a preacher, but if he steals from the collection plate, he's just a thief."

David Hailey wasn't a thief, he was a murderer, and Granny Abby hadn't had much patience with murderers—or at least not cold-blooded ones. "A man gets liquored up and kills somebody in an argument, and he'll most likely be sorry enough when he sobers up, and it might even shock him into lifelong sobriety. But a man who kills when he's cold sober, that's a different story, Lydia Ann. Best hang him as soon as the trial's over 'cause it'll save trouble in the long run."

Lydia often wondered if she didn't plan on going into defense work in reaction to Granny Abby's opinions. Certainly Granny Abby had thought so and hadn't been the least bit disapproving. She'd said she'd rather Lydia had a mind of her own even if it was foolish than be a milksop who always did what her elders told her. Being elderly didn't guarantee wisdom; it was just a damn good indication of it.

Amanda Hailey would never be elderly. That beautiful red hair would never dull with gray; her youthful milk-white complexion would never wither; and the firm young body Lydia had seen in the autopsy pictures would never go slack and soft. She would be forever young to those who remembered her. And to the budget committee, except for Roy O'Brien, she would be forever foolish and sinful. Lydia choked back a sob. She hoped Amanda had enjoyed her sin because now she would never learn to enjoy virtue.

Amanda Hailey was dead at nineteen. Dead at the hands of the man who had pledged to cherish her. Dead at the hands of the man Lydia Ann Fairchild had pledged to defend.

Lydia drew a shaky breath and felt John Lloyd tuck his handkerchief in her hand. She looked up and felt her lips quiver. She would bet Amanda Hailey had never seen such warm caring in a man's eyes as she now saw reflected in John Lloyd's.

"It's not fair, John Lloyd," she whispered.

He didn't answer, but then there was no answer he could give. Not even John Lloyd Branson, orator, could argue that life was fair. It was simply better than the alternative.

She blew her nose and stared over the balcony railing as a young woman began to sing "Beyond the Sunset" in a clear, pure voice.

"Amanda loved sunsets."

Lydia jerked at the sound of Hailey's voice, so low as to be almost indistinct, and turned to look at him. "What did you say?" she whispered.

His gray eyes were warm with memories. "She loved sunrises, too. And thunderstorms and sunshine, cold winters and hot summers. She loved life in all its contrasts. But she hated that song and everyone knew it. I think God will forgive me if I'm angry that whoever arranged the services chose it. Even if He doesn't, I'll still be angry."

Maybe if David Hailey hadn't added that last remark and his eyes hadn't gone cold, Lydia wondered later if she wouldn't have done what she did. On the other hand, maybe she would have anyway. Either way, she didn't believe she'd ever regret it.

Sometimes a person had to stand up and be counted.

"Stop the music!" she shouted, standing up and leaning over the balcony before she changed her mind. The organist, the soloist, and a hundred mourners—although Lydia doubted many of them were actually mourning—craned their necks to look up at her. Most had surprised or shocked expressions on their faces, but one, an older woman with a very short haircut, looked indignant, while a balding man with a square, strong body looked angry.

"Miss Fairchild, what are you doing?" demanded John Lloyd, tugging at her arm.

"God bless America, Branson," growled Miller, who was sitting on Hailey's other side. "The judge said no trouble and I don't think he exempted Miss Fairchild from that order."

"Hush up, both of you!" Lydia hissed as she pulled her arm free of John Lloyd's grip. "Amanda Hailey didn't like that song," she called down to the bewildered soloist. "Sing another one. Sing . . ." She looked over her shoulder at David Hailey.

" 'Onward, Christian Soldiers,' " he replied.

"Sing 'Onward, Christian Soldiers'," she ordered.

"Young lady, that's not a proper song for a funeral," said the short-haired woman.

"Amanda Hailey liked it and it's *her* funeral, not yours," retorted Lydia.

"Sit down, Mildred. You never liked Amanda in the first place and I had a screw loose for ever agreeing to let you handle the arrangements," said the balding man. He pointed to the soloist. "Linda, sing it and sing it loud. Amanda liked the rafters to rattle when she played music."

The organist hit the opening chords, and Lydia sank back in her seat. She was shocked—a little—at her own audacity, but somewhere in the back of her mind where memories lurked she heard Granny Abby's voice: "Good girl, Lydia. You've got grit."

She turned to David Hailey and her smile died on her face. Tears spilled out of his eyes and rolled down his cheeks. "Thank you, Miss Fairchild."

Lydia turned back to stare over the balcony. She couldn't watch him cry because she still saw no remorse in his eyes. And grief alone didn't count.

The wind shrieked around the gravestones, set the bare branches to rattling like dry bones, and scattered petals from Amanda's few funeral wreaths across the frozen ground. Skirts and trousers and coat hems flapped against shivering legs, and men doffed their Stetsons and Resistols not so much out of respect for the dead as to deny the wind possession of their expensive headgear. Few besides her husband and his official escort accompanied Amanda Hailey to the cemetery, but those who did huddled together against the wind behind the single row of metal folding chairs rather than claim an empty seat close to an officially defrocked minister who was also a murderer. Sympathy for the bereaved did not extend to those responsible for their own bereavement.

Lydia sat between David Hailey and John Lloyd at the cemetery. She could feel the curious eyes staring at her, but curious looks weren't responsible for the hot, itchy feeling in the middle of her back. Mildred Fisher was responsible for that. Mildred was standing behind her, and Lydia knew the woman was staring at her with all the disapproval of the self-righteous. She also knew Mildred was only waiting for the graveside services to end before pouncing. She hoped the woman was prepared. Chastising Lydia Fairchild was a different proposition from chastising a young girl caught between her husband and her husband's congregation like Amanda Hailey had been. Lydia didn't have any divided loyalties; she was on Amanda's side, period.

If Mildred Fisher wanted a fight, she, Lydia Fairchild, would give her one.

With the last amen, she bounced up from the metal folding chair only to feel John Lloyd's arm go around her waist and clamp her to his side. "What are you doing? Let me go! I can hardly breathe."

"If you cannot breathe, then you cannot talk, and if you cannot talk, then you will not make a spectacle of yourself as I very much suspect you are about to do," he said in a low voice without his usual drawl. "I do not trust your nascent self-control."

"I'm not going to start a fight," she gasped.

His sigh was long—and long-suffering. "It has been my experience that you seldom start fights, Miss Fairchild, but you never hesitate to respond to provocation, and you have a very broad definition of what constitutes both response and provocation."

"I suppose you don't consider mauling me as provocation," she panted as she considered whether or not to kick him and reluctantly decided not to. The only leg within range of her boots was his left leg, the one in which he had been shot by a person unknown—at least unknown to her. Everyone else in Canadian knew, but no one, least of all John Lloyd Branson, would tell her. She wondered if that wasn't a greater provocation than merely being manhandled.

"Sometimes your vocabulary is deficient, Miss Fairchild. To maul is to handle roughly, to bruise, or to injure by or as if by beating. I hardly think a firm embrace qualifies."

"I hate it when you sound like you've read the *Oxford English Dictionary* from cover to cover."

He arched one eyebrow in that maddening show of utter control. Even his muscles obeyed him without question. "I do own a set, Miss Fairchild."

He would!

"I sure am enjoying your little vocabulary lesson, Branson," said Maximum Miller. "But I think we better get the preacher out of here. The press is waiting outside the cemetery like a pack of vultures, and judging from the way they're all staring at your clerk, somebody must have told them about her interrupting the funeral. After the preacher I'd bet she's the next item on the menu."

Lydia glanced over the prosecutor's shoulder. The press had outnumbered the mourners in the funeral cortege, and although Sheriff Taylor and his deputies had kept them a cemetery's length away during the graveside service, it was obvious that law and order was breaking down. The press was flanking the line of deputies and jogging toward the mourners as fast as the weight of their Minicams would allow.

With a last warning glance at Lydia, John Lloyd freed her and grasped David Hailey's arm. "Let us wait a minute more, Cleetus, until your vultures are close enough to catch our scent. Then we shall dash to our limousine waiting less than twenty feet away, stranding the media with no prey and a hundred yards or more from their own vehicles. A successful retreat is often a matter of timing."

However, another set of vultures was closer. Roy O'Brien planted himself squarely in front of David Hailey. "You son of a bitch, you didn't have to kill her." He turned his face toward John Lloyd. "You better not get him off, Branson, or . . ."

"Or what, Roy?" asked John Lloyd.

"Just don't do it," O'Brien finished, but it didn't take a psychic to read the threat in his red-rimmed eyes. As far as the truck driver was concerned, David Hailey was dead meat if he went free.

"Get out of here and don't be talking to the defendant, O'Brien," said Schroder, the first words Lydia had heard the taciturn investigator say the whole afternoon.

A weeping Agnes Ledgerwood, her face looking every year of the age she tried to hide, took O'Brien's place. "If I hadn't seen you with my own eyes, I wouldn't have believed it, Reverend Hailey. I've been church secretary for five years and I would have sworn on the Bible that you didn't have any meanness in you. I just don't understand any of this, and I don't sleep at night for feeling guilty and I don't understand that either."

"Quit whining, Agnes," exclaimed Mildred Fisher, nudging the church secretary out of the way to confront Hailey. "How dare you make our church a laughingstock! Everyone is making jokes about that business with the manger. Why didn't you just leave her where she fell? Why didn't you?"

"That's enough from you, too," said Schroder, turning his shoulder and pushing past her, tugging David Hailey along with him.

It wasn't enough for Mildred. "And you," she said, grabbing Lydia's arm as she followed Schroder and jerking her around. "Acting disrespectful in a church."

"Disrespectful is open to interpretation," Lydia said in an imitation of the lofty tone John Lloyd always used when correcting anyone, usually her. "And I'll thank you not to grab at me," she added, jerking free of Mildred's clutching fingers and trying to step around her.

Mildred matched Lydia's sidestep. "But what do you know

about respect? You're just like *her*! A harlot! Living with John Lloyd Branson like you're doing."

"Judge not, Mildred," said Hailey.

"If you had judged the way you should have, none of this would have happened," retorted Mildred.

"A harlot?" Lydia asked slowly, feeling her face turn bright red.

"Miss Fisher, as prosecutor, I'll have to ask you not to approach the defendant," said Maximum Miller, caught between being cordial to a state's witness and knowing the judge would hang him out to dry if he didn't shut Mildred Fisher up.

"Did you call me a harlot?" shouted Lydia.

"Mildred," John Lloyd said in as deadly a tone of voice as Lydia had ever heard him use. "Do not cast slurs on Miss Fairchild's character, or you will deal with me, and I do not think you want to do that."

Lydia stepped closer to the angry woman. "I would rather be a harlot than a self-righteous, judgmental bitch like you."

She shoved past Mildred, tromping on the woman's feet in her hurry to get to the limousine before her newly born self-control failed, and she slapped Mildred Fisher across the mouth.

Mildred screeched and fell back into the arms of an effeminate-looking man in his middle forties. "Virgil! My bunions!"

Lydia swore that Mildred's brother, Virgil, smiled and winked at her before helping his limping sister to a waiting car.

AD INTERIM

HE PACED HIS CELL, FIGHTING TO CONTROL HIS SORROW AND his fear.

There were none so blind as those who would not see, and none clung to their blindness with greater tenacity than Mildred Fisher. And none were more afraid than Mildred. She had built of her life a prison and feared to unlock its door. She could argue theology with the most learned men, but misunderstood the nature of God. She could quote endless Bible verses without error, but overlook the simplicity of their message. She would work tirelessly raising money for new hymnals or washing dishes after the Wednesday church supper. She visited the sick, was the first to take food to the bereaved, and supported the foreign-mission program with small contributions. She was a pillar of the church, but she was a hollow pillar, too weak to support the weight of a sinner who sought to rest against it.

The key to Mildred's prison was love, and she feared it.

He had failed in his ministry. He had not taught Mildred Fisher to love.

Nor had he made the blind to see.

No one saw through his act of sacrilege to the love beyond it.

CHAPTER THIRTEEN

JENNER CLAIMED A SEAT IN THE FIRST ROW BEHIND THE prosecution's table, not because he was a law-enforcement officer and thus automatically on the state's side, but because it gave him the best view of Lydia Fairchild's profile. Sometimes he even got a full-face view when she turned her head to look toward Maximum Miller. She had to be the most gorgeous woman in the Panhandle, from her long blonde hair and blue eyes almost the color of turquoise to the tiniest bones in her feet, which just happened to be connected to legs that went on forever. If he had to be Sergeant Schroder's temporary partner, if he had to mix with the scum of the earth, which murderers were, if he had to sit in endless trials, then the privilege of watching Lydia Fairchild was his compensation.

He wasn't sure what to call his fascination with John Lloyd Branson's legal clerk. Any heterosexual male would suffer an attack of lust at the sight of any woman as well put together as Lydia Fairchild whether they admitted it or not, and Jenner admitted it. But lust didn't explain his fascination. Lust was a mile wide and an inch deep. It was all surface. You saw a woman and wanted to jump her bones and sometimes didn't even know why and didn't care enough to find out. Lust lasted as long as it took a man to ejaculate.

So it wasn't lust—or rather only the smallest part—but it wasn't love either. At least not the kind he shared with his wife: the having babies, raising kids, paying bills, laughing together at a silly TV show kind of love, the comfortable kind of love where you finished each other's sentences. He had a feeling Lydia Fairchild could finish her own sentences, thank you very much.

No, he didn't love Lydia Fairchild. He fantasized about her the way some men did about owning a Rolls-Royce, but that was as far as it went—just a fantasy. If he were the kind of man to interest Lydia, then he wouldn't be Larry Jenner, and he was satisfied most of the time with who he was. He guessed the bottom line was that he liked Lydia, admired her, enjoyed looking at her, and wished her well.

And maybe, just maybe, that was love in its broadest definition, and he didn't think love ought to be defined too narrowly.

Maybe during the lunch break he'd run down to the library and look it up in the *Oxford English Dictionary*.

In the meantime he'd kick back and enjoy the trial, beginning with the Panhandle's own forensic pathologist, Dr. Patrick T. MacElvoy, all five foot six inches of him if you included his elevator shoes and inch-long red flattop. The only ingredient missing was one of his cheap, smelly black cigars hanging out of his mouth. The pathologist smoked incessantly except when wearing his surgical mask, and Jenner had heard that MacElvoy had slit a hole in his mask just big enough for his cigar and smoked anyway if his current patient had been lying around for a few days without benefit of refrigeration. If he worked on a fresh body, he sang operatic arias instead. Jenner had heard the arias but had never seen the doctor with a cigar stuck through his mask. Jenner made a point of only attending autopsies on fresh bodies.

"Dr. MacElvoy, would you tell us the mechanism of death of Amanda Hailey?" asked Maximum Miller.

The pathologist cleared his throat and turned his body so that he was speaking directly to the jury. "A blunt object crushed the squamous portion of the right temporal ridge above the mastoid bone,'' he answered, pointing to his own head. ''The skull is real thin there.''

''We wish to introduce into evidence State's Exhibits One, Two, and Three, Your Honor, which are photographs showing the size and location of the fatal wound,'' Miller said with a glance over his shoulder at John Lloyd.

''No objection,'' said John Lloyd.

''Objection!'' Lydia said a heartbeat later.

Judge Myers frowned. ''Which is it? Objection or no objection?''

John Lloyd rose. ''Miss Fairchild has recently developed the irritating habit of speaking out of turn, Your Honor, and as she is not presently licensed to practice law, her capacity here is strictly as a legal aide and henceforth a silent one. The defense has no objections.''

He sat down to an eruption of angry whispers from Lydia. Surreptitiously Jenner leaned forward to listen, and every reporter among the spectators did, too.

''Those pictures are prejudicial, John Lloyd, and unnecessary besides. A drawing would do as well and not cause the jury to wish they had skipped breakfast. Why don't you object, damn it?''

Jenner wondered, too. Every defense attorney tried to keep autopsy photographs out of the jury's hands if they possibly could. No point in showing the jury in living color what a brutal bastard your client is.

''The photos are necessary to the defense,'' said John Lloyd.

''But the prosecution will pin those photos on a damn bulletin board in the courtroom where nobody will miss them!''

''Exactly what I am hoping, Miss Fairchild.''

''But I don't understand!''

''Trust me, Miss Fairchild. My client does.''

''He doesn't know any better!''

''But he has faith.''

''Faith,'' repeated Lydia, throwing up her hands and leaning back in her chair in defeat. "Oh, God, are we in trouble."

"John Lloyd, if you're through conferring with your legal aide, we'll continue this trial," said Judge Myers.

"You may continue the trial," said John Lloyd, inclining his head toward the judge.

"I'm glad you gave permission," said Myers. "You know, John Lloyd, sometimes I don't think you remember who's the judge and who's the lawyer. You ought to work on correcting your confusion. Mr. Miller, Mr. Branson has graciously consented to continuing, so get with it."

Maximum Miller was damn good, thought Jenner, as he watched the prosecutor approach the witness. If a person didn't know any better, he would think Miller was as calm as Lake Meredith on a windless day. And if he hadn't seen him slip a couple of Tums in his mouth, Jenner would think so, too. The assistant district attorney of Potter County and special prosecutor for Texas vs. Hailey was a badly puzzled man.

"Do you have a conclusion as to the cause of death, Dr. MacElvoy?"

"Blunt-force trauma. Homicide."

Miller picked up the rock. "Do you have an opinion as to whether this might be the murder weapon?"

"There's no *might* about it," said MacElvoy, unconsciously stroking the end of a cigar that stuck out of his pocket. "That is the murder weapon. It matches the wound and I even found a chip from the victim's skull adhering to it."

Maximum Miller nodded gravely, but Jenner saw him sneak a quick look at the jury to gauge their reaction to the pathologist's testimony. Apparently satisfied, he introduced the rock into evidence, then turned toward the defense table. "Your witness," he said to John Lloyd.

John Lloyd stood, tugged his vest down, and studied the pathologist. How long Jenner wasn't certain, but long enough to have everyone in the courtroom holding their breath.

"In your estimation, Doctor, and I will accept your estimation on the basis of your credentials and experience, how much strength is required to murder a woman of Amanda Hailey's size in the manner to which you testified?''

Jenner heard Lydia Fairchild let her breath hiss between her teeth and knew that John Lloyd Branson was in for another grilling by his legal clerk. Accepting the pathologist's findings closed the door to a rebuttal witness on behalf of the defense. He wondered what had happened to the famed John Lloyd Branson. He was defending his client worse than a first-year law student. Jenner saw Maximum Miller chewing another Tums and knew the prosecutor was wondering the same thing.

Even Dr. MacElroy had a puzzled look on his face. ''Not all that much strength would be required. Like I said, the bone's real thin there. Of course, murdering someone with a fist-size rock like this one is might be a little awkward.'' He picked up the rock to demonstrate. ''Not much killing surface is exposed unless you grip the round part, in which case this elongated blunt end with all the blood and tissue dried on it sticks out between your fingers like a brass knuckle with a spike on it. That is exactly how our murderer held it. Also, the blow was struck square on, no angle to the wound, which is another indication that he held it in the way I described. He brought his arm back parallel to the floor, swung forward across his body, and *crunch*—drove the blunt tip of that rock through the bone and into Amanda Hailey's brain. More strength would be required than if the murderer had better leverage, like holding the rock like a knife and stabbing downward with it, but not all that much. If you begin with your arm stretched out and slightly back, then swing it around, you got centrifigual force working in your favor. Takes the place of brute strength.''

The courtroom was deathly silent, and a couple of women jurors were a little paler than when the trial started. Jenner felt a little pale himself and wished the pathologist wasn't so graphic.

''Could you determine the approximate time of death, Doctor?''

MacElvoy stared at him as though he thought the attorney had lost his mind. ''Not on your life, son, not on a body that had been lying in a sleet storm for four or five hours. A sleet storm will lower the body temperature faster than anything I know except maybe being dumped in a tub of ice water. I did check stomach contents, found out when she last ate, and using that fact and the testimony of the circumstances—when she was last seen alive—came up with an educated guess that she died between eleven-thirty and twelve-thirty. You want it narrowed down anymore, you're gonna have to wait until you die so you can ask St. Peter at the Pearly Gates."

"I see," said John Lloyd, turning away to face the jury, looking at each face in turn before asking another question. "How tall was Amanda Hailey, Dr. MacElvoy? In feet and inches, please. Not everyone is familiar with the metric system."

"Oh, she was a little bit of a thing, just a smidgen over five feet. I can figure it out exactly if you want."

"Thank you, Doctor, but *smidgen* will do." John Lloyd turned suddenly to face the spectators. "Now will you point to five or six people in the courtroom sufficiently tall enough and strong enough to have murdered Amanda Hailey?"

Maximum Miller was on his feet. "Objection, Your Honor. That question is immaterial, irrelevant, and so improper it leaves me speechless."

"That's about as unlikely as John Lloyd's using words of one syllable instead of three or more, Mr. Miller, but I do agree with you about the question. Objection sustained," drawled the judge.

John Lloyd walked across the courtroom to stand by his client's shoulder. "My apologies, Your Honor. I would not dream of asking an improper question."

"If you were under oath, John Lloyd, I'd charge you with perjury for that statement, but since you're not, I'll have to let it pass. Get on with your cross-examination and confine your questions to issues raised in direct examination or matters covered by the autopsy protocol."

"Certainly, Your Honor. One last question, Dr. MacElvoy. Did you find any foreign material on the victim's fingers?"

"I found lipstick smudges on the index, middle, and ring fingers of the victim's right hand."

"Did you find any foreign material under the victim's fingernails, Doctor?"

"Not a smidgen, Mr. Branson."

"No further questions, Doctor. Thank you."

MacElvoy was already pulling a cigar out of his pocket as he stepped off the stand when Maximum Miller stood up. "I have one more question on redirect, Doctor, so keep your seat."

MacElvoy looked longingly at his cigar before replacing it in his pocket. "Let's have it, Cleetus."

"In your professional opinion, would the defendant, David Hailey, be of sufficient height and strength to have murdered his wife without difficulty in the manner you have described?"

MacElroy looked at the preacher and nodded his head. "No doubt about it, Cleetus."

The minute the judge excused him, MacElvoy scooted up the aisle whistling an aria and unwrapping a cigar, seemingly satisfied with his testimony, but Jenner noticed an uneasy expression in Maximum Miller's eyes. He wondered why the prosecutor was acting as nervous as a kid on his first date. Miller ought to be dancing a jig over Branson's shooting himself in the foot. All the defense attorney did was point out how tiny and helpless Amanda Hailey had been against her tall and strong-looking husband. All Branson did was help the prosecution's case.

But why the hell should he do that?

Jenner pushed the worry out of his mind. Worrying was Maximum Miller's job, and he was doing a good job of it judging from the way he was eating antacid pills. Jenner wondered if a person could overdose on Tums.

Miller inserted the crime-scene video into the VCR.

"Now, Sergeant Schroder, would you tell the jury where this video was taken?" asked Miller, returning to the counsel table.

Jenner didn't listen to Schroder's reply but watched the jury instead. He could follow the progress of the film by the expressions on the various faces. There were a few drawn breaths and hard swallows when Amanda Hailey's body first appeared on the TV screen. A young woman in the last chair in the first row of jury seats momentarily closed her eyes. Jenner didn't blame her. The closest most middle-class women got to murder was in the movies, and no matter how good the special effects were, Hollywood came in second best when it came to dead bodies. There was just no mistaking the real thing.

The faces lost their expressions of revulsion and discomfort when the video began replaying the scenes in the bedroom, but then Jenner understood that. An empty bedroom was a lot easier to take early in the morning than a dead body.

Maximum Miller turned off the video, asked a few more questions about the blood tests made on the rock and fingerprints on the jar of cold cream, which he entered into evidence, then got down to business.

"Sergeant Schroder, was the vanity bench in the bedroom tipped over?"

"Yes, sir."

"Is that consistent with a body falling backward off the bench?"

"In my opinion, yes."

"Is the victim's wound consistent with an assailant standing behind Amanda Hailey while she was sitting at her vanity?"

"I believe so, yes."

There were a lot of "consistent withs" in the rest of Miller's questions, because that was the only way the courts would admit a crime-scene reconstruction. An investigator couldn't simply say that he believed the murder happened in a so-and-so manner; he had to say the murder was "consistent with" it happening in a so-and-so manner. Sometimes Jenner thought trials were exercises in convoluted euphemisms.

He glanced at the defense table. Lydia Fairchild was leaning forward slightly, her eyes focused on Schroder and her fingers silently tapping on the table. John Lloyd Branson, however, was leaning back in his chair, his hands folded loosely over his belly and his eyes half closed. As much as the defense attorney had already screwed up, Jenner figured he at least ought to pay attention.

After Maximum Miller had wrung Schroder dry with every possible "consistent with," he turned him over to Branson, who straightened, blinked as though just waking up, took a sip of water from a glass sitting on the defense table, cleared his throat, and finally stood.

"Sergeant Schroder, I believe you stated, and we all saw, that the sliding glass door in the bedroom was open?"

"Yes, sir."

"Was the bedroom cold when you observed it the first time?"

"Yes, sir."

"Was it freezing cold or merely chilly?"

"It was pretty cold."

"Did you make any attempt to obtain the exact temperature, Sergeant Schroder?"

"No, sir."

"So you have no way of knowing whether it was open for an hour or two hours or three hours or all evening?"

Schroder opened his mouth to speak, caught himself, and shook his head instead. "No, sir."

"Is it consistent with the evidence for Amanda's assailant to enter by the glass door, kill her, and exit the same way, leaving the door open?"

"It is consistent, yes."

"Is it consistent with the evidence for the assailant to enter from the bedroom and exit by the sliding glass door?"

"That's consistent, too."

"Is there any way, consistent with the evidence, that we can determine how long the glass door was open and whether it was used by the assailant to enter, to exit, or both?"

Schroder hesitated, then shook his head. "No, sir."

Maximum Miller stiffened and Jenner heard him expel a deep breath. He was amazed at the prosecutor's self-control. He ought to be dancing around the courtroom shouting hosannas because Glen Williams would testify that David Hailey came around from the back of the parsonage carrying his wife. There were only two exits in the back of the parsonage: the back door, which was locked from the inside, and the sliding glass door off the bedroom. It was all on the tape Schroder made during the interview, the tape Branson had already listened to. Branson was setting himself up to get stiffed when Williams testified. Hailey entered by the bedroom door and exited by the sliding glass door and that's all there was to it. The door was no big mystery.

Apparently Branson must have remembered, too, because he turned abruptly to another subject. "Sergeant Schroder, what is the object we saw in the middle of the bed?"

"A copy of the budget report."

"Your Honor, if the prosecution does not plan to enter that crumpled budget report, the defense requests the right to do so."

"Mr. Miller?" inquired the judge.

Maximum Miller slowly pushed himself up. "We plan to enter it when we call our fingerprint expert, Your Honor."

John Lloyd nodded. "That will be satisfactory, Your Honor. The defense just did not want any foreign object not admitted."

He turned back to the homicide detective. "Sergeant Schroder, are the fatal wound and the tipped-over vanity bench also consistent with Amanda Hailey being struck by a taller person while she was standing up facing her assailant and then falling sideways over the bench as she was dying?"

Schroder scratched his head thoughtfully. "I suppose it is consistent with the evidence."

"The fatal wound is on the right side of Mrs. Hailey's skull, Sergeant Schroder?"

"That's correct."

"Then if she was standing facing her assailant, the assailant was most probably left-handed. Is that true, Sergeant?"

Jenner tried to remember if the preacher was right- or left-handed while Schroder shifted his weight from side to side in the witness chair. "I suppose that would be probable."

"If, however, Amanda was sitting down facing her mirror

and her assailant was behind her, then the assailant was most probably right-handed. Is that true, Sergeant?''

The homicide detective shifted once more and his bushy eyebrows started drawing together in a frown. Jenner could see his right eyelid beginning to twitch.

''I suppose that would be probable.''

''Objection, Your Honor! Damn it, Branson, you can't have it both ways,'' said Maximum Miller, his chin jutting out belligerently.

''What is the basis of your objection, Cleetus?'' asked the judge.

''I suppose you are right, Mr. Miller,'' said Branson as he pushed a yellow legal pad over to Hailey and handed him a pencil. ''Write your name, Reverend Hailey.''

''Just a minute, John Lloyd,'' said Judge Myers. ''I have an objection before the court.''

Neither Branson nor Maximum Miller nor anyone else in the courtroom paid any attention to him. There was another deadly silence with everyone including the court reporter watching the defense table, where David Hailey wrote his name with his right hand, then switched the pencil and wrote his name again with his left hand. From what Jenner could see from where he was sitting, except for the slant of the letters, both signatures were identical. David Hailey was ambidextrous.

''Apparently I can have it both ways,'' said John Lloyd.

Lydia Fairchild covered her face with her hands and sank forward until her head rested on the defense table. Jenner could hear her murmuring ''No, no'' in a monotone.

AD INTERIM

David Hailey watched John Lloyd lean back in his chair again after casually holding up the legal pad for all to see. He heard the murmurs of the spectators and knew if he raised his head and looked to his left he would see the jury staring at him, this man accused of murdering his wife. He also knew that certain members of the court were staring at John Lloyd with bewilderment in their eyes. If he was an object of revulsion, John Lloyd was at least an object of disapproval and bewilderment. If his actions were misunderstood, John Lloyd's were equally misunderstood—even by Lydia Fairchild.

And by himself.

He heard the judge call for a noon recess and stood up, waiting for the bailiff to escort him back to the holding cell where he would be away from accusing eyes. For all that he had tried to hold on to his faith and to his belief in the path he had chosen, he was frightened. He saw prison walls beckoning to him and tasted the first bitter fruit of despair. Perhaps John Lloyd was not a shepherd but a wolf in sheep's clothing.

He felt a hand touch his arm and flinched back.

"Reverend Hailey, trust me," said John Lloyd.

He looked into the attorney's eyes and saw none of the lackadaisical attitude he expected. Instead he saw an intensity of purpose that shamed him. John Lloyd Branson had not lost faith in his cause and was convinced of the rightness of his course.

"Do you know the truth?" Hailey asked, curious to know if this man saw beyond the shadows cast by sacrilege.

He saw the lawyer's eyes sharpen and sensed the terrible will behind them. "I know the minor part of the truth, although not all of that, but the most important truth still eludes me."

"And what is that?"

"Why you substituted your wife's body for the Virgin Mary."

"I cannot tell you."

"You are determined to continue along the way you've chosen?"

"I must. I am a minister first and your client second."

He saw John Lloyd close his eyes briefly and felt relieved, as though a spotlight had been turned off. He could not stand much more of this man's scrutiny without weakening, and that he must not do.

John Lloyd opened his eyes. "I will try to serve both our purposes, but I warn you now that I will not allow justice to be suborned."

"Would you allow it to be suborned in the name of God?"

"Justice and God are synonymous in my eyes, Reverend Hailey."

As he watched John Lloyd turn to leave the courtroom, David Hailey wondered for the first time what he would do if the jury found him innocent, as he was very much afraid they would do if John Lloyd had indeed guessed part of the truth. How would God and justice both be served then?

CHAPTER FOURTEEN

LYDIA RAN DOWN THE THIRD-FLOOR HALL OF THE COURTS buildings, shoving her way through reporters, and made it to the elevator ahead of John Lloyd. She punched the button to close the door and leaned her head against one wall. The skin of her face felt so tight, she wondered if it would burst like a ripe plum and expose the tendons and tissue beneath it. At least no one would recognize her if she looked like a refugee from a horror movie and she wouldn't be pestered by reporters or John Lloyd Branson.

She felt the elevator jerk and looked around to see the end of a wooden cane sticking between the slowly opening doors. She hit the "close" button again with one hand and grabbed the cane with the other. The doors started to close, hit the cane that for all her jerking remained between them, and opened again. Suddenly there was no resistance on the other end of the cane, and Lydia stumbled backward, hit the wall of the elevator, and slid to the floor.

"I trust you are not bruised, Miss Fairchild," said the owner of the cane, stepping onto the elevator and hitting the "close" button.

Lydia scrambled up. "How did you get through the reporters?"

He cocked an eyebrow. "I merely suggested that Maximum Miller had the details of David Hailey's alleged escape, but that I had no comment on the subject."

"You *lied* to the press!"

"Not entirely. I did call it an *alleged* escape."

"You sneaky, low-down—"

He held up his hand. "Miss Fairchild, watch your language."

She shook his cane in his face. "Don't you dare chastise me, you . . . you hypocrite!"

"I assume you are confused by my uncharacteristic behavior this morning," he said, stepping back from the wildly shaking cane.

"Yes, I'm confused! For God's sake, John Lloyd, a beginning law student knows better than to paint himself into a corner by asking a witness a question he doesn't already know the answer to."

"But I did know the answer, Miss Fairchild. I had observed Reverend Hailey and knew he was ambidextrous."

Lydia stared at him with her mouth open until she felt her tongue drying out. She closed her mouth and swallowed as she mentally tried several responses before settling for the simplest one.

"Why?"

"A very open-ended question," he said as the elevator doors opened. "Ah, the first floor. Miss Fairchild, at the risk of seeming an invalid, may I have my cane now, or do you still plan to bludgeon me?"

"Would it do any good?" she asked, thrusting the cane at him.

"Only to remind me that you are a woman not to be taken lightly, a fact that you believe I have ignored."

"Haven't you?" she asked bitterly, stepping out of the elevator and whirling around to face him.

He led her over to a bench against one wall, pulled her down beside him, and took her hands, rubbing his thumbs lightly over her knuckles. "Not intentionally, Lydia."

"Lydia?" she squeaked. She cleared her throat and tried again. "Lydia?" This time her voice was too breathless, but she supposed it was better than sounding like a mouse with its tail caught in a door.

He smiled, and she caught her breath at its sweetness, then narrowed her eyes. She wasn't sure she believed in a sweet John Lloyd. Sour was more his style.

"As you have often pointed out to me, I only call you Lydia when my guard is down and I am acting 'human' in your words. When I retreated into myself these past days, it was not because I took you lightly. It is a characteristic of mine to withdraw when I am considering a puzzling case—and this is a most puzzling case."

"No, it isn't, John Lloyd. You're just reading all this theology into it. It's voluntary manslaughter just like I told you," she said.

"Lydia, did your mother never tell you not to interrupt a man when he is laying bare his soul?"

"Uh, no. Or she may have and I don't remember. Actually, John Lloyd, my mother was always so glad when I brought home anyone in pants who wasn't on probation for some form of civil disobedience that she never gave me any advice at all. I think she was afraid I would do the exact opposite."

"Your mother is a wise woman. You do tend to be obstinate. However, I am not your mother, so I will tell you to be silent while I am confessing. And I am confessing. I am thirty-eight years old, Lydia, and I have never shared confidences with a woman before. I have had relationships, yes, but the limits were clearly defined and never did those limits include more than superficial emotions. Certainly they never included sharing my philosophy and my love of justice."

He drew a deep breath, and she thought of a swimmer preparing to dive underwater. "I have known for some time that I was fighting a rear-guard action against you, that my self-imposed limits were crumbling faster than the walls of Jericho, but that does not mean that my character has altered, only that I can no longer shield myself. I am still what I was before you first entered my office, Lydia, a man who finds it difficult to confide my innermost thoughts. I have always weighed my legal strategies in solitude and must learn to do otherwise. It is an unsettling experience for me."

She felt tears sting her eyes and clog her throat. She leaned over and kissed his cheek. "Thank you, John Lloyd."

His face was solemn, as solemn as any she had ever seen in church, and she felt her stomach tighten in anticipation. "I say all that to say this. I wanted to give you a happy Christmas, but instead I have given you doubt and distrust and loneliness. That was not my intention. Neither was it my intention to take you lightly, but I find I have done that also by my behavior. But in this instance I can do nothing else. I must defend David Hailey and I must do it my way. Call it my gesture of goodwill toward men."

"Then why aren't you defending him, John Lloyd? Why has every question you've asked been double-edged? And why, damn it, did you tell God and Maximum Miller that the preacher could have killed Amanda with either hand?"

John Lloyd looked away. "Lydia, I can have it both ways, but Maximum Miller cannot. He must commit to one course or the other, but not both. And"—he closed his eyes—"and I must make David Hailey appear guilty to save him."

"But I don't understand!" cried Lydia, leaning toward him. "All you have to do is suggest a reasonable doubt to the jury and they cannot convict him of murder."

He turned back to her, a look of resignation in his eyes. "No, Lydia. Doubt is a corrosive emotion. It will not serve my purpose. In this case the jury must commit to an act of faith in order to serve justice. And justice must be served."

"I still don't understand," she said. "Why can't you explain your strategy in words of one syllable? I'm bright. I can comprehend."

"I cannot explain an act of faith, Lydia, and I do not altogether understand it either. I am feeling my way along a path that becomes visible to me only as I take each step. I cannot explain what I cannot yet see. It is the Christmas season, Lydia. It is the season for faith."

"You are asking me to have faith in you, but you won't

try to explain what all these . . . these religious feelings have to do with the law?"

"Christmas is also the season for giving without expectation of receiving."

He released her hands and retrieved his cane from the bench beside him and stroked his hands down the smooth wood. Lydia realized that the cane looked very much like a miniature shepherd's staff, and she remembered sitting on her Granny Abby's lap and looking at all of the pictures in her enormous Bible. So many of the men in those pictures carried a shepherd's staff. She wasn't sure whether it was nostalgia for a time when it was so easy to believe in faith or an ingrained sense of trust in John Lloyd, but she impulsively clutched at his coat sleeve.

"All right, John Lloyd, I'll follow where you lead, but . . . but like your difficulty in confiding in another person, I'm not good at surrendering my own judgment. It's part of *my* personality. Something to do with wanting to be independent, I guess."

She heard the slightest hiss of air escape from his lips and knew that he had been holding his breath. Imagine John Lloyd Branson so uncertain of himself and his persuasive powers that he held his breath. It was almost enough to make her wish she had no reservations about her pledge—or that she hadn't voiced them.

"Miss Fairchild, I will accept what you have given me. It is more than I expected, but less than I wished. For the moment I will be satisfied."

She noticed that he was back to calling her Miss Fairchild, so she supposed his guard was up again. Unfortunately, so was hers.

Lt. Clyde Seale, the fingerprint expert, was tall, thin, and laconic, with bushy gray hair, thick glasses, and an armload of charts, photos enlarged to poster size, and diagrams. Lydia had heard that prosecutors loved him because he never said one word more than absolutely necessary in answer to a question. Loose lips *may* sink ships, but they *absolutely* sink cases. Lawyers love talkative witnesses only when they are testifying for the other side.

Maximum Miller slowly rose to his feet with a glowering look at John Lloyd. One pocket of his coat was ripped half off, the result of a misjudged grab by an out-of-state reporter inexperienced in the care and feeding of the assistant D.A. Lydia had heard whispers to the effect that Maximum Miller had yelled so loudly at this effrontery that the reporter had turned to run, tangled his feet in one of the many electrical cords plugged into every available socket to charge up TV lights, and done twenty feet down the hall on his belly accompanied by three portable banks of lights and the Channel 7 anchorman who hadn't moved out of the way quickly enough. The prosecutor's subsequent remarks regarding reporters and John Lloyd's ancestry and his sexual practices were deemed too obscene for broadcast. Bobby Benson had immediately called a press conference to placate irate reporters only to discover that they were too busy exchanging their favorite Maximum Miller–John Lloyd Branson stories to bother attending. The ponytailed reporter was heard to remark that he hadn't seen this much action since he covered a rock concert that ended in a riot.

Still, Bobby Benson must have felt his assistant needed guidance, because the district attorney was now sitting next to Maximum Miller and looking worried. Or rather, Lydia assumed, worry accounted for the sweat he kept wiping off his forehead. It certainly wasn't the temperature in the courtroom, which hovered somewhat above that of a meat locker.

"Lieutenant Seale, did you examine the bedroom of Amanda Hailey for fingerprints?" asked Maximum Miller.

"Yes, sir."

"Would you tell the jury the location of fingerprints?"

"Yes, sir."

Maximum Miller waited, but the lieutenant didn't say anything else. The entire courtroom heard the prosecutor's sigh. "Lieutenant, would you point out on a diagram of the room where you found fingerprints?"

"Yes, sir," replied Seale, and methodically sorted through

his various instructional aids until he found a drawing on a piece of poster board.

Lydia leaned forward to examine the drawing after it had been entered into evidence. She had read the lieutenant's report, but she hadn't realized how devastating the evidence really was until she saw the diagram. Amanda's prints were found on the cold cream jar, the vanity bench, the top of the vanity, the closet door, the inside knob of the bathroom door, and nowhere else. David Hailey's prints were found on the closet door, a drawer that held Amanda Hailey's underwear and nightgowns, one of which had blood spots on the right shoulder seam, and the metal door frame of the glass door just above the handle.

Lydia wished Amanda Hailey hadn't been such an obsessive housekeeper. The woman must have washed down every wall and polished every surface at least three times a day.

In Lydia's opinion the only bright spot in Seale's testimony concerned the crumpled budget report. Partial prints of David Hailey appeared on the back of the paper as well as on the front side. Prints of Mildred Fisher, Agnes Ledgerwood, Virgil Fisher, and Glen Williams also appeared on the front and back edges.

"Lieutenant Seale, to your knowledge, did Fisher, Ledgerwood, Fisher, and Williams explain the presence of their fingerprints on the budget report?" Miller asked with a quick look at the defense table.

Lydia elbowed John Lloyd. "Object! Seale didn't question the witnesses. Schroder and Jenner did. Seale's evidence is hearsay."

"Miss Fairchild, I have bruises from your use of your elbow during yesterday's testimony. A simple tap on my shoulder will suffice."

"Quit chewing me out and object!"

"John Lloyd, do you have an objection?" asked Judge Myers.

"See, even the judge thinks the question is improper," hissed Lydia.

John Lloyd stood. "I have no objection, Your Honor."

Lydia saw Maximum Miller's mouth gape open before he

snapped it closed, while Bobby Benson stared at John Lloyd with an expression of total disbelief. She could identify with that reaction. She didn't believe it herself.

"You may answer the question, Lieutenant," the judge directed while staring at John Lloyd with a mixture of concern and suspicion.

"I understand from talking with the other officers that Ms. Fisher and Mrs. Ledgerwood both handled all of the reports as chair of the committee and church secretary. Virgil Fisher and Glen Williams were seated together on one side of the table at the budget meeting and each passed the report to Hailey."

Maximum Miller nodded. "As secretary Agnes Ledgerwood made copies and Mildred Fisher passed them out. Like a schoolroom, where you pass worksheets down the row so that the teacher won't have to pass them out individually. Is that correct, Lieutenant?"

"Yes, sir, I believe so."

"Your witness, counselor," Miller said with a pleased look.

In Lydia's opinion he ought to be pleased, since he had managed to slip in testimony explaining away any fingerprints except for David Hailey's. She took a deep breath and pushed away her confusion about John Lloyd's tactics. Not that they didn't *want* the jury to know that the budget report in question was David Hailey's; in fact, it was *necessary* that the jury know, or her theory of the sequence of events would be weakened, but it went against the grain to make it so easy for Maximum Miller. And John Lloyd Branson never made things easy for any prosecutor. Trying to figure out why he was doing it now gave her a headache to accompany her queasy stomach.

John Lloyd rose and walked to the large easel, where Seale's diagram was displayed. He studied it, tilting his head this way and that until the courtroom was once again breathless with anticipation. Lydia was breathless, too, but in her case it was due more to distrust. There was no way to refute the fingerprint expert's testimony, and she didn't understand why John Lloyd wanted to try. All he would accomplish would be to emphasize the evidence. Besides, the defense needed those fingerprints as badly as the prosecution did.

"Lieutenant Seale, were there any fingerprints in the bedroom or on the budget report that you were unable to identify as belonging to the deceased, the accused, or the witnesses?"

"No, sir."

John Lloyd waggled his finger at the lieutenant. "Come, sir, are you testifying that there were no other fingerprints anywhere in that bedroom or on that report?"

Lieutenant Seale shook his head. "Not that I could identify."

John Lloyd whirled from the chart to face the witness. "Then you did find more prints?"

"No, sir."

"Lieutenant, as much as I can appreciate a man of few words, having a bent in that direction myself"—there was loud laughter in the courtroom at such an exaggeration—"but perhaps you could be a trifle more forthcoming. What did you find that you could not identify?"

"Smudges."

"Ah, smudges," repeated John Lloyd. "Perhaps you would be so good as to tell the jury where you found these smudges."

"On the outside of the crumpled budget report and on the handles of the glass door."

"And do you have an opinion, based on your experience, as to the nature of these smudges and to their possible cause?"

"Objection, Your Honor," said Bobby Benson. "The answer would be pure speculation on the part of the witness."

"Tut, tut, Mr. Benson. I allowed Mr. Miller to ask an improper question a moment ago because I was interested in justice and believed justice better served by allowing the jury to hear why the budget report had fingerprints other than Mr. Hailey's without the necessity of recalling Sergeant Schroder. Surely, as district attorney, you are not any less interested in justice?"

"For Christ's sake, Bobby, will you sit down?" Lydia

heard Maximum Miller whisper to his boss. "You haven't studied the case file. There's nothing about those smudges that can hurt us, and your objection just makes you look like you don't know what the hell you're doing. Seale *is* an expert, after all."

"I withdraw my objection, Your Honor," said Benson, blotting the sweat off his forehead with a wrinkled handkerchief.

Judge Myers gave a lengthy sigh. "I wish both sides would remember who is the referee in this case and address their remarks to me." He pointed to the witness with the stem of his pipe. "You may answer the question, Lieutenant."

"In my opinion, the smudges were possibly fingerprints smeared too badly for identification, or possibly fingerprints that simply were unidentifiable because of the surface. The door handles were a bumpy, decorative metal, and the budget report had been wet."

"But you did succeed in lifting Mr. Hailey's fingerprints from the report. Why would some prints be blurred and others clear?" asked John Lloyd.

The lieutenant pushed his glasses back up on his nose and leaned forward with a piece of paper in his hand. "If I could demonstrate, Mr. Branson?"

John Lloyd waved his hand. "By all means, Lieutenant."

Lydia rose halfway out of her chair before sinking back down. Perhaps she was wrong. Perhaps John Lloyd had some brilliant idea in mind that she hadn't thought of: a mysterious outsider perhaps—except that none of the evidence supported such a theory.

"When a person crumples a sheet of paper into a ball such as was done to the budget report, he kind of rubs his fingertips over the paper in the process. He doesn't crush it with straight up-and-down motions of his fingers. Then he generally squeezes it against his palm and that would tend to smear prints. The prints I did lift from the report in its crumpled state were almost indentations, as if the person had suddenly dug his fingers into the crumpled ball—like he was mad about something. All of those prints were those of the defendant, David Hailey."

"Thank you, Lieutenant," said John Lloyd, and returned to his seat, a faint smile on his face.

While Maximum Miller was calling Agnes Ledgerwood to the witness stand, Lydia leaned close to John Lloyd. "Why did you do that? Why did you question him at all? We're not arguing that David Hailey's fingerprints weren't in that bedroom or on that report. All you did was paint a picture of a violent man squeezing a paper ball and wishing it was his wife's neck."

"Voluntary homicide does call for strong emotion, Miss Fairchild," he replied, patting her hand. "Trust me."

Lydia barely held back an exceedingly profane expression containing a certain four-letter word as she jerked her hand away and folded her arms to listen to Agnes Ledgerwood. It was almost verbatim what had been on the tape except that Maximum Miller steered away from any questions about the secretary's feelings of guilt. Other than as an expression of Agnes's guilty conscience for judging young Amanda Hailey so harshly, Lydia didn't see any purpose in the jury hearing it. In fact, maybe it was best they didn't. The defense was based on presenting as black a picture of Amanda Hailey as possible, a woman who finally drove her husband to murder. Sympathy for the victim had no place in that picture.

John Lloyd stood up and began his questions without any of the dramatic pauses that he had used with previous witnesses.

"Amanda Hailey played loud music?"

Agnes swallowed and twisted a lace-trimmed handkerchief. "Yes. Sometimes I thought the girl was deaf to play that music so loud. I could hear it clear over in my office. I don't know what it would have been like this spring with the windows open."

"But you won't know, will you, Mrs. Ledgerwood, because Mrs. Hailey is dead?"

Agnes's chin trembled. "I guess I won't."

John Lloyd walked over to the photograph of Amanda Hailey propped against the wall opposite the jury box. It was poster size and showed in gruesome detail the bloody depression in the young woman's head. Agnes Ledgerwood's eyes followed the lawyer's progress until he stopped beside the photograph, then she quickly jerked her head around to look at the floor in front of the prosecution table.

"I believe you testified that Amanda Hailey wore clothes inappropriate for a minister's wife?" John Lloyd asked.

Agnes nodded. "Yes, she did."

"And Mr. Hailey did not object to his wife buying jeans and slinky robes and, in one case, a tight leather skirt?"

Agnes swallowed, her eyes inadvertently turning to John Lloyd. "I never heard him say."

John Lloyd's black eyes watched the secretary like a predator ready to pounce, and Lydia straightened, wondering what he was up to now. "Did Amanda Hailey buy those clothes after her marriage, Mrs. Ledgerwood?"

The secretary's eyes darted around the courtroom as though she was looking for an escape. "I don't know."

"I believe Mr. Hailey dated Amanda for some weeks before marrying her. Surely you had an opportunity to observe her wardrobe during that time. Did she possess those inappropriate clothes before her marriage?"

"I . . . I'm not sure. Perhaps she did."

John Lloyd nodded, looking down at the photo of Amanda Hailey's wound and then suddenly leaning over to trace its outlines. Everyone else's eyes followed his, and Lydia cringed. Damn it, what was he doing?

John Lloyd straightened. "I believe the salary paid Mr. Hailey is quite modest, is it not?"

Agnes eagerly nodded. "Yes. He said he had no need for more money."

"So there was no money in the Haileys' personal budget to purchase a more appropriate wardrobe for Amanda? In other words, did she not make do with what she had before the marriage?"

"I . . . I guess so."

"Objection, Your Honor. Mr. Branson's questions are irrelevant," said Bobby Benson.

"Your Honor, I am merely covering an issue raised by Mr. Miller during direct examination. Much was made of

Mrs. Hailey's clothes. I was attempting to clarify the matter."

Maximum Miller jerked on Benson's coat and Lydia heard him mutter something to the effect that John Lloyd's "digging his own grave. Don't take away his damn shovel."

Benson stood up and wiped his face again. "I withdraw my objection."

"Mr. Benson, I wish you would quit changing your mind. It's disruptive. Continue, John Lloyd, but watch it. I'll stop you myself if you fish too far from shore."

John Lloyd turned back to the witness. "I believe you testified that Amanda Hailey argued with her husband in public that he should render more to Caesar. By Caesar, did she mean the minister should pay more attention to wordly matters?"

"I assume so. That's the usual interpretation."

"What specifically were the subjects of the arguments?"

"On one occasion she said he was too busy to be a scout master, that it was the responsibility of the boys' fathers and he shouldn't let them avoid it. I can't remember what she said on all occasions, but the gist was that the congregation took advantage of him and that he needed to remember he had a duty to be a husband to her, too."

"None of those arguments seem out of the ordinary for a wife. I believe most wives take umbrage if they believe their husbands are being taken advantage of, and certainly they all believe that men have a strong tendency to neglect their families and it is the duty of the wives to see that they do not."

He paused for a moment as if to let this new interpretation set in, then continued. "Did Mr. Hailey object to Amanda's concerns?"

"Well . . ."

"Did Mr. Hailey object, Mrs. Ledgerwood?"

"No," she said, bowing her head.

"Did he object to her clothes or to her music?"

"No. He was very tolerant."

"So he had no reason—no motive—to be angry with Amanda Hailey. Do you agree with that, Mrs. Ledgerwood?"

She took several deep breaths before answering, and Lydia saw tears gathering in her eyes. "No, he didn't."

"Do you, Mrs. Ledgerwood, of your own personal knowledge, know of any reason for Mr. Hailey to murder his wife?"

"No, I don't," she said between sobs.

Lydia stared at John Lloyd. Not only had he set up Amanda Hailey as a caring wife, but he had painted David Hailey as an indulgent husband, leaving the jury no reason to believe that the preacher had lost his temper and whacked Amanda in the head. Exactly the opposite of what the jury had to believe to vote for voluntary manslaughter instead of murder. Voluntary manslaughter rested upon the jury believing that David Hailey killed his wife while acting out of a sudden passion.

John Lloyd Branson wasn't digging a grave for himself; he was digging one for the Reverend David Hailey.

AD INTERIM

"AGNES!"

David Hailey heard the murmurs of the spectators and the admonitions of the judge, but he heard them from a distance. He saw Maximum Miller rise and the bailiff start toward him, but he saw them move in slow motion. It was a gift he had always possessed, this ability to mute sounds and to slow down motion so that he might not be distracted. He had overheard his parishioners speak of his charisma, but he knew it was nothing more than what his mother had once called his one-track mind. He could concentrate on one goal at a time, one subject at a time, one person at a time, to the exclusion of all else. He was a minister to the exclusion of all else. And Amanda would not let herself be excluded.

It was why she was dead.

"Agnes," he called again, pushing thoughts of Amanda aside.

Reluctantly Agnes looked toward him, her eyes so full of confusion and self-doubt that he felt tears fill his own eyes.

"Reverend Hailey, I'm sorry, but I don't understand why I should be."

Silently he willed her to say more until he realized that she had nothing more to say. He sensed that she was close, so very close, to understanding. Of all his congregation Agnes was the one who seldom accepted anything at face value. All of a sudden he felt a terrible fear.

"Agnes, keep your own counsel and don't interfere!"

He barely had time to see her startled look before the bailiff reached him. He felt himself forced back into his chair by the female bailiff and a young uniformed police officer, who snapped handcuffs around his wrists.

CHAPTER FIFTEEN

THE PREACHER HAD CRAZY EYES, JENNER DECIDED AS HE tested the handcuffs to make certain they weren't too tight. Crazy eyes like that Russian monk's—Rasputin, wasn't it? Jenner remembered seeing his picture in a world-history textbook at Amarillo High. He didn't remember a hell of a lot from that course, but he remembered that monk. Except that Hailey's eyes were gray or gray-blue instead of black, they burned just like Rasputin's. Eyes like that could burn a hole right through a man. No wonder that church secretary had stumbled out of the courtroom like the devil himself was on her tail. Very likely he was, and his name was David Hailey.

"Mr. Hailey, I don't allow outbursts in my courtroom," said Judge Myers, his pleasant-looking face as stern as those of Jenner's fourth-grade schoolteacher, who could scare nine-year-old boys into good behavior without raising her voice. "John Lloyd, if you cannot control your client, I will be forced to have him removed to the holding cell, where he may watch these proceedings on video until such time as he regains a proper respect for this court. Do you understand, Mr. Hailey?"

Jenner saw the preacher's shoulders slump as though whatever was setting him on fire had burned itself out. "I will be quiet, Your Honor."

"See that you are," snapped the judge. "Mr. Miller, call your next witness."

"I call Mr. Hank Gregory," said Maximum Miller.

Jenner leaned over David Hailey. "Take it easy, preacher. You pissed off the judge, and that doesn't do your side any good." He couldn't figure out why he had warned Hailey. He didn't like the man and hoped the jury would send him down for at least twenty years' hard time.

Hailey looked up. "Thank you, but don't trouble yourself worrying about me. I'm not really dangerous except to the unrepentant."

Jenner went back to his seat next to Schroder. "Did you hear that guy? The unrepentant? I don't care what Maximum Miller says. The preacher is several bricks shy of a full load. And I don't think Branson has counted his own bricks lately either."

"You taken up being a psychiatrist?" asked Schroder.

"Listen, Schroder, you've been sitting in that witness room until today. You've missed a lot."

"I've heard about it from some of the cops who've been watching the trial on their breaks, and Special Crimes has a pool going on the verdict at a buck a chance. Everybody's betting on how many years Branson will get for his client. Pick any number between one and ninety-nine."

"What did you pick?"

"I ain't a gambler. I bet on a sure thing."

"What was it?"

"Quiet down, son. I want to listen to Hank Gregory. I might want to hedge my bet."

Jenner watched Hank Gregory walk feebly to the witness box and sit down. The old man looked even older than he had three weeks ago, and it didn't help that his lips were blue from the chill in the courtroom. Jenner hoped Gregory finished his testimony before coming down with a killer case of pneumonia.

After a few preliminary questions, Maximum Miller paused dramatically, something he was as good at as John

Lloyd Branson, and then got down to the business of hanging the preacher.

"Mr. Gregory, when you saw Mr. Hailey carrying his wife's body from the parsonage, did you form an opinion as to his state of mind?" asked Miller, turning to face the jury, all of whom were leaning so far forward that Jenner wondered how they kept from falling facedown on the floor.

"Son, I didn't know my own state of mind right at that minute. Figured maybe I'd suddenly gone senile and was having visions. Wasn't until Roy O'Brien started cussing that I figured if I was having a vision, then everybody else was having the same one."

"When *did* you form an opinion, Mr. Gregory?"

The old man rubbed his chin and thought a minute. "I reckon it was when the preacher dressed up his wife in the Virgin Mary's clothes and set her on that bale of hay. That's when I figured he was either crazy as a hoot owl or mean as hell. I decided on mean 'cause he didn't really act crazy in spite of what he was doing. He was just as calm as a man pitching feed to his cattle in the wintertime. He was just doing what had to be done. Then he looked up at all of us watching him like he expected us to say something. Not one tear did he shed, Mr. Miller. Not one damn tear."

"Your witness, counselor," Maximum Miller said quietly. Jenner thought that even the assistant D.A. looked a little shook, and it took a lot to shake up Maximum Miller.

John Lloyd stood up. "Where was everybody sitting at the budget meeting, Hank?"

Hank Gregory raised his thin white eyebrows at the unexpected question and peered at John Lloyd as if trying to figure out what the attorney was after. Gregory had lived all of his life in Hemphill County and must have known Branson since the lawyer started wearing Western-cut three-piece suits, which Jenner thought was probably the minute he stopped wearing diapers. Nobody in the courtroom, with the possible exception of Maximum Miller and the judge, knew better than Hank Gregory that a wise man walked carefully around John Lloyd Branson and he damn sure watched his answers.

The old man leaned back in the witness box, apparently satisfied that the lawyer's question didn't hold a bear trap. "I was sitting next to Roy O'Brien and on Mildred's right. There's kind of an agreement between the members of the budget committee that somebody sits between Mildred and Roy." He squinted one eye shut in thought. "Let me study a minute, John Lloyd. I wasn't expecting you to ask me that question so I ain't thought much about it."

"Take your time, Hank."

The old man rubbed his cheek for a few seconds, then nodded to himself as if satisfied. "The preacher was sitting at one end of the table like he always does, and Mildred was sitting at the other end like *she* always does. Let's see now, I reckon Virgil was sitting next to his sister since she likes to keep an eye on him, and then there was Glen Williams and Agnes Ledgerwood next to him. That would put Agnes to the preacher's left. That all you wanted to know, John Lloyd?"

"Not quite, Hank. Did anyone leave during the meeting?"

"I reckon you mean during the fight?" Hank asked with a grin on his face.

"Objection, Your Honor," said Maximum Miller, jumping up like a jack-in-the-box. "Improper cross-examination. Branson's asking questions about topics not covered by direct examination."

Jenner noticed that Miller didn't say that Branson's question was irrelevant, just that it was improper.

"I believe that Mr. Miller did mention the budget meeting, Your Honor, which gives me the right to question this witness about events that occurred during it."

Judge Myers shook his head at the prosecutor. "Mr. Miller, you left the door open again and John Lloyd figured he was invited in. Objection overruled."

John Lloyd turned back to Hank Gregory with the closest thing to enthusiasm Jenner had seen the attorney display so far. "Yes, Hank, I mean during the fight."

"Well, I'll tell you, John Lloyd, I left. I was having trouble with my stomach and didn't figure hearing Roy O'Brien and Mildred get into it over what the preacher's wife was wearing would do my bellyache any good, so I went out on the porch for a smoke. Wasn't but a minute until Glen Williams came out and went to his car for his cigarettes. Mildred won't allow smoking during the meetings and gives anybody a dirty look for even carrying a pack in his pocket. Me and Roy O'Brien don't care if we ruffle her feathers, but Glen's a politician and don't need to be making an enemy of Mildred. Anyhow, Glen comes back and we had us a cigarette and jawed about nothing in particular for a few minutes until Mildred comes whipping out of the parsonage, pulling on her gloves and looking madder than a wet hen. Then we knew the fight was over."

"What happened next, Hank?" asked John Lloyd.

"Well, pretty soon Virgil comes meandering out on the porch, lit up, and took a couple of puffs—waiting to give Mildred time to cool off, don't you see—then goes wandering off after his sister. That's when Roy O'Brien comes out to join us. We all figure we got time for one more smoke before Virgil can persuade Mildred to come back and finish the meeting."

"And Agnes and Mr. Hailey stayed in the house?"

"No. The preacher took his wife back to the bedroom before the fight started and was the last one to come back in the house. Agnes? Well, I guess Agnes trailed after Virgil. No, that's wrong. Agnes came out of the house a minute or two before Virgil and went after Mildred. Virgil followed her. Didn't neither one of them look anxious to catch up with Mildred. I've seen molasses run faster on a cold day than them two. Anyhow, they came dragging her back and we got the meeting started again. Must have been five minutes before the preacher came back."

"From his bedroom?" asked John Lloyd.

Hank Gregory shook his head. "Nope, through the front door like a cold wind and his hair full of sleet. Said he'd been over to the church to pray for forgiveness." He grabbed the sides of the jury box and leaned over to stare at the preacher. "Maybe God will forgive you, but this old man ain't about to, not for murder and not for sacrilege."

Judge Myers waited a heartbeat for John Lloyd to ask that

Hank Gregory's last comment be stricken from the record, but the attorney remained silent. "The jury will disregard the witness's last remark," the judge said finally with a quizzical look at the defense table.

That ruling was like locking the barn door after the horse was stolen, decided Jenner. There was no way in hell the jury was going to forget what Hank Gregory said.

John Lloyd clasped his hands behind his back, and Jenner noticed that his knuckles were turning white. Maybe he was more upset with himself than he let on for allowing a witness to get out of hand. He ought to be if he wasn't. The attorney had heard the tapes and knew the preacher had been outside. Why in hell had John Lloyd Branson asked that question in the first place?

"In your opinion, Hank, was Mr. Hailey angry with his wife during the committee meeting?" asked John Lloyd.

Hank opened his mouth, then closed it again, a bewildered expression on his face. "No. But he must've been, or else he had no excuse for killing her except for pure meanness."

"Thank you, Hank," John Lloyd said as he sat down, leaving everyone in the courtroom wondering how he ever made a living as a defense attorney when he seemed to be doing a bang-up job convicting his own client.

Maximum Miller took a long time calling his next witness, staring instead at John Lloyd Branson. He wasn't the only one. Everybody else was, too. Except for Lydia Fairchild, who huddled in her chair hugging her stomach and looking sick.

"Call Mildred Fisher," Miller finally said, and Jenner reluctantly switched his attention from Lydia Fairchild's pinched white face to the older, harder, less attractive but considerably more confident one of the budget committee chairwoman.

Mildred Fisher folded her hands with their polished nails—red this time, Jenner noted—and tilted her chin up as she waited for the first question. She wore a long-sleeved navy blue dress of some bulky knit with a red patterned scarf around the neck. In Jenner's opinion it wasn't much of an improvement over the masculine suit she'd worn the first time he saw her. Like her brother's, Mildred's skin was dead white, but it resembled marble rather than skimmed milk. Or maybe that was a judgment made on the basis of character rather than physical appearance, but at any rate, Jenner thought, she looked awful in navy blue and red.

Her wardrobe aside, Mildred Fisher was Maximum Miller's kind of witness: absolutely sure of herself and answering his questions as quickly as he could ask them. Not that there was much new that Jenner didn't already know. Even Mildred's account of the fight was consistent with Roy O'Brien's, except she put a different spin on it so it sounded like she was defending herself against an unwarranted attack.

"Then Roy O'Brien took me to task for my pointing out to Mrs. Hailey that her robe was inappropriate. Of course, Roy had known Mrs. Hailey before her marriage and was completely uncritical in his judgment. I think he saw her as a young girl and didn't realize how embarrassing it must be for a minister to see his wife sashaying around in practically nothing when there were other men around. Even if her reputation had been pure, her behavior would have raised eyebrows. As it was, everyone thought the worst except Roy. He never saw a thing."

"Could you be more specific, Miss Fisher?" asked Maximum Miller. "What was there to see?"

For the first time Jenner saw Mildred Fisher hesitate. It wasn't much of a hesitation, just a second to lick her lips. On the other hand, most predators licked their mouths just before taking the first bite of their prey.

"She touched men. You just should have seen her hugging all the men in church old enough to be her father. How can men keep their minds on the sermon under such circumstances?"

"Can you tell us of your own knowledge what Amanda Hailey's reputation in the community was, Ms. Fisher?" asked the assistant D.A.

"A tart!"

With that remark ringing in the jury's ears, Miller turned over the witness to John Lloyd.

The defense attorney stood up behind the counsel table,

his right hand resting on Lydia Fairchild's shoulder. One look at her face told Jenner that her boss's gesture wasn't a sign of affection. Lydia's face was as red as Mildred Fisher's lipstick and her fists were doubled up. If there was another outburst in the courtroom, it wouldn't be David Hailey who made it.

"Ms. Fisher, I am not a gourmet cook, nor do I pay particular attention to the food section in the daily paper, but I was under the impression that a tart was a form of pastry, a small open pie with a sweet filling, to be precise."

The woman's face turned splotchy, as Jenner had seen it do before. "It also means a loose woman!" Mildred Fisher must have a set of the *Oxford English Dictionary*, too.

"A prostitute?" suggested John Lloyd.

"Yes!"

"A prostitute takes money in exchange for sexual favors. Do you know of your own knowledge that Amanda Hailey was a prostitute?"

Mildred sat staring at him, her face now an unattractive red.

"Do you know of your own knowledge that Amanda Hailey was a prostitute?" repeated John Lloyd. "Do you know of your own knowledge of an occasion when she exchanged sexual favors for money?"

"No!"

"Do you know the name of any man with whom Amanda Hailey slept either before or after her marriage?"

"No! But her reputation was terrible."

"Because she hugged church members old enough to be her father?"

"Yes."

"Did you ever observe Amanda Hailey embracing men of her own age, or did she reserve her physical affection for those males she considered father figures?"

"I never saw her hugging young men, but that doesn't mean she didn't."

"You can only testify to what you have personally seen and heard, of course," agreed John Lloyd. "And as to what you have personally seen, did you ever witness the minister chastising his wife for her behavior?''

''Mr. Hailey was far too well-bred to call down his wife in public.''

''Then he did not openly chide Amanda when he escorted her from the budget meeting?''

''Of course not.''

''Then he did not glare at her disapprovingly, or jerk her out of the room, or snarl some order to her that others could barely hear as many other embarrassed men might do?''

''No!''

''Then he was not angry with this young, spirited, and affectionate girl who only interrupted the meeting to serve coffee and to remind its members of the late hour and her husband's need for rest?'' asked John Lloyd, moving around the defense table and limping over to the photo of Amanda's wound.

''You make her sound like a goody-goody,'' snapped Mildred, following him with her eyes. She caught sight of the photo, then glanced away.

''Perhaps goodness, like beauty, is in the eye of the beholder, Ms. Fisher,'' said John Lloyd, returning to his seat. ''I have no further questions for this witness, Your Honor.''

Mildred Fisher marched from the courtroom with a straight spine, squared shoulders, head held high, and the meanest look on her face that Jenner had seen in quite a while. He figured John Lloyd Branson ought to watch his back or take up wearing a bullet-proof vest.

Virgil Fisher, on the other hand, wouldn't scare a rabbit. In fact, given his twitching nose and receding chin, a rabbit would probably think he was a litter mate. As a witness, Jenner thought he was a dud for both sides. He even denied having an opinion as to whether or not the preacher was angry with his wife, but then Jenner figured Virgil Fisher didn't have much practice having opinions of his own.

John Lloyd stood up and straightened his coat. ''Virgil, do you know of any man with whom Amanda Hailey had or was having an affair?''

Virgil's nose twitched. "No, I don't, John Lloyd, but there was talk."

"Do you know if Mr. Hailey had also heard this talk?"

"Oh, it wouldn't have made any difference. Reverend Hailey never listened to gossip and always preached about bearing false witness if anyone said anything unkind about another person."

John Lloyd nodded thoughtfully. "Then perhaps we should go on to another subject. After your sister left the parsonage, I believe you and Agnes Ledgerwood followed her. Did you see the minister during this time?"

"No, we didn't see anyone. Heavens, it was sleeting. Why would anyone be out without a reason?"

"And your sister did not mention seeing the minister to you?"

"I doubt Mildred would have noticed the Second Coming, John Lloyd. She was much too angry."

"And you found her at your car in the church parking lot, and she was still angry?"

"No, we found her in the nativity scene trying to pull down the Virgin Mary's robe to cover her feet, and she had a few words to say to me about donating a mannequin with painted toenails. She said it reminded her too much of Amanda Hailey. Heavens to Betsy, she was mad, but she hadn't said a word to me about the mannequin being inappropriate up to that time. I didn't know what to say to her, so I took the path of least resistance and said nothing."

Jenner would bet Virgil had worn ruts in the path of least resistance.

John Lloyd casually strolled over to the photograph of Amanda Hailey's wound. "Virgil?"

Mildred's brother obediently turned his head to look at the attorney, flinched at the sight of the photo, and carefully averted his eyes.

"We have heard much about Amanda Hailey's costume that so shocked your sister the night of the budget meeting. As a connoisseur of women's apparel, would you describe the garment?'' John Lloyd asked as if he hadn't noticed Virgil's reaction.

Virgil smiled. ''It was a simple caftan of cheap gold velour with a front zipper and long loose sleeves, and it was floor length, of course.''

''Velour being a relatively heavy and opaque material?''

''Yes, sir.''

''So an observer could not see Amanda Hailey's body through the material?''

''Oh, no!''

''Was the front zipper open to reveal Amanda Hailey's cleavage?''

''No, it was zipped up to the throat.''

''It was then a modest garment worn in a modest manner with no flesh revealed that might incite a man to passion?''

''Not in the manner you mean, but Amanda Hailey would have attracted attention whatever she wore. She was a redhead, and natural redheads are so statistically rare—less than five percent of the population—that it is difficult not to notice them.''

''Then you saw nothing immodest about her garment that would disturb her husband?''

''*I* certainly didn't.'' He left no doubt in anyone's mind who did.

''Then is it not possible that Mr. Hailey removed his wife from the budget meeting, not because he was upset with her, but to prevent her from being unduly criticized by your sister?''

''I hadn't thought of that, but I believe it entirely possible, Virgil said with a thoughtful nod. ''Yes, I do—and I'm so happy. Murder over a caftan is so trivial, don't you see?''

John Lloyd's face grew solemn. ''Yes, I *do* see, Virgil.''

AD INTERIM

He could sense Lydia Fairchild's growing distress by her restless gestures: crossing and recrossing her legs, tapping her fingers, twisting in her chair, rubbing her temples and the space between her eyes, but most of all, the paleness of her face, as though sorrow had bleached out all color. She was much like Amanda in that respect. Amanda would lose the healthy pink color that so many mistook for blush. Her lips would be colorless and look shrunken rather than full. Only the tiny freckles on the top of her cheeks and across the bridge of her nose, like the faintest dusting of gold dust, saved her from being the same dead white as Virgil Fisher. And her eyes—grass-green eyes that could glitter like emeralds or look as soft as velvet.

Lydia Fairchild possessed no freckles that he had noticed, and her blonde hair lacked the vividness of Amanda's, looking instead as if God had fashioned it from silvery moonlight. But her eyes, those beautiful eyes like sky-blue turquoise set between black lashes, lent color to a marble face.

He knew as surely as though he had been told that Lydia Fairchild had not wanted John Lloyd to defend him although she had agreed to help him. He knew also that she had never resolved her conflict, and to that conflict was added another. She did not understand the path that John Lloyd had chosen, and not understanding it, she followed reluctantly. She did not share his faith.

Neither had Amanda always shared his faith, depending instead on love.

In the end love had not been enough to save her.

CHAPTER SIXTEEN

LYDIA RAISED HER HEAD AS JOHN LLOYD ROSE AND CROSSED to stand beside the photograph of Amanda Hailey's fatal head wound. Roy O'Brien turned his head to face him, but rather than averting his eyes away from the photo, as all the other witnesses had done, he studied it. His chin quivered once before he tightened his lips and his face flushed a dull red.

"Roy—" began John Lloyd.

"You can call me Mr. O'Brien," he interrupted. "I'm particular about who uses my first name."

"Did Amanda call you Roy?" asked John Lloyd

"Yeah, but don't read anything into it that ain't there. Amanda called everybody by their first names. She even tried it with Mildred, but the old bitch took a strip of hide off the girl. Told her it wasn't respectable."

"I believe you came to Amanda's defense the night of the budget meeting?"

"Yeah, somebody had to, and her husband damn sure wasn't. He just said Mildred like that was going to stop her. He should have known better. He was the one who was always telling us we were no different than the people the Bible talks about. He should have taken that a step further, then he would have known that if we ain't no different, we sure ain't no better either. Judas betrayed Christ and Peter denied him three times. Aaron, the brother of Moses, is the man who made the golden calf that the children of Israel worshipped while God was busy handing down the Ten Commandments. Hell, we're still betraying each other and denying we know somebody if we think it might cause us trouble, and we sure do know how to worship the golden calf except we call it money or power or fame."

He stopped and wiped his hand over his face. "The preacher always expected us to be a little more divine than we are or were or probably ever will be. Just calling somebody's name in that voice of his ain't gonna stop a fight if a person's got their dander up. Although, to be fair, it worked most of the time. But it didn't work this time, and he should have called Mildred down."

"Mr. O'Brien, do you know of any lovers Amanda Hailey might have had before or after her marriage?"

"No! Because there weren't any! It was all talk, and I don't even know how it got started, but none of it was true."

"Do you know if Mr. Hailey had heard this talk?" asked John Lloyd.

"Of course. He'd heard it because Amanda told him, and I was there when she did it. We were all sitting in a booth in the truck stop where she worked. She fiddled with her hair and twisted around like the seat was too hot, then just blurted it out. Said she didn't think it was fair for her to marry him without his knowing that folks talked about her. Then she slipped off the engagement ring with the tiny diamond and held it out to him."

"But Mr. Hailey married her anyway?"

Roy O'Brien laughed. "God Almighty, John Lloyd, didn't you ever burn for a woman? Well, the preacher did, and lust makes for mighty poor judgment. He told her the talk didn't matter and things would work out." O'Brien leaned forward. "But nothing was working out. People, mainly Mildred, were still talking; Amanda was still feisty and funny and not keeping her head down to avoid drawing fire, and worse than that she was acting like a wife. She made sure he didn't skip meals. If you called the parsonage late at night, Amanda answered the phone and you better have a damn good reason for disturbing the preacher's sleep. She watched out for him like a guard dog."

John Lloyd hesitated, studying Roy O'Brien, then asked one more question. "If Mr. Hailey did not believe the gossip about Amanda, and she was fulfilling her role as a virtuous woman who watched over her husband and cared for him, do you have an opinion as to why David Hailey might have killed his wife?"

Now it was Roy O'Brien's turn to hesitate. He rubbed his forehead and glanced at the minister, then glanced away. "When you put it that way, I'll have to say I don't know. But I do know one thing, John Lloyd. The last time I saw Amanda alive, David Hailey was hauling her back to their bedroom. The next time I saw her he was carrying her out of that same bedroom and she was dead."

Lydia bowed her head again, unable to look at John Lloyd. Her head was pounding and her nausea was almost more than she could stand. She wondered if Maximum Miller had any Tums left.

She looked up as John Lloyd slipped into his chair. The last witness was Glen Williams. He was also their last chance to throw a monkey wrench in the prosecution's case. If John Lloyd screwed up this cross-examination like he had the others, then David Hailey's next stop would be the Texas Department of Corrections in Huntsville. Of course, he could always appeal on the basis of incompetency of counsel. She rubbed her forehead, where her headache was the worst. John Lloyd Branson, an incompetent attorney? It wasn't logical, rational, or believable. In fact, it was impossible. It violated everything she knew about the man.

But incompetency was better than the alternative: that John Lloyd Branson was deliberately and with malice aforethought sabotaging his own client. It was impossible! It was *sacrilege*!

"Please," she whispered as John Lloyd rose to cross-examine Glen Williams. She wasn't certain to whom she was speaking. John Lloyd hadn't heard her, and she doubted that even God could sway John Lloyd Branson short of striking him dead.

"Glen, how far away were you when you saw David Hailey pick up something from the border of the flower bed?" asked John Lloyd.

"I was perhaps thirty feet away when I saw him pick up the stone," Glen said in a deliberate manner. If John Lloyd was going to make points off Glen Williams, he would have to work at it.

"Was there a light near the flower bed?"

"No, but the streetlights were on as well as the spotlight on the nativity scene and another on the front of the church. There was sufficient light for me to see that Hailey was not leaning over to tie his shoe."

"What was the weather like at that time, Glen?"

"It was sleeting."

"A light sleet or a heavy one?"

"I'd call it heavy," said Glen.

"And sleet is frozen or partially frozen raindrops? Is that correct?"

Glen smiled. "If you say so, John Lloyd. I'm certainly not about to argue definitions with you."

"And frozen raindrops would be ice? Is that correct?"

"Again I'm not going to argue with you. Sleet is ice or mostly ice."

"Is it not true, Glen, in your experience, that ice reflects light?"

Glen Williams saw the trap but couldn't figure a way to avoid it. "Yes, it does, but the light would have had to come from behind me in order to reflect back in my eyes."

"I believe the streetlights were behind you, Glen," said John Lloyd quietly.

Glen sighed and capitulated. "That's true. The sleet was reflecting light, but I could still see Hailey picking up a stone. I wasn't blinded by any means."

"In a heavy sleet storm that was reflecting light back into your eyes, and from thirty feet away, you saw David Hailey pick up a rounded white object. Is that correct?"

Glen sighed again. "That is correct."

John Lloyd picked up two exhibits that were lying on a table near the court reporter. "Glen, can you swear without a shadow of a doubt in your mind that you saw David Hailey pick up a stone, or did you see him pick up this budget report, which was crumpled into a ball resembling the stones from the border of that flower bed?" He held both objects out, one in each palm. "Can you swear under oath and without a shadow of a doubt that it was the stone rather than the budget report, a rounded white object we already know from previous testimony was still wet when examined after the murder?"

John Lloyd stepped closer to the witness box and lowered his voice. "Can you swear in front of Almighty God that it was one and not the other?"

Glen Williams finally shook his head. "I can't swear to either one, John Lloyd. I assumed it was a stone, but it could've been the budget report."

Lydia would have felt faint with relief if she had been the type to feel faint in the first place. She did admit to feeling as limp as a wet noodle. John Lloyd had done it! He had planted doubt that the prosecution's scenario of the crime was correct. He wasn't incompetent. He wasn't sabotaging his client.

Now if he would just sit down and shut up while he was ahead.

But apparently John Lloyd had no intention of shutting up as he wandered over to that same horrible photograph. "Glen, would it be consistent with the evidence to say that a wet, crumpled ball of paper caused this wound?"

Glen clenched his jaw just enough to make a muscle jump, but he didn't avoid looking at the photograph. Of course, he was a prosecutor himself; he had seen gory photos before. "No, John Lloyd, it would not be consistent with that wound."

Lydia felt her muscles begin to tense up again as John Lloyd failed to thank the witness and return to the counsel table. "Please, God, don't let him ask another question."

God apparently failed to hear her prayer or else John Lloyd ignored his maker. "In your capacity as district attorney, in which you must weigh facts when preparing to prosecute a case, would you consider it more consistent with all the physical evidence of which you have knowledge to presume that David Hailey picked up this *wet*, crumpled budget report rather than a stone?"

"I would have to say no. It is not more consistent."

"Then you are testifying that it is less consistent?"

"No, I'm not saying that either, John Lloyd. It's six of one and a half-dozen of the other. I observed that David Hailey had been outside during the time he was absent from the budget meeting. I also observed no one else entering Amanda Hailey's bedroom except David Hailey and therefore he must have dropped the report on the bed where I saw it while I was guarding the crime scene until Sheriff Taylor arrived, at which time I informed him I was a witness and would not be prosecuting the case. But it is not *more* consistent with the evidence to presume that he dropped the report in the flower bed while picking up a stone when he was outside during the break. It is not *more* consistent with the evidence to presume that he then noticed after the meeting that he had dropped it, picked it up, took it to his bedroom where he suddenly decided to undress his wife's body and deposit it in the nativity scene."

"But it is not *inconsistent* with the evidence?" John Lloyd insisted, but in Lydia's opinion it was already too late.

"It is if you consider that David Hailey knew the routine of these meetings as well as anybody. He knew every fight between Mildred and Roy ended with Mildred stomping off and her brother and Agnes trailing after her. He knew that Hank and I would immediately go outside for a smoke and Roy would join us as soon as he put Mildred in her place. He knew that he might be observed by at least three people. If it hadn't been sleeting, there would have been six witnesses."

"Why would there have been three more witnesses if it had not been sleeting?" asked John Lloyd.

"Hank and I and later Roy stayed on the porch, and there's a thick latticework on the end of it closest to the flower bed. Between the lattice and the sleet and not paying attention, we might not have noticed Hailey sneaking around the corner of the house."

"Would it be consistent with the evidence to presume David Hailey picked up the stone and dropped his budget report during the five-minute period when the rest of the committee returned to the house but he did not?"

"I didn't testify that it was five minutes. It was more like two or three. Five minutes is a hell of a long time when you're sitting around a table waiting for somebody and hoping nobody gets in a fight in the meantime, but then it has been my experience that witnesses don't always make accurate estimates of time unless they are looking at a clock or happen to check their watches, which I don't personally remember anyone doing. So no, it would not be consistent with the evidence. In fact, it would be a lot less consistent."

"Would you explain why?" asked John Lloyd.

"Because it wouldn't make any sense for him to murder his wife, then go back outside, walk around the house, and enter from the front door."

"Would it make more sense if you knew that one of the other witnesses testified that Mr. Hailey told her he was praying?"

"Yes! That would be consistent with my knowledge of the defendant. He always prayed when he felt he had committed some penny-ante sin. It would be consistent with his character for him to pray for strength to resist temptation. It is also consistent with the evidence that God didn't grant his prayer."

Glen Williams leaned back in the witness chair, a sympathetic expression on his face. "You should have quit while you were ahead, John Lloyd."

For the second time since the case of Texas vs. David Hailey began, Lydia Fairchild bolted out of the courtroom before the judge adjourned the proceedings.

Lydia heard John Lloyd opening his office door and rose to her feet to stand by the attorney's rolltop desk. Getting out of her chair had taken almost more effort than she had energy for—as if she was a very old woman. And perhaps she was.

Perhaps age was more a matter of losing one's illusions than the toll of mounting years. As long as a woman believed in someone besides herself, whether it was God, or a friend, or a child, or a man, she stayed young inside where it counted. No man was an island, according to John Donne. No woman was either. When the bell tolled for the death of John Lloyd's soul, it tolled for her also because she had believed in him.

"I thought that you might come here," he said, closing the door behind him. "Although I did look for you at home."

"I caught a ride back to Canadian with Judge Myers's court reporter and asked her to drop me off here. Your home is for our private lives. This office is for our professional lives."

"And you have concerns about our professional lives?" he asked, walking toward her.

The sound of his footsteps was uneven, more so than usual, and she noticed the lines of strain on his thin face. Both revealed the effort he made to walk with no more than a slight limp. She silently moved aside so that he would at least sit down at his desk. Nothing personal in her concern. She would do the same for a serial murderer.

"I will stand, Miss Fairchild. I am neither so tired nor in so much pain that I need to be treated as an invalid. Besides, experience has taught me that mobility is the best defense against your right hook."

"I can do without your levity, John Lloyd. And I'm not in the mood for your macho male bullshit either. I know your leg is hurting, so you might as well sit down. I promise I won't hit you. And"—she held up her hand—"don't snarl at me for mentioning your leg. You were shot at some unspecified time in the past by some unspecified person and it left you permanently affected. Not disabled, not handicapped, and, for God's sake, not crippled, but affected, and I'm tired of tiptoeing around your denial. I never thought any less of you as a man because you limped."

She surreptitiously wiped her damp hands on her wool skirt and braced herself for an outburst of wounded pride. She might be totally repulsed by John Lloyd's betrayal of his ethics and of her trust, but she still found herself hoping she hadn't humiliated him.

He walked around her and lowered himself carefully into his high-backed padded chair, stretching out his leg with a groan he didn't bother muffling. He leaned his head back and closed his eyes. "Thank you, my dear."

"What?"

He opened his eyes. "I said thank you. Even a man such as myself occasionally suffers from vanity. I do not like references to my affliction from others because I do not like being an object of pity. In your case, however, I had another reason. I'm older than you by some fourteen years and I did not want you thinking of me as a crippled old man. Therefore I refused to allow you to mention my leg or to fuss over me as women are wont to do. I did not want your sympathy. Vanity, pure vanity. Now that you have confessed you do not find my masculinity lacking, which I assure you, my dear, it is not, I shall dispense with my masquerade."

She wobbled on shaky legs to her own chair and sank down, unable to think of anything to say. "I'm speechless. I . . . I'm at a loss for words."

He waved a hand in the air. "Please, Miss Fairchild, you are sounding painfully like Mrs. Dinwittie. Saying something like 'Thank you, John Lloyd' or perhaps even 'I'm flattered' will suffice."

"I am," she said, then felt tears running down her cheeks. "Damn you, John Lloyd. Why did you wait until now to tell me? Why didn't you tell me sooner? Were you holding back just in case you needed some emotional blackmail and decided this was the time? First all those things you told me yesterday when I was so angry with you, and now this. Did you know how upset I've been? Did you decide that a little sweet talk to gullible Lydia would calm her down? Did you think I was so weak-minded that I would overlook what you're doing?"

He reached over and took her hand despite her efforts to avoid him. "Exactly what is it am I doing, Lydia?"

She shook her head until her hair lashed her cheeks.

"Don't call me Lydia! That won't work either. You committed sacrilege, John Lloyd!"

"Sacrilege?" His eyes widened slightly as if he was surprised. "Perhaps you would care to explain that charge."

She waved her free hand toward a huge book on her table. "I looked up the word in your unabridged dictionary. It means the desecration, profanation, misuse, or theft of something sacred."

"Lydia, I am familiar with the definition. What I am questioning is your usage."

She counted on her fingertips. "You profaned the canon of legal ethics, you misused your profession, and you stole something sacred."

Her tears were blurring her vision so badly that she could hardly see his face. Which was probably just as well. She couldn't tolerate one of his quelling looks. "The canon of ethics says you must defend your client to the best of your ability. I've watched you in court before. I've measured your ability, and this time you're not even coming close to using the skill I know you have. You are deliberately sabotaging your client's case with every cross-examination. You have deliberately erased all doubt in the jury's mind that David Hailey killed his wife in a fit of passion. You have refuted all motives and left him looking like a psychopath. And that performance this afternoon with Glen Williams . . . Well, I just don't have words to describe it."

"I doubt that, Miss Fairchild. Your facility for finding words to express yourself has never been lacking—and certainly not this evening."

She noticed he was back to calling her Miss Fairchild again and decided he was on the defensive. She wiped the tears from her cheeks. "You said yesterday that justice must be served. Did you mean that you believe David Hailey is guilty of murder instead of voluntary manslaughter? Did you decide that you will see justice served by selling your client down the river? Answer me, damn it!"

"What did I steal, Lydia?"

Now she was Lydia again, and she wished he'd stop trying to confuse her. "What are you talking about?"

"You said I stole something sacred. What did I steal?"

She sniffed and wiped her face on her sleeve. "I thought you were so wonderful, John Lloyd. Oh, you're pompous and stubborn and a stuffed shirt sometimes, but somehow—and don't ask me to explain—all those traits make you endearing. You're brilliant, and I thought you were so passionate about the law. I was even jealous. I wondered if you would ever feel that much passion for me."

He fished a handkerchief out of his breast pocket and handed it to her. "What did I steal, Lydia?"

She took the handkerchief and held it over her eyes to blot up the tears as they fell. "My trust, John Lloyd. My belief in you. How can I believe in someone who commits sacrilege?"

He released her hand and she told herself she didn't feel bereft. The silence lengthened, and finally she uncovered her eyes to look at him. He sat with his head bowed over his clasped hands, his elbows resting on his knees.

Gingerly she touched his shoulder. "John Lloyd? I have to resign. I can't work with you when my conscience is so at odds with"—she hesitated—"the rest of me."

He raised his head to look at her. "You may, of course, continue as my houseguest until you are able to book a flight back to Dallas. At Christmas that may take some time."

"I've arranged to stay with Mrs. Dinwittie."

"I see."

She shoved back her chair and got up to pace back and forth, twisting his handkerchief between her fingers. "Is that all you have to say? Aren't you going to defend yourself? Aren't you going to explain how I'm wrong? Aren't you going to explain why you've deliberately blown our voluntary manslaughter defense?"

He looked up at her with expressionless eyes. "Your defense, Miss Fairchild, and a very well-reasoned one. Your explanation for the presence of the budget report on the bed was brilliant. It is even, I believe, accurate. David Hailey did pick up that report rather than a stone, and Amanda Hailey did die during the time of the break. But your defense was never my defense, and the key word for my rejecting it is *believe*. You believe David Hailey guilty and marshaled all the facts to support your thesis of voluntary manslaughter just as you believe I am guilty and have marshaled all your facts to condemn me. What you see as sacrilege is instead an act of faith, a belief that David Hailey is a man of strong religious convictions who was deeply in love with his wife. Such a man would not kill and certainly would not profane a religious symbol."

He rose and picked up his cane. "Therefore I intend to ask for an instructed verdict of not guilty. I proved David Hailey is not guilty of manslaughter because there was no evidence of sudden passion, and Maximum Miller cannot prove the premeditation necessary for a murder conviction. The judge will be forced to grant our plea."

Lydia felt as though she was the one on the receiving end of a right hook, and for a moment she felt like doubling over until she could recover from the shock. But it wasn't her breath she had lost.

"My God, John Lloyd, what have I done?"

"I believe, Miss Fairchild, that like David Hailey's congregation, you looked at the evidence and found it consistent with guilt. However, I am not David Hailey, and you have misjudged me."

"I'm sorry, John Lloyd. I should have known better. I *did* know better, but I couldn't reconcile what my head and my heart were telling me when they both were saying different things. You were so secretive, nearly as secretive as David Hailey." She looked up at him. "Why didn't you tell me what you were doing? Why didn't you trust me?"

"It was not a question of trust, Miss Fairchild. I do not exaggerate when I say I would trust you with my life. But it is not my life that is at stake. It is David Hailey's. You are a very poor liar, and I had to mislead the prosecution. I could not fool Maximum Miller for the time I have fooled him if he had not been convinced that you believed me to be doing a poor job defending my client. Of course, I never expected you to accuse me of sacrilege."

"You used me! Again! And for no good reason! What

difference does it make if you fooled Maximum Miller or not? The result is the same: an instructed verdict."

He clasped her shoulders, his eyes as black as anthracite coal and burning with as clean a flame. "It does make a difference, Miss Fairchild. I had to buy time. I have temporarily checked Maximum Miller, but the game is not over. He will counter, but first he must study the board, and I shall use that time to persuade David Hailey to break his silence and tell me why in the damnable hell he so mistreated his wife's body! Unless I know that I will lose this case. A murderer will go free and a soul will be forfeit. If I had allowed our personal interests to jeopardize the cause of justice and redemption, I would indeed be committing sacrilege and you would be right to despise me."

Lydia knew she would hurt tomorrow, but for now she was numb. She had misjudged him, and he had used her in the name of a higher purpose. She wasn't sure which was worse, her accusation or his callousness, or if they had sinned equally, and it didn't really matter. They had wounded each other, and one of them had to make the first move toward reconciliation. "We were both wrong, John Lloyd. Can we forgive each other and put this behind us? Can we go on working together?"

He looked at her and she had no sense of what he was thinking. "I don't think so, Miss Fairchild. I don't have your youthful resiliency to heal myself. Get your coat and I'll take you to Mrs. Dinwittie's."

She was reaching blindly for her coat when he spoke again. "And, Miss Fairchild."

"Yes?"

"Not a word about my using contractions, please."

AD INTERIM

John Lloyd explained his decision to ask for an instructed verdict. "You have gambled and lost, Mr. Hailey, and now I must extricate you from this dangerous game in which you are presently engaged."

"I don't consider it gambling, and it is certainly not a game, not when a soul is at stake."

"If you find that analogy offensive, consider this one. I have succeeded in making a silk purse from a sow's ear, but at any moment a sharp eye may detect the swinish bristles and Maximum Miller has sharp eyes. I have done what I could to help your cause at no little personal expense to myself, I might add, but you must break your silence. It will avail you nothing, and I must know the whole truth."

"How long before you ask for an instructed verdict?"

"Maximum Miller has asked for a recess until after New Year's Day; to 'develop further leads that have just come to my attention' is his excuse. He is preparing to do a microscopic examination of the silk purse, and without your help I may very well be left holding deep-fat-fried pigskin. I must know the meaning of your act of sacrilege, Mr. Hailey."

" 'For he knoweth not that which shall be; for who can

tell him when it shall be?' Ecclesiastes, chapter eight, verse seven, John Lloyd."

"Perhaps you are also familiar with Ecclesiastes, chapter eight, verse six: 'Because to every purpose there is time and judgment, therefore the misery of man is great upon him.' The time for your purpose is over and judgment must be meted out."

David Hailey closed his eyes. "I'll wait."

He heard John Lloyd leaving his cell and gave in to his terrible fear. What if he was wrong?

CHAPTER SEVENTEEN

"INSTRUCTED VERDICT!"

Maximum Miller's fist came down on top of his desk and rattled his computer. Jenner figured either Miller's fist or his voice rattled every desk in every office on this entire side of the building.

"That son of a bitch is going to ask for an instructed verdict!" shouted the assistant D.A. as he swiveled his chair from side to side, staring first at District Attorney Bobby Benson, then at Sergeant Ed Schroder, then finally at Sergeant Larry Jenner.

"Well, Cleetus, you said the best you could do was voluntary manslaughter anyway, so it doesn't matter if the jury does it on their own or the judge orders them to," said Benson, blotting his forehead and trying to find a comfortable position in the molded-plastic chair.

Jenner knew it was a measure of Maximum Miller's standing that the meeting was in his office instead of Benson's larger, more comfortable one. The reputations of elected officials more often rested on the skills of born prosecutors like Maximum Miller than it did on their own courtroom performances. The smart ones knew it, and no one had ever said that Bobby Benson was dumb.

Maximum Miller rubbed his hands over the top of his balding head, pursed his lips, and stared at his boss. Benson squirmed uncomfortably in his chair, either because his butt was going numb or because his assistant's eyes were skewering him, Jenner couldn't tell which. As long as he wasn't on the receiving end of one of Miller's glares, he didn't much care.

"Bobby," said Maximum Miller, and Jenner braced himself. Any time the prosecutor used a soft tone of voice all hell was about to break loose. "Bobby, that sneaky, sorry, skinny S.O.B. is going to ask for a *not guilty* verdict!"

Benson swayed backward in his chair, probably blown there by the force of Miller's voice, Jenner decided. "How can he do that, Cleetus? I've never seen such an inept performance in all my trial career. He proved your case for you. He proved that there was no one else in that bedroom except Hailey. He transformed Amanda Hailey into Donna Reed, and I didn't think anybody could do that. And he proved that the preacher didn't exhibit any signs of sudden passion. He proved murder!"

"Bobby, you got two things wrong." He held up a finger. "One is that John Lloyd Branson was inept. He acted like it, he fooled Lydia Fairchild, and damn near fooled even me, but Branson is *never* inept. Two"—he held up a second finger—"is that he proved my case. He did no such thing. He shot it so full of holes that I don't have enough fingers and toes to stop them up."

"I don't know how you can say that, Cleetus," said Benson. "Are you sure you aren't just gun-shy of Branson? He has gotten the best of you a few times."

Maximum Miller popped a couple of Tums in his mouth. "You're damn right I'm gun-shy," he mumbled, sipping coffee to wash down the antacid pills. "That's because the sneaky bastard carries concealed weapons. But if you'll listen a minute, Bobby, I'll tell you what Branson did to our case. You listen, too, Schroder, 'cause you're gonna be responsible for finding me corks to plug up the leaks."

He belched and leaned back in his chair. "First off he proves that we don't know the exact time of death. Now that doesn't mean shit except to the jury, because nobody but God or a witness with one eye on the victim and one eye on his watch knows the exact time of death. Too many different factors involved. But a jury doesn't know that or they don't believe it, which amounts to the same thing in the end. All those crime-of-the-week shows on television or murder mysteries written by ignoramuses who don't know enough to call a pathologist make life miserable for real prosecutors."

He scratched his head. "Where was I? Oh, yeah, the time of death. Now when Branson brought that up, he created himself a window of opportunity. The preacher could have killed his wife during the break or after the break, we don't know. Then he brings in that goddamn crumpled budget report. Did you notice that slick as Glen Williams was, he never managed to explain why that budget report was wet?"

"Well, Cleetus, surely there's an explanation," said Benson, looking worried for the first time.

"Sure there is and Branson stumbled up on it. I think Glen Williams saw the preacher pick up that budget report instead of a stone just like Branson believes. That means Hailey had to off his wife during the break. But"—he held up his hand—"we got a problem with that, too. Did you notice how Branson kept asking about the fight? Did you notice how he kept asking where everybody was, where they were sitting and who was where and when?"

"I noticed that," said Benson. "But that fight between that Fisher woman and Roy O'Brien didn't have anything to do with the preacher. He wasn't even there. He was back in the bedroom."

Schroder spoke around the cigarette hanging out of one corner of his mouth. "It wasn't the preacher he was asking about. He wanted to know where everybody else was. All six members of that budget committee were outside, and by my count, four of them were running around the church grounds mostly out of sight of everybody else."

Miller slapped his desk again. "You get the gold medal, Schroder. Branson managed to suggest four other people with the opportunity to grab a rock out of that flower bed, sneak around the parsonage, slip through that door, and whack the preacher's wife. The whole thing wouldn't take more than three minutes at the most. So who have we got? We got Mildred Fisher in the manger scene; we got Glen Williams going to his car for cigarettes; we got Virgil Fisher and Agnes Ledgerwood going after Mildred, but they both leave the porch a minute or so apart. And we got the preacher who has been outside long enough to get sleet in his hair. Do you know who we haven't got?"

"Eyewitnesses," said Schroder, mashing out the last half-inch of his cigarette in Miller's ashtray.

"Exactly! No one saw the preacher kill his wife. Now that would be all right if nobody else could have killed her. But Branson dropped four more suspects into our laps. We can't convict the preacher of murder if we can't eliminate all of the other possibilities. And we can't—right now. We can't convict him of voluntary manslaughter either because we can't prove sudden passion—right now. If the prosecution closed tomorrow, John Lloyd Branson would be on his feet demanding an instructed verdict from the judge before the seat of my pants hit the chair. And you know what? I think he'd get it. I think the judge would order that jury to hand down a verdict of not guilty on the grounds that the state can't prove the case. And the judge would be right because we can't prove shit—right now."

Bobby Benson looked more than worried; he looked sick. "Cleetus, if we let that preacher walk, I'm dead meat in the primary election. I'll be the district attorney who lost the Virgin Mary case. They'll preach about me in every church in town, probably including my own. There'll be letters to the editor. Nobody understands technicalities like instructed verdicts. You can't explain them in a thirty-second sound bite." He leaned over and pulled his hair with both hands. "My opponent will cut off my balls and make calf fries out of them."

Maximum Miller leaned over and patted Benson's shoulder. "Quit tearing your hair, Bobby, or you'll end up reflecting light off the top of your head like I do. And stop worrying.

I'm not going to let you lose the primary. The first thing your opponent would do when he took office would be to fire me, and I'm not about to see the justice system of Potter County in the hands of somebody that stupid."

The district attorney closed his eyes, and Jenner thought he mumbled a prayer. "Thanks, Cleetus. I knew I could count on you."

"Bobby, I'd fight this even if you weren't running for re-election, because that mealymouthed preacher killed his wife even if I can't prove it one hundred percent, and I'm not letting that son of a bitch Branson get him off!" He stood up and grabbed his coat off the back of his chair. "Schroder, you and the Hardy boy get your butts in gear. We're heading for Canadian, and we ain't coming back until we find the smoking gun. And, Schroder, I'm driving. There's no way in hell I'm riding in the backseat of your car again."

Jenner wasn't certain that riding in Miller's Suburban was much of an improvement over riding with Schroder except that the Suburban was cleaner—if you didn't include the air. Between Schroder's Camels and Miller's big black cigars, Jenner figured he'd die of secondhand smoke long before they reached Canadian. Or hypothermia, since he had his head hanging out the window and his face had gone numb about twenty miles back.

"You having hot flashes, Jenner?" Maximum Miller asked from inside a wreath of smoke encircling his head. "Or you got another reason for trying to freeze our asses off?"

Jenner pulled his head back inside, coughed once, and wheezed, "Smoke."

Miller glanced at Schroder. "Smoke? Did he say smoke?"

Schroder stubbed out his cigarette. "Get rid of your cigar, Cleetus. Any time you can see the air and you ain't in Los Angeles, Jenner gets choked up. I think maybe he's allergic to tobacco smoke."

Schroder voluntarily stubbing out his cigarette for any reason except to light another? Jenner couldn't believe it.

"How the hell did you end up with a partner who's allergic

to smoke?'' asked Miller, putting out his cigar. ''I would have thought you'd be a little more choosy, Schroder.''

''I'm not his partner,'' protested Jenner. ''I'm just on temporary assignment.''

''I'm used to him now and I figure he can't help it—it's like being born with flat feet,'' said Schroder.

''I'm not your partner,'' Jenner said again a little louder.

''Sounds to me like you're getting sentimental in your old age, Schroder,'' said Maximum Miller. ''Or else an old mother hen, taking a kid like that under your wing and training him as a homicide investigator.''

Jenner tried one more time. ''I'm not his partner. I'm temporary help.''

''He's got good instincts, Cleetus. Or will have when he's seasoned a little more. I'm not getting any younger. It's time I started looking around for somebody to pass along all my experience to. I think of it as an apprentice program.''

Jenner choked, then stuttered, ''I-I'm not his p-partner.''

''You got something caught in your throat, Jenner?'' asked Miller.

''Yeah. Outrage,'' shouted Jenner.

''Well, shut up about it. It's Christmas. I don't like my holidays spoiled by outraged cops. I don't know what you've got to bitch about anyhow. Schroder and I put out our smokes.''

Jenner chewed on his outrage the rest of the way to Canadian. Silently.

Maximum Miller parked in back of the Hemphill County Courthouse. ''We'll start with Glen Williams. It's nearly lunchtime, and I can't take the Fishers or Agnes Ledgerwood on an empty stomach. Come to think of it, Mildred Fisher is hard to take on a full stomach.''

They found Glen Williams loading a paper plate with snacks. ''What are you three doing here on Christmas Eve? I've already testified to everything I know for a fact and half of what I guessed.''

''It's that other half we're interested in, Glen,'' said Maximum Miller, plucking a potato chip off the D.A.'s plate and scooping up onion dip from a bowl sitting on a table loaded with cookies, cakes, candies, sliced turkey, molded salads, raw vegetables and dip, and a gigantic bowl of eggnog.

"You're interrupting the courthouse Christmas party, Cleetus," protested Williams, holding his plate out of Miller's reach and backing away. "For Christ's sake, can't this wait?"

The prosecutor reached for his own plate and proceeded to load it up. Maximum Miller was a Rotarian and had practice making the most of a paper plate and a buffet. He popped a piece of raw cauliflower dipped in ranch dressing in his mouth and crunched, all the while looking at the other man.

Williams heaved a sigh. "All right, Cleetus, I know when I'm beat. Help yourself to the goodies and come into my office."

"Don't mind if I do, Glen. Schroder, you and the kid load your plates and we'll ask questions while we eat. That way we won't waste any time."

Jenner would have complained about a thirty-year-old man being called a kid, but he figured Maximum Miller suffered from the same selective deafness as Schroder. Neither one of them heard anything they didn't want to hear.

"Glen, did you see anybody or think you saw anybody when you went to your car for your cigarettes?" Maximum Miller asked a few minutes later when they were all sitting in the D.A.'s office with the door closed.

"If I had, I would have testified to it yesterday, Cleetus, but I didn't see anybody. It was cold as hell and the wind was blowing forty miles an hour, so I wasn't exactly interested in seeing who might be admiring the scenery."

"You didn't see the preacher messing around the flower bed?"

"It's that damn wet budget report that's got your bowels in an uproar, isn't it, Cleetus?" asked Williams, putting his plate down on his desk and folding his hands. "I don't blame you. That budget report is going to stick in the jury's mind like chalk on a blackboard. I tried my best to draw Branson away from it, but I couldn't lie. I don't know what I saw David Hailey pick up, not for absolutely certain. I'm sorry."

"Did you see the preacher pick up his copy of the budget

report when he took his wife out of the meeting?'' asked Schroder.

Glen Williams screwed up one eye and thought about it, then shook his head. ''I didn't notice, Sergeant. The whole thing was embarrassing if you want to know the truth, and I tried to look anywhere but at the preacher. I wish Mildred Fisher would find some hobby other than trying to run everybody else's business. I never saw anybody who was so damn sure she was in the right and that God backed her up. Anyway, I know that I left my copy of the report lying on the table, and I seem to remember several other copies lying there, too, when the meeting broke up, but I couldn't swear to whom they belonged. I can tell you somebody who would know, could probably remember which corner of every paper was facing east.''

''Who?'' asked Maximum Miller, one hand full of angel-food cake poised in midair.

''John Lloyd Branson. That guy's got a photographic memory.''

Maximum Miller dropped his cake, icing side down, in his lap.

It took him all the way to Hank Gregory's farm five miles outside Canadian on a farm-to-market road in need of maintenance to recover his composure. By the time the prosecutor parked in front of a white farmhouse hugged by bare cottonwood trees, Jenner thought it might be safe to talk to him.

''Uh, Mr. Miller, you weren't serious about staying in Canadian until we found something, were you?''

Maximum Miller swiveled his head around to glare at him. ''You got a problem with that?''

Jenner shrugged his shoulders. ''Well, it's Christmas Eve.''

''I know what the date is.''

''Tomorrow's Christmas.''

''You got a point, Jenner? If you do, spit it out. If you're just making conversation, shut up. I'm tired, I'm frustrated, and my second-best pair of pants I just picked up from the cleaners have a three-by-five-inch grease spot. Who the hell ever heard of using Crisco to make icing? It's a good thing I dropped that cake. It probably would have clogged up my arteries and I would have had a heart attack and spoiled Glen's Christmas party worse than I did."

"I want to spend Christmas with my kids, and tomorrow's my day off," Jenner blurted out.

"Why didn't you say so in the first place instead of walking around the subject like it was a piece of cow manure? You know, Jenner, you're gonna have to learn to speak up for yourself. Anyhow, no, we're not spending Christmas Day in Canadian. We're going home tonight. I try not to agitate my wife any more than I absolutely have to, and my working Christmas Day wouldn't set right with her." Miller's wife stood about five feet tall and weighed maybe a hundred pounds. She was the only person Jenner knew of who could scare the prosecutor.

"I can get a room at the motel and stay over and poke around, maybe pick up some gossip, Cleetus," said Schroder. "I ain't got any plans for Christmas."

"I thought maybe you'd come over to the house tomorrow morning, Schroder, and watch the kids open their presents, have dinner with us. If somebody doesn't help me eat that turkey my wife's fixing, she'll be serving it as leftovers until New Year's."

Jenner heard the invitation come rolling out of his mouth, but he didn't believe what he was hearing. He didn't even much like Schroder, for God's sake, and here he was inviting the fat slob for Christmas. All that secondhand smoke he'd been breathing since he got stuck as the investigator's temporary partner must have killed most of his brain cells.

Miller and Schroder sat staring at him with their mouths open. Jenner guessed they didn't believe what they were hearing either. He casually shrugged his shoulders. "It was just a thought, is all. I mean, don't feel like you have to come, Schroder. You probably wouldn't enjoy it. The kids make a lot of noise and pester the grown-ups by showing off their toys. . . ."

"I reckon I'll come, son." Schroder opened the passenger door and slid out. "Come on, Cleetus, get a move on. We got to get back to Amarillo early. I got a few gifts to buy."

He trudged toward the farmhouse faster than Jenner had ever seen him move.

"Now, Schroder, you don't have to—"

He didn't finish his sentence as Maximum Miller suddenly gripped his shoulder. "Don't say another word, Sergeant Jenner," said the prosecutor softly. "You just earned yourself a nice shiny star in your crown when you get to heaven. Now don't tarnish it by discouraging Schroder. When you give somebody a present, don't be telling him how to enjoy it."

CHAPTER EIGHTEEN

"WOULD YOU LIKE ANOTHER CUP OF TEA, MISS FAIRchild?"

"No, thank you, Mrs. Dinwittie," Lydia said with the closest thing to a smile that she could manage. Actually, what she wanted was a drink, preferably of bourbon, but if that wasn't available, she would take anything with caffeine whether it was tea, coffee, or any soft drink, provided it wasn't of the dietary variety. What she didn't want and would, in fact, regurgitate if she had to force down another cup, was Mrs. Dinwittie's herbal tea. Lydia hated herbal tea. If living to a ripe old age meant she had to subsist on herbal tea and tofu, she would gladly give a year or two on the far side of seventy in order to enjoy caffeine, alcohol, sugar, salt, fat, and red meat on this side of thirty.

"My, aren't we just as cozy as two bugs in a rug?" asked Mrs. Dinwittie with a smile.

"We certainly are," said Lydia, forcing her mouth into an answering smile. They were, too. Mrs. Dinwittie's house was slightly larger than a postage stamp, and every room was stuffed with matching early American furniture. She had never seen so much maplewood and pseudo–Revolutionary

War artifacts in such a small area in her life. Even Mrs. Dinwittie's wastebaskets were covered with scenes from Valley Forge. Lydia felt as though she ought to be wearing knickers and knee socks and big buckles on her shoes just to match the decor. Jeans, a Texas Rangers sweatshirt, and tennis shoes seemed so out of place.

Of course, she *was* out of place. It was Christmas Eve and she was five hundred miles from her parents' home in Dallas, sipping herbal tea with an acquitted ax murderess.

She blinked and felt a tear catch on her eyelash. She had cried more in the last twenty-four hours than at any time since she was ten years old and broke her leg jumping off the garage while pretending to be Wonder Woman.

"Mrs. Dinwittie, would you happen to have any bourbon? It's the cocktail hour and Christmas Eve. We should celebrate. You know, 'tis the season to be jolly, goodwill toward men, and all of that," said Lydia, wiping her eyes on the tail of her sweatshirt.

"Oh, my, Miss Fairchild, I'm afraid I don't have any alcohol in the house. It created such problems between Mr. Dinwittie and me that I swore I'd never even have cooking wine around."

"Oh, yes, I'm sorry, Mrs. Dinwittie, I forget your experiences with the cocktail hour aren't as pleasant as mine." Lydia thought that had to be the understatement of the year. Mr. Dinwittie had been, from what she had heard, the champion drunk in the state, and a mean one at that. He had used Mrs. Dinwittie for target practice until the evening Mrs. Dinwittie had had enough of ducking bullets and had wielded an ax instead.

"Of course, Mr. Branson doesn't have a problem with alcohol," continued Mrs. Dinwittie.

Lydia wiped her eyes again. "No, he doesn't."

"And he's a man with clean personal habits. Not a hair out of place describes Mr. Branson."

"He's always so neat that he makes me feel like a slob sometimes," said Lydia.

"That's why I just couldn't stop looking at the cobweb hanging off his ear—"

"Cobweb?"

"—and poor Mrs. Higgins, his housekeeper, had to take a week off to recover from seeing Mr. Branson climbing down the attic stairs with that cobweb waving in the breeze."

"Cobweb?"

"But of course it's just so difficult to keep attics clean, and there's no reason to, I suppose. No one entertains in an attic, certainly not when you own such a large house as Mr. Branson does, although I nearly cry when I think of him rattling around that big old place all by himself. His grandmother's been dead for just years and years, you know."

Lydia thought that carrying on a conversation with Mrs. Dinwittie was like trying to listen to the radio when someone kept changing stations with no warning. "Wait, back up. What about the cobweb?"

"It came from the attic, of course. I hope you don't think Mrs. Higgins would allow such a thing in the rest of the house. She's just as neat as a pin."

Lydia closed her eyes and counted to ten before looking at Mrs. Dinwittie. "I mean, what was John Lloyd doing in the attic? It doesn't sound like the sort of place he'd go to."

"He went up to get the Christmas ornaments. For the Christmas tree? My, and isn't it a beautiful tree? He asked Mrs. Higgins and me exactly where he ought to put it, you know, and I had to help him decorate it. Mrs. Higgins just wasn't up to it, I'm afraid—the shock and all—and he doesn't have much experience along those lines since he hasn't had a tree since his grandmother died."

"He never put up a Christmas tree?" asked Lydia, trying to visualize John Lloyd Branson in his three-piece suit and Phi Beta Kappa key crawling around in a dusty attic.

"He always said Christmas was a time of sharing, and he had no one to share with. Oh, not that he didn't give, Miss Fairchild. He always buys Mrs. Higgins and me the nicest gifts, and he always buys toys for any child whose family is going through difficult times. He gets lists of names from all of the churches and the schools to make sure no one is left out. But nobody knows this except the preachers in town and the superintendent of schools—and me, of course—so don't tell anyone."

"Christmas is about giving without the expectation of receiving," said Lydia slowly.

Mrs. Dinwittie clapped her hands. "Why, that sounds just like Mr. Branson."

Lydia blinked away more tears. "He said it to me. I didn't take him very seriously. I mean, it sounds like the sort of thing you say at Christmas."

"You should have taken him seriously, Miss Fairchild," Mrs. Dinwittie said, nodding her head sagely—if a Kewpie doll could ever look sage. "He was so excited this year. I just never saw him act like that. I even heard him whistling once, just happy as a lark. And the shopping he did! He bought Christmas music, the manger scene on the mantel, the evergreen on the staircase, and the presents. I never saw a man buy so many presents for a woman. He even bought a bottle of your favorite bourbon. He didn't wrap the packages, though. I did. Bless his heart, he was so embarrassed. He said you always expected him to be perfect at everything he tried, but he was just *awful* at gift wrapping."

Lydia didn't even try to blink back the tears; there were too many. "You mean all those presents under the tree were *mine*? But, Mrs. Dinwittie, there must be a hundred of them!"

"I don't think so, Miss Fairchild. I only counted sixty-seven—although he might have bought others and had the store wrap them."

"I . . . I suppose he can take all of them back," said Lydia, trying desperately to speak despite her quivering chin.

Mrs. Dinwittie tipped her head to one side as though considering the possibility. "I don't think he would do that, Miss Fairchild. No, I don't think so at all."

Lydia nodded, wiping her eyes on her sleeve. "I don't think so either, Mrs. Dinwittie. People might feel sorry for him, and John Lloyd would rather die than be pitied."

"He's a proud man, but then you know that, don't you?"

"Yes, I know that."

"Well?" asked Mrs. Dinwittie, her little black eyes twinkling behind the pink lenses of her glasses. "Are you going to let him get away with it?"

Lydia watched Mrs. Dinwittie drive off and felt the butterflies in her stomach turn into dive-bombers. She must be crazy. There was no other explanation for why she was standing on John Lloyd's front porch about to enter his home without knocking. He would probably have her arrested for trespassing or breaking and entering, but nothing ventured, nothing gained, as Mrs. Dinwittie would say. She took three deep breaths, opened the door, stepped through, and slammed it behind her.

"John Lloyd Branson! Come out, come out, wherever you are, and fight like a man!"

"Miss Fairchild, you would do well to imitate Mrs. Dinwittie's manners rather than her speech. She would never burst into a man's home without an invitation."

Lydia whirled toward the fireplace. "I was afraid you"—she stopped, felt her heart begin a drum roll, and finished her sentence in a breathless rush—"wouldn't let me in." He was beautiful standing there with the firelight turning his bare chest pale gold or maybe it was just the wedge-shaped patch of blond body hair in the center of it catching the light. She'd seen John Lloyd without his shirt before—that day last summer when he had stripped it off to bind up her bullet wounds—but he'd been wearing more then than black pajama bottoms. Then, too, being shot had distracted her from appreciating what a really gorgeous physical specimen he was without his shirt. Broad shoulders, nice pecs, lean but muscular chest, flat belly—

"Miss Fairchild!"

She jerked her head up. "What?"

His face was rosy, but whether from the firelight or from temper she couldn't tell. "I said, I hope you do not believe I would leave a lady standing alone in the dark on my front porch."

"Well, it wasn't a lady. It was me. And it wasn't dark. Your porch light was on."

She saw his chest rise as he took a deep breath. "Miss

Fairchild, do you suppose you could put aside your usual flippancy for the duration of this argument? And I presume there will be an argument—at least on your part—since you did issue what sounded like a challenge as you entered."

"I'm not going to let you get away with it!"

"Get away with what, Miss Fairchild?"

"Firing me!"

"I did not fire you. I merely accepted your resignation."

"Don't get technical!"

He took another breath. "I can see this will be a more lengthy discussion than I anticipated. Please sit down, Miss Fairchild, while I put on something more presentable."

"No," said Lydia, slipping off her coat and walking toward him. "I don't want you making a strategic retreat to your bedroom for a stuffed shirt. If you're self-conscious, I'll strip down, but you're not leaving this room!"

His gaze slipped toward the hem of her sweatshirt, which she had already raised past her belly. "That will not be necessary, Miss Fairchild." He turned his back to gaze at the other end of the room. "State your case, please. It is late and tomorrow is Christmas . . ."

"And you have nowhere to go. And I have nowhere to go, so we might as well spend the day together like you planned. Did Mrs. Higgins remember to thaw the turkey? I suppose we are having turkey since it's traditional and you're very, very traditional. I hope so, anyway, because the other sort of traditional entrée is goose, and I hate goose. The meat tastes greasy and it doesn't have decent drumsticks. And pies? Did Mrs. Higgins bake a pumpkin pie? If she didn't, I will. I make a very good pumpkin pie and—"

"Miss Fairchild."

"—and my mincemeat pie is good, too, because I always use brandy instead of rum because I think it tastes better. But I won't if you'd rather have rum. I can compromise. And what about the cranberries? Did Mrs. Higgins buy fresh cranberries because I don't like—"

"Miss Fairchild!"

She flinched. "You don't have to yell, John Lloyd. I'm

right behind you and there's nothing wrong with my hearing."

He took several deep breaths this time. "Apparently there is, Miss Fairchild. I distinctly remember telling you that there was no point in our continuing this ill-conceived venture of ours. We are obviously too incompatible to work together successfully, so I think it best if we end this discussion before it degenerates further."

Lydia felt her stomach tighten and the dive-bombers take off again. She clenched her teeth. She would not lose this argument, damn it. "That's not what you said."

He looked over his shoulder at her. "What isn't?"

He used a contraction! She felt the dive-bombers land and turn off their engines. "You didn't say we were incompatible. You said you didn't have my youthful resiliency to heal yourself. I remember. I have a good memory. Not photographic like yours, but I do remember almost anything a person says to me, and that's what you said." She stepped closer until she was almost touching him. "So I'll heal you instead. I'm sorry I mistrusted you, and I didn't really mean it when I accused you of sacrilege. I didn't understand what you were doing and I overreacted. I do that when someone hurts my feelings."

He turned around then. "I do not recall saying anything to hurt your feelings, Miss Fairchild."

She twisted her hands together. "It's not what you said, John Lloyd. It's what you did. You didn't treat me as an equal. You used my own principles, my own belief in justice, against me. You turned me into a performing monkey."

"I explained why it was necessary," he began.

"I know you did! I remember, and I even have to agree with your reasons. I *am* a bad liar and not a very good actress, and you did ask me to trust you, but that doesn't excuse you. Not once—*not once*—did you say you were sorry. Even trained monkeys bite when they're mistreated."

"And you drew blood, Miss Fairchild," he said. His jaw clenched and his eyes began to glitter—or maybe it was just a reflection from the fire, but she didn't think so. He was angry, and that was the first hopeful sign—besides the contraction—that she'd broken through the walls again.

"After all the time you've known me, you dared to accuse me of deliberately violating my client's rights. Yet you expect me to accept your apology and go on as if nothing was said by either of us? You expect me to apologize for my tactics when I warned you beforehand that I couldn't explain because I didn't fully understand myself? You expect me to take you to my bosom, never knowing when you're going to sink your viperous fangs in my heart?"

She met his eyes. "Yes. And I expect one more thing. I expect you to never use me again as a *thing* like David Hailey did to his wife in the name of some undefined, unexplained higher purpose."

He narrowed his eyes, studying her face. "And just why should I agree to all this, Miss Fairchild?"

She licked her lips, suddenly feeling nervous again. "Because if anyone else had used me as you did, I would have slapped his face, called him a bastard, and walked out. I certainly wouldn't have been hurt. And if anyone but me had accused you of sacrilege, you would have fired them and shrugged off the whole thing, but you would not have been wounded. We can only hurt each other when we care. To quote Mrs. Dinwittie, I don't think we should throw out the baby with the bathwater."

He went suddenly still, and she thought of a wolf poised to leap upon a helpless prey. "Please, Miss Fairchild. None of Mrs. Dinwittie's deadly homilies. I don't want to risk misunderstanding you."

She turned her back. She was about to climb out on a limb and saw it off behind her, and she thought it might be easier to do if she wasn't looking at him. She'd be afraid to risk crawling out on that limb at all if John Lloyd Branson hadn't just used five more contractions.

"Because I think I love you, and you might love me—maybe."

She heard the clock ticking, the wind blowing against the windows, and the beating of her own heart, but she didn't hear a single sound from John Lloyd Branson. She straightened her shoulders and tilted her chin up a little higher. When one makes a complete and utter fool of oneself, the only thing left to do is to walk out with dignity.

She actually took a step toward the door when she felt his hand grasp her arm. "I've not ever known you to sound so uncertain of yourself, Miss Fairchild." His voice was deep and soft, and his drawl so pronounced, he seemed to be drawing his words out to twice their length. "And I've never known you to be afraid to spit in my eye. Turn around, Lydia, and tell me to my face."

She froze for a moment, then slowly turned around, walking toward him until she could go no farther, get no closer, then slid her arms around his neck. "Do I always have to be the one to meet you more than halfway?"

He smiled as he wrapped his arms around her and squeezed so tightly she could hardly breathe. "No, my dear, but this time I do think I'll have the last word."

She looked into his black eyes, and for the first time she could see over the rubble of all those walls to what lay beyond. "I love you, Lydia Fairchild."

Her last conscious thought was that perhaps John Lloyd Branson couldn't gift-wrap any better than a grade-school child, but his kissing was strictly postdoctoral.

"John Lloyd?"

"Uh-hum?" He lazily opened one eye but never altered his rhythm of stroking her bare back, bare hips, bare legs, and wherever else his hand happened to wander. It was very distracting.

She lifted her head off his arm and raised herself on one elbow. "John Lloyd?"

"Uh-hum?" he mumbled again, opening his other eye and letting both drift below her collarbone and down her torso, or what part of her torso wasn't lying snugly against his.

"You never apologized for using me."

His gaze slowly reversed itself until he met her eyes. Then he grinned and she caught her breath. She wasn't used to

John Lloyd acting so lighthearted. Maybe it was all that blood flowing somewhere besides to his brain.

"I suppose you did not intend a double entendre, Miss Fairchild."

She blushed from her hair line to the top of her breasts, which only made him chuckle. She never imagined that John Lloyd Branson might shed his straitlaced Puritanism with his pants. It only proved that you never really knew a man until you slept with him.

"This is a little too new to me"—obviously not to him, but she wisely kept that thought to herself—"to be my usual flippant self, John Lloyd, and that brings up another point." She ignored his raised eyebrow and smirk. The man had a hithertofore unexpected dirty mind. "Don't you think the present situation calls for something a little more intimate than Miss Fairchild? I feel like a Victorian governess in a pornographic novel."

He chuckled once again. "I never imagined your taste in literature included works of such dubious value. Lydia," he added softly and without a smile.

She bent her head to kiss him, allowed herself to be pulled into his arms and rolled over until she was on her back and John Lloyd was leaning over her with a very serious look in his eyes, before she pushed at his shoulders. "You haven't apologized yet."

"Damnation, Lydia, this is a most inconvenient time."

"John Lloyd, I'm not exactly uninvolved here either, but I want my apology so I can concentrate on what I'm doing—or rather what you're doing or are about to do."

"I apologize," John Lloyd said with a frustrated look in his eyes.

"You promise? Cross your heart and hope to die?" she asked suspiciously. "You won't treat me like a thing anymore like David Hailey did to his wife in the name of some undefined and—" She broke off with a gasp. "John Lloyd, that's not your heart you're crossing!"

He raised one eyebrow again. "But, my dear, you specifically instructed me to cross *your* heart—and I am."

"But that's not my heart, John Lloyd. My heart is in the

center of my chest, more or less, not off to one side.'' She sucked in a deep breath. ''But I don't suppose it matters just as long as you're in the general vicinity.''

''It is the intent that matters, Lydia,'' he said. ''I promise never to treat you like a thing as David Hailey did in the name of some—Damnation!'' He rolled over to the side of the bed and sat up. ''That has to be the answer—or part of the answer.''

Lydia threw back the sheet and scrambled over to him. ''What answer, John Lloyd?''

''Why David Hailey committed sacrilege.''

''Oh, no!'' she cried, grabbing him from behind and tumbling him over backward. ''Damn it, John Lloyd! It's not a convenient time!''

CHAPTER NINETEEN

Canadian—December 26

JENNER STRETCHED OUT IN THE BACKSEAT OF MAXIMUM Miller's Suburban and took a deep breath of unpolluted air. There was still a lingering smell of stale tobacco, but nothing his nasal spray couldn't handle. The smell of cow manure was worse, but as far as he knew he wasn't allergic to that. He allowed himself a soft—very soft—chuckle at the memory of Maximum Miller slipping on the frozen ground and sliding feetfirst into Hank Gregory's manure pile. The old man had tried to tell him that it could have been a lot worse if the manure pile hadn't been mostly frozen, but the prosecutor hadn't been in any state to listen. Schroder had driven back to Amarillo with Miller sitting in the passenger seat wearing one of Mrs. Gregory's blankets and all of the windows open. Even with his clothes and shoes rinsed off and double-wrapped in plastic, the aroma inside the car had everyone hanging their head out the window and hoping nobody sideswiped them.

And it was all for nothing. Hank Gregory didn't have anything to add other than that he couldn't remember who still had budget reports after the break. He couldn't even swear that he had one since he hadn't bothered to read it in the first place. The roof had to be fixed, he knew there was money to do it, and he didn't see any sense in arguing about it, except that Mildred Fisher just liked to argue on general principles.

Jenner unfastened the button on his uniform pants, since they seemed a little snug around the waist this morning. He couldn't have gained any weight from eating just one gigantic Christmas dinner and a few small snacks, so the cleaners must have shrunk them. He belched in complete contentment and closed his eyes.

He felt someone shake him. "Jenner, you asleep?"

He opened one eye and promptly closed it. He wasn't up to facing Schroder's sappy face. "No, I'm checking my eyelids for cracks," he mumbled.

Miller chuckled. "Checking his eyelids for cracks. That's a good one, Jenner. A man's got to keep his sense of humor in this business. Ain't that right, Schroder?"

Jenner didn't figure Miller was speaking from experience, since he hadn't had much of a sense of humor about the manure pile, and Schroder was about as humorous as walking on grass burrs in your bare feet.

"He'll do all right, Cleetus. He's just worn out from yesterday. Kids were all excited and rambunctious over their presents."

Jenner nearly choked. Damn right his kids were rambunctious on Christmas. But they wouldn't have been if Schroder hadn't given Jeremy, his four-year-old, a drum, and not a little drum either, but a great big son of a bitch. The blasted thing sounded like a crack of thunder every time Jeremy pounded it—which was a damn sight too often.

If that wasn't bad enough, he'd given Chuck, the seven-year-old, a guitar, and not just a guitar but one with an amplifier. Between the drum and the guitar, no one heard ten-year-old Melissa's baton—one of a set of six—go through the front window, bounce off the porch, and crack the windshield on Jenner's brand-new used car. Jenner couldn't figure out why the Lord hadn't seen fit to send the baton through the drum and bounce it into the guitar.

"Uncle" Schroder's gifts had been the hit of the day.

Jenner cringed just thinking about the kids calling the burly detective *Uncle* Schroder. A stranger might get the idea he was related.

He had to admit, though, that Schroder had enjoyed himself. He even smiled without looking like it was an effort.

"We'll tackle Roy O'Brien first," said Maximum Miller. "Much as he despises the preacher, if there's anything detrimental, maybe he'll remember it if we jog his memory."

"We better take what he says with a grain of salt, Cleetus," said Schroder, sucking on an unlit cigarette. "We don't want him stretching the truth."

Miller threw him an outraged look. "I hope you're not suggesting that I'd condone perjury."

"I ain't saying that at all, Cleetus. I'm just warning you that O'Brien's pretty hot under the collar about this murder and that's liable to make him more apt to think he saw things that maybe he didn't see at all."

"Don't teach me how to suck eggs, Schroder. I've been distrusting witnesses since I became a prosecutor and that was two days after I passed the bar exam, which damn sure wasn't yesterday." He turned his head and hollered over his shoulder. "Hey, sleepyhead, wake up! You got the directions to O'Brien's house. Tell me which way to go, and I hope to hell he doesn't live on a farm."

"Or if he does, that he doesn't have a manure pile," Jenner muttered under his breath, as he pulled himself up and reached in his pocket for the directions that Glen Williams had given them.

"Did you say something, Jenner?" asked Miller suspiciously.

"Yeah. Turn right at the next corner and go two blocks. It's a white frame house with a big cottonwood in the front yard."

"You got to learn to speak up, Jenner," said Miller, slamming on his brakes and swinging the big Suburban around the corner. "Nobody likes to strain their ears when somebody's talking."

Jenner wisely decided to keep his mouth shut.

They found Roy O'Brien under the hood of his truck.

"I got an oil leak somewhere," he informed them, wiping his hands on a greasy rag. "I'm running more oil through this rig than I am diesel. I'm an independent trucker. I can't afford to have my rig out of service."

Maximum Miller had minimal interest in Roy O'Brien's oil leak. "We want to go over your testimony, Mr. O'Brien. See if there's anything you maybe forgot."

O'Brien shook his head. "I didn't forget anything. I told you everything that happened."

"Did the preacher look angry when he hauled his wife out of the meeting?" asked Schroder, puffing on his cigarette. Jenner stood downwind of the smoke.

O'Brien absently wiped his hands again, then scratched his chin. Finally he shook his head. "I gotta be honest. He didn't. In fact, he was real gentle with her—like she was a child and he didn't want to scare her. That's what I can't understand. How can a man be so gentle one minute, then murder his wife thirty minutes later?"

"We don't figure he waited thirty minutes," said Schroder. "We got some conflicting testimony about that."

O'Brien nodded. "I know. It was in the papers. I figured I could read the papers once I was through testifying. Something about the budget report, wasn't it? The paper wasn't real clear."

"Do you remember who still had budget reports in front of them after the break?" asked Schroder.

"Sure," said O'Brien. "I got a real good visual memory. Everybody had theirs but Hank Gregory. I didn't think much about it 'cause Hank never reads them anyhow, just listens to Mildred Fisher read out the totals. Hank's eyes aren't real good anymore."

Maximum Miller rolled his eyes toward the heavens. "Shit!"

He was still mumbling under his breath when they pulled up to Agnes Ledgerwood's neat brick home. "I might have known that bastard would have asked about those budget reports if he'd thought it was important. But he didn't so I figure he knew all along it was Gregory's report that was missing. He didn't see much point in throwing suspicion on an old man with one foot in the grave, so he didn't say anything. He didn't even point out that Gregory was standing on that porch by himself for two or three minutes while Glen Williams was running out to his car for cigarettes."

Jenner didn't have any doubt who Miller was calling a bastard. "Maybe Branson figured old man Gregory is innocent."

Miller whirled around in his seat. "Hell, yes, the old man's innocent! And so are all the others, but Branson wasn't so generous with them. The fact is, Jenner, in spite of all the criticism of Amanda Hailey, I don't see anybody mad enough at her to ventilate her skull. Except maybe Mildred Fisher, but Mildred Fisher still had her budget report if O'Brien can be believed—and I think he can or Branson would have pounced on Fisher. And the preacher had been outside and was late coming back to the meeting. Plus"—Miller stabbed his finger in the air—"where was the preacher while Mildred was killing his wife? In the church praying like he told Hank Gregory? Or waiting until Virgil and Agnes dragged Mildred Fisher back to the meeting and the men finished their smokes and the coast was clear with no witnesses to accidentally see him pick up that rock?"

"What about that wet budget report?" asked Schroder.

"Screw that budget report!" yelled Miller, slamming his hand on the steering wheel and letting out a yelp. Jenner hoped the prosecutor hadn't broken any bones in his hand because then he'd bitch about it all the way back to Amarillo.

"The preacher couldn't have stolen Gregory's report when he came back to the meeting and realized his was gone because Roy O'Brien was sitting between him and Gregory, and O'Brien would have damn sure remembered."

Miller chewed on his unlit cigar. "Damn it, Schroder, there's got to be an explanation for that budget report and we just haven't thought of it yet. Branson just threw it out to mislead us and it's working.'' The prosecutor sounded worried.

Suddenly Jenner sat up. ''Wait a minute! We're taking O'Brien's word for it. Nobody else can remember. But O'Brien was mad as hell and maybe—just maybe—he was confused. He was sitting between the preacher and Hank Gregory and knows that there wasn't a report in front of one of them and he just remembered the wrong one. Like he said, he wasn't paying a lot of attention.''

Miller and Schroder looked at each other, then both shook their heads. ''Pretty weak, Jenner,'' said the prosecutor reluctantly. ''And I can't go back and ask O'Brien because that would be leading the witness, and that witness is too damn willing to be led as it is.''

''You didn't let me finish,'' said Jenner. ''There might be another reason that Branson didn't ask everybody about that budget report.'' He paused dramatically.

''Well, spit it out, damn it!'' roared Miller. ''I'm not giving out Academy Awards for dramatic delivery.''

''Because Branson already knew that it was the preacher's report that was missing. And don't you remember that Hank Gregory's fingerprints weren't on that report?''

Miller grinned, then started laughing and pounding his fist on the steering wheel. ''Sergeant Jenner, I take back everything I ever said about you. You're gonna be a hell of a detective one of these days.'' He punched Schroder's arm. ''You were right about the kid after all, you old reprobate.''

''We still ain't out of the woods,'' mumbled Schroder. ''We ain't proved nothing but a negative.''

Maximum Miller opened his door. ''Think positive, Schroder. There's something there and we just got to find it. Let's go see what the church secretary can tell us.''

''But I can't tell you anything else, Mr. Miller,'' Agnes Ledgerwood said a few minutes later as she served them coffee and slices of rich, dark, rum-soaked fruitcake smothered in real whipped cream. Jenner wondered if he'd make it back to the Suburban without his pants button popping off and rolling under the church secretary's picture-laden coffee table. He chewed, swallowed, and set his plate on the coffee table next to the morning newspaper. Another witness was keeping up with the trial. He didn't see what good it did keeping witnesses from listening to one another's testimony. They could read it all in the paper.

"I didn't see the preacher while I went after Mildred, and I certainly didn't see anybody pick up a stone out of that flower bed," said Agnes. "I was just worried about getting Mildred out of that manger scene and back in the house. She was so cold, her hands were shaking." A note of irritation crept into her voice. "I don't know why Mildred was so upset about that mannequin's painted toenails. She jumped in the middle of me just the day before because I'd made a fuss about the same thing. Sometimes I think Mildred just likes to cause a fight."

Jenner thought she was probably right.

"Can you think of anything that happened during the day of the budget meeting that might have set the preacher off, Mrs. Ledgerwood?" Maximum Miller asked with a note in his voice that could possibly be called desperation. "Any disagreement with his wife that you overheard that he might have brooded over?"

Agnes Ledgerwood looked down at her fingernails, which Jenner noticed had been trimmed down to the quick—or bitten off. The preacher's little escapade had evidently worried his secretary into chewing her nails. She looked older, too, as if she had given up her struggle against age.

"Reverend Hailey never brooded, Mr. Miller," said Agnes, finally looking up at the prosecutor. "He always tackled problems head-on so they wouldn't fester."

"He sure tackled this one head-on," Miller said after they had finished their fruitcake and waddled back to the Suburban. "About two inches behind the ear." He put the big vehicle in gear and drove toward downtown and the Fishers' dress shop.

Jenner slid out of the backseat and looked across the street. "Hey, there's Branson's office over there. He and the Fishers are neighbors. Wonder if he's up there watching us?"

"I don't give a damn if he is," said Maximum Miller, slamming his car door. "Damn bastard. Sending us on a wild-goose chase after that budget report. He's probably heard all about us biting his baited hook—town's too small for him not to find out—and he's sitting up there behind his rolltop desk chuckling to himself in a Texas drawl." He popped a Tums in his mouth and belched.

If he had heard about the manure pile, Jenner figured Branson was doing more than chuckling. He was rolling around on the floor in his three-piece suit laughing his damn head off. In a Texas drawl.

A tiny bell tinkled over the dress-shop door when Maximum Miller pushed it open. Mildred Fisher looked up from her position behind the cash register, the bright, hard smile on her face quickly turning to a frown when she saw Jenner in his uniform.

"Go through that door in the back wall and wait in the office, please. I don't want any customers seeing a police uniform. It's been a nightmare all month with women coming in to 'browse' and asking all kinds of questions. I don't know why people can't mind their own business."

Jenner figured Mildred Fisher was a pot calling the kettle black, since he hadn't heard of her ever being reluctant to give advice when nobody asked.

The dress shop's office was in sharp contrast to the sales area, which was carpeted in pale blue with white paneled walls touched with gold trim. The office had brown linoleum, peeling plaster beige walls, battered filing cabinets, and a desk in need of refinishing. A white metal table against one wall held a coffeemaker and two cups. Evidently Mildred Fisher didn't believe in providing free coffee to browsers or anyone else.

Virgil Fisher looked up from the desk where he had been adding up sales tickets. His nose twitched. "Mr. Miller, Officers, welcome to my private quarters. I'd ask you all to sit down, but as you can see, there's only one extra chair. Mildred doesn't believe in encouraging visitors to the bookkeeping area." He looked around the office and his nose twitched again. "Grim, isn't it? Mildred doesn't believe in spending money where it can't be seen."

Jenner decided there was a hell of a lot Mildred didn't

believe in, most of it having to do with creature comforts and hospitality and kindness. He remembered how poor and mean the parsonage had been and thought that Mildred Fisher liked to pinch pennies just to prove she had the power to do it.

"If you've come to ask about that budget report, Mr. Miller, Virgil and I both had ours all the way through the meeting," said Mildred Fisher, stepping into the office and folding her arms.

"Just how did you know what I wanted to ask, Ms. Fisher?"

"Good heavens, this is a small town," Mildred said in a voice she might have used to lecture Amanda Hailey. "There must have been ten women from the courthouse who came in after you people interrupted the Christmas party. Those ill-fitting doors to the offices in that old building leak sound like a sieve. Besides, it was in the paper."

Maximum Miller didn't bother trying to smile. He didn't like Mildred Fisher to begin with, and he didn't care to have her lecture him. "As a matter of fact, Ms. Fisher, we don't want to know about the budget report. We've solved that little problem to our satisfaction. We're interested in what you and your brother know of any disagreement the preacher and his wife might have had prior to the budget meeting."

Mildred smiled and Jenner decided her smile was worse than Schroder's. "Well, I suppose it was bound to come out sooner or later. I was naturally reluctant to discuss it since it concerns a relative, but apparently I have no choice. I didn't deliberately conceal it, just didn't mention it because I had hoped it had nothing to do with the murder. It happened much earlier in the day and I just didn't see the connection."

She hesitated, and Virgil burst in. "Now, Mildred, that had nothing to do with it!"

Miller glared the twitching little man into silence. "What happened, Ms. Fisher?"

Her eyes opened wide in mock innocence. "Why, Mr. Hailey caught his wife in my brother's arms."

"Bingo!" shouted Maximum Miller.

CHAPTER TWENTY

Amarillo—January 4

LYDIA TOSSED HER HEAD SO THAT HER NEW DIAMOND EARrings caught the light in the courtroom. She had never owned a diamond anything before, and she couldn't quite subdue her impulse to show off. She had even put her hair up in a loose French roll so that her ears would show. Her turquoise-blue wool suit was also new, as were her shoes, bag, white silk blouse with a froth of lace at the neck, and a briefcase with not just her initials but her whole name in gold letters. All Christmas presents from John Lloyd—along with several other complete ensembles, jewelry, books, a compact disc player and library of music, and more underwear and nightgowns than she could wear in a year—all verging on the indecent.

And everything fit perfectly, including the underwear, which made her suspect that John Lloyd Branson had spent a great deal more time in the past few months studying her body than her mind and wondered why she had never caught him at it. Of course, he *was* devious on occasion. But *not* sacrilegious.

She turned to give him a flashing smile, but he was staring at the other counsel table. "What's wrong, John Lloyd?" she asked, turning to follow his glance.

He stroked his chin, a thoughtful expression in his eyes. "Maximum Miller is smiling. This is most unusual, Miss Fairchild. Never trust Maximum Miller when he is smiling. What is even more suspicious, he is not eating Tums."

Lydia sighed. She was Miss Fairchild again, which meant John Lloyd was settling down to business. Which they both had to do, of course. She just wished he didn't switch from personal to professional so easily.

She studied the prosecutor. He did look pleased with himself as she saw him pat Bobby Benson's shoulder. The district attorney seemed more relaxed, too, as though he was a condemned prisoner who had received a reprieve from the governor just before the executioner plunged the lethal injection in his arm.

"What is it, John Lloyd?" she asked.

He glanced at her briefly and for the space of a heartbeat she saw that burning, intent look in his eyes that meant he was about to reach for her, but it vanished before her thighs had a chance to build up a good tingle.

"Maximum Miller and his cohorts, Sergeants Schroder and Jenner, were in Canadian over the holidays, Miss Fairchild. I spoke with Mrs. Dinwittie early this morning to ascertain what, if anything, had occurred during our absence, and she informed me that our worthy opponent had been skulking about town."

Lydia felt her cheeks turn pink. They hadn't exactly been absent; they simply hadn't left John Lloyd's house until this morning. "How did she find out?"

"Mrs. Dinwittie has her sources and I do not like to inquire too closely as to what or who they might be, Miss Fairchild. She is a admirable woman in many ways, but she does tend to become agitated when questioned."

"And it isn't a good idea to agitate Mrs. Dinwittie?"

"Mr. Dinwittie discovered it to be a very bad idea on one occasion, Miss Fairchild. I try not to follow his example, particularly now when I have reason to find life very pleasant.''

Lydia blushed again. She had no doubt as to what that reason was.

When Maximum Miller called Mildred Fisher to the stand, Lydia felt John Lloyd stiffen like a hunting dog when it first catches the scent of a bird about to fly up its nose.

Maximum Miller rose, glanced toward John Lloyd with just the faintest trace of a smirk on his face, and turned to the witness. ''Ms. Fisher, would you tell us in your own words what you witnessed in the foyer of the business wing of the Church of the Holy Light around two in the afternoon the day of the murder?''

Mildred folded her hands on top of the rail of the witness box, and Lydia thought they looked like the claws of a predator. Her fingers were long and thin and her red nails just a bit too long. She was wearing another navy and red ensemble, this one a suit, and she didn't look any better in the colors than she had the last time she testified.

''My brother, Virgil, and I stopped by the church to pick up the copies of the budget report. I always like to have them ahead of time so that I can prepare my presentation.''

Lydia curled her lip. How much time did it take to read a simplified budget for a church she bet didn't have more than one hundred and fifty members in the congregation, if that many? Mildred just had a control problem. She liked to control people and had a problem if she couldn't.

''I was in the church office talking to the secretary, Agnes Ledgerwood, about the meeting. I wanted to make sure that Agnes had called all of the committee members and told them the correct time. Meetings I chair start on time and I don't like members dragging in late.''

''If you could cut to the chase, Ms. Fisher,'' said Maximum Miller, shifting from foot to foot with impatience.

''Yes, of course. I'm sorry. You're not interested in *my* activities.''

The emphasis on ''my'' was so pronounced that chairs creaked as the spectators leaned forward. Lydia heard that rude, ponytailed reporter with the nasal accent mutter, "Hot damn, here it comes."

"I picked up the budget reports, admonished Agnes about calling promptly, and walked out of the church office into the foyer. What I saw shocked me so much that I dropped the reports on the floor."

"And what did you see, Ms. Fisher?" asked Miller, leaning forward a little himself.

"I saw Amanda Hailey embracing my brother and *kissing* him. Her hands were all over him. I was speechless for several seconds."

Lydia would bet her new diamond earrings that was the only occasion in her life when Mildred Fisher was speechless.

"When I found my voice, I yelled out, 'Stop that, you hussy!' Well, she did, then stood there looking at me without a speck of color in her face. She didn't know I was around and I guess it nearly shocked the life out of her. I walked over and slapped her face and told her that my patience was at an end. I intended to tell her husband."

"And did you tell Mr. Hailey?" asked Maximum Miller.

"I didn't have to. He was standing in front of his office staring at his wife. He had seen the whole thing."

"What did Mr. Hailey do?"

"He walked over and took Amanda's arm and then looked at Virgil. He told Virgil that he would make certain this sort of thing never happened again."

"In your opinion, was the minister angry?"

"I should say so! He was furious. His face was red and his jaw was clenched. I told him how horrified I was and how inexcusable his wife's behavior was. He just looked at me and looked at Virgil and told us both that he hoped we would not speak of it."

"What did your brother say, Ms. Fisher?" asked Maximum Miller, sitting down and propping one elbow on the arm of his chair.

Mildred hesitated, then burst out, "He didn't say a word, Mr. Miller. He was red in the face and completely mortified.

Just imagine how you would feel if a woman practically raped you. I just grabbed his hand and pulled him out of there. He was so embarrassed that he wanted to skip attending the committee meeting, but I insisted. When you're innocent, you should hold up your head and go about your business."

"Your witness, Mr. Branson." Maximum Miller's voice was practically a purr.

John Lloyd didn't move and he didn't speak. He sat looking at Mildred Fisher while the seconds ticked by. Acting on the premise that physical intimacy didn't preclude certain preintimacy reactions, Lydia was ready to elbow him in the ribs when he finally spoke. "Where were Amanda Hailey's hands on your brother's body, Mildred?"

Lydia heard several gasps from the spectators and felt a little uncomfortable herself. And protective. She didn't want Mildred Fisher making Amanda Hailey sound like a slut.

The older woman's face turned splotchy, and she cleared her throat. Detailing the location and involvement of various body parts during a passionate clinch between two people wasn't something Mildred Fisher had expected to do.

"She touched his shoulders and his chest. I didn't *stare* at them! I saw them and then I yelled."

John Lloyd rose slowly. "I believe you just said that you were speechless for several seconds. How many seconds?"

Mildred twisted in her chair, saw the photo of Amanda's head still leaning against the railing, and jerked back around. "I don't know! Perhaps five."

"One can observe a great deal in five seconds, Ms. Fisher. Surely you saw more."

Mildred's face turned a dull red and her lips twisted. "I saw her touch his . . . his private parts."

"Touch or grasp?" asked John Lloyd.

Mildred looked down at her hands. "I don't know. I saw it so briefly, then closed my eyes and yelled."

"No further questions, Ms. Fisher," said John Lloyd.

Lydia leaned over to whisper in his ear. "Why did you stop? My God, that's the most ludicrous story I've ever heard."

John Lloyd's face held no expression at all. "I stopped,

Miss Fairchild, because she is telling the truth about what she saw. Mildred Fisher would never talk in public about a woman touching a man's genitals if I had not forced her to do so. She is the wrong generation and the wrong character to speak lightly of such matters. I cannot refute her testimony."

She clasped his arm. "John Lloyd, she's lying! She's got to be. Amanda Hailey wouldn't come on to Virgil Fisher. My God, you've seen him. I don't want to sound ugly, but most women wouldn't have him as a gift if he came with a million dollars in his pockets. He certainly doesn't compare to her own husband."

John Lloyd tapped his fingers on the counsel table while he studied her face. She didn't have a clue as to what he was thinking, but she knew his agile, *devious* mind was concocting a defense of some kind. She just hoped it was devious enough to save David Hailey's bacon.

And speaking of David Hailey, she peered around John Lloyd to see what the Panhandle's very own Elmer Gantry was up to. The answer was nothing. He was sitting as mute as ever, his hand shading his eyes. She noticed his hand looked thinner than it had before Christmas. Whatever secrets David Hailey was hiding within himself were slowly devouring him—at least physically. She felt suddenly as though the minister was shrinking before her eyes.

"The state calls Virgil Fisher," said Maximum Miller, and the entire courtroom turned around to watch Mildred's brother scuttle through the door and down the aisle, fumble open the gate in the railing, or bar, that separated the spectators' seats from those who had business with the court, and finally crouch in the witness box. His nose twitched more than usual, his chin seemed to recede even closer to his prominent Adam's apple, and his hazel eyes appeared to be more red-rimmed and weak. He truly looked like a frightened rabbit trapped in the middle of a busy freeway who knew he was seconds away from being roadkill.

"Mr. Fisher, did the Reverend David Hailey see you in a passionate embrace with his wife, Amanda?" asked Maximum Miller.

Virgil's eyes darted around the courtroom to avoid the sight of the prosecutor's stern face. "Yes."

"Was this embrace also observed by your sister?"

"Yes, but Mildred misunderstood!"

"Then Mildred Fisher did not observe Amanda Hailey kissing you, did not observe Amanda Hailey touching your chest and genitals?"

Virgil turned an ugly crimson and closed his eyes. "It wasn't what it looked like!"

"Did your sister observe Amanda Hailey touching your chest and genitals? Yes or no, Mr. Fisher?"

Virgil bowed his head; his voice was muffled when he answered. "Yes."

"And her husband saw these actions also?"

"Yes."

"Did Amanda Hailey touch and fondle you earlier in the day at your store, and did your sister warn her against such intimacies?"

Virgil jerked his head up to look at the prosecutor. "Yes, but Amanda was just being friendly. She always touched and hugged people."

"And when she touched and hugged you in the foyer of the Church of the Holy Light, was she just being *friendly*?"

Virgil opened his mouth several times, blinking his eyes in unison, but no sound emerged from his narrow mouth.

"Was she just being friendly, Mr. Fisher?" Miller demanded in a louder voice.

"I . . . I don't know."

Lydia cringed in her seat while Maximum Miller studied the pitiful man in the witness box. The portrait of Amanda Hailey slowly emerging from the testimony of both Mildred and Virgil Fisher was obscene—and she didn't believe it any more than she would believe Donna Reed molesting her children off camera. But believing and proving were two different acts: one only required instinct while the other required empirical evidence.

"In your opinion, was Mr. Hailey angry when he caught his wife and you in this embrace?"

"Yes, very angry."

"Did he ask you not to speak of it to anyone?"

"Yes."

"Why didn't you tell Sergeants Schroder and Jenner of this incident when they questioned you after the murder, Mr. Fisher?"

"I was humiliated and embarrassed."

"Your witness, Mr. Branson," said Maximum Miller.

Lydia clutched John Lloyd's arm, whispering frantically in his ear. "He's lying, John Lloyd. Make him recant."

John Lloyd loosened her clutching fingers. "He is not lying, Miss Fairchild. Surely you can hear the ring of truth in his voice."

Lydia let go of his arm and drew a shaky breath. That was the problem. She *could* hear the truth in Virgil Fisher's voice. Damn it, John Lloyd should have followed her advice and gone for voluntary manslaughter after all.

John Lloyd stood up, his face as stern as Maximum Miller's had been. "Virgil, the truth is a very fragile thing, easily broken and its pieces scattered. A tone of voice, a certain reflection when answering a question and the truth shatters like fine crystal. But, unlike crystal, one may collect the pieces and delicately restore truth and it sparkles again without cracks."

He paused, his gaze flickering toward Maximum Miller before returning to Virgil. "Your sister believes she told the truth. She believes she held fine crystal in her hands. But she did not. She held a jelly glass instead because her personality and her convictions led her to confuse cheap glass with fine crystal."

Virgil Fisher stared at John Lloyd as though mesmerized, then nodded, his eyes suddenly bright, almost shrewd. "That's exactly right, John Lloyd."

"You also confused a jelly glass for fine crystal, did you not, Virgil? You confused Amanda Hailey's friendliness with passion?"

"Yes," Virgil admitted with a sigh. Lydia saw Maximum Miller start to rise, then collapse into his chair again.

"Did you embrace Amanda Hailey?"

"Yes."

"Was she a willing participant?"

"When she thought it was a friendly hug, but when I kissed her, she tried to push me away," said Virgil earnestly, his eyes fixed on John Lloyd.

"Her touching you was in aid of trying to escape your embrace?"

"Yes."

"And when pushing against your chest did not work, Amanda took a stronger defensive action? Mounting an assault on a man's genital area is a time-honored and effective way for a woman to defend herself, is it not?"

Virgil nodded. "It was effective with me."

There was nervous laughter from the spectators, and Lydia heard the ponytailed reporter's voice raised in heartfelt agreement: "Damn right!"

"Then your speechlessness when confronted by David Hailey and your sister was more the result of physical discomfort than of failure to defend an innocent woman's actions?"

"Absolutely, John Lloyd!" said Virgil.

"In your opinion, Virgil, did Mr. Hailey also misunderstand the embrace?"

Virgil leaned forward. "No, he didn't. He saw everything, including Amanda's trying to push me away. He was angry, but at Mildred, not Amanda. He was very gentle with his wife, and . . . and gentle with me, too. He gave me a pitying sort of look and told me he hoped this never happened again."

John Lloyd glanced at David Hailey, who had at last straightened and was watching Virgil Fisher. "One other piece to be replaced, Virgil, in our chalice of truth. David Hailey frequently uses biblical references when speaking. Several witnesses mentioned this in their statements. What were David Hailey's exact words when he told you and Mildred not to speak of what had happened?"

"He said not to bear false witness against Amanda."

"You have obeyed his counsel, Virgil," said John Lloyd solemnly. "You have not born false witness against Amanda Hailey."

AD INTERIM

HE CLOSED HIS EYES AND WHISPERED A PRAYER OF THANKS-giving. Virgil Fisher had rendered unto the Lord the truth. He had cleansed his soul. But the greater truth still remained unrevealed. Others still steadfastly denied what their hearts knew. Others still stood in danger of hellfire. He must also be steadfast. He must wait. He must trust that others would finally see the truth and render it unto God.

And Mildred, poor Mildred. He must redouble his prayers that she pluck away the scales that blinded her to love.

CHAPTER TWENTY-ONE

"DAMN IT ALL, CLEETUS! WHY DIDN'T YOU OBJECT WHEN Branson let loose with that business about truth and crystal and jelly jars?"

Bobby Benson paced around Maximum Miller's office as best he could in a space Jenner judged couldn't be much more than ten by ten with a desk, a credenza, a bookcase, and four chairs taking up most of the room. The district attorney was in a towering rage and most of it was directed at his assistant.

"That whole speech sounded like a closing argument to me, Cleetus. You should have cut Branson off!"

Maximum Miller slumped in his chair, watching his boss weave around chairs as he paced from window to door and back again. After several more repetitions in slightly different words of his contention that the prosecutor had royally screwed up, Benson finally dropped in a chair and started pulling his hair.

Miller swiveled around in his chair to face his distraught boss. "A prosecutor isn't after a conviction for conviction's sake, Bobby. We're supposed to reveal the truth. That's what Branson was doing with Virgil Fisher and he was damn clever about it, too. He gave that scared little shit a way to save face. He allowed Fisher to view his sexual harassment of Amanda Hailey as a little misunderstanding. He allowed Fisher to claim that he honestly believed Amanda Hailey would welcome being mauled. And you know what? I believe it, too. I don't think Virgil intended to force himself on the preacher's wife. I think he let his fantasies get out of hand."

Miller rubbed one hand over his face as if to wipe away defeat. "I'll tell you something, Bobby. I wish I had handled Fisher the same way Branson did. Know why I didn't? Because I fell into the same trap as Mildred Fisher. I believed what I wanted to believe because it fit my notions. I didn't stop to think that maybe my notions were wrong."

"You mean you don't think the preacher killed his wife?" asked Jenner, shocked that Maximum Miller would doubt his own case.

"That ain't what I said, damn it!" yelled Miller. "I still think that Hailey did it, but I don't think we have a goddamn clue as to why. I was looking for evidence to support voluntary manslaughter, which I've said all along is the best we can hope for, but I was wrong. This isn't voluntary manslaughter. It's deliberate murder. That conclusion is more consistent with the evidence, but I could no more tell you why Hailey offed his wife than I can tell you why I always put on my pants left leg first even though I'm right-handed. Maybe he did it for one of those reasons that the witnesses claimed. Maybe he felt trapped between her and his congregation. Maybe he got frustrated because he couldn't dictate her every damn move. Maybe he was jealous and just kept it to himself. I don't know. But I do know one thing. I have to have a motive to use in my closing argument. The jury expects it. I have to go over all the testimony and all the evidence and consult a fortune-teller if that's what it takes, but I have to come up with some logical, rational explanation for a murder committed by a man for reasons I don't think are rational to anybody but him, even if I knew what those reasons were in the first place. And if I can't think of a logical explanation, I better come up with an emotional one that the jury will buy."

"But I thought you said Branson would ask for an instructed verdict," said Benson, straightening up and smoothing his hair down.

"He may, Bobby, but I have to be prepared. The defense takes over tomorrow and I don't need to tell you that Branson hasn't told us shit about his witness list because he doesn't have to. He could call a psychologist who's an expert in religious mania. He could call a theologian. He could call Saint Peter to testify for Hailey and we wouldn't know it until we saw the halo."

He unwrapped a package of Tums. "In other words, I don't *know* what's gonna happen from here on out, but I'll be damned if I'll get caught with my pants down and my boxers showing again. I'm gonna make notes on a closing argument on the front side of the page in my legal pad and notes for an argument against an instructed verdict on the back side of the page. In the margins I'm updating my résumé for when you lose the primary and I get fired. Now everybody get out of here so I can think about what the hell I'm going to do."

As he walked out of the office, Jenner's last sight of Maximum Miller was of the prosecutor chewing his antacid pills and looking as if they didn't help his bellyache at all.

"Schroder, what do you think will happen tomorrow?" he asked the burly detective, who, he suddenly realized, hadn't said a word all afternoon.

"Nothing."

"What do you mean, nothing? Who do you think Branson will call as witnesses?"

"Nobody."

"Nobody! Schroder, you're crazy as shit."

"Wait till tomorrow and see if I'm wrong."

Schroder was wrong.

But so was Maximum Miller.

John Lloyd Branson didn't call a psychologist or a theologian or Saint Peter.

He called an anthropologist.

Not that Dr. Peter Millhiser was Jenner's idea of what an anthropologist ought to look like. He didn't have white hair, didn't peer through thick glasses, didn't drone pedantically in answer to every question. Millhiser was in his late thirties, tall, wiry, wore contact lenses, Levi's, and cowboy boots, and spoke with a Texas drawl as thick as John Lloyd's. He did have white hair, but it made him look younger instead of older, maybe because it was such a contrast to his deep tan.

"Dr. Millhiser, could you define culture in layman's terms, please?"

Millhiser pursed his lips. "Roughly speakin', John Lloyd, culture is everything we're taught that makes us behave and believe the way we do whether we're talking about the language we speak or the attitudes we accept or the sports we like or the institutions we support or the church we go to. It's all part of the definition. For example, baseball is an American cultural institution. We aren't born loving baseball or knowing how to play it, but it's a part of our culture. We are exposed to it almost from birth on TV and radio and in the newspaper. We are *taught* baseball. Same thing with believing in the Bill of Rights or the Constitution."

"You mentioned attitudes, Dr. Millhiser. Would you be so good as to give us an example of an attitude that might be considered cultural rather than innate?" asked John Lloyd.

"Most anthropologists believe that ninety-nine-point-nine percent of attitudes are cultural instead of innate, John Lloyd, with you being the possible point-one percent. Never have figured out a way to explain you otherwise." He grinned when the courtroom erupted in laughter. "Anyhow, you want an example so the jury will understand what we're talking about. Okay, I'll keep it simple. Men aren't supposed to cry, except maybe when their mama or their wife or their child dies. Doesn't matter if a man is hurting or loses his job or finds out his wife is leaving him, he's not supposed to cry. Why not? Because it's unmanly. It's not that way everywhere in the world, but it's that way here. It's a socially transmitted attitude. It's cultural. Been some attempt to change that attitude, to persuade men it's all right to be sensitive and cry, but I don't see it succeeding. The attitude is too deeply embedded in the culture of this country, and it's damn hard to jettison your culture. You can rebel against it, you can deny part or all of it, but you can't make it go away."

"And you said religion is part of one's culture?"

The anthropologist nodded. "Absolutely. Maybe one of the strongest elements of a culture are its religious beliefs. Lot of wars have been fought over religion."

John Lloyd paused, and Jenner saw him take a deep breath. "Speaking hypothetically, Dr. Millhiser, in your opinion, how difficult would it be for a minister who has followed that calling for a number of years, and who holds the pulpit in a small community of traditional religious beliefs, and who exhibits no symptoms of mental illness suddenly to not only kill his wife, but to commit an act of sacrilege in front of witnesses? Your opinion, Doctor, as an expert in cultural anthropology?"

Millhiser eased forward in the witness box and turned to face the jury. "The smaller a community, the stronger are the cultural bonds among its members, generally speaking, and the more difficult for the individual to violate community standards. For a minister to break the taboo against murder held by the community, and also to break the taboo against sacrilege held not only by the community, but by his own religious culture, would be almost impossible without some reason that overwhelmed his fear of censure and his fear of spiritual retribution. I can't stress enough how powerful religious taboos are in any culture."

Jenner leaned over to whisper to Schroder. "Maybe this guy isn't Saint Peter, but he's as close as you're going to find without a halo. What I can't understand, though, is why Branson is bringing up the sacrilege angle. That doesn't have anything to do with the murder."

Schroder gave him a pitying look. "Son, haven't I taught you anything? If Branson harps on an issue, then you can bet it's important, but be damned if I can figure out how. Maximum Miller can't either. I just saw him eat some Tums."

Jenner watched the prosecutor's rhythmic chewing and wondered if he ought to buy stock in whatever drug company manufactured the antacid pills. Might be a good investment the way Miller was probably driving up sales.

Schroder jabbed him in the ribs. "What the hell is Branson playing now? He just asked how old the Virgin Mary probably was when she had Jesus."

Jenner turned back to the witness in time to see Millhiser scratching his head like a man trying to think of a diplomatic answer to a question he knew might land him in deep trouble. "I'm no theologian, John Lloyd. I don't know what the religious answer is supposed to be. I can just tell you what we know about the culture of that place at that time. The general consensus is that women of that period in that part of the world probably weren't fertile until the age of eighteen or nineteen. Disease and/or diet are the generally accepted reasons. That doesn't mean they didn't go through puberty until then. It just means they weren't fertile."

"Then they did not marry until then?" asked John Lloyd.

Millhiser waggled his finger. "Now I didn't say that. Generally they married earlier and were certainly betrothed earlier. By the way, a betrothal was considered damn near as binding as marriage."

"Was physical intimacy common during these betrothals?"

Millhiser chuckled. "May have been. May not have been. No way to tell. Those folks didn't write sexual confessions and call them autobiographies the way we do now. One thing for sure, though, and that was it wasn't socially acceptable to have a baby outside wedlock. Your sweetie got pregnant, you were expected to marry her pretty damn fast."

"And if the man did not believe the child was his?"

"He broke off the betrothal and the woman became an object of public scorn."

"Yet Joseph did not put away Mary when she told him that she was pregnant," remarked John Lloyd.

Millhiser grinned, but Jenner noticed he looked a little uneasy. "You're getting into theology again, John Lloyd. Angels appearing in dreams and all that. I'm not going to step into that stretch of quicksand except to say that it appears to me from reading the gospel of Matthew that Joseph was a mighty confused man. He obviously didn't want to believe that Mary had betrayed him because the evidence was that Mary was a virtuous woman and I think he loved her. When he had his dream of the angel appearing with the news that Mary was pregnant with the messiah, he must have been relieved. He could believe the angel because his religious culture had predisposed him to believe despite all the evidence to the contrary that virgins don't get pregnant. His religious culture taught him to have faith, and faith doesn't rest on logical proof or material evidence—not in his culture, or our culture, or any culture I'm familiar with."

John Lloyd put his hands behind him and rocked back on his heels. "Yet, Dr. Millhiser, Joseph's faith was consistent with the evidence of Mary's virtuous reputation."

The anthropologist looked pensive for a moment. "I guess it was, but it was inconsistent with what Joseph must have known about the birds and the bees. Myself, I've always thought that Joseph's actions were a sign of a strong faith and a strong love even if the Lord did send him a personal message. Joseph always had the option of disbelieving that angel."

"In your opinion as a cultural anthropologist, would you agree that an individual immersed in his religious culture is as capable of acting according to the dictates of his faith in our rather irreverent modern world as was Joseph, even if those actions are misunderstood?"

Millhiser stroked his chin. "Well, John Lloyd, I think I could write you up a pretty good paper in support of that thesis."

"Your witness, Mr. Prosecutor," said John Lloyd.

Jenner nudged Schroder. "Maximum Miller's boxers are showing again. How can he refute that witness without saying the Bible stretches the truth?"

Schroder's eyebrows were one solid fuzzy line across his forehead as he sat frowning at no one in particular that Jenner could see. "He can't, son," the burly detective finally said. "And he can't ask for that testimony to be stricken on the grounds that it doesn't seem to be relevant either. The jury won't like it. We walk real easy around religion in this part of the country. It's part of the culture, you know,'' he said, nodding his head.

Maximum Miller stood up, scratched his head, rubbed his hands together, stepped out into the river—and avoided the quicksand. ''Dr. Millhiser, in your career as a cultural anthropologist, haven't you ever observed religious taboos broken by ministers?''

''Sure have, but not very damn many. We just hear about the bad apples.''

''So it's not impossible for a minister to break a religious taboo?''

''Nope, just a whole lot less likely than for the ordinary person to do so.''

''In your opinion?''

''In my opinion,'' agreed Millhiser.

CHAPTER TWENTY-TWO

Canadian—January 5

LYDIA WAITED UNTIL NEARLY MIDNIGHT BEFORE SHE SLIPPED out of bed, grabbed a robe, and padded into John Lloyd's living room. He stood in front of the fireplace staring at the mantel. He neither moved nor spoke when she gently touched his shoulder.

"John Lloyd, aren't you coming to bed? It's late and we have to be back in court tomorrow."

He finally turned and she caught her breath. He looked weary, but more than that, he looked defeated. "Miss Fairchild, for the first time in my legal career I have failed my client. Don't misunderstand me. I have lost cases before and seen my clients go to prison, but I have never felt that I failed to present an adequate defense. I have never felt that I have failed to explain to a jury the underlying motives for a client's behavior—until now. The most important case of my career and I have failed! It is a new experience for me and a very humbling one."

She rested her hands on his shoulders. "John Lloyd, you

haven't failed. The judge will grant our plea for an instructed verdict. David Hailey won't go to prison."

He turned away and stretched out his arms until his hands rested on the mantel and let his head hang down. "How can I persuade a jury if I cannot persuade even you, Miss Fairchild?"

"Persuade a jury of what? You won't be making a jury argument. Maximum Miller hasn't proved his case. The judge will order an instructed verdict of not guilty."

"That is not good enough. It will not free him of the charge of sacrilege."

Lydia looked around, expecting to see stone walls and rushes on the floor and knights in armor cleaning their lances because she certainly felt as though she had been transported to the Middle Ages.

"For God's sake, John Lloyd, you must think you're arguing before an ecclesiastical court. David Hailey is charged with *murder*, not sacrilege!"

John Lloyd straightened to face her, his eyes burning with fervor or fever, she wasn't sure which although she preferred the latter. Fever meant a physical illness. She could handle physical. What she couldn't handle was religious zealotry. It wasn't part of her culture.

"Miss Fairchild, he is innocent of murder, but that was always the lesser crime of which he stands accused by the world. Thou shall not kill is the sixth commandment. The first five concern man's relationship to God, and David Hailey sinned against God by disposing of his wife's body in the manner that he did."

Lydia stumbled to a chair and sat down. She wondered why she ever fell in love with John Lloyd Branson when she could have chosen somebody less complex, more like herself. Or if she had to choose somebody totally different, why didn't she choose a football player? She bet a quarterback didn't sit up nights berating himself over that one last touchdown pass he *didn't* throw if he had already won the game seven to zip.

"John Lloyd, it isn't your responsibility to save David Hailey's soul. That's his job description. He's the preacher.

You're the lawyer." She broke off as one of his statements suddenly burst in her mind like a rocket. "What do you mean he's innocent?"

"I have always believed that, Miss Fairchild. And I have always been aware of David Hailey's calling. It is why he has remained mute and it is why I called Dr. Millhiser to testify. I wanted the court to know the strong cultural and religious expectations of that calling. Simply put, David Hailey is a shepherd who must lead his flock to God, not force them. He has not defended himself because he feels he must give the murderer an opportunity to ask forgiveness of God. He believes that once the murderer has redeemed his soul, then a confession will follow."

Lydia stared at him in disbelief. "That is absolutely the thinnest, most unbelievable, damnest argument I've ever heard, John Lloyd. I'm glad you're not making it to the jury."

He reached down and caught her hand, pulling her out of the chair. "But I am, my dear. Now that I know why he committed sacrilege, I believe I can convince the jury to free him on all charges. More important, perhaps my argument will convince the murderer of the error of his beliefs and he will offer a quick prayer for forgiveness, then render unto Caesar for secular justice."

Lydia shook her head and wondered if it was too late to fall in love with a quarterback. "John Lloyd, you're crazy, you're over the edge, you've stepped in that quicksand Dr. Millhiser was talking about and it's swallowed you up. You can't even keep up with what *you* believe. A few minutes ago you said you didn't know why David Hailey committed sacrilege."

He glanced at the grandfather clock, then turned her around and gently urged her toward the stairs. "It is past midnight, Miss Fairchild. It is now January sixth. The day of epiphany. Do you know what that means?"

Lydia smiled in resignation. "Generally, but I'll bet you're going to tell me specifically."

He ignored her comment, but then she expected that. When John Lloyd defined words, he tended to be hard of hearing. "Epiphany was the day the Magi revealed the divinity of Christ to the Gentiles. Epiphany also means a sudden manifestation of the essence of something. You are neither Magi nor angel, Miss Fairchild, but you manifested the essence of David Hailey's motive for sacrilege."

"What?"

"On Christmas Eve you pointed out that I used you for some noble and undefined cause just as David Hailey used his wife. That was the beginning of my epiphany, but I could not entirely discern his purpose—until tonight when you attempted to change my mind by pointing out the error in my thinking. David Hailey attempted to do the same thing for his flock but somewhat more subtly. You both failed, but that does not invalidate the purity of your intent."

"What intent could I possibly have in common with that twit?" demanded Lydia.

"Love, my dear."

"I don't understand, John Lloyd," she said as he walked her up the stairs.

"You will tomorrow, Lydia, when I make my closing argument."

She stopped in the bedroom doorway, bracing herself against its frame. "John Lloyd, do you think quarterbacks read the *Oxford English Dictionary*?"

After Maximum Miller finished a hellfire-and-brimstone summation for the prosecution, it was the defense's turn.

John Lloyd wore his string tie with his three-piece western-cut black suit. He always wore a string tie when he gambled, and in spite of his air of confidence during the drive to Amarillo, Lydia knew he saw his closing argument as a gamble. Whatever his closing argument was. He never had told her, and after he promised he would not keep secrets from her again. No, that was wrong. He promised he wouldn't use her again. He had said nothing about not keeping secrets and she hadn't thought to demand it. Pretty sneaky of him.

She wondered if quarterbacks were that sneaky.

She turned around and located all the members of the budget committee. She hoped John Lloyd's plan worked, but she doubted it would. That sort of courtroom confession only happened in Perry Mason stories.

She leaned across John Lloyd's empty chair. "I may have misjudged you, Mr. Hailey. I'm sorry."

He smiled. "You didn't know me, Miss Fairchild. You were not part of what Dr. Millhiser described as my culture."

She gestured toward the spectators. "I may not be, but your budget committee is. They're all here for this finale just like they were all present at the last finale. Tell me, Mr. Hailey, which one is it? I promise I won't jump up and point my finger. I'll let you and John Lloyd finish this little passion play of yours, but I just want to know. Which member of the budget committee murdered your wife?"

He didn't pretend not to understand her. "I don't know, Miss Fairchild."

"Ladies and gentlemen," began John Lloyd, and Lydia turned to watch the last act. "My client stands accused of murdering his wife. The state contends that he picked up a stone after the budget meeting and crushed her skull, then carried her body out of the bedroom through the sliding glass door and callously dumped it in the nativity scene. We will admit that he carried her body from the bedroom and that he placed her in the nativity scene, but *not* for a callous reason, as I shall shortly explain. Neither will we admit that he picked up a stone and murdered his wife."

John Lloyd walked to the jury box and rested one hand on the railing. "Let me first digress to summarize what had gone before this fatal night. David Hailey, a minister, marries a young girl, who at nineteen, if we accept Dr. Millhiser's testimony, is approximately the age that Mary might have been. But Mary, the woman who will give birth to Christ, is a woman of virtuous reputation. Amanda Hailey, on the other hand, is reputed to be not virtuous, a slut in common terms. Yet David Hailey does not believe it, and his belief rests on the evidence of her behavior. She does not spend his meager salary on new clothes even though she must be aware that her own are not appropriate. She watches out for him, sees that he eats regular meals, receives sufficient rest, and guards his time against unwarranted encroachment by his flock. These are the actions of a loving wife."

John Lloyd waved a finger in the air, his voice rising. "Not one—*not one*—of the witnesses could testify of their own knowledge as to the existence of a lover now or in the past. Neither could a single one of the witnesses testify to seeing or hearing David Hailey chastise his wife. On the contrary, he defends her and excuses her behavior as that of a typical woman of her age. These are the actions of a loving husband."

He lowered his voice, and Lydia saw everyone in the courtroom leaning forward so as not to miss a word he was saying. "That is the situation that existed on December second. A loving wife and a loving husband—and a congregation disapproving of one and disappointed in the other. With that background in mind let me recount the real sequence of events that occurred that night. David Hailey breaks up an argument between his wife and Mildred Fisher by escorting his wife to their bedroom. It is the second altercation between Mildred and Amanda that day, yet *not one* witness testifies that David Hailey is angry with his wife. But David Hailey had been angry earlier in the day as Virgil Fisher testified. David Hailey had been angry with Mildred Fisher. It is reasonable to assume that he still possessed some of that anger that night. Although a minister, he is still a man. But as a minister he is obligated according to his religious beliefs to ask forgiveness for that anger. He goes to the church to pray, leaving Amanda in their bedroom after perhaps calming her for a few minutes. What happens next? After watching the video of the crime scene and reading the autopsy protocol, I believe the evidence is consistent with my account of the next few minutes."

He walked away from the jury box, then turned back. Lydia noticed that every juror's eyes followed him. "So what happened next?" he asked again. "I believe Amanda Hailey sits down at her vanity to remove her makeup. We know this because her jar of cold cream was found on the floor near the glass door. We also know that she never lived long enough to cream her face because no foreign substance such as cold cream was found under her fingernails, but lipstick was found on her fingertips. Therefore Amanda Hailey sits down and removes her cold cream from her vanity drawer, where she surely keeps it as she is an immaculate housekeeper and would hardly clutter the top of her vanity. Before she even has time to unscrew the lid, the glass door opens and someone steps in. Amanda rises, frightened perhaps that someone dares to walk into her bedroom without knocking, throws her jar of cold cream at the intruder, realizes the intruder is not a stranger, and reacts with a gesture many women might use under similar circumstances. She presses her hand over her mouth, thus leaving lipstick on her fingertips. That gesture of surprise and concern and perhaps fear of what she has done costs Amanda Hailey her life. The intruder takes three or four quick steps, brings his or her arm up, and smashes the pointed end of the stone against Amanda Hailey's skull. Amanda falls, knocking over the vanity stool, and the murderer flees, leaving the glass door open to weather as cold as a merciless heart."

Lydia shivered. She could almost feel the cold wind whipping through that open glass door, blowing sleet on that old, worn carpet, dampening the edges of the cheap drapes, and further chilling the already cooling flesh of Amanda Hailey. She noticed one of the women jurors doing the same thing and knew that up to this point at least the jury believed John Lloyd.

"Let us leave Amanda Hailey in that bedroom, dying or already dead, and return to the budget committee, gathered again around the dining-room table after a break during which all were outside, and at least five were, at one time or another, alone. The meeting adjourns and Reverend Hailey accompanies the members outside, where Glen Williams testifies that he sees the minister pick up a round white object from the flower bed. David Hailey hurries inside while all the others except Virgil Fisher go to view the nativity scene."

John Lloyd paced in front of the jury, his limp more pronounced than on previous days as though the story he was telling were a heavy burden. "Let us return with David Hailey to the bedroom where he discovers his wife's body and sees the bloodstained stone. What he had feared when he picked up the crumpled budget report and saw a stone missing is indeed true. One of his flock has stoned his wife to death for her perceived misdeeds. He undresses her and carries her naked body to the open sliding door, which he pushes open still further, thus leaving his fingerprints on the metal band above the handle. The murderer, who undoubtedly wore gloves and thus left smudges, only needed to open the door wide enough to step into the room. David Hailey needed it open all the way in order to exit carrying his wife's limp body. He carries her to the nativity scene and replaces the mannequin of the Virgin Mary with Amanda's body."

John Lloyd stopped and turned to face the jury. "Why, why, why did a minister commit such an act of sacrilege?" He paused and Lydia saw several jurors shaking their heads. "Because as a minister David Hailey focused on convincing his congregation that the followers of Christ were ordinary people like themselves. They were not the plaster figures the centuries have made of them; they were the small businessmen, the ranchers, the secretaries, the local government officials, the blue-collar workers of their day. Mary, who has been turned into a saint, was first a young girl pregnant out of wedlock, in danger of being put aside by her espoused husband, Joseph, and who must have been the subject of unpleasant gossip just as Amanda Hailey had been. By placing Amanda's body in the nativity scene, David Hailey demonstrates that the gossip was untrue, that rather than punishing a sinner, the murderer has broken the sixth commandment. David Hailey, as a minister, subject to the religious culture he has been taught, believes that it is his duty to allow the guilty time to recognize their transgression and render an accounting to God before he renders them up to Caesar in the form of the police. Thus he has stood mute not because he is guilty, but because he is innocent. To David Hailey, standing mute is an act of faith."

John Lloyd walked slowly back to the defense table and stood behind Hailey, clasping his shoulders. "This account is consistent with the material evidence, but more important, it is consistent with the behavior of David Hailey over the five years that he has stood behind the pulpit of the Church of the Holy Light. I do not need a personal message from God to convince me of David Hailey's innocence. I know the truth when I see it."

Lydia clasped his hands when he sat down and flinched at their coldness. It was as if all his warmth had been spent in his closing argument and nothing remained but a chilled, weary man sitting in a hushed courtroom.

She heard Maximum Miller rise and glanced at his solemn face. "Your Honor," said the prosecutor. "It is the duty of the prosecution to uncover and reveal the truth. I believe that John Lloyd Branson has usurped that duty. I believe that he has this day revealed the truth. I further believe that Caesar has demanded enough of David Hailey, and I, as counsel for the State of Texas in this matter, ask that all charges against him be dismissed."

AD INTERIM

HE HEARD THE JUDGE DISMISS THE CHARGES, HEARD HIM adjourn the court, even heard some of the reporters' shouted questions, but at the same time he heard nothing but the sound of his own cry when he saw Amanda's body and the lonely scream of the wind as it blew through the open glass door.

He felt the jurors patting his shoulders, clasping his hands; felt the heat of the TV lights as cameramen jockeyed for the perfect shot; even felt the hands of spectators pushing at him from behind; but at the same time he felt nothing but the weight of Amanda's dead body and her chilled skin under his hands.

He smelled the tang of peppermint mouthwash on a juror's breath, smelled the sourness of clothes worn too long by another, even smelled the sweet flower scent of Lydia Fairchild's perfume, but at the same time he smelled nothing but cold wind and lemon furniture polish and the sharp, metallic odor of Amanda's blood.

He saw the courtroom; saw the judge's bemused face, the open mouths and excited eyes of spectators, the brooding features of Maximum Miller; even saw John Lloyd's weary, questing expression; but at the same time saw only Amanda's slack face, dimmed eyes that would never see another sunset, and the bloody hole behind her ear.

He wondered if John Lloyd knew that the saintly, forgiving shepherd he had described would never forgive the murderer, not for stealing Amanda's life, but for stealing away all his memories of her alive.

He tasted his own tears and they tasted of failure.

He failed to forgive, and he failed to lead to forgiveness. Once more he had expected more of the divine than real men are capable of, and once more his expectations were destined not to be fulfilled. The guilty had not stepped forward and now Caesar's armies were gathering, soon to march forth under blind justice's banner with the exhortations of her most devoted follower ringing in their ears. John Lloyd Branson would see justice appeased.

CHAPTER TWENTY-THREE

"LISTEN HERE, BRANSON, IF YOUR BOY STOOD UP AND CONfessed he'd killed his wife after all, I couldn't charge him with murder again without running into problems with double jeopardy, so why are you so damn set on baby-sitting him?"

Jenner leaned against the wall between Bobby Benson and Schroder in Maximum Miller's office listening to the exchange between the assistant D.A. and John Lloyd Branson, and for once he was on Branson's side. David Hailey looked to be in need of a baby-sitter. For a man who had just gone from being a candidate for a lynching by popular demand to being a serious contender for sainthood, the preacher didn't look very happy. In fact, he looked like a man who just had dirt kicked in his face.

"Besides which," continued Miller, "I'm not crazy about you listening in while I question Hailey. Next thing I know you'll be signing on as defense attorney for whomever we arrest after the preacher here opens up and tells us what he knows."

"I will not be defending Amanda Hailey's murderer," said John Lloyd. "I have a conflict of interest."

Maximum Miller froze in the process of lighting one of his cigars. "What? Explain yourself, Branson—and in words of no more than two syllables, please. I'm not up to translating your speech into colloquial English this morning."

John Lloyd folded his hands over the top of his cane. "In the vernacular, I want in on the action. I want to be there when Sergeant Schroder arrests the murderer. I want to *see* justice done. I want vengeance."

Miller put his cigar back in his pocket and leaned back in his chair, studying the attorney. "That was pretty good, John Lloyd. I didn't hear more than three polysyllabic words in that little speech. I always knew you could be succinct if you tried. But you sounded more like the victim's husband ought to be talking. Vengeance for the victim is generally the first thing the family thinks of."

"Due to his calling, David Hailey thinks in terms of forgiveness, with retribution a poor second. I am not so merciful. I despise those who use God to justify their own heinous crimes."

"So you want vengeance for God?" asked Miller. "Seems to me that you're walking a pretty fine line yourself, John Lloyd."

"God does not require my assistance. Justice, however, may. I submit that my familiarity with this case and my lack of sentiment toward the participants are weapons you should not disregard. Miss Fairchild once accused me of being an Old Testament man. I submit this is an Old Testament crime and that I am uniquely qualified to help you solve it."

"Oh, for God's sake!" cried Lydia Fairchild, leaping out of her chair.

"I believe that is the point, Miss Fairchild," remarked Maximum Miller, raising one eyebrow at her outburst.

"No, it's not! Maybe all of you ought to remember that human beings murder for sex or money or power. Religion is just their cover. Even the Crusades, in spite of all the rhetoric, had as much to do with territorial claims and looting as they had to do with religion. God is a scapegoat for man's greed or lust."

"I believe that is what I said, Miss Fairchild," said John Lloyd.

"No, it wasn't. You were talking about religious mania. Somebody killing because they believe God told them to. I don't think so. I think the murderer used that stone because it was a convenient weapon, not primarily for its religious symbolism."

"Well, before we get bogged down in a theological discussion, I suggest we ask Mr. Hailey who he suspects," said Miller. "We'll worry about the whys and wherefores after we have the son of a bitch in jail."

"He doesn't know!" Lydia protested. "I've already asked him."

"Is that right, Hailey?" demanded Miller.

The minister shook his head. "I left Amanda and went to the church to pray for forgiveness for my anger with Mildred and my impatience with Amanda. And I had been impatient with her when we reached our bedroom. I'm not the saint that John Lloyd painted me. It had been a day of revelation for me, and I didn't welcome any of the revelations. I saw at last that my parishioners were not going to accept Amanda as I had hoped. Of course, they were not in love with her and I was. There would have to be a compromise on both sides, and neither side was willing because neither side believed they were at fault."

Jenner saw the minister raise a shaking hand and rub his forehead. Poor bastard. He had been between a rock and a hard place.

"I left the bedroom through the glass door, leaving it closed and unlocked. I guess Amanda was too upset to lock it again. I walked to the back door of the church and let myself in. I saw no one."

"Then you did pick up that budget report after the meeting?" asked Schroder.

Hailey looked up at the burly sergeant. "Yes. All the rest was just as John Lloyd said."

"All right, Branson," said Schroder. "You were in that dining room looking at that table. Who's budget report was missing?"

"Hank Gregory's. I never brought it out in the trial because he is the only person whom I did not suspect."

"You're taking one thing for granted, John Lloyd. You're taking for granted that everyone sat at their same places when the meeting reconvened," said Lydia.

"They did, Miss Fairchild, or at least Hank and O'Brien and the preacher did. O'Brien told us when we questioned him after Christmas. Hailey, how about it? Anybody change places?"

Hailey shook his head. "No, Mr. Miller."

"Good," said Lydia. "That eliminates everybody then. I know who the murderer is."

Jenner never saw so many men with their mouths open all at the same time. Even Branson dropped his jaw. If Lydia Fairchild had stripped off her blouse, he didn't think she could have shocked the room's occupants more. He wasn't shocked, however. He remembered Lydia Fairchild during the investigation into the death of the museum curator. Even Branson had slipped up on that one, but Lydia Fairchild hadn't. She was one sharp lady.

He scratched his back against the door frame and waited to see who would find his voice first. He wasn't surprised when John Lloyd spoke. Nobody could accuse Branson of not having an agile tongue.

"Miss Fairchild, perhaps you would share your epiphany with us?"

Jenner wondered exactly what *epiphany* meant but was afraid to ask.

Lydia smiled and perched on the edge of Miller's desk. "Let's talk motive, gentlemen. Who had a motive to kill Amanda Hailey?"

"Mildred Fisher," said Miller promptly. "She was absolutely convinced that Amanda Hailey was a slut and was destroying her church and that the minister didn't intend to do anything about it. And she had means and opportunity. *And* she was sitting next to Hank. She could have appropriated his report when she realized she had dropped hers outside. Hank wouldn't pay any attention because he never read them anyway. *And* she went back into the house before all the others except Virgil and Agnes, and I'll bet they were too busy walking on eggshells around Mildred so they wouldn't upset her again that they never noticed what she did. She must be getting a little nervous with all this talk about that report."

"And I suppose you're going to tell me Mildred stoned Amanda because she thought she was doing God's will by killing a slut?"

"That's about the size of it," agreed Miller.

Lydia rolled her eyes toward the ceiling. "You people should get a life."

"But Mildred Fisher is right-handed," Bobby Benson said suddenly, looking proud of himself. "And Branson proved the murderer had to be left-handed."

Lydia swatted away his words as though she was swatting flies. "That's immaterial, Mr. Benson. You are correct only to the extent that yes, the killer held the stone in his left hand. Think about the sliding door. If you are standing outside, you must pull the door to the right to open it. Grasping it with your left hand would be awkward and unnatural if you are right-handed. Also you would be standing with your body twisted when you did open it, and the murderer had no time to clumsily turn his body and step through the door. He had at most five seconds to enter, take the four or five short steps across that tiny room, and crush Amanda Hailey's skull while she was still reacting after throwing her cold cream at one of the budget committee. So if the murderer is right-handed, he switches the stone to his left hand to open the door but has no time to switch it back to his right hand. Of course, my scenario is unnecessary because the murderer *is* left-handed."

"Who are you talking about, Miss Fairchild?" demanded Schroder.

"Don't rush me, Sergeant Schroder," said Lydia. "Listen to all of my reasons. They may help you get a confession, which is the only way you'll be able to arrest Virgil Fisher. There's no proof, you see."

Jenner joined the other men in dropping his mouth to the level of his knees. Wimpy Virgil Fisher who was afraid to smoke in front of his sister? Scared little Virgil Fisher who wouldn't defend Amanda Hailey against his sister's charges? Virgil Fisher? Not hardly.

"Who first told you of the fight during the committee meeting? Virgil Fisher. Have you listened to his taped statement carefully, Sergeant, and compared it to subsequent statements? He leaves the impression that no one left the room and that after five minutes the minister returned and the meeting resumed. He knows that someone will mention the break, but most of the attention will be focused on the fight and Hailey's taking Amanda to the bedroom—as was the case. On the other hand, he didn't attempt to hide the fact that he left the meeting early—to warm the car for Mildred because he knew that Glen Williams had seen Hailey pick up something from the flower bed. He must have been one scared bunny when he learned John Lloyd effectively refuted Glen's testimony. I think it's interesting that neither Mildred nor Virgil mentioned the assault on Amanda earlier in the day until attention had to be focused back on the preacher."

"How do you explain Virgil's admitting he was the one at fault?" asked Schroder.

"Two reasons. One, he didn't know why the preacher wasn't talking and he couldn't take the chance that he might suddenly break his silence. Two, everybody loves a repentant sinner, and religion had been the focus of this case all along. Oh, yes, and three, he made his sister look bad. Virgil Fisher has been such a joke that nobody really looked at him—and that's why he killed Amanda."

"Sex, Miss Fairchild?" asked John Lloyd, his face expressionless.

Lydia blushed, and Jenner looked quickly back at John Lloyd. He wondered if there was something going on between the two of them and shook his head. Stiff-necked, stuffed-shirt, hidebound, old-fashioned Branson wouldn't put the make on his legal clerk.

Lydia cleared her throat. "Yes, sex. I think Amanda Hailey must have been the only woman who ever paid much attention to Virgil, and he simply didn't understand that she put him in the same category as Hank Gregory: a safe man. He fantasized about her, and when he saw her in the church, alone, he acted out his fantasies—and was rejected. Not only did Amanda reject him, but the whole humiliating episode was witnessed by Mildred and the preacher. 'Don't bear false witness,' warns David Hailey, but what about the truth? Would Amanda Hailey, the young and foolish bride with the reputation for being outspoken, carelessly mention it? I don't think Virgil was prepared to take the chance. I think that's when he began planning to murder Amanda Hailey."

"Just a minute, Miss Fairchild," said Maximum Miller, chewing on an unlit cigar. "I might buy your story up to this point, but the evidence won't support a premeditated murder charge."

Lydia shook her head. "The evidence won't support a charge of any kind. No witnesses, no fingerprints, no trace evidence, nothing to indicate Virgil Fisher committed murder *except* that he is the only one outside of the preacher who had the opportunity to do so with absolutely no risk of being seen."

John Lloyd folded his hands and casually crossed his legs. Jenner wondered what he was thinking. Surely no lawyer, particularly one as full of himself as John Lloyd Branson, would sit quietly while a third-year law student demolished his case.

"Miss Fairchild, please elucidate your reasons for believing that Virgil planned the murder. I would be most interested in your interpretation."

"Think about it, John Lloyd. Virgil knew the meeting would be held in the parsonage. He assumed with good reason that Amanda would not be present. He knew absolutely that Mildred and Roy O'Brien would get into a shouting match about something because they always did and that everyone else would leave the room for a cigarette. He further knew absolutely that Mildred would leave the meeting in a huff and he and Agnes would have to bring her back, giving him the opportunity to substitute Hailey's budget report for the stone in the flower bed. Remember that he was the last one to leave the house and remember that he knew Hank Gregory never read his budget report. He placed Gregory's copy in front of Hailey's chair so the missing budget report wouldn't be noticed until later. Then when he left early to warm up the car, he slipped around the parsonage first, killed Amanda, and went on to the parking lot. Amanda was dead so she couldn't talk. Mildred *wouldn't* talk—except to him, of course—and the preacher would be under suspicion for murder."

"How could he be sure of that, Miss Fairchild? If the preacher had done what he should have, which was run out of the house screaming that his wife had been murdered, he might not have been arrested," said Maximum Miller.

"Mr. Miller, that sounds like something one of the detectives on TV might say," chided Lydia. "Of course he would have been arrested. He was the last person to be seen with Amanda, and with Virgil leaving the door open, the body temperature would be altered, making it difficult to determine the time of death. It would be anyway according to Dr. MacElvoy, but I'm betting Virgil didn't know that."

"Surely Virgil Fisher didn't depend on Reverend Hailey finding the budget report to make him look even more suspicious?" asked Bobby Benson. "Why did Fisher even put it in the flower bed?"

"The preacher picking up that report was a lucky break for Virgil, but it didn't matter one way or the other. The police would have found it—with Hailey's fingerprints on it, and Hailey would still be in trouble."

"Then you're contradicting your boss?" asked Benson. "You're contending that Virgil murdered Amanda after the budget meeting? What about the cold cream jar? What about the fact that Amanda hadn't taken off her makeup?"

"How long was Amanda sitting in that bedroom by herself? Twenty minutes? Thirty minutes? That's not very long if you're a woman and you're upset with a man. You need that long to cry, to pound the pillow, to pace the floor, to plan what you're going to say when you see him again." Lydia clenched her hands together suddenly and her voice wobbled. "Well, that's what I would do, and several people have told me that I'm a lot like Amanda. What I wouldn't do is immediately change into my nightgown and cream my face. I'd have to calm down first."

She swallowed and closed her eyes briefly. "Another thing. Amanda didn't freeze because she had thrown a cold cream jar at a member of the budget committee. She didn't put her hand to her mouth because she realized she'd committed another indiscretion and her husband would be upset. She threw a cold cream jar in an unconscious reaction to someone stepping into her bedroom. She froze afterward because she was terrified. I don't think a man can appreciate a woman's reaction to being sexually mauled. She feels . . . fragile. And violated and frightened of it happening again."

Maximum Miller broke an uncomfortable silence by scooting back his chair. "What say we go talk to the little shit. Schroder, the budget committee still upstairs in the courtroom with the bailiff and a couple of cops?"

"Yeah. With a couple hundred reporters sitting outside the locked door like a bunch of vultures."

Miller tucked in his shirt and slipped on his coat. "Don't worry about it. I know how to handle vultures."

"How's that, Cleetus?" Schroder asked before Bobby Benson could do more than open his mouth.

"You sneak into the courtroom through the judge's chambers." Miller slapped his boss between the shoulderblades. "Now, Bobby, leave your hair alone and have a Tums."

Jenner caught Schroder's arm as the investigator started through the door. "Hey, how did you bet in that pool on Branson?"

The detective shrugged. "I told you I always bet on a sure thing. I picked not guilty. I won one hundred and ninety-seven dollars because nobody else in the pool bet on it. Thought I might buy the kids one of them fancy keyboards that makes all the extra sounds."

"What kids?"

"Yours."

Jenner walked along with David Hailey behind John Lloyd and Lydia because nobody was going to let Sergeant Larry Jenner ask any questions anyway and the preacher looked like he needed a friend, but mainly because the back view of Lydia Fairchild was not half-bad and he could enjoy it without getting lasered by one of Branson's warning looks. Always providing Branson didn't turn around and catch him in the act.

"What if he doesn't confess, John Lloyd? What can Schroder and Maximum Miller do?" asked Lydia, taking hold of his arm and practically winding herself around it. Jenner figured that if Branson were human, he'd break out in a sweat and stumble over his cane about now. The front side of Lydia Fairchild creating static electricity on a man's coat sleeve, particularly while his arm was in it, was probably more effective than aspirin for preventing heart blockage. Might be dangerous for anybody with high blood pressure though.

"There is very little Cleetus and Sergeant Schroder can do in that event, Miss Fairchild. As you pointed out, there is no evidence against him. And while we are on the subject, may I compliment you on your brilliant deductions?"

Lydia smiled at him. "Elementary, my dear Sherlock."

He arched an eyebrow. "Does that make you Watson, my dear?"

"Of course not. Watson was a man."

He leaned over and kissed her, and not a leisurely kiss either, Jenner noticed. "Good. I should not enjoy kissing a man. Also Watson's deductions were frequently wrong." He raised his voice. "Sergeant Jenner, did your mother never tell you it is impolite to stare?"

Jenner stumbled. "No, but you have."

"See that you remember it. And, Sergeant?"

"Yes, sir?"

John Lloyd stopped in the doorway leading from the judge's chambers to the courtroom, where Jenner saw the six suspects looking extremely unhappy. "Sergeant, before our fearless leaders begin interrogating our prospective guests in an effort to select one to win free lodging, courtesy of the state of Texas, will you please step to the front of the bench and ask all of the suspects to hold their gloves in the air?"

"Why?" asked Lydia.

"Because, Miss Fairchild, I believe Sergeant Jenner should have a speaking role in the final act of our pageant. He is too often used as comic relief. Sergeant, do you accept?"

Jenner nodded. "Yeah. I don't think it'll do any good, but I accept. What the hell, Branson. I like to gamble every once in a while."

"John Lloyd, you can't believe—" began Lydia.

"Now, Sergeant!" ordered John Lloyd, pushing him toward the bench while grasping David Hailey's arm.

Jenner staggered to the exact center of the court, caught himself, and straightened. His one part, even if this play was going to close the same night it opened. "Ladies and gentlemen, I want all of you to hold up your gloves—now!"

Schroder turned around. "What the hell are you doing, Jenner?"

Miller grabbed the detective's arm. "Shut up and cross your fingers! Or pray. That might be more appropriate."

One by one the suspects held up their gloves. Glen Williams wore black felt ones while Hank Gregory's were of heavy leather. But Jenner wasn't interested in Williams or Gregory or even O'Brien. He watched Virgil Fisher instead as the suspect reached in his pockets. He concentrated so hard that he nearly missed Agnes Ledgerwood's whispered comment: "Mildred, what happened to your lovely gloves? The leather's all dried and shriveled."

"Agnes!" shouted David Hailey. "Be careful!"

Agnes looked up, her face slack with surprise, but only for a split second. Then she understood and backed away.

Jenner thought later that it was to Miller's and Schroder's credit that they didn't waste time arguing, just rushed for Mildred Fisher like two aging linebackers. It was too bad—or maybe it wasn't—that Mildred Fisher may have been a little older than both of them, but nobody could fault her physical condition. She shoved Agnes Ledgerwood to the floor, leaped over her, and ran down the aisle toward the aging and overweight pair. Just as it appeared they would collide, Mildred did a sidestep into the front row of seats, went over the railing to the top of the prosecution table, and launched herself from there to the floor and toward the door to the judge's chambers,—and Lydia Fairchild.

Jenner ran toward the door just as Lydia yelled, "She's mine!" and executed the best flying tackle he'd ever seen. Maximum Miller claimed later that Texas A&M could have won the national championship his senior year if Lydia Fairchild had played for the Aggies. He also allowed that Mildred Fisher wouldn't have made a bad running back in her younger days.

AD INTERIM

I HAD SUSPECTED MILDRED, OF COURSE, ALTHOUGH LYDIA Fairchild had convinced me I was wrong. Had John Lloyd not been so astute, it is possible poor Virgil might have gone to prison. I believe Mildred would have confessed to save her brother, but I am no longer as sure as I once was. As John Lloyd would say, the evidence is consistent with her remaining silent for fear Virgil might spend too much money while she was in prison. Had she not been so miserly, she would have thrown her leather gloves away rather than try to clean them. John Lloyd tells me blood is quite difficult to remove, particularly when it has dried. He believes Mildred hid her gloves in the nativity scene after the murder and could not retrieve them until after Special Crimes left late the next day. I remember vaguely wondering during the trial how Mildred knew Amanda polished her toenails. It was too late in the year when we married for Amanda to wear sandals, and Mildred did not see her feet that night at the budget meeting because the table was between them. She could have only seen Amanda's bare feet if she had been in the bedroom that night. John Lloyd and Lydia both missed that point. I am glad. A little humility would be good for John Lloyd's soul.

I was not surprised that Agnes had been the one to actually notice the gloves. Agnes is always an observant person.

Lydia Fairchild was angry with John Lloyd. She said he should have confided in her. His remark that he might have been wrong did nothing to soothe her feelings. She knows as well as I do that John Lloyd Branson is seldom wrong. His claim that his theory rested on less evidence than hers also failed to win him back his place in her good graces.

She reminds me so much of Amanda. That is why I am so surprised that she assumed Amanda would have cowered before Virgil. I cannot imagine Lydia Fairchild cowering. And she was wrong about Amanda. My wife would have thrown her cold cream, then attacked Virgil with her hand mirror. As I imagine Lydia Fairchild would have done in her place.

Lydia is also wrong about me and was overwrought when she slapped me after Mildred was arrested. I should not have struck Virgil for forcing himself on Amanda as she insisted would have been the right thing to do. I was a minister first and a husband second.

I am not certain what she meant when she said she had not misjudged me after all.

EPILOGUE

IT WAS LYDIA'S TURN TO STARE INTO THE FIREPLACE AND his to seek her out. She heard his halting step on the staircase and wondered what his first words would be.

"What did you mean by your statement to David Hailey that you had not misjudged him after all?"

Those weren't the words she had hoped to hear. "You're asking me to confide in you? Is that always the way it's going to be? I talk and you listen. Then I make a fool of myself, which you knew all along I would do, and you leap in with the right answer and look wise."

She felt him rub her shoulders and would have jerked away except every muscle in her body was stiff from tension and his hands felt good. "I'm sorry, Lydia, but until Mildred held up her gloves and Agnes gave her away, I truly thought I might be wrong. Your deduction was more reasonable, more rational, more scientific, and more consistent with the evidence, and I didn't want to cast doubt on you. If you were right, you deserved all the accolades those men would have given you. If you were wrong, I didn't want to be the one proved right at your expense. I'm glad it was Maximum Miller who received the credit and not me, although I understand Schroder is insisting he share it with Sergeant Jenner."

"You could have stopped me," she said, feeling her thighs begin to tingle. He was serious. He had used contractions and he never did that unless he was angry or unsure of himself. Or of her.

"I had no opportunity since you proposed your theory in the presence of five other people. I will not call you down in public like a child. Or at least not about something you believe in so strongly."

She turned around and put her arms around him, settling her head on his shoulder. "He's a cold man, John Lloyd. I thought so the first time I met him, and I think so now."

He smoothed her hair. "Holding a conversation with you can be a challenge, Lydia. You skip from subject to subject like a bee gathering honey. I assume you are answering my question."

She lifted her head to look at him. "He's a cold man. He says he loved Amanda, but he used her body like it was a blow-up doll, and for what? To shame his congregation into admitting they were wrong? To persuade someone so utterly bad as to kill a young girl that she should ask forgiveness? He put his congregation before his wife. He put the group before the individual. All in the name of a higher love. There is no higher love, John Lloyd, than one individual loving another. Love starts there. We love the family, the neighbors, the people in our community because we first loved one person."

She rested her head against his shoulder again. "I could never be like David Hailey."

"You judge him harshly, Lydia. He lives according to the dictates of his own conscience."

She closed her eyes, thinking of Amanda Hailey. "I do, too, John Lloyd. I told him at the beginning I was on his wife's side."